Love & Freedom

Sue Moorcroft

First published 2011 by Choc Lit Limited
Penrose House, Crawley Drive, Camberley, Surrey GU15 2AB, UK
www.choclitpublishing.com

ISBN 978-1-906931-66-7

Prin 8EX

For my mother
Connie Moorcroft
(Mum, thanks for not being any of
the mothers in this book)

Acknowledgements

At the precise moment that I needed help from an
American woman who was living in England, I met the
lovely Amanda Lightstone in BBC Radio Cambridgeshire's
Chat Room. Since then, she has thoroughly and patiently
answered dozens of questions and corrected my American
English, enabling me to have Honor, an American
heroine, in this book. Thank you, Amanda! And thanks
also to members of her family who provided additional
information and insights.

Further grateful thanks go to:

Twitter followers who supplied information on web design
and hacking. In a particularly special bit of Twitter magic,
I also found Donna Sessions Waters who so generously
helped me with American law, even identifying what was
missing from my idea and making it whole. Valuable
additional information was provided by Lynn Spencer.
Stephen Hooper, who was my background source of
information regarding the career of Martyn Mayfair.
Roger Frank and Mark West, my beta readers, who
don't normally read the type of book I write but rose
manfully to the task and helped make this a better book.
Kevan and Suzanne Moorcroft for driving me around

Connecticut; the Reverend Marion Hubbard for talking to me about a small town in west Connecticut and mailing me an incredibly interesting book; Cynthia de Riemer for background information about US/UK English relating to property; Trevor Moorcroft for never missing an opportunity to bring my novels to the notice of his many friends and colleagues and suggesting that they buy one; Ashley Moorcroft for the word 'relationshippy'. And to Paul Matthews, for taking Honor's walks and bus rides around Brighton with me and providing on-the-spot information whenever I texted with questions. I would have taken him on the rollercoaster but he had a hangover.

As always, huge thanks to the Choc Lit team, who are such a pleasure to work with.

Chapter One

'Excuse me, you're burning.'

The man in Honor's dream, whoever he was, was right – her face, arm and thigh felt as if they were on fire. She'd been dreaming of falling asleep too close to a furnace. Could it be on a boat? Because she could hear seagulls, too. And feel the seasickness.

'Quit yanking on my arm, you're making me queasy,' she tried to protest. But the words clung thick and sticky to her lips.

The voice grew louder. 'Wakey, wakey. Come on, lady! You're burning.'

Waves of nausea swelled sweatily up her body as she tried to prise up her heavy eyelids. The sun blazed into her eyes and she scrunched them shut again. 'Please don't,' she whimpered.

The voice was deep, coaxing. 'Just help me to help you inside.'

She squinted one eye open again as the dark figure of a man bending over her moved around to block the sun. 'I think I'm sick,' she whispered as sweat trickled between her breasts. 'Real sick.'

'If you weren't before, you are now,' the silhouette agreed, cheerfully. He had a cute English accent. She was familiar with the English way of making jokes about serious stuff but she hoped he realised that she really was sick. Desperately. Colours-melting, brain-whirring sick.

What was a great, tall Englishman doing filling her vision, anyway? She groped through her memory.

She was in England …

The whirring in her head became the hiss of the ocean and the furnace became the sun. She was lying on a wooden lounger on a patio overlooking a road and the ocean beyond, with a stranger crouching beside her. And she felt bad.

'Get up,' the stranger persisted. 'You're being barbequed.'

'Right.' It halfway made sense. She made to sit up but cried out. Parts of her *had* fallen into a furnace! The patio swooshed alarmingly and she clamped a hand to her mouth.

The man jumped up and retreated. 'Do you need a bathroom?'

She scrunched her eyes and hoped that he would understand that she meant, *Yes! Quick! I dare not nod my head or remove my hand to speak.*

'Can you stand?'

'Mmm ...' Maybe. But when she attempted to drag her feet to the ground black spots danced behind her closed eyelids. She froze.

'OK, I'll carry you. You try and keep it all in until we reach the bathroom and I'll try not to hurt you.'

'Ah-ah-ah-WOOOH!' Honor's eyes flew open as her side burst into flames, taking her mind off her nausea. 'Careful, for Chrissake, I'm on fire!'

'I'll bet. I'm trying not to touch your burns but you've got to get indoors.'

She shut her eyes again as the man surged to his feet beneath her with an impressive expulsion of breath, just like a weightlifter. A door opened and the furnace receded. She unscrewed her eyes, almost expecting to see long, white hospital corridors instead of a vaguely familiar house interior. 'Have I been in a fire?'

She felt a rumble of laughter in his chest. 'It's not that bad. I found you asleep in the sun and it looks as if you've been there way too long. Even the English sun can burn you once in a while, you know.'

Fresh sweat flooded down her face. She gulped. 'Bathroom–'

'Got it. We're here.'

Just in time.

'The doctor's just arrived.' His voice came muffled through the bathroom door.

So the man was still here. During the misery and pain of delivering her innards to the toilet, Honor had kind of forgotten about him. She held back her hair, sweat leaking down her forehead and behind her ears. And despite flames licking her skin whenever she moved, she was shivering like a frightened puppy. 'OK,' she managed.

Cautiously, she inched to her feet, ran water in the basin and washed her face with the tiniest little pats, then swilled out her mouth.

Another rap at the door. 'Hello? This is Dr Zoë Mayfair. Can you let me in?'

'It's not locked.' Honor hung over the basin, breathing hard. She couldn't straighten; her right side had been set in hot glue.

And then there was a neat woman in the tiny room with her, flushing the toilet, looking into her face, turning her cautiously to frown sympathetically at her skin. 'Let's see if we can get you out of here so that I can examine you. Have you stopped vomiting?'

'For now.'

'Martyn, the bedroom's at the back, isn't it?'

'Yes, through here.'

Allowing herself to lean on the dark-jacketed arm of the doctor on one side and – gingerly – the bare arm of the man on the other, which struck almost as hot as her own miserably scarlet limb, Honor weaved to the blue bedroom with white furniture, like a doll's house, that would be hers for the next four months and where most of her cases stood waiting to be unpacked.

Scared her skin might split, she sort of oozed down on to the edge of the bed.

Dr Mayfair was coolly efficient. 'Right, Martyn, I don't think we need you in here. See if you can find a jug to fill with cold water and bring a glass. She needs fluids.' The door clicked. 'Poor you.' Dr Mayfair was all sympathy. 'The first hot spell of the summer and you have to go and fall asleep in it. The sea breeze makes the sun deadly.'

'Jetlagged, I think. I didn't set out to sleep.'

'No doubt you're sore.' Doctorly understatement, like when they said, 'There will be a scratch,' and then thrust a massive needle into the heart of one of your joints. 'Your skin's quite inflamed and you'll be feeling dehydrated. Let's get some fluids into you and something on that blistered skin.'

'You bet,' Honor murmured, watching Dr Mayfair open the door to take from manly hands a jug and glass, suddenly realising that all she wanted in the world was to feel that cold clear liquid easing down her throat.

'Just sip,' the doctor cautioned. 'Or you won't keep it down.' She pulled up a bedroom chair and watched with a little furrow between her eyes as Honor sipped. She'd discarded her jacket around the back of the chair and her white blouse looked crisp and cool, her short mousey hair neatly bobbed, making Honor aware of her own sweat-draggled clothes and hair frizzing around her face.

Dr Mayfair turned to the fat black bag at her feet. 'So you're here on holiday? From America?'

Honor began to nod, but stopped when pain jabbed its fingernails into the backs of her eyes. 'I live in Connecticut. I've rented this house for the summer.'

The doctor turned back, her hands full of sachets of white

cream. 'You've rented it from my sister, Clarissa, in fact. Martyn, who found you, is our brother. She'd sent him down to do the welcome thing and check that the place was in full working order because you caught her on the hop. She'd hardly put it on the market as a holiday rental when you booked it for four months.' She wriggled her hands expertly into surgical gloves and snipped open the first sachet. 'Pity you weren't wearing sleeves because the burn's extended behind your shoulder. Can we get the top off …? Ah, I see, the straps loosen.'

'This is an antibiotic cream, for mild burns. It'll take away some of the pain, cool the inflammation and help you heal. I'm afraid you're going to be sore but Martyn caught you before you got to the hospitalisation stage.'

'That's goo – ow! OW!'

'I know.' The doctor might be sympathetic but she wasn't to be deflected from her aim of slathering the thick white cream over Honor's puffy red skin. 'Keep drinking water. Cool baths might help but don't put any oils or salts or foams in. And stay out of the sun, obviously. You're pale skinned and freckly so you'll probably need to be careful for the next month. Get yourself some high-protection sun lotion or sun block – and use it so that this doesn't happen again. You can expect to feel better in a week or so, but you'll have skin loss. Do you have any medication for pain or inflammation?'

Wincing miserably, Honor shook her head.

'I can leave you half-a-dozen of these – ibuprofen. Take two now, two at bedtime and two in the morning, then you'll need to get more. Do you have any family in the area?'

'Probably not the way you mean.' And as the doctor hesitated, Honor added, 'I think I do, through my English mother, around Brighton. While I'm over here I hope to look them up.'

'Sounds interesting. Have you registered with a local doctor?'

'I hadn't planned on getting sick.'

Dr Mayfair smiled. 'I presume you have your health insurance card? I suggest you do register – I'll give you a list of the local practices in Rottingdean and Brighton. Most patients from Eastingdean and Saltdean register in Rottingdean, as it's between here and Brighton. And you might need to see a practice nurse because you're going to have trouble reaching around to those blisters on your shoulder. Do you think you'll be all right alone?'

'I think so. Maybe I'll call a cab in the morning and get taken to a local drug store.' Honor paused, focusing her fuzzy mind on all the information she'd absorbed on her annual vacations in England. 'You call it a pharmacy, right? Where I can get Tylenol or something? And I need a supermarket. I don't have food, yet. I really just landed.'

'They won't know what Tylenol is, you'd better ask for ibruprofen.' The doctor snipped open a fresh sachet. 'Or maybe it would be better if I lent you Martyn for an hour. I'll send him in and you can give him a list.'

Honor felt her face – the rest of her face that wasn't scarlet already – flood with colour. 'I can't give your brother a list of errands.'

The doctor began on Honor's neck. 'We all do. It's not as if he has a full-time job. And what else are little brothers for?' She raised her voice. 'Martyn?'

He must have been waiting in the hallway because it was only a moment before Honor's rescuer took a step into the room. It was hard to think of him as anyone's 'little' brother as he had to duck his head to get through the doorway. His stubble was as dark as the straight hair that fell either side of his face and flicked across his forehead above near-black eyes, like a Manga character. Exotic cheekbones and a sculpted jaw; he didn't look remotely like his mousey, middle-sized, middle-aged sister. 'I can go now,' he said, 'but tomorrow I start a job that will last five days.'

Dr Mayfair pretended amazement. 'Five whole days? All at once?'

The eyes glistened with amusement. 'Three, really. The other two are for travelling.'

'I thought five was a lot, for you.'

Honor was shocked. A guy only being able to get three days of work? It seemed mean to tease him about it. But Martyn seemed able to shrug off his sister's barbs and his dark gaze shifted to Honor. 'So, what sort of thing do you want apart from the ibuprofen? Bread? Tea? Milk? Maybe some ready meals?'

A new wave of nausea swelled Honor's ribcage and, as Dr Mayfair had finished with the cream, she began to shift herself carefully towards the pillows, desperate to drop her head on to their cool, clean softness. 'That is so great of you. Maybe some plain cookies. I don't feel like real food.'

He hesitated.

She thought back to all the summers she'd spent around London with her dad, Karen, Zachary and Jessamine and the cookie/biscuit confusion in which they always found themselves. 'McVitie's Digestive Biscuits,' she specified. And, with a sigh of relief, closed the eyes that felt hung with ten-pound weights.

She must have flickered into sleep for a few moments because Honor was alone in her room when next she heard the doctor's calm, clear voice. It was coming from the other side of the door. And she was teasing her baby brother again. 'I thought you were calling me out to minister to a girlfriend – so I'd finally get to meet one.'

Martyn gave a deep, incredulous laugh. 'Yeah, right.

I invite a girlfriend over from America and *let her rent Clarissa's place*? You think that's going to end well, Clarissa having the perfect excuse to turn up at the door at will?'

Dr Zoë gave a theatrically regretful sigh. 'I can see the disaster potential. But we all think it would be nice to meet one or two of your personal beauty parade of women.'

'Clarissa met Rosie.' Martyn sounded as if he were trying not to laugh.

'Ouch. There's something that really didn't end well. When Clarissa–!'

'Exactly.' A pause, as if they were both reflecting on the situation, whatever it could be, between Clarissa and the unknown Rosie. Then Martyn returned to the subject of Honor. 'No, I just found the American quietly cooking. Clarissa asked me to come down. Like you, she gives me a list of jobs every time she sees me.'

Dr Mayfair's laugh was warm and sisterly, making Honor think suddenly of her Jessamine and Zachary; she hoped that her own big-sister-act was a little heavier on the sensitivity. 'I know, we put on you. But you don't mind helping Clarissa's tenant out, do you? I know you get fed up with the tourists, but she needs a hand.'

'I don't mind.' His voice began to move away, down the hall. 'She's pretty. At least, the bits of her that haven't been fried extra crispy are.'

Chapter Two

Morning. The sun glared through the window. Inch by painful inch, Honor peeled herself from the sheets. The skin of her right arm, shoulder, neck and cheek felt as if it had shrunk to fit someone two sizes smaller, stinging viciously. '*Son* of a *bitch*!' she hissed.

Glugging down the last of the cold water from the white bedside table, she eased from the bed and tottered along the hall to the bathroom. The shower unit, the kind that hung over the bath, provided a deluge of water. It took a bit of experimentation to make it bearable because anything the warm side of lukewarm made her feel as if she were being basted like a Thanksgiving turkey, but then she stood for a long time, letting the flood soothe her savaged skin and trying not to wish she was at home in Hamilton Drives, where Jess would have clucked and sighed then taken care of her.

Dabbing herself dry and spreading more of Dr Mayfair's magic cream over her boiling scarlet patches, she wondered how to dress. Certainly nothing that had to be hauled over her head – ooh, ow. No.

Sorting through a suitcase, she was able to locate a loose, pale green shirt to ease cautiously up her burned arm, 'Ow … ow … ow …' so that it burst none of the water-filled bubbles clustered as ugly as frogspawn on the crest of her shoulder. A bra was out of the question. It would be torture.

On her way to the kitchen she noticed a key glinting on the doormat by the front door. Martyn must have posted it through after letting himself out. She'd tackle bending over to retrieve it later.

The kitchen was large for a compact home, meant for eating in as well as for the preparation of food. At the side of the single-storey house – she must remember to refer to it as a bungalow – it gave a close-up view of the fence that ran between this property and the next, yet light danced through it on to yellow walls and white counters.

In the fridge, she discovered milk, cheese, eggs, pineapple juice, sunflower spread, a pre-packed salad and a cooked breast of chicken. In a cupboard: tea bags, instant coffee, wholemeal bread, sugar, McVitie's Digestive Biscuits, crackers, several tins of soup and a box of cereal.

Best of all, on the kitchen counter along with the ibuprofen and the receipts, stood a giant container of green aloe aftersun gel – spray on. 'What a guy,' she marvelled. 'Brains as well as looks.' She unbuttoned and carefully slid down her shirt, closing her eyes as she sprayed the pulsing area that she hadn't been able to reach with the cream. Bliss.

Buttoning up, she picked up the receipt and saw it came attached to a note in a spiky hand.

Honor,
Hope what I brought will keep you going until you can shop. Clarissa says that if you need anything else, to ring her. Hope you're OK soon.
Martyn Mayfair.

Having consumed a bowl of cereal and three cups of coffee, wincing whenever the steam brushed its cruel fingers across her tight red cheek, Honor was in the middle of revising the plans she'd had for the day – unpack, shop, get her laptop online, explore – and postponing most of them until she'd recovered from her sunburn, when she heard the front doorbell.

On the doorstep was a woman wearing pink-and-blue

gym clothes and an impatient expression. She did manage a smile, though. 'Hello, I'm Clarissa, you're renting the bungalow from me.'

'Oh, hi!' began Honor, stepping back, because it was unreasonable to keep somebody standing on the doorstep of her own house. Bungalow. Clarissa evidently needed no invitation, anyway, because by the time Honor closed the door behind her, she was already in the living room that fronted the bungalow, had dropped into a pink swivel chair and was spreading paperwork on the seat of the small cream sofa.

She opened the conversation with a corresponding lack of ceremony. 'Thought I'd check you're OK. Are you OK? Martyn realised you weren't up to signing the tenancy agreement when he found you getting sunburned, so he left it with me.' She selected a set of papers and a pen.

Honor lowered herself gently on to the vacant half of the sofa. 'Sure, I'll sign it now. I was so stupid to fall asleep in the sun and was lucky your brother found me and called the doctor. She's your sister, right?' The resemblance was clear. Both women were small and stocky, their hair identical shades of mouse. Maybe it was just the men in their family that got the dark, brooding movie-star looks.

'Right. Zoë. If you're sure you're up to this?' Clarissa held out the pen. 'It's exactly the agreement that I emailed to you to read over, so you just need to sign ... and I'll sign ... I've dated it from when you moved in. That's good, thanks.' Then she added, ingenuously, 'I just got the agreement off the internet, so I hope it's OK. But you feel trustworthy, to me.' Her smile flashed again, a glimpse of a softer side under her brisk manner.

The daughter of a lawyer and until lately an employee in an industry in which every agreement was a shrine to proper procedure, Honor was bemused. But she just said, politely,

'Sure, I'm good for it. Ouch!' Extending her arm too far to pass the paperwork back, her shoulder burned as if a Band Aid had been ripped from her skin.

Clarissa made a sympathetic face. 'Will you be all right? I can call Zoë again–' But she glanced at her watch as if checking she could spare the time.

'I'll be fine. I just need time to recover. Zoë fixed me up and Martyn helped me out with food and medication. It was so great of him to do that because he doesn't look exactly–' she searched for something to adequately encapsulate why Martyn Mayfair didn't look like anybody's personal shopper –'domesticated.'

Her choice surprised a laugh from Clarissa. 'The only thing domesticated about Martyn is that he lives indoors. Although, I suppose, he does know how to open tins or buy food that doesn't need much cooking.

'It's good to know he uses his time for something more useful than seeing how attractive he can make himself to women.' And then she shrugged and softened the words. 'Martyn's one of the good guys, if you don't mind his lifestyle and his occasional explosions.' Her kid brother so dismissed, she returned to the purpose of her visit. 'We have a small information point for visitors at the community hall so I picked up some things I thought might be useful to you – timetables for the buses and for the trains from Brighton, and a couple of maps, so you can find your way around. It's only a few minutes' walk to the local shops – I've marked them in red.'

'Thank you!' Honor was touched. 'Between you, your family has provided almost a welcome wagon. The bus schedule will be really useful because I need to look for temp jobs and driving here is damned scary.' Then, as Clarissa rose, 'Wait, I need to pay Martyn for the things he bought for me.' Making no sudden movements, she fetched her bag from the bedroom, glad she'd stopped at the airport ATM for currency.

Clarissa hung around only long enough to take the money. 'Thanks – but I have to go. My contact details are on your copy of the tenancy agreement. Call if you have a problem.'

'Thanks again–' Honor began. But Clarissa was already halfway out of the door. After watching through the window as her landlady ran down to her car and reversed neatly out of the gravel drive, Honor stood looking out at the patio with its white-painted concrete balustrade and the concrete steps dropping to the drive and front lawn. Built on an incline, the bungalow was the top step of a kind of giant stairway with its own garage tucked niftily beneath it; then down to the lawn, down again to the coast road with its growling traffic and the grassy cliff top beyond and, one last giant step over the cliff to the blue ocean dancing with jewels from the morning sun. She was going to like it here, she decided. She hadn't moved home often but she knew familiarity was just a question of finding new habits to get into.

Of letting go of the idea that Hamilton Drives, either her town-centre apartment or her dad's blue clapboard house, was 'home'.

If she hadn't let herself get burned she could have run across the road – there was a crossing right outside – and found the way down to the beach.

But, she sighed, there were some boring necessities to take care of, even if she felt like crap and her sunburn throbbed like a dragon's roar. Firing up her laptop on the mobile internet signal, which would do until she could get properly hooked up, she trawled through her credit card and bank accounts, clicking on *change details* and tapping in her new address in Marine Drive, Eastingdean, Brighton, East Sussex, United Kingdom, with a sense of adventure.

Switching to a sense of guilt, she opened her email account

and selected *Stef, Jess, Zach* and *Dad* from her address book for the *To:* line.

Subject: A little space

Hi,
With everything that's happened, recently, I'm sure you're not too surprised that I've decided to take some time out, away from Hamilton Drives. You don't have to worry about me. I've rented a little house and I have my severance pay so I'm all set.

She reread the last line and wondered whether to say something about being back soon. Then she shrugged – which made the dragon roar harder – and simply added:

Lots of love
Honor x

And pressed 'send'. There. That ought to reassure everyone at home in Connecticut. She wasn't sure whether Stef had internet access in his new place but someone was bound to pass the message on.

Chapter Three

The job had gone well and Martyn drove home, wipers swiping. In the few days he'd been away the weather had broken and cloud rolled like a dark grey blanket over the rooftops but even the rain gusting in diagonally from the sea couldn't spoil his mood. He'd spent some time with a scantily clad woman, which was always good.

Queuing down the swooping road that was fast becoming a river he sang along to the radio, splashing over the speed bumps and past the *Welcome to Historic Rottingdean* sign, the cricket club, the pond, threading around delivery vehicles blocking access to the eclectic mix of shops in Rottingdean High Street. Finally, he reached the crossroads that made the seaside village a traffic nightmare and turned left on to the coast road and the climb up to Saltdean then Eastingdean.

His black BMW X5 was taller than some vehicles but still he had to concentrate in order to negotiate the starbursts of tail lights in the gloomy downpour, so that it took him a few moments to notice the woman who appeared at the top of the steps from the undercliff and waited patiently at a pedestrian crossing.

Once he did notice he found he couldn't look away.

An inability he held in common with a group of lads getting off the school bus, across the road.

And three men walking down the hill.

And several other drivers.

Because she was soaked to her all-too-visible skin. And it was Clarissa's damned tenant, again. Not a week since she'd passed out with sunstroke and here she was bringing the traffic to a halt looking like Miss Thunderstorm on a glamour calendar, her light blue top clinging to a neat little torso and bra-less breasts. Wow.

Absolutely, completely wow.

Hastily yanking on the brake so that he couldn't run into the car in front, he looked some more. Very nice.

But, he supposed, unless she was an exhibitionist – which would be interesting but seemed unlikely – she wasn't flashing at the locals intentionally. And if her, um, assets caused a traffic accident it would be a horrible way for her to discover her mistake. Humiliation wouldn't be in it. He pressed the button that lowered the window. 'Hi!' he shouted. The woman was preparing to cross the road. What was her name? 'Honor!' And then, more loudly, 'Honor!'

Finally, she looked around. Hesitated, then gave a tiny wave as she began to cross in front of him. Her hair was wound up behind her head except for the sodden strands that clung to her cheeks and she clutched something against her abdomen, a plastic carrier bag folded carefully around it. The teenage boys began a howler monkey appreciation of her unwitting display and she turned to regard them uncertainly.

'Get in and I'll run you up to the bungalow,' he called.

Indicating her drenched clothes, she smiled but shook her head. 'I'll ruin your upholstery. It's not far and I can't get any wetter.'

'Please. Get in!' The boys were sticking their fingers in their mouths to whistle. No doubt invitations in schoolboy street-mouth would follow. Whichever way he looked at it, getting her into his car was a good thing.

Finally, shrugging – oh, wow again – she veered around to the passenger door and hopped up beside him, blinking the rain away. As the interior light flashed on her eyes shone green with brown streaks, like little gooseberries, as they studied him. 'I've been exploring in Rottingdean and didn't notice the storm coming up. I'm as wet as all get out and I was having such a great time, till then. Rudyard Kipling's garden is there.' Her enthusiasm invited him to marvel along with her.

'That's right,' he managed. He was staring. He tried not to but it was as if her breasts were magnets and his eyes, heavy as metal, were being dragged away from her face. And his cheeks were aching with the effort of not pulling his smile into a wildly appreciative grin. Really, it was a sin to cover all that beauty up, but he was getting physically uncomfortable in his jeans and had to find a way to stop himself drinking her in because women could be quick to note the direction of a man's stare and slow to accept responsibility for it. With an inner groan of protest, he manoeuvred out of the seatbelt and then his jacket, clearing his throat. 'Here, put this on.'

'It'll only get wet–'

'You need it more than me.' The queue of vehicles behind him had begun to toot and honk because the BMW was blocking the road – or maybe they were objecting to him removing Honor's body from the landscape – so he slipped back into his seatbelt and concentrated on indicating and pulling away as she snuggled into his jacket.

'I don't think the English climate likes me. This is the first day I've been out since getting burned and the weather let me get right into Rottingdean and then broke on me. Thank you for stopping. I wasn't certain it was you, right off. You look a little different today, without the stubble.'

'I had to shave for a job,' he replied, trying to keep his eyes from flicking back to check that he really had been so stupid as to give her the means to hide what had been deliciously revealed.

'Oh ...? Nice SUV, by the way.' She glanced around the interior, curiously. 'I want to thank you for helping me out, Friday. If you hadn't woken me I could have ended up in the hospital. And you were so kind, fetching my groceries. Your sister Clarissa came by and I gave her the money, which she's keeping for you. She's been so helpful about getting me a bus schedule and everything.'

'No problem.' Martyn drove up the hill. The road swooped down and up again before he could swing the X5 into the bungalow's drive, halting in front of the garage. And, before she could move, 'I'll walk you to the door.'

She looked surprised. 'You must have been one hell of a boy scout.'

He was beginning to think that himself. But, somehow, no matter how sexy and appealing she looked with fabric clinging to curves that were a gift to mankind, he didn't want her to show him anything she wasn't willingly letting him see. Without stopping to examine the thought, he jumped out into the needles of rain, chilly against his overheated skin, ran around the car and opened her door. She began to pull off his jacket. 'Here—'

He gritted his teeth against temptation and hooked the fabric back around her shoulders. 'Not yet.' Ignoring her puzzled frown, he ushered her up the steps and across the patio, hunching against the weather as she fumbled with the unfamiliar key. Only once she was safely in the hall did he let her hand back his jacket.

'Thanks again. You are so kind. I'll go get dry – I must look like a drowned rat.'

His eyes flickered south and this time he couldn't hold back his grin. If Eastingdean ever held a wet T-shirt competition she would ace it. 'Believe me, you look fabulous.'

Honor watched the Englishman run through the driving rain and drop out of her sight as he took the stairs, reappearing in seconds in the drive below. He had a nice vehicle for a guy without a proper job. But maybe the BMW belonged to whoever he'd been working for? She'd wanted to ask him about his work but it hadn't felt as if he'd welcome the intrusion, so intent as he'd been on his self-imposed task of helping her, pretty much insisting that she got into his SUV and then practically stuffing her into his jacket. He seemed unable to even carry on a conversation as he'd concentrated grimly on his personal mission of delivering her to her front door. Maybe he had some kind of OCD problem – Outmoded Courtesy Disease, ho ho.

She grinned, wiping a chill trickle of water from her neck. He had one hell of a look without the thick stubble, with that cleft chin and the suggestion of a dimple beside the corner of his mouth, so tall, and his hair cut so casually around his face. On Friday she hadn't really been in a condition to appreciate his wow factor.

But that guy was a ten. Maybe even an eleven. And when he smiled he went totally off the scale.

She sighed, squelched into the bathroom and tugged the cord that turned on the light. And froze. 'Holy crap!' Her eyes and mouth became aghast circles as she gazed into the large bathroom mirror.

At the saturated T-shirt that had turned transparent in the rain.

Slowly, she put her hands over her eyes. Oh no. Martyn's OCD had been Openly Chest Distracted.

Chapter Four

Luckily, she need never see Martyn Mayfair again. Nor the schoolboys on the hill or the drivers whose keen gazes she'd assumed to be cheerful English sympathy at her poor, saturated state. But who had actually been ogling her boobs.

Because she could always jump over the cliff.

Or move right back to Connecticut.

But that would mean giving up on her big idea for the summer. Honor eased off her sodden T-shirt and flung it to the floor. She had to stay. Which meant she'd probably have to face Martyn Mayfair again because his sister obviously gave him tasks connected with her rental property.

She set the shower at a notch above lukewarm, which she could take now without setting her sunburn pulsing, stepped under the water and closed her eyes in misery.

The fabulous smile that had half-blinded her had actually been a lascivious grin, the light in his burning dark eyes had been laughter. Savagely, she scrubbed shampoo into her hair. Tomorrow, she planned to find a temp agency. But first, she'd buy a big umbrella against the English weather that suddenly threw in a storm in the middle of a heatwave.

Unable to resist the draw of the rolling ocean, Honor began the next day by strolling along the great concrete walkway called the Undercliff Walk to Rottingdean, a popular route, judging by the walkers, runners, mothers with buggies and owners with dogs all enjoying the return of the sun, albeit accompanied by a horizontal breeze.

The cliffs, rising up on her right, were white. She'd never seen chalk cliffs close up before and it was like walking beside an enormous, badly cut cake – complete with falling crumbs, judging from the chunks of chalk littering the ground. The scale and grandeur took her breath away.

To her left, over great bulwarks built as protection from the incoming tide, the beach was made of rocks, from breakwaters of great boulders to millions and trillions of pebbles, which every wave rattled like a moment of applause. As she walked, she took deep breaths of the salty wind that whipped her hair and filled her ears. It tasted like freedom.

She loved, loved, *loved* England.

She resisted the temptation to wander into Rottingdean village which, yesterday, she'd half-explored, cute and quirky and anything but rotting. Instead, she took one of the cream-and-red buses from the shelter outside the White Horse Hotel, a typically English bus with two decks stacked on top of each other. The 'double decker' reminded her of all those summers spent in London and, as then, she climbed the steep spiral stairs. Why would anybody travel downstairs when they could look into gardens and over roofs?

Much of her sunburn recovery time had been spent with her guidebook, learning that the city of Brighton and Hove – 'London-by-the-sea' – was made up of Brighton, Hove, and over thirty other areas, including Rottingdean, Saltdean and Eastingdean on its edge. But it felt like no other city, with the waves down below the cliff as they stopped-and-started their way along the coast road.

Then came Brighton Marina, with twinkling rows of boats and cubed apartment buildings and beyond it shone a great white structure, projecting into the waves and bearing a huge sign, *Brighton Pier*. Ringing the bell for the driver to stop, she scooted down the twisting metal stairs and jumped from the bus.

Her guidebook's glossy photographs of the pier hadn't prepared her for its size, running out to sea like an ornately fenced runway decorated with a series of white-iced cakes and silver pepper pots and, bizarrely, a colourful, full-sized, fun fair of carousels and roller coasters perched on the end. Skittish green waves slapped and tickled the great legs. For several minutes she held back her hair in the breeze and drank in the grandeur, and the confusion of people, laughing, calling, shading their eyes, streaming in and streaming out.

But her severance pay was going to melt like the ice cream clutched by the nearby squealing children if she didn't earn something to help it along, and so she turned her back and took out her map.

She was unprepared for the number of *people* in Brighton, surging away from the shore across the coast road under strings of lights and old-fashioned lampposts, jostling along the sidewalks – pavements, she must remember. The bustling streets of fabulous white Regency buildings, cheek-by-jowl with art-deco architecture and modern shopping centres, climbing inland from the sea, were a lot different to the sedate streets of Hamilton Drives.

She bought a cheap, plasticky, non-contract cell phone with £20 of air time, then followed her map to the first employment agency on her list, taking only minutes to establish it as the wrong kind of agency – no fun, temp jobs there, just a condescending woman who didn't understand why Honor wouldn't want to use her degree or her qualifications as a financial advisor.

After eating a sandwich and drinking English tea – hotter and stronger than she remembered – by the statue of naked children cavorting with dolphins in Brighton Square, she allowed her feet to wander into the Lanes, part of the original village of Brighton left standing when the French burned the rest down in a raid in 1514. The streets were only a few feet across and, despite the milling tourists shouting to one another and taking photos with their phones, Honor could imagine herself back in the sixteenth century, when the walls had never seen their current bright white coats and the air was redolent of horse, hawkers and whores.

But, brought back to her twenty-first century self by her reflection in the window of a shop full of bright, stretchy dresses and glittery tops, she frowned to see that her grey T-shirt and blue jeans made her stand out in the throng of summer tourists like a pigeon in a city full of parrots.

Twenty minutes later she emerged from the shop, not so much a parrot as a glorious bird of paradise in a short, black, stretchy dress shot with gold, a rainbow-striped shrug tied between her breasts – loosely in deference to the remains of her sunburn – and gold gladiator sandals. Her hair swung from a band of multi-coloured sequins and mini chandeliers of black iridescent beads hung from each ear.

Jeans and T-shirt crammed into her backpack, she swung along to the next agency and in through the glass doors, talking brightly, as she approached a man with curly hair and blue eyes. 'Hi! I'm looking for temp work. Clubs, restaurants or shops would be good. Offices and boring stuff – bad.'

He invited her to the seat in front of his desk. 'I'm Aaron. I can help you. We have temp jobs opening all the time.'

'That's great. I'm depending on you.'

'Then I'd better not let you down.' Responding to her flirtatiousness by giving her his full attention, he whizzed through her details, hopping his cursor about his computer screen. 'Qualifications?'

Honor shrugged. 'I dropped out.'

He looked unsure. 'So ... none?'

'None.' She dismissed her degree in History from American University, Washington DC and her Series 7, 63 and 66 licences from the Financial Industry Regulatory Authority. 'But a lot of experience of waiting table.' She'd worked in restaurants all through school, her dad wanting her to learn financial responsibility and Karen being intent on her contributing to her keep. 'Available for work straight away, flexible hours and I have a UK passport.'

'Great!' he beamed. 'And a UK bank account?'

She hesitated. 'No.'

'Ah. We can't pay you without a UK bank account.'

Her smile faded. 'I'll take cash.'

'I'm afraid we don't handle it.' His pushed his computer mouse aside.

'Not even for an admin fee?'

His blue eyes were sympathetic. 'Just not at all, I'm afraid. We don't hold cash in the office. I'll leave your registration as "to be completed" and if you can get a bank account opened, just come back.'

She'd hardly been walking for five minutes when her brand new mobile phone rang, making her jump. 'Hello, this is Aaron – from the agency? Listen, I'm not really allowed to do this–'

'Yes?' Honor prompted, hopeful that he was going to say he knew how to get her a bank account.

'But I wondered whether you'd like to be shown a couple of the clubs, here in Brighton, where the jobs don't come through the agency. Maybe tonight?'

She wanted a job but she hesitated over translating the social conventions from English to American. 'Like a date?'

He cleared his throat. 'I just thought ... it can't be any fun to be the new girl in town and I can introduce you to some of my friends ...'

'Casual?' she suggested.

He sounded relieved. 'Absolutely.' Then, when they'd arranged to meet near the pier, his voice dropped and he began to gabble. 'Um, nine o'clock-see-you-there.' The line went dead. Maybe his supervisor had come along.

Honor was pleased to discover that the first bank she tried, the HSBC, was perfectly willing to open a UK account. It just took a whole lot of passport photocopying and a few pounds per month service charge. She left feeling that she'd ticked the tiresome tasks on today's To Do list and could enjoy herself with a clear conscience.

The breeze was waiting for her on the seafront, teasing free her hair as she checked carefully for traffic coming on the 'wrong' side of the road. Joining the stream of pedestrians chattering their way across to the pier, she passed the food kiosks under a leaded roof like a layer from a pagoda. She took her time exploring the mighty structure, the shops and the bars, gazing out at the fire-destroyed West Pier further along the beach, a sulking black skeleton, derelict and disconnected from the shore. The two piers were like a study in life and death.

She walked between the banks of games machines in the arcade and watched carousels with their spinning cargo of laughing people. When she reached the roller coaster's rattling roar she looked back to marvel at how far she was from the shore. It was a bizarre place for a fun fair.

After several hours, she followed her nose and her empty stomach to a kiosk selling fish and chips. She hadn't eaten English fish and chips since her last trip to England, a five-day break with Stef, who had decided London sucked, to Honor's bitter disappointment, calling it 'fat-red-bus-ugly-black-cab city'. He saw no point visiting Buckingham Palace if he couldn't take tea with the Queen or even her fancy-assed soldiers and felt stupid outside Westminster 'tube station' – which he insisted on calling the subway – when he demanded, 'So where's Big Ben?' and a laughing stranger pointed straight up, to where the enormous clock tower hung over them.

Growing up, family vacations had made London a place

to be consumed, inhaled, embraced, with its old bridges and gargoyles glaring from the architecture. Her dad had shared with Honor not only a love of English history but also of the people, who seemed to know that the family name, Lefevre, was pronounced 'Luh-fay' and not 'Luh-feev-uh', as was the tendency at home. Garvin Lefevre liked the English a lot.

Which, presumably, was how she'd ended up with an English mother.

She sighed, trying not to miss him, watching the seagulls balancing on the wind, thinking of his email that she'd received that morning:

Honor,
I know you're angry right now, but you also know that running away never solved a thing. Why don't you come home? I've seen Stef and he asked me to give you a message. Here it is:
'Aw, babe, gimmee a BREAK!'
This isn't what you are going to want to hear but I do think you ought to consider at least contacting him.

Honor's eyes followed a white-and-grey gull as it landed on the curlicued rail, pausing with wings outspread then folding them neatly. 'Thing is,' she told the gull, refusing to be spooked by its expressionless black eye and businesslike yellow beak, 'they think that I'll go back and do what's right.'

But those days were done.

When she finally wandered back to the entrance through the fading daylight, the pier sparkling under its night-time net of lights, she'd begun to wish her arrangement to meet Aaron undone. She scarcely knew the guy and her conscience was twanging. His employers wouldn't be pleased if they knew

26

he was moonlighting at finding people jobs.

Hugging herself against the increasingly frigid evening she was no longer even certain what he looked like. Very ordinary, maybe, with mousey curls. Clean shaven ...

'By the time I got here, I was convinced you wouldn't show up.'

Honor jumped. Aaron was grinning before her, saved from ordinariness by wide-open blue eyes. And quite tall. She thought suddenly of Martyn Mayfair – no, that was tall. 'I brought some friends along.' He introduced two couples in a rapid-fire burst of names that she couldn't possibly remember and they gathered around with friendly smiles and began to walk, chattering about America, holidays at Disneyland, cousins in Texas.

Honor was grateful to Aaron for providing safety in numbers. 'Where are we going?'

'A venue called Ali Spangles. You'll love it,' said a girl wearing a cute trilby hat.

'It's really cool,' added the other.

It seemed a long walk before they entered the club up six steps and a black passageway sprinkled with star-like lights. She tried not to mind that her sandals kind of stuck to the floor. Electronic dance music blared. With a shout of, 'Going to dance!' the two girls straight away thrust themselves through the crowd towards the dance floor, their men in train.

Honor watched them go, wondering. Aaron bought her a drink but was just standing there, quiet. She made an attempt to re-establish the dialogue. 'So – you like this club?'

His gaze quartered the room. 'I come a lot.'

'Do you dance?'

He glanced at her. 'No, sorry.'

Honor began to revise her opinion of the manners of Englishmen.

His gaze continued its methodical path. Then his face lit up. 'Come on, there's the guy I want you to meet.' He tugged her across the room as if he were a child and she his balloon bobbing behind, until he reached a squat, dark man with other men standing either side. 'Jermaine! How's it going, man?'

Jermaine nodded. He looked like the local gangster, cool as hell in his black shirt and jacket and his entourage taking a respectful step back because he'd entered a conversation. 'Good. You got some business?'

Aaron's hand tightened around Honor's fingers as she began to think about freeing herself. 'My friend here wants work waiting on tables.'

'I could help with that,' nodded Jermaine, looking at Honor.

'She's American and can't get a bank account, so—'

'I got one this afternoon,' Honor put in.

A frown clanged down over Jermaine's eyes. He turned to Aaron. 'She got one this afternoon,' he repeated, icily. The entourage stepped closer.

Aaron glared at Honor. 'You never told me!'

'You didn't ask.'

He put his lips against her ear. 'Listen, Jermaine owns three clubs and employs a lot of people. Know what I mean?'

'I don't think I want to know.' Anxiety stiffened her voice.

Aaron's anger faded and he snorted a laugh. 'I don't know what you're imagining – but Jermaine has jobs for waitresses who would prefer to be paid in *cash*.'

'Ah.' Honor finally got it. 'Without troubling the tax authorities.'

He winked. 'You didn't hear that from me.'

'No, not *precisely*.' She tweaked her hand free, smiling politely at Jermaine. 'Goodnight.' And turned to wriggle back through the throng.

Aaron caught up with her at the door. 'What the hell is wrong with you? You made me look a bloody fool.'

'I bloody guess I did.' She knew she hadn't popped the 'bloody' in the right place. Cursing in English took practice and she was upset. 'But you offered to *show* me around not *hawk* me around. You get a nice commission off that guy?' This time, when she stalked away, Aaron didn't follow. She paused outside, shivering, to drag on jeans and socks under her dress, her T-shirt over it, and change into tennis shoes.

Shoving her lovely gold gladiator sandals in her backpack, she set off to find a taxi rank, jogging gently beside the traffic along the sea front under the strings of lights, chanting under her breath, 'Honor, you will not be so gullible. You will wise up. Just because they speak English doesn't mean they're not foreigners.'

England wasn't perfect.

Chapter Five

She slept badly, frustrated that she'd got herself into a fix and angry that Aaron, even if only as Jermaine's flunkey, was apparently prepared to make a quick buck out of exploiting those without the right paperwork.

At seven, she abandoned the quest for sleep and checked her email. Her smile at seeing a message from her sister turned to a frown when she saw the subject line: *A message from Stef*

Hi Honor,
I saw Stef's dad, Will, and he gave me a message for you. He says, please won't you go and talk to Stef? xxx

Honor clicked *reply*.

Hiya Jessie,
Thanks for trying to help and please tell Will that I'm sorry – but I said everything I need to say to Stef. And Stef knows it.

She signed out of her email account quickly, in case Jess was up late in her chaotic bedroom with her latest Lord & Taylor purchases spilling everywhere, and came up with something else Honor didn't want to hear.

The English weather had decided on sun this morning, falling in a tempting patch on the corner of the front patio near the house. She dragged the wooden lounger into its warmth. Such early sun wasn't hot enough to bother her recent burns so she wasn't risking another self-inflicted dermabrasion. Drinking coffee and eating one of the bananas bought on the rain-curtailed trip into Rottingdean, she watched the glitter of the ocean through the gaps in the early traffic.

She was feeling pleasantly relaxed when she heard rapid footsteps and Martyn Mayfair appeared in the drive below in running gear, long strides quickly covering the ground between the gateway and the steps. She froze. Ouch! The wet T-shirt episode.

Before she could escape, he reappeared right in front of her, almost tripping over the splayed wooden legs of the lounger. 'Hell!' His breath was coming just about quickly enough to show he'd been running. 'What are you doing there?'

'I rented the place.' She forced herself to speak calmly, thinking hard about not thinking about wet T-shirts.

He smiled. 'Sorry – I suppose I expected you to be indoors. Clarissa sent me to see if you're over the sunburn.'

'Boy. Does she always take her landlady act so seriously?'

He shifted from leg to leg, keeping his muscles warm. 'How are landladies meant to act?'

She considered. 'Aloof.'

'In Eastingdean? You must be joking. Nobody's aloof in case they miss something interesting. So, you're enjoying the better weather?'

'Much better than the rai–' She faltered.

'Yeah, the rain. Probably best to forget about the last time it rained.' He bounced on the thick soles of his running shoes, fiddling with his watch, and she was certain it was to hide the laughter in his dark eyes.

But if he was prepared to pretend amnesia, then she was glad to do the same. 'I saw a lot of runners on the Undercliff Walk, yesterday. Looks great to run by the ocean on such a lovely morning.'

'It is, I do it most days. Want to run with me?' He kept his legs moving, his denim-blue sports pants moulding and clinging to well-muscled thighs.

She sat up, exhilarated by the idea of a run. 'Will you wait, while I put on my running gear?'

'Sunblock would be good, too. This is for you, by the way.' He took out a small white envelope. 'When you sent the money for the groceries, you overpaid by ten pounds.'

'Oh.' She flushed. 'I thought I ought to include something for your trouble. Don't you do that, here?'

His eyes danced. 'We don't tip friends – but thanks. You get changed and I'll jog around out here to keep warm.'

She ran indoors, dropping the envelope in the kitchen. She couldn't make him take a tip if he didn't want it but she wished he would.

Pulling on sweatpants and a long-sleeved sweatshirt and slathering her face and neck with sun block, she hooked on a navy-blue New York Yankees baseball cap, swinging her hair in a ponytail through the gap at the back. When she stepped outside he was jogging up the terrace steps, looking cool and breathing evenly.

'I'll keep moving while you stretch.' He pivoted on the top step and jogged down.

Right. Stretches. Although she ran regularly, back home, she'd never really bothered with the stretching part; she just began slowly and let her muscles warm that way. But, hey, if he took running that seriously … She bent slowly, rolling her spine up and down three times, then completed a few lunges and twists. A couple of hamstring stretches against the brick wall and she was done.

'OK. Let's hit the beach.' She trotted down the steps behind him.

He set off to the nearest set of pedestrian lights, running slowly on the spot until the traffic stopped, then leading the way over the road and down the first set of concrete steps, all the way down to the Undercliff Walk.

'Whoo! This is great,' she called, falling into an easy stride beside him between the stony beach and the rising chalk cliffs, sucking in the salt air. The sun kissed every ripple in the ocean and the traffic noise from the road above was whipped away by the wind. The day was fresh and new, and loping gently at her side was a man who, she was ready to admit to herself, could make her heart rate gallop without a running shoe in sight.

'Ready to pick it up?' Martyn accelerated smoothly and his long legs began to carry him effortlessly and rapidly away from her.

'No way!' She laughed, the tightness of her legs making her wish she'd warmed up more thoroughly. 'You're a hell of a lot taller – than – I – am.' Her breathing became disobedient and she slowed to let it kick back into rhythm.

He circled to let her catch up. 'Sorry, Pocketsize Woman.' He didn't look sorry. His eyes glittered with fun as he began to skip. 'Come on! You must be able to keep up with me now.'

'It would be easier to keep up with a kangaroo!' Her breathing went all to hell again as she began to laugh at the expressions on the faces of passersby as he bounced along at a pace that still had her running pretty hard. But she found her flow after the first half-mile and when Martyn gave up skipping and settled back down to run she began to enjoy the rhythmic pat-pat-pat of their feet on the concrete. The sun, the dancing sea and the fluttering breeze combined to inflate a balloon of happiness in her chest, a glad-to-be-alive, glad-to-be-here-and-not-dealing-with-all-the-crap-in-Connecticut feeling.

Martyn's respiratory rate still seemed about half that of hers but she was running fluidly, taking time out to watch the waves running up over those millions and millions of little round stones, and it didn't seem long before they reached the slope up to Rottingdean, the White Horse Hotel peering down from the top.

Martyn made for the steep steps curving up beside the slope, past the wall studded with big pebbles, just like the walls of the cute little houses she'd learned were called flint cottages. Gritting her teeth against the aches in her thighs and knots in her calves, Honor ran up behind him. At the top he turned and jogged back down past the cushions of wildflowers that studded the corners of each step. Heart rate and breathing getting jerky, Honor followed. Up, down; up, down. Her legs began to burn. Then he jumped down on to the beach and began to run back the way they'd come, but on the stones.

'You're kidding me,' Honor said under her breath. She pounded back across the concrete while he ran a couple of hundred yards on the incredibly shifting surface. Her legs got heavier. Unappreciative now of the dancing ocean, the beach and even the way that the undulating crest to the white cliffs brought the road above into view, buses looking like toys, her breath rasped and she tried to tug up her sweatshirt's long sleeves.

Her attention was diverted when Martyn jumped fluidly back up on to the concrete, reached over his shoulders with both hands and, without breaking stride, pulled his top off, baring his upper body to the sun. He cantered on, his top bunched in his hand.

'That's a cheat,' she gasped.

He turned his head and grinned. 'I don't mind if you take yours off.'

She snorted, which interrupted her breathing again and made him laugh, and wished she'd worn a running bra, so that she could have. And then she let herself drop just a half-step behind so that she could watch him as he loped easily along.

She had to blink.

None of the gym-freak's overdevelopment marred his body, but every tautly defined muscle was visible beneath his skin. So many muscles, all rolling in perfect harmony. He was a running sculpture, a perfect specimen. Jessamine, who wallowed in lovely romantic novels, would have called him a force of nature; Honor thought him more a work of art.

But even being in the presence of live art couldn't take Honor's mind off the way her legs were turning to string. She gave a silent groan as Martyn turned for the steep steps up the cliff to the road. She would have preferred one of the slopes on the last lap towards home. But, whooping in great lungfuls of air, she made it up.

She nearly cried when he turned and skipped down again. Womanfully, she gave chase, refusing to let him see how unfit she'd let herself get. Maybe hitting thirty should have been a clue that she needed to step up her running and her dance classes, but her hours at VPV Finance had got longer and longer as she'd battled the shrinking of her client list. Not normally good at knowing when to quit, that's when she'd asked Vic if he wanted her to be the staff member he had to 'lose' in that financial year.

And Vic had said yes so fast, Honor had been crushed. But she'd hung on to negotiate a generous severance package in lieu of notice. And, right there, was when she'd decided: Get away, Honor.

Pounding around a corner, she followed Martyn up a ramp into an underpass, their footsteps echoing *blam blam blam*. Over a path and car park and suddenly they were into a lush green park, a valley between ribs in the landscape. The residences of Saltdean rose in tiers like spectators at a football match.

She salvaged enough breath to call, 'Wow!'

People trekked through the park towards them, following the paved way on the floor of the valley, carrying backpacks or lunch boxes. Surely Martyn must slow up? Or risk scattering people like bowling pins. Her legs thanked him in advance.

But, 'This way,' he threw over his shoulder. And, to her horror, he set off up the slope on the right of the valley.

Once more, she thought she might cry.

And then she thought she might quit.

But she set off after him, knees throbbing, thighs aching, breath burning. Then he turned at the top and she saw that he was going to zig-zag the whole damned way along the sloping side of the grassy park. Her legs gave. Which pretty much meant the rest of her had to give, too.

Gasping for breath, she flopped to her knees and twisted on to her back, wafting the waist of her sweatshirt to let in blessed cool air, legs trembling like jello. Jelly. She was in England and this English rat bastard had driven her to this, so they must be trembling like jelly.

He returned, laughter finally making him breathe hard. 'I thought you were never going to give up. You ran way farther than I thought you could.' He took both her hands, pulling. 'You have to cool down and stretch or you're going to be too stiff to move.'

She whimpered. 'Stiff is OK. Stiff is good.' But she let him drag her up and they jogged slowly down the grassy slope, towards a skateboard park and along flat ground. They slowed and slowed until at last they were walking. He shrugged back into his sweatshirt and linked his arm through hers. 'Five minutes walking, stretches, then I'll buy you a smoothie.'

She groaned at the delicious prospect of something thick and cold easing her throat. But the burn did leave her calves as she walked and even her knees firmed up. The stretches he made her do were more comprehensive than the ones she'd sketched at the bungalow but, at last, he let her lie down on the slope in the dappled shade of a tree whilst he went to the kiosk beside the play park.

Pressing an orange-and-passion-fruit smoothie into her hand, he dropped down beside her. 'I really shouldn't have let you run like that. I knew within about thirty seconds of leaving your place that you were unfit. I just wondered how long it would be before you admitted it.'

'I hate you,' she managed, taking tiny sips and trying to hold the liquid at the back of her throat to ease the burn. 'Every time I found a rhythm, you ran me up steps or up a hill.'

He sucked his straw, his breathing almost even already. His hair blew back from his face and a morning shadow hollowed his cheeks. 'Works on the glutes.'

Her chest was still heaving. 'That's how you got that butt, huh? I guess mine could use the work.'

A spark ignited in his eyes. 'I think I would have noticed.'

She changed the subject. 'How are your sisters?'

'Zoë and Clarissa? They're the ones you've met. I have Nicola and Beverley, too.'

'Four sisters! Poor you. Any brothers?'

'Nope. Mum just had girls until–' He drank instead of completing his sentence, the dull orange liquid sinking slowly in the bottle.

'So you were raised in a houseful of women?'

He laughed. 'It made me strong. They were all so bloody bossy I had to stand up for myself.'

'I thought Zoë was a little ... *decisive*, when you called her for me but Clarissa ...! She takes "decisive" to a whole new level. Was your mom the same way?'

He grinned between sips. Then sighed. 'I might as well

tell you, as it might help you not to put your foot in it with your landlady. And there's always somebody in Eastingdean ready to rake up ancient history because the Mayfairs are official gossip fodder. Thing is, those I call my sisters – well, none of them are.'

Honor levered herself on to her elbow. 'Were you fostered?'

He shook his head. 'It sounds really Catherine Cookson, but Clarissa's my natural mother. She had me when she was sixteen so the other three are really my aunts and the person I've always called "Mum" was my grandmother. "Dad" was actually my grandfather.'

Honor hid her surprise. 'I've heard about that situation. I guess that the arrangement made things … easier on Clarissa.'

'Expect so. I tagged on to the end of the family and Clarissa carried on with her life, her education and her youth. It saved me being a complete embarrassment.'

Honor sensed he was waiting for her reaction. 'Your Mum-Gran was pretty generous.' She tried to say the English 'Mum' naturally but it sounded totally fake.

His eyes softened. 'She was wonderful. She and Dad are gone now and I miss them. They didn't want Clarissa to suffer for a moment's wildness, the kind other girls got away with.' He paused. 'I remember the day that Mum explained it all to me. It was a hell of a shock – but then nothing seemed to change. Maybe there had been some idea that Clarissa would take me over at some unspecified future date, perhaps when she was in a settled relationship. But she didn't get married until I was at uni.'

'A new guy wouldn't have wanted you, anyway. The new partner always wants a clean slate and their family to be all perfect and symmetrical.' Honor rolled back down on the grass and watched a puff of white cloud sailing over the washed blue sky.

Sinking on to his stomach and elbows brought his face level with hers, making her aware of his proximity in a way that undid the cooling accomplished by the smoothie. 'Maybe. Clarissa did eventually decide she wanted me, long before she married Duncan. But I liked living with comfy Mum rather than spiky Clarissa and so Clarissa was hurt.'

'Fighting over you! Lucky guy.'

He laughed. His eyes were fixed on hers. 'It didn't feel lucky. First I was Clarissa's "mistake", but then, when her friends began to settle down and have babies, she looked around for me as if I was a handbag she'd put away until it came back into fashion.'

His hair hung around his face in quills. It was *just* long enough, Honor decided. Long enough to be sexy and cool and swing almost in his eyes, not so long as to be surfer-dude. It lay just so. Women would kill for hair like that but guys didn't even seem to notice their amazing good fortune. His eyes, apart from being dark, were full of intelligence and wry humour. And interest. It burned in his eyes and intrigued her. 'So what did she come out of college as?'

'A schoolteacher in drama and dance. But she didn't have the understanding disposition for the schoolteacher bit, so now she gives dance classes privately. You know, the kind of thing adults do in the evening and at weekends and kids do after school.'

'I certainly do know. I was one of those kids mad on tap and ballet, graduating on to street dancing. Maybe I'll take a class with her.'

He closed one eye against the sun, as if he were winking. 'Dancing would build up your stamina. And Clarissa would love it.

'I get on with her OK, now,' he went on. 'Except for her incessant complaints about my life. When I dropped

39

out of uni, we could hardly be in the same room because I asked Mum if I could live with her while I got on my feet and Clarissa wanted me to finish my degree and pick up a graduate's salary. We had some shocking arguments.'

Honor remembered the explosions Clarissa had mentioned.

'Clarissa said that Mum shouldn't let me live there for nothing,' he went on, 'with my head in the clouds. Mum said, "I let you live your own life and make your own choices. And you lived that life for some time before you chose to take any notice of Martyn. Now he's going to make his own choices and take opportunities and make mistakes, too." So Clarissa had to accept it.

'She's still circling "good jobs" in the paper for me, though. And, because I help her out by designing flyers for her dance classes and keeping up her website in my spare time – of which I have plenty, as she never hesitates to remind me – she drops heavy hints about the benefits of working a forty-hour-week in design.'

'And Clarissa never had any other kids?'

'No. It would probably have been different if she had. Maybe she would have found a way to start calling me her son instead of her brother. But she's born and bred in Eastingdean and, having once agreed to the rewriting of the family history, it was hard to make the change.' His smile twisted.

She snorted. 'I know about small towns. Back home in Hamilton Drives, one half of the town is never happy unless it's picking busily over the lives of the other half. How about your dad? Is he around?'

'My natural father, he was a tourist. Nothing romantic about Clarissa's story, just teenagers letting testosterone get ahead of what little sense they had.' His grin flashed.

'Aren't you *curious* about your natural father?'

He shrugged. 'I suppose I have been. I'm a giant next to Clarissa, and much darker, so it was no surprise when she told me that I look just like him.'

And kind of understandable that, if he'd had towering calendar-guy looks like Martyn's, the absent tourist father might have found Clarissa a pushover. 'Didn't her parents track him down and make him pay child maintenance? Or even marry her?'

'All Clarissa knew about him was that he was called John and came from Leicester.'

'Oh.' She began bending and stretching her legs, feeling stiffness setting in already. 'That would make it tough for you to find him.'

'I never felt the need. He doesn't know about me. I just think of him as a sperm donor.' Then he smiled, his teeth even and white. 'I've churned out my entire life story. Sorry. Incredibly boring.'

'I appreciate being put in the picture.' She sat up and turned her face to the sun. Lying down next to him, so close, was making her feel skippy inside.

A sprinkling of mothers let tiny children play on the climbing frames below, perhaps on their way back from dropping the older kids at school. But then she noticed a woman with long black curls and a multi-coloured crocheted poncho shading her eyes and gazing up at Martyn and Honor. 'Friend of yours?'

Martyn turned to look and the woman waved enthusiastically. 'Shit, it's Robina.' He turned away, embarrassment curling his face.

Honor stared at the woman, who was hovering as if considering climbing up to join them. 'That's an unusual name.' She paused, waiting for him to fill the silence, give her information about Robina. And, when he didn't, 'She seems to know you.'

He cupped the side of his face as if to prevent the image of wildly waving Robina burning itself on to his retinas. 'Sorry, but can we ignore her? She can be a giant pain and it's the best way. Honestly.'

'What kind of giant pain?' Honor itched to respond to someone so obviously available for communication. 'Will she come up here to talk?'

He groaned. 'Hope not! She wants to be in my life. She wants to *be* my life! She owns a tearoom, the Eastingdean Teapot, and I used to go in there, but I stopped because … You know how it is, when someone likes you too much.'

Intrigued and astounded, Honor turned to look at him and the slot of tension that had appeared between his eyes. 'How does someone like you "too much"?'

His hand remained a barrier between his eyes and Robina, who had stopped waving now and was just watching. 'She sits with you uninvited when you visit her tearoom, makes you special cakes, writes you poetry, gives you presents, calls at your flat or lurks around bushes watching your flat, she follows you on Twitter and makes you a page on Facebook, she *walks through the park when she knows you'll be out for your morning run*, she hangs out wherever she thinks you might turn up.' He sighed. 'I can hardly cross the road to the pub any more, because she'll be waiting to try and burrow into me, like a parasite.'

'Wow. I find that bizarre.' As Honor watched, the woman turned away, hair flying behind her. The disappointment in her slumped shoulders tugged at Honor's vulnerable heart. 'You mean she's like a stalker?' She knew she sounded incredulous but … well, it was pretty incredible.

'Just like one.' He risked a glance and visibly relaxed when he saw Robina stumping away. 'Zoë told me that you were over here to trace your family?'

Honor could sympathise with his obvious desire to change

the subject but her curiosity kept her watching Robina. 'It's not the only reason but, sure, I might look for my roots, while I'm here. My mom's English. She left me when I was a baby. I've always wondered about her.' She paused. The woman was passing from sight now, skirting the back of the cream art deco building with the swimming pools in front, which Honor had seen from the road before – Saltdean Lido. Honor moved her gaze back to Martyn. '*Obsessed* about her, my family would say. So, yeah, I could try and talk to her. My dad was over here on vacation from law school when they met at the Reading Rock Festival, and he let himself be enchanted by her, a wild child of rock music, champion of personal freedom – *completely* unlike him. Nowadays he practises law and is buttoned up in a major way. But back in the day, apparently, he was so enchanted that when the wild child told him she'd missed a period, they went through a Druid handfasting ceremony at the Autumnal Equinox, on Primrose Hill. And he took the wild child back to the States in time for him to begin his final year at law school.' She shook her head. 'And that was when all the trouble started.'

'Trouble?' He sat up and hooked his arms around his knees, his shoulder brushing hers, warm and firm. Seriously firm. UK dictionaries probably said: *toned – see Martyn Mayfair*.

She swished the last drops of the smoothie in the bottom of the bottle and drank it down. 'The handfasting had no standing in law, of course. I guess that Garvin Lefevre isn't the type to lose his marbles, even when he falls instantly in love.' She tilted her baseball cap over her eyes against the climbing morning sun. 'But, apparently, my mother started to call herself Mrs Lefevre and Grandma said that she didn't care whether they'd married in the eyes of Mother Earth, they had to be married in the eyes of the State of Connecticut before she could call herself that. They didn't get along, particularly when my mom kicked up a storm because she wanted a home birth, which, like, nobody did in New England in the seventies. She wanted to go to bars and gigs and my dad was always at school or studying, so I guess it was pretty hard on her and she didn't much like America. And I guess she didn't like being my mom either because, three weeks after I was born, she took off. I understand why it would have been hard to take me – I'm American and the FBI takes a dim view of foreigners swiping our citizens, even when the citizen is the foreigner's kid. But I'd kind of like to know why I wasn't important enough to make her stay. Or even stay in touch.

'Dad was relieved to see her go, I think, though he was in the middle of exams and probably didn't know which way was up. Grandma took me over – just like yours – and Dad married a good American girl, Karen, a few years later.

'So, there you have it – I'm a mistake, too.'

Chapter Six

'It happens,' he said, quietly. She was looking away, now, watching mothers pushing buggies, toddlers trying to keep up. Now she was no longer sunburn red, tiny freckles kissed her nose. Her ponytail was a toffee-coloured cloud, but when he had found her on the patio this morning her hair had hung loose over her shoulders, not in waves but in ripples. He liked her hair. He liked her pixily determined chin and short, straight nose. But not as much as her pretty mouth. She had a seriously pretty mouth. Her lips were glistening with the last of the smoothie and it begged to be licked away.

She was no cover girl; her beauty was too quirky, too expressive. Too dependent on the pretty mouth that he couldn't stop watching as she said, 'I was five and Dad and me were a unit, when they got married. Karen was a good stepmom but, of course, she couldn't love me as much as she loved her own kids. Sometimes she'd act as if I'd been a lot of trouble and get Dad to take me off somewhere, like she was saying, "This one's your child, sort her out." She carried on with her career until she was pregnant with Jessamine, and Jess was a difficult baby and Zachary followed quite soon, so Grandma carried on caring for me when Daddy wasn't home until I went to junior high when I was twelve. Old enough to get the school bus and old enough to watch Jessie and Zach.'

'Watch them do what?' He couldn't resist teasing her for her American terminology.

A smile flickered across her eyes. 'I watched them do just about everything – helping them if it was a good thing, stopping them if it was a bad thing. You say "babysit", right?

'You know how you get that child in a family, the one who is older and more self-possessed, who runs lots of errands? Well, that was me, because when I was responsible and helpful, Karen didn't make other arrangements for me. So it was a lot easier on everyone.' She turned her fine green gaze on him and smiled. 'You can't fault her logic – I'm not her kid. Families do you in, don't they?'

He commiserated with a touch to her hand. Her nails were manicured and her fingers dainty. 'Mum would have called you "a fine-boned lady". That was her greatest compliment because she was like my sisters – short and sturdy, like peasant stock. And I'm a big guy.'

She laughed. 'You sure are.'

His glance flickered contemplatively to her mouth. But he just took her hand and surged to his feet. 'Ready to go?'

She winced. 'Ow! Ooh,' as she began to use her legs, so he led her back out of the underpass and along the undercliff to Eastingdean at a snail's pace. He should never have kept running when he knew she was blown; it didn't seem like such a good joke, now, because she was walking as stiffly as a heron. And it was taking forever to get back to Eastingdean.

'All I can see from here is the top of your cap,' he observed, when she seemed to be walking more easily.

'Doctor's orders were that I cover up in the sun for a while.' She glanced up. 'I don't think I ever said thank you for dragging me in from the sun and calling Dr Zoë. You were the good guy, looking after things for your sister, and you got a sick American to take care of. One more thing to hold against Clarissa.'

The undercliff was busy and he sidestepped a small child on tow behind a large black dog and steered her to a slope up to the road. 'I'm being kind to her, at the moment, even when she pulls all the sister-mum crap. Her husband did one, a few months ago.'

Her eyebrows dipped. 'Did one what?'

'Did a runner. Went off with another woman.'

They'd reached the clifftop and the traffic and the breeze combined to make it difficult to hear each other so they'd crossed the road to the bungalow before she answered. 'Poor Clarissa. I didn't know about her husband.'

'She and Duncan were going to live in the bungalow.' He nodded up at it. 'They moved in with Nicola while they did this place up so Clarissa's still there, because when Duncan took off Clarissa had to take the mortgage on her own. That's why she's renting the bungalow out. Nicola's between relationships – none of my sisters but Clarissa ever bothered getting married – so she's happy to share living expenses. But I still feel bad for Clarissa.' He watched Honor's behind as she walked up the terrace steps. 'Duncan Wells had always been a problematic bastard but the crunch was when another woman came on the scene. So Clarissa embraced being single again, and went back to calling herself Mayfair.'

Honor halted at her door. 'Horrible for her.'

He tilted the baseball hat gently off her head, sliding it slowly down her ponytail and stretching around her to hang it on the door handle. Now she was in the shade her skin was safe. And the damned hat would only get in the way when he kissed her.

But she was still frowning over Clarissa's troubles. 'You're obviously on her side when it matters. That's real important.'

He propped his hand on the doorframe. 'She drives me mad, but of course I'm on her side. She was hurt. Also, she gave me hell.'

'Gave *you* hell?'

He shuddered at the remembered purgatory. 'Straight

after Duncan left, it came out – in the worst way – that I was in a relationship with a married woman, Rosie. In my defence, the first I knew of it was when Rosie's husband turned up, threatening to kill me.'

'Wow,' she breathed. 'That sucks. How could you not know?'

'Exactly Clarissa's point. But it seems that the endless lies and deceit that come with having an extra-marital affair can be used to blindside the lover as well as the husband. I honestly didn't know. I was so pissed off with Rosie. Apart from subjecting me to a horrible scene and making me look an idiot, she involved me in hurting her husband, which I hated. She didn't wear her wedding ring, she stayed out all night – how the hell was I *supposed* to know?'

'Maybe she wasn't all that married? Like – separated, or something?'

'It's true that they were only "kind of" married, according to her. But that message didn't seem to have reached her husband … Anyway, I've sworn off married women. I don't need them.' He dismissed Rosie and her excuses. His primary interest in this conversation was wondering when it would pause long enough for him to get to know that pretty mouth.

Which was no longer smiling. Instead, Honor sighed. 'So this would be where I tell you I'm kind of married, too.'

He took a look into her eyes. There, too, the smiles were gone. His heart began a slow float downwards, hardening his voice as he straightened up and stepped back. 'And you don't wear a wedding ring, either.'

Her smile was defensive. 'They're not compulsory.'

Anger ripped through him, firing words from his mouth. Not loudly. Quietly. Like a ticking bomb. 'Maybe they ought to be – to stop poor bastards making dangerous assumptions!'

And before he could soften, explain it was disappointment that made him snappy and that he was prone to speaking first, thinking later, she unhooked her cap and opened the door. 'Assumptions are always dangerous. If they weren't assumptions, they'd be intelligently researched conclusions, wouldn't they?'

And the door shut, firmly, in his face.

Chapter Seven

From the way that his eyes, heavy with desire, had been fixed to her mouth and, damn, pretty hot, she'd known he wanted to kiss her. His spurt of anger told her just how much.

A kiss would probably have been a bad idea. For all kinds of reasons.

Like Stef. Stef. And ... Stef.

She could have told him that she and Stef were living separate lives but right now a man in her life, particularly an angry man with barriers against married women, would complicate her already knotty situation. And she knew little about Martyn Mayfair other than that he kept turning up in shining armour to rescue her from dragons – well, sunburn and thunderstorms – and he had a stalker, which was sad and, as she was pretty freaked by the whole Robina thing, an out-of-left-field complication.

There was no reason for her to feel affronted that Martyn had thrust her from him like a dog that had rolled in something stinky.

So she should just stop.

She sighed. Well, stop then, Honor.

But, before he'd turned so harsh and unforgiving, she'd been all set to drown in those dark eyes and let his lips make real the connection they were obviously both feeling. And as for that incredibly English way he said 'bastard' – barzstard. Not basstard. Cute ... She shook herself. Stop! Really, stop. Not going to happen.

A long soak in a hot bath went some way to easing her stiff muscles. Then, after a quick lunch, she fired up her laptop and resolved to work through her inbox to punish herself for wishfully thinking herself kissed by a specimen of almost perfect male physical beauty. First the mail she'd let build up from friends and recently ex-coworkers demanding to be told exactly what the hell she thought she was doing, pinging back the same breezy paragraph to each: *Hi! I'm fine, just enjoying a little time out before deciding where I go from here. Be sure to see you sometime.*

But the concern from loved ones was harder to deal with. She clicked first on *Zach*:

Hey Honor, you OK? Dad's stressing. He rang me, checking whether you were hanging with me down in Texas but I told him no. But if you do want to hang here, I'll still tell him no, if you want. Zach
PS I keep hearing that everyone back in Hamilton Drives is so amazed. I knew Stef's stunt would make it hard for you but you kind of took people by surprise by leaving.

She moved on to *Jessamine*:

Honor, I saw Stef and he's totally subdued, wishing he was back in the days when his worst crime was blowing up a mailbox. ☺ *He says to tell you that he loves you and knows he deserves to be punished but he misses you like crazy and wishes you'd go see him. Love you, sis. Jessie xxx*

Honor smiled, picturing Jessie, the image of blonde, pretty Karen, throwing her arms around Honor and delivering those kisses, heavy on the lipgloss.

She left the hardest till last. *Dad*:

Honor, honey, I'm not going to pretend that I'm in favour of you hiding out from your errant husband but I guess that's a conversation for another day. Until you've got this fit out of your system, can we please continue to check in with one another? Regularly? Karen says Hi.

I love you.

She returned, *I love you, too. I'm really fine, Dad.*

When she'd conquered her inbox, restless emotions and incipient muscle stiffness sent her to put up her hair and slap on her sun block and walk out to explore Eastingdean while the sunshine lasted.

Most commercial activity in Eastingdean was centred on The Butts, a broad road, off Marine Drive, of pubs, fascinating stores and places to linger. Honor suppressed a childish snicker at the idea of a street named The Butts. The British didn't use the word 'butt' in quite the same way as Americans but if she were ever to open a shop here it would have to, just *have to*, sell panties and boxer shorts. She could call it *Cover Your Butts*. Or *Beautiful Butts*. *The Butts for butts*. *The Butts Store*.

On the first corner of The Butts was a block of shops called Starboard Walk, studded with enormous pebbles row on row on row. The rest of the stores – no, *shops* – that lined The Butts were an eclectic mixture of more flint, plain red brick, rendered and painted in white or cream with the occasional pink, or the cross between a house and a zebra that was mock-Tudor.

The butcher's shop and the one that sold fruit and vegetables were worthy only of a glance and she noted the fish and chip shop for when she hadn't just eaten. Across the road from the Eastingdean Teapot, the tearoom that Martyn had said belonged to his stalker, she browsed happily around a leafy, peaty garden shop that sold spotted Wellington boots, neat packs of seed, and baskets of hanging plants swinging gently as they waited to be bought.

Her favourite, though, she found at the point where the

shops were petering out – Pretty Old. The shop front was stained dark, the bevelled glass windows shone, and the air smelled of dust and beeswax as she stepped inside. From somewhere in the recesses she thought she could hear a radio but, although a tinkling bell announced her as she closed the door, nobody emerged to help her.

It wasn't exactly an antique store, not like those she'd seen in London's Chelsea. In Hamilton Drives the sign over the door would have said something about 'collectibles'.

But, wow. It was crammed with cool stuff.

In cabinets crouched old telephones, from froggy-looking examples in two shades of green to brittle black, dials yellowed with age and a funny cord that looked as if it had been covered in cotton.

Then came the photographs. Faded photographs in tones of grey or shades of sepia; weddings and christenings, parades, family groups and solemn babies in long gowns, all framed in tarnished silver or wood smoothed by age. Even better was an album of postcards that were embroidered in faded silks and sometimes edged with lace.

She picked it up and breathed in the smell of old.

Old paper, old ink, old lives. It was exactly the kind of history she loved best: the kind you could touch, just on the edges of living memory. Inside the album's back cover was written in a childish cursive script: *Mary Brownlee, The Rise, Eastingdean, East Sussex.* Was Mary Brownlee still around? Probably not, she realised, sadly, if her precious collection had ended up in this hushed, musty shop.

Each postcard had its own embroidered message: *Happy Christmas. Happy Birthday. To My Darling Wife. To My Little Girl. Don't Forget Me.* Honor turned each thick page gently, reverently, *Souvenir de France, Right is Might,* until she reached the final one, *RFA 1917, my heart it wings to thee.* The colours were muted by the years but every stitch was beautiful and precise, just as it had been set almost a century before.

'Lovely, aren't they?'

The quiet voice came from right beside her and Honor jumped so hard she almost dropped the precious album. A woman in her sixties twinkled at her, eyes almost disappearing in her smile, cheeks as round as red apples. If her ears had been pointed, Honor would have suspected her of being a hobbit. 'Sorry, did I startle you? You're looking at First World War silks. They were embroidered for the servicemen. What you're holding is a collection of cards a staff sergeant in the Royal Field Artillery sent home to his wife and daughter.'

'They're gorgeous.' Honor stroked a page. 'How much would you charge for the book?'

Hobbit woman crinkled up her face again. 'I'm afraid it's expensive. The collection will soon be a hundred years old, which is rather a magic figure, in antiques. And all together like that in the album, they sort of tell a story, don't they?'

Honor waited.

The screwed-up face screwed up even more. 'I couldn't take less than two hundred pounds.'

'Wow. I'd have to think about that.' Regretfully, Honor closed the album and slid it back on to the shelf by a framed photo of girls in drum majorette uniforms, hems well below their knees.

The lady nodded, sadly. 'I know. Expensive.' Then her face scrunched up again with a pained smile, as if she were gently disappointed in Honor but was too gracious to make it plain. 'Do enjoy browsing.'

Honor did. By the time she finally tore herself away from the shelves of beads, bobbins, boxes and brassware, she felt dazed. Holding bits of history in her hands had made her covet so many that, like a child confused by the largesse of a toyshop, she hadn't bought a thing, just allowed herself a last loving flick through the postcards in their creased old hide binding. Maybe, just maybe, if she could get herself a job, she could justify buying that fabulous collection.

Outside, the sunlight made her blink as she crossed the street to return down the other side. In a recess almost opposite Pretty Old stood a wooden community hall. She was fascinated to learn from the glassed-in notice board that the hall was home to a whole bunch of groups and events: a visit to Rottingdean's windmill – she'd seen it, big and black on a ridge above Rottingdean village, but hadn't figured out how to get to it. A talk by a local author. Tai Chi for the over fifties. How to make dough animals for the under tens. And Zumba! The Zumba classes back in Hamilton had taken place in an air-conditioned dance studio with a polished floor and a wall of mirrors, rather than in something that looked like a large shed, but she couldn't see how it could be too different. She'd loved the combination of aerobics and Latin music and, forgetting that her muscles were already stiffening from her run, she shifted her weight right as she went up on the ball of her left foot. *Yeahhh … Zumbahhh!* Ow … butt cheeks!

Maybe Zumba would have to wait.

She turned towards the Eastingdean Teapot. OK, it was giving in to curiosity but, after hearing Martyn's stories about Robina, she just had to walk through the troughs of many-coloured petunias and the green chairs and tables. Menus were sandwiched in sturdy acrylic holders and parasols flapped their white fringes in the breeze like big crazy spiders.

The tearoom, set behind the teagarden, was like a parlour, furnished with mismatched wooden furniture and smelling as sweet as fruitcake. On the walls hung cookie tin lids and pretty plates. Pickles and conserves in hexagonal jars with lace caps waited for buyers on a counter that divided the tearoom from the kitchen and behind it a teenaged boy washed glasses and a blonde woman in a hairnet rushed around.

In the middle of the kitchen stood the woman from the park, Robina, in jeans and a richly embroidered green velvet top, a black apron slung around her hips, recognisable from the bubble of black curls held back from her face by a black bandana. She didn't look much of a stalker, icing chocolate flowers on to greaseproof paper.

Honor watched, fascinated by the fluid swoop-twist movements that created the petals and the dab that joined them in the middle. After a few clusters of swoop-twist petals, Robina glanced up. 'Would you like to sit down? We'll take your order at the table.' She smiled and Honor thought she had never seen such huge brown eyes, nor amazingly bee-stung lips.

After everything she'd been told she'd half-expected horns and cloven hooves, so it took her a moment to respond to being not only in conversation with Robina but it being quite normal and friendly. 'Sure. Thanks.' She settled on a wheel-back chair with a rose pink cushion at the last free table, glancing around at a lone man taking up the whole of a table meant for four by spreading out his broadsheet newspaper; two young mums talking earnestly as they shovelled food into their toddlers; and three tables seemingly populated by one party, judging by the way that they talked across the divides as they ate.

The teenager emerged from the kitchen with a pad and pen. ''Lo. What can I getcha?' He had the same big brown eyes as Robina, but his hair was flat and sandy and he didn't have her lips. Honor found herself being glad – lips like that were for girls.

She glanced at the menu. 'A pot of hot tea, please, and

maybe some cake or pie.'

He indicated a table beside the wall, tiered with cakes under clear plastic covers. 'We got carrot cake, lemon drizzle, pineapple upside down, date and walnut, and chocolate cupcakes, apple pie and cherry with almond tart. You can have cream, custard or ice-cream.'

'They all look delicious.'

'Yeah.' He wiggled his pen, glancing sympathetically at a toddler who was crying at being trapped in his highchair.

'Are all these cakes made right here?'

'Yeah.' He nodded vaguely at the kitchen. 'Or there's desserts on the menu. No more cream teas, the last of the scones have just gone.' He wiggled his pen again.

'I'll have cherry and almond pie, with cream.'

'OK.' He scribbled, then disappeared back through the flap in the counter into the steam of the kitchen, sliding his feet along the floor as if too weary to pick them up.

Honor waited, gazing around at the lace at the window and the stack of white crockery on the counter, the survivors of many sets, judging by the mix. Robina was still intent on her task, giant icing bag twisted in her hands. The woman in the hairnet kept up a steady stream of conversation and sometimes Robina answered. The lone man folded up his newspaper and left his empty cup but no tip. Three middle-aged women took the table.

Then the door shot open. 'Rufus! I've got fifteen minutes, be a love and get me a big fat mug of black coffee and one of your mother's enormously risen scones, quick as you can, good boy.' Clarissa. Martyn's sister-mother. Well, now. Wasn't that interesting?

A smile touched Rufus's face like a watery sun as he selected an enormous mug and carried it to the coffee machine. 'Too late for scones. Got cupcakes, lemon drizzle–'

'Damnation. Is one of those cupcakes chocolate? I need

something to sweeten me up before I teach tap to unwilling little girls and boys in Hove.' She glanced around the tables.

Honor lifted her hand. 'Hi, Clarissa.'

Clarissa waved back. 'Oh, Honor. Sunburn better? May I join you?' She hooked her bag over the back of the other chair and nearly snatched the coffee and cupcake from Rufus's tray.

'Much.' Honor smiled at Rufus as he put down in front of her a white china teapot, matching cup and saucer, a tiny milk jug and some sachets of sugar. 'Thanks.'

'Everything OK at the bungalow? I can send Martyn round if you need help with anything.' Clarissa blew over the surface of her coffee. Her hair curled beside her cheekbones and although she set about her cupcake with deadly efficiency, she didn't look as if she carried a spare pound. If she'd given birth to Martyn at sixteen she must be in her late forties but her skin was smooth. Maybe it was because she didn't smile enough to get wrinkles.

Honor poured her tea. 'Everything's great. I love the view over the ocean.'

'You wanting the place for four months was a bonus because it cuts down on tons of paperwork and stuff. Have no idea what I'll do if I can't let it in winter. Panic.' She fired out her sentences between bites.

Honor picked up the fork that came with her cherry and almond tart. When she took her first mouthful of pastry, the cherry leaking bloodily through the cream, she couldn't suppress an, '*Mmm ...*'

'Good?' Clarissa nodded. 'She's a genius with pastry, Robina.' She indicated her cupcake. 'And cake. Robina's the one with the dark curls.'

In the interests of local community harmony, Honor elected not to ask Clarissa if she knew about Robina's passion for Martyn. 'She's Rufus's mom?'

Robina, overhearing, looked up with a beaming smile. 'Yes, he's my little Ru – Sophie, can you put the icing in the fridge, please? – and he helps us out here when he's not at school.'

Honor glanced at her watch. 'Isn't it school time, now?'

Robina put down the icing bag and picked up a whisk and a bowl to cradle in her arm. 'Only sports day, so I kept him home. We're a person short because Kirsty, who usually works here, is in hospital with one of those strange viruses. She's really ill, poor Kirst. So Rufus is more use here than running round a track. Aren't you, little Ru?'

Rufus shrugged, face impassive as he accepted money from the mums and toddlers as they left.

Honor suspected Rufus would have enjoyed sports day, given the opportunity.

'So.' Clarissa wiped the last of the cupcake from her fingers with a jolly yellow napkin and sank back into her chair with her coffee. 'How are you liking England?'

'I love it.' Honor smiled, even though Clarissa didn't. 'I'm going to make myself a real pig over English history, that's for sure. I've been browsing the Pretty Old store, up the street, lusting after an album of postcards sent home by an artillery staff sergeant in World War I. But I have to resist spending that much money until I get a job. The cards are called silks and they were embroidered by Frenchwomen for the servicemen–'

'How much did she try and skin you for?'

Honor halted. 'Excuse me?'

Clarissa fished around in her bag for money. 'Peggy, at Pretty Old. What did she want to charge you for the album?'

'Two hundred pounds.'

Clarissa jumped up, dropping money for the cupcake and coffee on the table. 'Got to run. See you.'

'OK–' Honor was left talking to empty air as Clarissa let

the door bang behind her. She shrugged and turned back to her pie.

Behind the counter, Rufus washed up as the woman who Robina had addressed as Sophie called, 'Remember to rinse everything under the hot, Ru,' which, as Honor could see, he was doing already. Rufus said nothing but pulled a gargoyle face at Sophie's back, making Honor choke.

He met her gaze with one eye through a gap in his hair and a corner of his mouth quirked up before he turned back to his steaming sink.

Honor was getting ready to pay her bill when Clarissa burst back in. 'Fifty quid?'

Honor jumped. 'What?'

'Peggy said she's sorry, she thought you were American. You can have the album for fifty quid.'

Honor felt her hackles rise. 'I am American.'

'But now you're living here you don't count as one so she won't rip you off. Call back into the shop if you want it.' And she was gone. Through an uneven square window Honor watched her run across the teagarden and down the road – did everyone run, in the Mayfair family? – in wonder that Clarissa would scrounge the time, when she was so obviously busy, to get her tenant a good price on an old album. Evidently, there was kindness in her.

Leaving the Eastingdean Teapot, Honor strode back up The Butts to Pretty Old and pinged through the door. 'Hello, dear,' cooed Peggy, from behind the counter, quite unabashed. 'Sorry about earlier. I thought you were American.'

Smiling sweetly, Honor said, 'I am. And I can only pay twenty.'

'You poor thing.' Peggy's smile was just as sweet. 'Because I can only sell for fifty.'

'OK. I'll surf around ebay.' Honor pivoted on her heel.

'Forty-five, then. Just to make up for me thinking you

were a tourist. Clarissa says your mum is English.'

Honor regarded Peggy, still beaming, perched behind a glassed-in counter full of medals and coins. 'Yes, that's right. I'm living in Eastingdean for four months. I might become a regular customer. Thirty-five.'

Peggy began to slide the album into a crinkled supermarket carrier bag. 'Call it forty, then. I don't want to get on the wrong side of the Mayfairs.'

Honor propped her hip against the counter, deliberately not taking the proffered bag. 'Are they scary? I've met three Mayfairs and they've all been good to me. Thirty-five.'

Peggy's creases multiplied in exasperation. 'Thirty-five, then, just this once.' Taking Honor's notes, she slid them into the cash register. 'It's not that there's anything wrong with the Mayfairs – it's just that they're involved in everything in Eastingdean. Zoë is the doctor, Nicola is the midwife, Beverley is a legal secretary. We all have to hope that they know how to keep their mouths shut.'

Accepting the bag, Honor raised her eyebrows. 'I guess they must understand that. The Mayfairs will have as much to hide as the next person.'

Peggy cackled, her eyes disappearing completely. 'One of the Mayfairs doesn't hide very much.' And she laughed until her cheeks shook.

Honor stared. Sometimes, British humour completely baffled her.

Chapter Eight

Next day, having spent the previous evening filling out endless forms at employment websites and receiving nothing in exchange but bountiful promises, Honor decided she deserved a break.

Waiting for the bus on Marine Drive, her heart gave an apprehensive hop when Martyn Mayfair popped up at the top of the beach steps on his morning run, the wind whipping his sweatshirt tight against his body. He didn't see Honor until he was headed firmly for the nearby pedestrian crossing and would either have had to make a visible detour to avoid her or actually cut her dead. She saw him hesitate, as if considering both of those things. 'Hi,' she said, neutrally, to make it easy for him to say 'Hi' back and run on.

'Hi,' he returned. But instead of running on he slowed until he was jogging on the spot. 'Going out?'

He didn't smile, so she didn't, either. If he was going to make it so obvious that it was only good manners that were forcing him to pass the time of day with her, she would do the same. 'I'm taking a trip to Brighton to the Royal Pavilion. It was George the Fourth's favourite home when he was Prince Regent.'

He cocked a sardonic brow. 'But Queen Victoria didn't care for it at all.'

She flushed. She was so used to Stef's zero knowledge of English history that the hint had just slipped out. 'I guess that sounded stupid.'

'No. Just as if you think I am.'

'Not at all I–' What was stupid was this snarky exchange. It wasn't as if she had a lot of friends in England and last

62

time they met they'd been so much on the same wavelength, running beside the ocean and then lounging on the sweet-smelling grass comparing unsatisfactory childhoods. Until ... 'Martyn,' she began impulsively, 'I want to talk to you about my marriage–'

'No, don't.' He held up his hands like stop signs, beginning to move off, jaw set.

'But–'

He actually let his legs stop moving. 'Don't sweat it. I liked you. You're hot. But there are a lot of *single* women with pretty faces and sweet bodies, sugar pants.' And he finally smiled, as if he knew that he'd irritated her and was glad. 'Here's your bus. Have a nice day.'

Honor jumped aboard the platform. 'Men who think they're drop-dead gorgeous are such a pain in the ass.' Without looking back to see if she'd irritated him in return, she rode along the coast road going over in her mind everything she'd read about the Pavilion so that she didn't have to think about Martyn Mayfair at all. Sugar pants. Huh.

It seemed weird that an honest-to-God palace should be at the side of a major road, traffic roaring by, but the bus let her off right outside it. Sucked inside by the onion domes, towers, minarets and cookie-cutter windows, she took the audio tour, revelling in every opulent room of hand-painted wallpaper and gilded plasterwork, wishing she could stroke the chair in which 'Prinny' had lounged on the long side of the banqueting table during lavish dinners with his cohorts and consorts, a towering chandelier of crystals and dragons above their heads.

She stood for ages in the kitchen that had seen the preparation of those indulgent meals, drinking in the lantern ceiling and the long wooden counters, imagining how it must have felt to tend the automatic spit or polish the gleaming copper pans.

The Pavilion was crowded with tourists, it being summer. She was frustrated by people talking as she tried to listen and gave herself a headache cramming the big black audio set against her ear to shut them out as she gazed at the lovingly restored gold plaster cockleshells of the music room's domed ceiling and listened to the story of the arsonist who had damaged so much splendour. But walking the shining palace gave her a chance to work off lingering post-run stiffness and losing herself in the past soothed her post-Martyn crankiness.

Right at the end of the tour, she noticed that the Pavilion had a function room, where a man who walked like the rear end of a horse and two women in the black dresses/white apron combination of waitresses everywhere were stacking silver-edged crockery into flat blue crates stamped Florence Events Catering. She passed by, left her visitor feedback and stowed her audio set, as politely requested, spent twenty minutes in the gift shop – she couldn't resist a Union Jack teapot – and stepped outside.

A small white van was parked on the flagstones and the women from the catering company were sliding the crates they'd been packing in the Pavilion through the back doors. On the open door was stuck a small notice: *Staff Wanted*. Honor hesitated. When one of the women looked up, she smiled. 'Is it waiting staff wanted? Because I'm looking for summer work two or three days a week.'

The woman looked at her as if she must be mad. 'Really? You need to speak to Lawrence – Lawrence! Lady here wants a job.'

The man, Lawrence, breathing hard, stacked the box he was carrying and rested his great big behind as if it, too, was too heavy for him to drag around. He studied her. 'I'm looking for daytime staff. Too many of my part-timers are students or young mums and want evening and weekend work – great for dinners and parties but no good for corporate. It's astonishing how many organisations experience sudden needs to shut away together a couple of hundred people. If you're flexible and you can cover the kind of corporate business that bursts out of nowhere, I could give you a trial.'

She shrugged. 'I'm pretty much without ties or schedules and I worked my way through school waiting tables.'

Lawrence pulled out a pen. 'Then I'll take your details.'

In two days, Honor was working for Florence Events Catering.

With her hair caught tightly behind her head and a full white apron over a plain black dress – that she had had to buy because she hadn't brought anything suitable from home – she ensured coffee pots and hot water urns were full when delegate hordes flooded out on caffeine and sugar breaks, cleared away when the tide flowed back into the conference rooms and prepared for the after-meeting treat of canapés and wine. In no time she could respond to, 'What's *that*?' with a helpful, 'Deep-fried mushroom risotto bites with parmesan mayonnaise,' or, 'Cajun chicken with spicy vodka and tomato dip.' A wooden charger protected her fingers from the heat of the square black stoneware plates, and cheerful unconcern protected her from the disdain of people who would have preferred a bag of chips.

She'd spent enough time in the corporate torture chambers to be amused at being on the other side of the tray, gliding serenely between suited shoulders, through the politics, backstabbing and plain old ass kissing, thanking her lucky stars that she wasn't the one networking like mad.

Honor's role carried little responsibility and no brainwork and that was just how she wanted it. But those were the only good things about the job. Though she'd looked forward to visiting Brighton hotels of all ages, styles and sizes, seafront or city, by the time she'd been with Florence Events Catering for almost two weeks she'd begun to dislike the way that the regular hotel staff viewed the events staff as intruders, every friendly overture to be repulsed and all co-operation to be withheld. Lawrence was way too visible, fawning over the client's event organiser, unsettling the chefs, barking at the waiting staff, big ass waggling in his dark suit. And though she worked only part-time, her feet ached full-time. And so did her back. And her hair had to be washed as soon as she got home or else it smelled like garlic, salsa or prawns.

So. Staying long? Didn't think so.

After a particularly crappy hot July Friday of seminar delegates being given hell all day by their bosses and passing it along to the servers, with interest, she made for the taxi rank on King's Road, though a minimum-wage job didn't justify her taking cabs.

Tired and overheated, she just wanted to shower, get a glass of cold wine with her meal and then maybe a walk along the undercliff in the cool of the evening. So she groaned when she reached the rank to see it empty of taxis but full of people. She sighed. The bus would be a hell of sweaty tourists and insufficient seats.

Her burning feet felt too big for her shoes as she dragged out her tattered bus schedule and started the trek to the nearest stop, the heat of the day seeping up from the flagstones to cling around her aching calves.

And then Martyn Mayfair's oversized vehicle hummed up beside her.

The window eased down. 'I'm on my way to Eastingdean, if you want a lift?'

She hadn't talked to him since the snippy conversation at the bus stop and could see his smile was forced. But, being a polite Englishman, he wouldn't drive by. And being a poor dragging waitress, she wouldn't repulse his olive branch. 'Damn right!' She climbed up into the passenger seat and collapsed. 'It's been a tough day so I really appreciate the ride. Thanks.'

She sank back to enjoy the air conditioning as he steered the vehicle back into the flow of the hundred other vehicles crawling slowly along the seafront, tourists stepping into the road as if the traffic wasn't there, licking ice-creams and exhibiting red shoulders.

'You've got a job?' He touched a button on the steering wheel and the music pouring from the stereo in the centre of the dashboard diminished.

'Conference catering. Very casual and not much fun and I'm pretty sure I'm not going to stick it another week. How about you?' She hoped that sounded like a friendly enquiry and not a dig.

He held back to allow a blue sportscar to come out of a side street. 'We've just been shooting on the beach.'

Her eyebrows flew up. 'On the *beach*? I thought you guys didn't carry guns?' Having served in a room overlooking the beach for much of the day, she was amazed that she hadn't heard gunfire and sirens.

He laughed shortly. Then he threw back his head and laughed harder, as if what she'd said was sinking in. 'Well, you know. It's tourist season – that means we can shoot them.' He slapped his knee, his laughter rocking around the confines of the SUV.

Well, good. Enjoy your stupid joke and don't tell me why it's funny. She shut her eyes. The English were nuts, the lot of them.

There was an email from Stef's co-worker, Billie, short and to the point.

Honor,

Because Stef hasn't got internet access he wrote you a message and asked me to pass it to you. Here it is:

How's the moral high ground? Hope the view is better than from here. 'Here' stinks. Come on, Honor, do the right thing – come see me.

Trying to make her the guilty one, which made her boil with fury. In the circumstances.

It also made her sad. And then mad at him for making her feel sad. He wasn't happy with how things had worked out for him but he'd got himself into a fix that she couldn't get him out of. Anyway, she had to get out of the habit of taking responsibility for him.

By the time she'd showered and eaten, the sun was setting, blazing a glitter path across the ocean to the shore, and Honor's feet had recovered enough for her to want to breathe the salt air. She tied up her damp hair and zipped herself into a light fleece jacket against the evening breeze, then crossed the road.

She strolled the undercliff walkway, squinting against the sun on the water that hissed in on the shingle beach and tinkled out again. On her other side, the chalk cliffs were pink in the sinking sun and studded with flint, clumps of thrift and little fissures where seagulls made their homes.

The undercliff was quiet. Nearer to Rottingdean there might be more tourists but below Eastingdean and Saltdean she met mostly dog walkers and a handful of cyclists as the walkway jinked to follow the shape of the cliffs.

She rounded a curve and saw a cluster of teenage boys, jeering and swearing and pushing someone around. The willowy boy being pushed was trying half-heartedly to joke his way out but the pushes turned to hard shoves that, even if delivered with a certain amount of laughter, had got to hurt.

It was Rufus, from the Eastingdean Teapot.

Honor slowed as the scuffle grew into a slapping fight. On the concrete path was an enormous chalk drawing of a penis. She paused to study it. 'Anatomically correct. Your science teacher will be proud. Hi, Rufus.'

Instant silence.

Rufus tossed back his disordered hair and hid a rock of chalk behind his narrow back.

The meatiest of the others, obviously the ringleader, shoved Rufus hard in the small of his back, making Rufus's head whip back. 'Don't be a wuss 'cos some Yankee Doodle knows your name, freak. Sign it.'

Rufus turned to face the boy, much heavier and taller than himself, glancing from him to the crude drawing. And then at Honor.

The bigger boy shoved Rufus again, hard, catching him this time at the base of his neck, making him wince. 'Do it! Fucksake. Sign it.' Miserably, ducking his head, Rufus brought out his chalk.

Honor summoned up her best school marm voice. 'He doesn't have the time. Robina asked me to fetch you, Rufus. I have the car up on the road. I don't know what the problem is but she's real pissed about something.' And then, catching a sneer snaking across the bully's face, ''Fraid the cops are sitting in your front room waiting for you. So you'd better come.'

As one, the meaty boy and two weedier hangers on stepped away from Rufus, as if cop contact would contaminate them.

Eyes wide, Rufus dropped the chalk and wiped his hands on his black jeans, leaving grey smears.

'Come on,' Honor snapped. 'Don't keep the officers waiting.'

'Yeah, don't keep the officers waiting, *freak*. Right, Yankee Doodle?'

'Right, butthead,' she agreed, amiably.

Rufus fell into step beside her as she marched off. When

they'd rounded the next fold in the cliff, Honor risked a glance back. 'Your friend isn't real smart but he does seem mean. Is he likely to give us more crap?'

Rufus sighed. 'Frog? Yeah. When he's had time to think about it, he'll probably follow us and try and get me in deeper with the cops. That's what that drawing was all about – there's been stuff in the paper about obscene drawings by the local kids.'

Honor winced. 'Um ... There are no cops, so, do you want to pick up the pace, there?'

'What?'

'Run!'

They broke into a run, Rufus outdistancing Honor in a few strides and having to steady down to her speed. 'So the police don't want me?'

'No,' Honor panted, as they made for the next lot of stairs up to the road. The cliff was tall, here, and the steps became a slope about halfway up. 'I just applied the rule we used to have in high school – if you're in trouble, pretend you have to attend to worse trouble someplace else.'

He managed a short laugh as he swung around the handrail and started the first flight. 'I thought Frog had set me up, somehow. It's good news that I'm not in trouble.'

'But the bad news is I don't have a car waiting.'

He doubled the pace, as lean and fast as a greyhound. 'That's OK. I can lose Frog.'

By the time they made the top steps, Honor's thighs were burning and she was wishing all over again that she'd taken the daily runs that she'd promised herself and maybe even signed up for those Zumba classes. But she hadn't made 'running away from mean teenagers' a fitness goal.

Rufus led her across Marine Drive and up a driveway. 'Isn't this private?' she called, her jello legs struggling with the pace.

He turned and frowned, his hair blowing over his face. 'Well, dur! The idea is to keep *quiet*.'

'Oh.' Horrified that she might be denounced as a trespasser but unwilling to turn back in case the pugnacious Frog had followed them up from the undercliff, she crept after him across the edge of a lawn, as far away from the big cream-coloured art deco residence as possible, through some spiky bushes that smelled of soap, through a hole in a wooden fence, almost falling at the other side where the ground dropped two feet. Now they were on another drive. This time, Rufus turned away from the house and in a minute they were out on a quiet residential street.

Honor threw another glance behind them. 'You think we're OK?'

'Yeah. Frog doesn't know that way.'

Honor felt her breathing begin to steady. 'So how come you do?'

Rufus grinned. 'I used to do a paper round along here. I found – well, made – that place to cut through.'

Nevertheless, she kept looking behind. 'So, that charming guy back there, why do you call him Frog?' The setting sun wasn't reaching over the houses and the shadowy street was lapsing into cool twilight.

'Toby French. He's the year above me at school. He's a big brave man as long as he's got his two Tadpoles with him.'

'I know the type.' She walked beside him in silence for a couple of streets. The lamps were coming on, now, burning orange in a sky like blue metal. 'Looks to me like he's giving you problems.'

Rufus shrugged and hunched his shoulders, jamming his hands in his pockets and walking faster. 'It happens.'

She tried to keep up. 'Happened to me a time or two but I had a badass friend and that helped a lot.' Stef. She pictured him in high school with his tawny hair blowing, his thumbs hooked in the pockets of his jeans. In the days when he'd been an asset and not a liability.

Rufus sniffed. 'Yeah? Well, I haven't got a badass friend.'

Pity. 'Maybe we can get you a badass reputation, then.'

He laughed without humour. 'I've got a reputation but not as a badass.'

Freak. Honor heard the word spewing from Frog's nasty mouth, remembered the way that Rufus had recoiled.

He led her down an opening and across the top of Saltdean Park, away from the beach, into one street after another. He was taking her back to Eastingdean. In fact, she suddenly realised, he was taking her in the direction of The Butts. 'Do you live at your Mom's tearooms?'

'Yup.'

When they reached the broad sweep of The Butts, he hurdled a trough of petunias and made for a passage up the side of the tearoom. Then he paused, shooting glances at her from the corner of his eye. 'I don't want you to tell my mum. About Frog.' He concentrated on his scuffling feet.

Honor leaned against the wall, tucking her hands into her pockets. 'Your mom makes great cakes,' she observed, as if just remembering.

'Yeah. Do you want to, like, come in or something?'

'Not if it's going to make your mom ask lots of awkward questions.'

'She will. She'll get–' He revolved his hands in the air as if juggling words and being unable to find the right ones.

'Will she charge around to Frog's house and try and sock him on the jaw?'

He shook his head. 'No, she'll charge round but put a spell on him or something. It's well embarrassing.'

Honor snorted with laughter. 'Like a witch? You're kidding me.'

'No, not really. 'Cos she's not a witch, although she once

bought a book of occult symbols,' he replied, gloomily. 'It would be cool if she could turn his eyes yellow or make his knob drop off or something. But she can't. She'll just rant and tell him that he's got bad Karma and I'm "her little Ru" and he'll wet himself making pathetic jokes about Kanga, Roo and Winnie-the-Pooh. Then he'll tell everyone at school that my mum's dead weird. Again. And I'm a freak.'

Honor twisted her ponytail with her fingers. 'I don't suppose this is his last year at your school?'

Despondently, Ru shook his head. 'He's got another year at least. Anyway, he lives near.' He nodded towards some unspecified location. Then, suddenly, 'Here's Mum.'

A small white van rolled up to the kerb and Honor saw Robina staring at them through the passenger window. As soon as the wheels stopped turning, she jumped out. 'Hello?' she said, to Honor, curiously.

The driver of the van was Sophie, the woman who worked with Robina in the Eastingdean Teapot. She climbed out of the other door.

'Hi!' said Honor, in her best American tourist accent. 'How are you today? We met already, didn't we? In your tearoom? I was just asking your son about the community centre and wondering whether to join some classes. You know, I'm new around here.'

Robina looked amused. 'I doubt Ru knows much about the community centre. We don't do joining in, do we, Ru? We're more … free spirits! Eh, Sophie?'

Sophie beamed. Her hair, now it was free of its hairnet, hung straight to her shoulders. 'That's us.'

'So, how was Crusty, at the hospital?' broke in Ru.

'*Kirsty* is still quite ill.' Robina frowned. 'Bloody doctors have no idea what's wrong with her. "It's a virus," they say, but they don't know which. Or how to treat her. They try her with no-good crap medicine and it has no effect. I took her St. John's Wort and echinacea.'

'Your friend sounds really sick,' Honor commiserated. 'I guess the St John's will help if she's feeling down and the echinacea is to help her immune system?'

Robina shifted on her leather-sandalled feet, then changed the subject, making Honor suspect that she had no idea about herbal properties and had simply grabbed a couple of things from the holistic health shop at Starboard Walk. 'So, Ru, my little Ru, I'm afraid you're going to have to help us out for the summer. Kirsty isn't going to be well enough to work for weeks.'

'Shit,' muttered Ru.

Honor looked into his lean, sad face. 'You weren't looking for a summer job?'

'I just got one.' He shot a defiant look at his mother. 'Taking money on a ride on the seafront in Brighton. It's really cool on the rides. It's wicked, Brighton.'

'But Kirsty's ill,' Robina pointed out, delving into a large, green canvas bag embroidered with peacocks. 'Me and Sophie can't manage, Ru.'

'Not on our own,' agreed Sophie.

'Put a card up in the window,' Rufus wheedled. 'Get someone.'

Pulling out her keys, Robina waved them around, as if wiping his words from the evening air. 'I can't get my head round interviewing and all that stuff. If I put a card up I'll be mobbed. C'mon, Ru, don't give me a hard time.'

Ru hunched even more. 'You just can't be bothered.'

Robina gave him a hug. 'Don't be grouchy, little Ru!'

Ru accepted the embrace but his brows lowered over stormy milk-chocolate eyes. Honor could see why he'd hate to give up a summer job on the Brighton seafront in favour of serving cake in his mother's tearoom. Eastingdean's aging holidaymakers wore comfy clothes and sensible shoes, whereas Brighton's rides would attract crowds of giggling girls with short skirts and high heels. The rides would be a lot better for him. He'd have fun.

She opened her mouth and words slid out. 'How about me?'

Robina cocked her head. 'You?'

'I'm working as a waitress for a catering company in Brighton but I'm looking for something else. I've worked in coffee shops before, when I was in school. I only expect to make minimum wage and I'm a local girl until September.' She already knew enough about Robina to know that what she was suggesting was not necessarily a good idea, but Ru was looking at her with such blissed-out hope that the words just kept on coming. 'My name's Honor Sontag. Why don't you give me a try?'

'Yeah, Mum, give her a try,' Rufus urged.

Robina frowned. 'What's wrong with the job you've got?'

'It stinks.'

Sophie giggled. 'She sounds OK, Robbie.'

Robina shrugged, as if who worked in the tearoom was of no importance, just so long as someone did. 'OK. Come tomorrow, about eleven.'

And she brushed past, up the passage to a side door with a light that came on as she approached, Sophie scurrying after.

Ru didn't follow. He leaned against the wall, his hair blowing in the wind until the door had shut behind his mother and Sophie. 'Good one. Thought I was going to be stuck with a crap summer.'

'You don't like working for your mom?'

'She's OK as long as other people do the donkey work and she's free to make her work-of-art cakes. Soppy Sophie does my head in, though. Crusty isn't quite so bad but Soppy is so giggly.' He grimaced. 'But watch her. She's sweet as pie only so long as Mum likes you.'

Honor pulled a face. 'Maybe I ought to reconsider–'

He grinned and amended, hastily, 'You'll love them.' And, as if to stop her thinking about the subject too deeply, 'Are you seeing that Martyn Mayfair? Him from the buses?'

Martyn's involvement with buses was news to Honor but maybe he drove a tour bus? It would explain why he was away from home for a few days at a time. 'I just rent my place from his sister.'

'I saw you out running with him.'

'Yeah, we did, once. He nearly killed me because he's superfit. I'm not dating him or anything.' Definitely no 'anything'.

Ru nodded. 'That's good, because Mum's got a thing about him. She can get … intense.'

'Oh-kay.' Unease slithered down her spine. She hadn't really considered Robina's stalky tendencies. 'Isn't she quite a lot older than him?'

'S'pose. She's not bothered about things like that.' His forehead settled into lines that he seemed awfully young to have.

Honor felt bad for him. 'Thanks for the heads up. So, what are you going to tell Frog, when he asks about the cops?'

He shrugged. It seemed the gesture most familiar to him.

'Tell him a tourist made a complaint,' Honor suggested. 'Just say something like, "I didn't know I'd hurt him" and refuse to give details. It'll be just enough to make him wonder.'

He managed a smile. 'OK. Thanks.'

Honor wished she could come up with something better to stop Frog picking on Ru. Although creating a badass reputation seemed a good idea in principle and it had worked for Stef, who rarely had to get physical to keep trouble at arm's length, she wasn't really sure how to go about it.

Chapter Nine

Martyn liked where he lived. It didn't sound glamorous to say that his place was over shops, but as Starboard Walk was right at the sea end of The Butts he had a fantastic view over the cliffs to the Channel. The small block had been renovated specifically to appeal to those discerning enough to patronise Belinda's hat shop, Holistic Harmony, a nice Italian restaurant and an upmarket confectioners, the kind that sold sugared almonds in cellophane tied with curly gold ribbon.

He liked the black iron external stairway that ran down past the flint-studded walls at one end of the block and the black iron balcony that bellied out at the other, with enough room for him to sit with the occasional beer and watch the waves and the road disappearing east towards Peacehaven or west to Saltdean, Rottingdean and Brighton.

Before he let himself out on Saturday morning, he did a quick check of the car park from his bedroom. And there was Robina, hanging idly around as if looking for something. He stepped back as she looked up. Waited until, with one last look, she wandered off with that *life has disappointed me* look.

To give her time to get clear, he opened his laptop and spent twenty minutes on Facebook, before he set off on his favourite run along the undercliff to Rottingdean; it didn't matter if it wasn't early because the day didn't threaten to be hot. An army of ragged white clouds marched before a scurrying breeze but it didn't feel as if rain was on the way. He'd lived all his life on this cliff top, and knew.

Locking the door, he turned to run down the iron stairway

only to find Clarissa on her way up. 'Oh cra– Hello,' he said.

She gave him A Look but didn't comment on his unenthusiastic greeting. 'I was hoping to catch you. Could you please call on our American friend?'

Oh. 'If you need me to.' He put the slightest stress on the word *need*.

Clarissa's sharpened gaze told him that she hadn't missed the emphasis. 'Not if you've got a full day,' she said, evenly.

'Running and volleyball. Then I have to talk to Ace.'

Clarissa's nose wrinkled. She had never met Ace Smith but disdained as an affectation his having rearranged his name from Jason, through Jace, to Ace. But if you were a Smith, you had to do something if you wanted to be memorable, in Martyn's view.

'So does that count as a full day?'

He debated staying where he was, towering above her, but decided it was unnecessarily combatant – exactly the trait he disliked in her – so jumped down several steps until their eyes were level. He even managed a smile. 'How about you tell me what it is you need help with and then I'll tell you whether I can do it?'

When she returned his smile, ten years fled her face. 'It's that brilliant digital thermostat thingy that Duncan put in at the bungalow. Honor "cain't figyure it out".' She put on a horrible American accent that owed more to Jesse James than to Honor's musical New England syllables. 'It's an unco-operative thing and you have to get it into a certain mode before the water will heat without the radiators.' She pulled a pamphlet from her pocket. 'I found the instructions. I've been asked to take on a tap class in Hove or I would have gone myself. The instructor is ill and I might be able to keep the class permanently, if I get them out of a hole, now.'

'OK.' He took the instruction leaflet and slid it into the pocket on the front of his sweatshirt. He supposed his path was bound to keep crossing with Honor's, what with Clarissa being her landlady and a pain in his backside. Prickly Clarissa. She was all attitude. Why couldn't she have explained about the class from the start instead of trying to guilt him into helping by hinting he had nothing else to do?

'Thanks.' She checked her watch and turned towards her white VW Beetle with pink-and-lilac heart decals streaming along the doors. She took dance classes at some funky gyms and thought it made her look cool, but the car didn't suit her. A Hummer would better reflect her personality, capable of barging past everything in her way.

As she drove off, he performed his stretches at the foot of the iron stairway, tightening his laces whilst he held position. Then he jogged along the pavement, over the crossing, across the grass and down the steps to the broad concrete promenade at the foot of the cliffs.

Setting the stopwatch on his watch, he set off, letting his stride lengthen, running smoothly, avoiding the litter of chalky rocks at the foot of the cliff lying in wait to twist the ankles of the unwary. The rhythm of his stride was as natural to him as his heartbeat.

Uh-oh. There she was, on a bench.

Not even subtle. Bloody Robina.

He picked up his pace.

And up she hopped as she saw him coming, tossing back her hair and moving into the middle of the walk to intercept him. 'Hi! Good to see you! I was just thinking–'

The wind whipped the rest of her words away as he powered up, tossing, 'Excuse me,' at her as he flew past, settling in for a hard run between Eastingdean and Rottingdean, the wind flipping his hair. People watched him. He was used to that. Weaving past buggies and children; past the underpass and on to the slipway below the White Horse Hotel, slowing, trotting up the stairs, down the slope, up the stairs, down the slope, on to the steep beach and, as the tide was out, down to the sea, careful not to turn an ankle on the pebbles. Then back the way he'd come, welcoming the wind to cool him until he turned into the underpass and around into the park to beat up and down the grassy slope, feeling his buttock muscles begin to burn and then his calves. Turn at the top, trot down, muscles relaxing. Turn, run back up.

He slowed, cooling down a level. Slowed again when he reached the tree that he and Honor had lounged beneath, its dappled shade dancing over her body. He checked his watch and ran on up the slope … turn … down. He was jogging towards the rubber courts now, where a volleyball net was being run between the posts. One of the men securing the net turned and waved. Martyn lifted his hand in return. 'Hey, Jamie.' Last one. Up … turn … down.

Then he trotted into the court, high-fived with Jamie, who he'd known since school, back when Jamie was thinner, shouting hellos, receiving a few good-natured insults in return. Throwing a pound coin into a box, he took a bottle of cold water out, making himself sip instead of gulp, taking up station at the back in the freezone, ready to return long serves. The blokes nearest to him, Tim and Elliot, grinned and said, 'All right?'

And he said, 'Yup. You?' That was all the conversation needed.

Saturday morning volleyball was shaped by who turned up; the game seemed to organise itself. They'd played fourteen-a-side a couple of weeks ago. Nobody cared. It was fun, an opportunity to run and stretch, dodge and return the ball. Martyn had no competitiveness for sport at this level – he just enjoyed hanging out with the guys. He didn't even know all their names and it didn't matter.

Jamie pinged the net and shouted, 'Everyone ready?'

Martyn's laconic, 'Just get on with it,' acted like a

commence-of-play whistle and the ball was punched up towards the sun.

The moment the old grey ball sailed towards Martyn he forgot all about his irritation with Clarissa and Robina. He jumped, he passed, he spun out of the way of a teammate with a shout of, 'Yours!' and he served with ferocious spikes. He got hot enough to yank off his sweatshirt, grinning through the resultant yowl of catcalls. He gave the impression that he was focused on nothing but the game.

But the impending visit to the bungalow floated around his mind.

He glanced up to where they'd talked together on the grassy slope. He'd done everything except stick a sign on his forehead saying *Interested!* He leapt high and punched the ball back over the net, where it clipped the corner of the court and squirted away before it could be returned. 'Yesssss!'

What was it with married women not wearing wedding rings?

After five sets the game broke up with as little ceremony as it had begun. The net and ball were bundled into Jamie's holdall and the players melted away in ones and twos. 'See you!'

'Yeah, next week.'

Martyn wriggled back into his top and drank the rest of his bottle of water. He felt good. The exercise had soothed him.

He strolled across the grass towards Marine Drive, the shortest route to the bungalow. The traffic, changing gear for the hill, seemed loud after the comparative calm in the park. His legs felt pleasantly worked and, for once, he walked, rather than ran, the whole way, even up the steps to the bungalow.

When Honor opened the door, she smiled her surprise. That mouth. Her smile punched right into his soul.

He dragged the – now dogeared – leaflet from his sweatshirt pocket and her smile faded. 'Oh shoot. I guess your si– Clarissa worked on you to come. I didn't mean to get you another errand to run. Just leave the instructions and I'm sure to be able to figure it out.'

'It's OK,' he found himself saying, as if he hadn't spent all morning fulminating about how not OK it was. 'I told Clarissa I'd make sure the thermostat's functioning.' For a moment their eyes locked and held, as if they were both remembering the kiss that never was, right here against this very door. And reaching unanimous agreement to move on.

In a white shirt and black jeans, her hair rippling from a ponytail high on her head, she was more of a turn on than all the women he met who spent their days in full make-up and sexy, expensive clothes. Someone else's wife or not, she was lithe and graceful and pretty as hell. And he still liked the shape of her mouth. The shape of all of her, in fact.

She stepped back to let him in. 'Sure, if you really have time to be the hero, it's in the hallway. I'm trying out for a new job at eleven so I don't have the time to argue.' She disappeared into the bathroom, leaving the door ajar, as he stooped to peer at the digital readout of the wall thermostat.

He could hear her rustling around. 'So, what's the new job?' He gazed at a diagram labelled in three languages.

'You'll hate it.'

'*I'll* hate it?' He looked at the little white plastic thermostat.

'I'm helping out at the Eastingdean Teapot. You know, taking orders, carrying food, bussing tables. *Clearing* tables.'

'You're joking!' He found the reset button under the plastic box of the thermostat unit and all the figures flicked off and came on again. When he turned, through the half-open door he could see her making big eyes at the mirror whilst applying her mascara in tiny flicks. 'Tell me you're joking.' He stabbed the mode button twice and heard the boiler hiss into life in the bathroom, then leaned his back against the wall and watched her some more.

'No …' The word elongated as she turned her face slightly and tickled the lashes at the corner of an eye. She studied the result, gave a little nod and put the mascara away. She squirted something at her neck and then a different something over her hair.

He tried to keep his voice calm and even. 'You're working for Robina? You know she's bonkers, don't you?'

She came out to plant herself in front of him. 'Only about you.'

'Does that make it any better? Bonkers is bonkers. Working with her might taint you, too.' He turned back to the thermostat. 'Let me show you this. It's a lot easier once you're let into the secret that the mode and reset buttons are hidden underneath this little flap, under the unit. So all you have to do to make changes is go to this mode and play around with the arrow buttons.'

For two seconds, her head was directly below his chin as she inspected the buttons. 'Ah, I get it, thank you. Is every woman who has a crush on you "bonkers"?' She took a step away but her perfume had already clonked him over the head. The hallway was too small for her to put much distance between them. He breathed the perfume in, unable to look away from her eyes; compelling, searching, flecked with gold. She should have been a lawyer – hypnotising criminals into confessing everything. Or putting their arms around her, lifting her off her feet and kissing that fascinating, fine-lipped mouth … 'No. It's just that Robina's–'

'–your stalker.' Her tone was solemn but her eyes twinkled, as if now that she'd had time to consider the matter she doubted his claims. 'Teenage crush behaviour is odd for a grown woman, I suppose. But she seems quite–'

'–bonkers,' he supplied.

'I was going to say *individual*. I'll make up my own mind about the rest.' She turned towards her bedroom. 'Are you heading home? I'm going to the Eastingdean Teapot, now. Shall I walk along with you? If that wouldn't make me bonkers …' She emerged with a jacket over her arm and two little books in her hand, one red and one blue.

'You don't need one passport to travel in Eastingdean,' he observed, 'let alone two.'

She collected her key from the hall table. 'No, but the employer needs to see the employee's passport for her to start work, in your country. So, I thought I'd bring both, just in case.'

'I don't remember seeing a US passport before.' He tweaked the blue passport from her fingers.

She held out her hand. 'I'll have that back, OK?'

'OK,' he agreed, but flicked through the pages. 'It's no different to a UK passport, really.' She probably thought her passport photo made her look stupid – women usually did think that – so he flipped to the photo page. Not too bad, really, although she looked younger and way too serious. He made to restore the passport to her waiting hand. Then paused.

'Hey,' he said. 'Honor's your middle name. Your first name is Freedom.'

Chapter Ten

She closed her hand around the little blue book. 'It's a name I don't use,' she snapped. 'I'm Honor. I've always been Honor. It's not that unusual, in the States, for well-meaning parents to give offbeat names or to have the kid known by the name that appears second or third on their birth certificate.' She ushered him through the front door and locked it behind him.

'Sorry.' His gaze was curious. 'Didn't mean to touch a nerve.'

She tucked keys and her passports into her bag. 'It's not that. It's just that people knowing always gives me a squirmy feeling because I'm kind of embarrassed. When I was young, other kids would poke fun when I got a new teacher and she called out for "Freedom Lefevre" instead of Honor Lefevre. Then there was the movie, *Cry Freedom*, and whenever that came around on cable it made all the other kids laugh.' She set off down the steps. 'I'm a little sensitive because it was the name that my mother gave to me then took her own freedom by leaving me. Ironic, huh? Dad hated it and it was him who picked Honor. He says that the names they chose indicated what each of them valued most. He and Grandma called me Honor and the Freedom part became just an irritating entry on my birth certificate.'

'And your passports,' he included, helpfully.

She frowned. 'I don't use the name *at all*. I just never got around to changing it legally.'

He fell into step beside her. 'But Freedom's a fantastic name. Freedom Lefevre. You sound like a porn star.'

She flicked him a glance. 'Gee, that changes everything.'

He laughed. 'OK, that didn't come out right. I meant to say that Freedom Lefevre sounds very hot.'

She breathed out, slowly. 'I'd still appreciate it if you'd just forget it. I'm already the odd one out around here, and I want to integrate, rather than to stand out with a stupid hippy name.'

'OK.' He shrugged.

'And I haven't used Lefevre since I got married – I'm Honor Sontag. OK?'

'OK,' he said, again, without inflection.

They turned the corner into The Butts and he halted at the end of the block. 'This is where I peel off.' He indicated a set of stairs like a fire escape up the side of a building.

She looked up at the door above, in the wall. 'Is this your place? It must be kind of fun to live over a shop.'

'I like it.'

Saying her goodbyes, she turned towards the Eastingdean Teapot but she knew her face was burning and wished he hadn't brought all the Freedom stuff to the surface. It had made her feel stirred up about her mom. Churning. Irritated. Angry.

How had she forgotten about Freedom being on her passport? She definitely wanted to be known as Honor. She pushed the passports right to the bottom of her bag.

'Helloo,' sang Sophie, from the white-tiled kitchen, as Honor pushed through the dark green door of the tearoom. 'Here's our latest helper.'

'Hi,' answered Honor, shortly, glad to have the opportunity to feel irritated with Sophie instead of with her mother.

Robina called from the other side of the kitchen's central island. 'I'm just going to run up to the butcher's for some fresh sausage meat for the sausage rolls. Back in five minutes.'

Sophie's pink shiny face grew pinker. It couldn't get any

shinier. Her default expression was a grin and she sprinkled her conversation with giggles. 'I'll look after you, Honor. Come through. We've just got lots of lovely local ladies in for their elevenses, at the moment, and we won't get busy for another half hour. I've got you an apron ready and, look, all the cleaning things are over here – and gloves because some of these cleaners would strip your skin. Robina's actually very save-the-planet but the kitchen has to be cleaned properly.' She giggled. 'Anyway, the job's easy, especially if you've worked as a waitress already. Menus are on the table and when the customers look ready, you take a pad and a pen and you go and ask them what they want – and then you come back to the counter and tell us!' She gave a tiny snort, like a giggly piglet.

Honor smiled, cautiously. 'What are "elevenses"?'

Another giggle. 'Morning snack. Second breakfast. Whatever you want it to be. Anyway,' said Sophie, suddenly becoming brisk, 'Kirsty says you have to fill out a form.' She led Honor out of the kitchen and into an office the size of a cupboard and selected a tatty blue folder from a pile, sorting through until she located a particular form. 'This is for people who haven't got a P45, I think.' She paused, doubtfully, form extended. 'I've never employed a foreigner before. Kirsty usually does all the admin stuff – she's brilliant at it.'

Honor pushed the form right back, seeing the opportunity to avoid revealing her stupid first name to Sophie and Robina. 'But I will have this P45 thing you need. I called Lawrence last night and he said that he'd send me my P45 and it would be straightforward for you. I'm not a foreigner because I have a UK passport, which he has already seen, so you don't have to,' she added, firmly.

'So that's OK then?' asked Sophie, vaguely. 'I could ask Kirsty when she comes home from hospital but she's been so poorly. So ...'

'So we're all set. I'll tie on my apron.'

'Brilliant!' beamed Sophie. Her interests obviously lay outside of the cupboard/office. Robina returned with her bag of sausage meat, Sophie became busy in the hot little kitchen and Honor was free to wait on the eighteen small tables, six inside and twelve out, where the customers proved to be friendly, probably because it's difficult to be miserable if you're eating cake to die for.

The cakes were legendary. Even customers who ordered a sandwich or homemade soup, jacket potatoes or a toastie, almost all succumbed to the sweet stuff as well.

Cakes were Robina's thing. The business model at the Teapot soon became clear as Robina serenely mixed, iced, filled and baked, and Sophie and Honor darted around her. Pinging sandwich toasters, hissing coffee frothers and bricks of cheese to be grated were not for her.

Luckily, Sophie was an octopus, turning things on, off or over, stirring, chopping, heating and beating, ever pinker and usually beaming.

Honor began to like her.

The coffee shop opened at ten in the morning and closed whenever Robina decided to shut it. Honor was meant to cover the busy time of eleven until four-thirty, five days a week, where most needed. She was getting ready to wind down her first shift when she checked her outside tables and saw that one had been taken over by three teenagers wearing ball caps and hooded sweatshirts.

She had no trouble recognising Frog and his Tadpoles. Snatching up pad and pen, she bustled outside.

'Hey, you guys,' she cried, as if she'd never been so delighted to see anyone in her life. 'And what can I get for you today?'

Frog narrowed his eyes. 'Hey, Yankee Doodle. We're waiting.'

'Uh-huh.' She nodded. 'And what can I get for you whilst you're waiting?' Then, because he looked puzzled, 'These seats are for customers. If you're not buying, you're not customers.' She smiled her widest, falsest smile.

Frog did not smile back. 'Where is he?'

She clicked her pen. 'Who?'

'The freak.'

Honor put on an owlish expression.

'Ru Gordon,' enunciated slowly.

'Rufus?' She cast a furtive glance behind her, lowering her voice. 'He's not here, today.'

The Tadpoles looked at Frog. Frog stuffed his hands into his pockets. Grey clouds were gathering out to sea. 'We came to see what happened last night,' he said.

Honor shrugged, plain stupid on the outside, boiling fury inside. 'You lost me.'

'With the freak and the cops.'

'Why do you call him the freak? Oh.' She looked around again. 'Oh, I get it! That's what happened, with that tourist, right? He just freaked out? Wow.' She shook her head gravely, noting, with satisfaction, the grins on the faces of Frog and the Tadpoles fading to frowns. Hamming it up, she hissed, 'You didn't hear it from me but he's still at the police station. Rufus said it was self-defence but, *y'know*.'

A pause for effect, then she hurried back into the tearoom and watched through the window as the three boys gazed at each other and made *what the fuck?* faces.

Content with her first foray into reinventing Ru as a badass, she danced into the kitchen and reached around to untie her apron. Robina looked up from sliding a heavy fruitcake into a green-and-white tin. 'We're stopping serving, now, so I thought that, as you're working out so well you could stay another hour and help us with the clean down.' She made it sound like a treat that Honor had earned by merit.

It turned out that 'help us with the clean down' actually meant 'help Sophie with the clean down', while Robina slid sponge cakes destined to become tomorrow's gateaux out of the oven and on to cooling racks, carrying them tenderly off to spend the night on a marble shelf in an adjoining pantry, safe from blasting bleach sprays.

Honor helped wash counters and polish stainless steel so that it didn't dry streaky, joining in when Sophie sang James Taylor songs as she worked. Her dad had just about every track that James Taylor had recorded.

'Time for a treat for the workers!' Robina sailed back into the kitchen and frothed up three mugs of coffee, then sandwiched together coffee cake with leftover chocolate frosting, spread some over the top, sprinkled the frosting with chopped nuts – blithely undoing much of the clean down – and led Sophie and Honor outside to one of the as-yet-to-be-sanitised green-painted tables.

Sophie seemed quite unfazed by having her kitchen mucked up in pursuit of a jolly calorific break. Robina obviously wasn't a routine kind of woman. At this rate, Honor would finish at nearer six than four-thirty. But, anyway. Having served delectable cake to other people for most of the day, she really did feel that she deserved a piece. Her waistline would forgive her, especially when she re-established her planned routine of running and dancing.

Following their lead, she propped her feet on the rungs of the table and tipped her chair just enough to relieve the pressure from the base of the spine, as the last few customers finished up at other tables, people strolled the street and the traffic built up.

'There he is!' Robina burst out, just as Honor took her

first bite of the beautifully moist coffee cake, the chocolate frosting melting like music on her tongue.

Sophie snorted. 'Oh, Ro*bina*!' Her brows curled crossly. 'You're really sad, sometimes, Robbie. A sad old bat.'

Honor paused mid-bite, astounded that Sophie could, apparently, be something other than sycophantically approving of Robina.

Robina's expression was tragic, her eyes welling real tears. 'Isn't he gorgeous? Look at those eyes. Look at that body! Isn't it knicker-wetting? I love him, I love him, I *love* him.'

Bewildered, Honor followed Robina's gaze. It was fixed on one of the cream-and-red buses that rolled down The Butts several times a day in the direction of Marine Drive. On the bus side was an advertisement for men's cologne from le Dur, a two-deck-high black-and-white image of a man whose dark stubble defined a cleft chin and hollow cheeks, his naked torso sculpted and spare, his stretchy, sketchy cotton trunks clinging.

'I love him,' Robina whispered.

Chapter Eleven

'Holy shit!' Honor inhaled half her cake.

Hacking and coughing through a suffocation of crumbs, she blinked streaming eyes to gaze at about fifteen feet of smouldering Martyn Mayfair as the image moved slowly down the street. 'Martyn's a *model*?'

'Don't we all know it?' sniffed Sophie, patting Honor between the shoulder blades with enough force to suggest she was mad about something.

'I sure didn't!' She looked over to Robina. 'And you, um ...?'

Robina, eyes still glued to the bus, was hugging herself and rocking. 'I'm in love with him. And he rips my guts out on a regular basis because he hardly seems to know that I exist.'

'Right.' Honor wiped her eyes. She could have told Robina that Martyn certainly did know that Robina existed – but, classic stalker avoidance, he was ignoring her. Refusing to engage. Refusing to feed her obsession.

She felt sorry for Robina but, wow. For his picture to be fifteen-feet high on a bus, Martyn must be 'someone'. Possibly he dealt with unwanted attention all the time. Images of his near-naked body were in the street for any crazy lady to drool over. Holy freakin' Joe. When he'd mentioned Twitter and Facebook he probably meant that people could 'like' his pages and join as 'fans'.

Slowly, her image of Martyn broke and reformed. It wasn't that he didn't have much work.

He just didn't have to work much.

She cringed when she remembered trying to tip him ten

pounds for shopping for her groceries. Zoë had just sent him off on the errand like he was her little brother. Not a male model, with his picture on the side of a bus.

Him from the buses. That's what Rufus had called him.

We've been shooting on Brighton beach. Shooting photos, dur-brain!

One of the Mayfairs doesn't hide very much. Honor had brushed Peggy's schoolgirl giggling aside as incomprehensible English humour but now … well, those tight trunks weren't hiding much of Martyn Mayfair.

The bus trundled off to pick up passengers in Saltdean and Rottingdean. 'And you're in love with him,' Honor repeated, blankly.

'It's not a hanging offence.' Robina seemed to be recovering, picking up her cake fork and plate, though her doe eyes were still red-rimmed. 'Neither of us are married or members of the clergy. We could get relationshippy.'

Honor tore her eyes away from the corner where the bus had turned out of sight towards Brighton – right outside Martyn's home, in fact. She tried to make herself sound not-shocked. 'No, you're right. There's no law against being in love.' And, then, feebly, 'Maybe one day he'll feel, uh, *relationshippy*, too.'

'Huh! Never.' Sophie's pinkness had drawn in to two angry patches high up on her cheekbones.

Robina glared, her eyes dark. 'He *might*.'

'Pigs might fly. Just give him up, Robbie. Relationshippy – you've always laughed at being relationshippy! You used to shout at Tucker for getting "all relationshippy" on you.'

Scowling, Robina folded her arms. 'Me and Tucker were relationshippy.'

Sophie made a rude noise. 'He might have been, poor sod, but you, not really.' And then, as if regretting her bluntness, she flung down her plate and threw her arms around her friend. 'Robbie, you know that there's no chance. He's years younger and he tries never to talk to you. Give up, darling. Give up. It's not going to happen.'

Dolefully, Robina began to sniff again. 'He used to be my friend.'

Sophie's voice sank. 'Well … he stopped by the Teapot for coffee, sometimes.'

'Decaff,' Robina nodded. 'He doesn't eat much cake or drink lots of caffeine. He has to take care of his body and his skin because it's his living. His face is his fortune.' She gave a watery giggle. 'Not just his face–'

'But he doesn't stop by any more, Robbie, does he?' asked Sophie, gently. 'Like, never.'

They finished the clean down quietly, even Robina spraying and wiping until the sweetness of cakes in the air was overcome by bleach and damp cloths.

Energetically applying elbow grease to the sinks, Sophie was obviously intent on springing Robina from her black mood. 'It'll be lovely to have Kirsty home tomorrow, Robbie, won't it?'

'Yes.' Robina didn't look up.

Sophie turned to Honor. 'Her sister will bring her, because we couldn't fetch her until evening.'

Honor polished the coffee frother. 'Is she coming out of the hospital and right back to work?'

'No! She won't be back at work yet.' Sophie rinsed her steaming cloth. 'She'll go straight to bed, I expect. Whatever the virus is, it made her really ill. The doctors said she could come out if she rested.'

'So she's coming here because she's still too sick to go home?'

Robina began blasting hot water into the mop bucket, the metal kind with a mechanism on top to squeeze the mop.

'She lives upstairs with me and Ru. Sophie, too.' The mop bucket clanged as Robina let it down on the floor. Dark hair was springing out all around her bandana that, today, was embroidered with the yin and the yang. 'When Tucker died he left the Teapot and the flat to me. Then Soph and Kirst moved in.' Robina splashed her mop into the bucket. 'Tucker was a good guy. But he was in a car crash.'

'It's three years, now,' Sophie explained, sadly, collecting the cloths and dropping them into a smaller bucket of bleach and cold water. She brightened. 'But when me and Kirsty moved into the flat, we took Tucker's place in the tearoom. So we all work together and live together.'

Honor smiled, wondering if Ru ever felt swamped by oestrogen. 'Wow. You and Tucker really were … relationshippy,' Honor tried out the word self-consciously, 'if he left you the Teapot, Robina.'

'It's a bloody big responsibility,' she grumbled, setting to with the mop as if she could clean the Teapot off the face of the earth if she rubbed hard enough. 'A business is worse than a small child. It always needs attention.'

Sophie gazed at her friend reproachfully, her hair beginning to escape its net. 'I think it was fabulous of Tucker to leave it to you. You've got no mortgage and me and Kirsty pay rent to you, on top of the profit that the tearoom makes.'

'But there's always plenty to pay out and it's a pain when I want to go away.' Robina stabbed the mop in the steaming water then trod on the gizmo that squeezed the water out. 'I've missed the Isle of Wight Festival, Download and Glastonbury, this summer–'

'Isle of Wight and Download festivals are on at the same time so you couldn't have gone to both, anyway.' Sophie dug her hands into her apron pocket as if digging in her heels.

'–*and*,' flared Robina obstinately, 'I'm missing Latitude right this minute!' She threw the mop on the floor, ripped off her apron and stamped out of the front door, leaving the 'closed' sign swinging behind her.

Sophie made a face. 'I don't think she'll get to the Global Gathering, either,' she whispered, as if Robina might be lurking in earshot. 'Because Kirsty usually keeps the Teapot open while we're away – Kirsty doesn't "do" festivals, so she's quite happy to stay here. But the Global Gathering's only two weeks from now.'

'You're talking about music festivals, right?'

Sophie picked up the mop, rinsed it and gave it a squeeze. 'That's right. Kirsty isn't going to be well enough.'

'And you can't stay behind, to look after the shop?'

Sophie propped the mop in the corner and hung up Robina's apron. 'Robina and me go together,' she said, firmly. 'And Little Ru, of course, but he often goes all sulky, so he's no company.'

Honor pulled off her own apron. 'Was Robina fixated on Martyn Mayfair when Tucker was alive?'

Sophie shook her head, freeing more of her hair to dance around her head. 'Oh no, she and Tucker were cool. Robina was happier with him than with anyone and he took care of her and loved her. She didn't get hooked on Martyn Mayfair until after Tucker died. Then she developed a bit of a crush on him.'

Thinking back to Robina's storm of grief on seeing Martyn's picture on the bus, Honor murmured, 'Some crush.'

When Honor finally stepped outside, the traffic had eased and the gulls were exchanging heartbroken cries. It was much later than she'd expected to finish work and she could smell something delicious. Despite the coffee cake, her stomach rumbled as she looked around to identify the source.

And there it was, right across the street, a glowing blue

Fish 'n Chips sign flashing in a window running with condensation. Her mouth watered. English chips had always been a huge favourite with her and Jess and Zach. Somehow tastier than American fries – although soggier, also – *fish 'n chips* couldn't be good for her but, right that instant, they were what she wanted most in the world. In moments she'd joined the patient queue that curled around the steamy interior where great fat fryers sizzled and a hot cabinet of golden battered fish and round crinkly pies sat above.

She ordered her fish and chips 'open' and watched the frying guy shake salt and vinegar over them, then set off to walk home, eating as she went. Very English. Especially the vinegar. Frankly? That was weird. But when in England, one should do as the English do.

She broke off a steaming hot battered morsel of fish and popped it in her mouth, hollowing her cheeks and puffing to try to make it cool enough to chew, glancing in shop windows and thinking how freaky Robina was about Martyn. And his picture sliding past Honor's astonished eyes on the side of that bus – wow. That had been something.

Nearing the Starboard Walk shops she glanced up at Martyn Mayfair's front door planted in the flint wall high above the street, with its access stairway, like a fire escape, cutting diagonally across the building to where the cars parked to the side of and behind the shops.

'You freak!' The words cut the evening air, making Honor jump. The voice continued more quietly, so that Honor couldn't make out the words. But the tone was as hissy as a rat. Soundlessly, she crept around the shrubs that divided the small parking area from the road. It was Frog she saw first, more distinctly as she drew nearer. 'Thing is, freak, you're beginning to get on my nerves.' Honor took another step.

Then saw Rufus.

The Tadpoles had him, spread-eagled against a wall.

Chapter Twelve

Only Rufus's eyes moved, desperately seeking escape. His green striped shirt was torn and hanging off one shoulder. His eyes kept coming back to Frog. Eyes full of fury and fear. And, worst of all, to Honor, resignation. He was steeling himself for whatever bad thing was coming and, judging from the way that the grinning Tadpoles had their ankles hooked around Ru's to spread his legs, what was coming probably involved a hefty kick where it really hurt.

From her position, Honor could see that beneath his baseball cap, Frog's face shone with the incomprehensible pleasure of the bully. 'And what do I do to people who get on my nerves, freak?' Frog's voice dropped. 'I teach them not to do it any more.'

Honor's stomach churned and she suddenly lost all desire for the fish and chips in her hand, so fragrantly mouthwateringly delicious seconds before. A long chip lay greasily across the top of the packet, glistening with salt. She extracted it and wiped it around the excess salt that had collected in the corners of the wrapping paper.

Two strides away, Frog was still winding himself up for attack.

Anger engulfing good sense, Honor moved forward. The expressions on the Tadpole's faces changed to astonishment as she stepped up beside and behind Frog but, before they could warn their leader, Honor reached around and jabbed the pointy corner of the salt-laden chip into Frog's eye, halting his nasty rhetoric mid-flow. 'So, frea-*eek*! Fucking hell!' Frog threw his hands up to his face, spinning instinctively to face his attacker, though both eyes were scrunching as he scrubbed at them furiously. 'What the *fuck*?' As he hopped back, Honor, following grimly, reached up and posted her steaming battered fish down the V-neck of his T-shirt.

Frog yelped in a whole new octave. 'Ow, ow-OW! That's fucking hot!' He beat blindly at his T-shirt and fish began to slither in smashed handfuls out of the bottom of the shirt and into the slung-low waistband of his jeans. 'Shit!' he howled, delving into his waistband to prevent hot fish from encroaching further.

Satisfied that Frog was safely occupied removing salt from his eyes and fish from his shorts, Honor turned her attention to the Tadpoles. Like most sidekicks, their bravado depended on their ringleader. Now that he was temporarily incapacitated their grins had turned to idiotic dismay. Utilising all the advantages of surprise, Honor stalked towards them with what she hoped was the manic light of battle in her eye, digging her fingers into her remaining chips. 'Let him go, morons.'

Like children caught with their fingers in the cookie jar, they jumped back and whipped their hands behind their backs.

Ru pushed free. 'Watch out for Frog.'

Honor swung around to see Frog advancing. Realising, with a heart sink, that the first instant of surprise had gone and that she'd put herself right in the middle of Frog and the Tadpoles, she lifted her bag of chips threateningly. 'Hold it, fuckhead.'

He scraped to an uncertain halt. But his eyes narrowed. 'What do you think you're going to do with a bag of soggy chips, Yankee Doodle?' He reached out and swatted the bedraggled remains of her meal from her hand.

'That's enough,' rapped a voice from above their heads.

With a flood of relief Honor watched the tall figure of Martyn Mayfair jog gently down his metal staircase. His eyes were fixed on Frog. 'Wind your neck in,' he snapped. 'You've tried to rough one younger kid up three-to-one and instead you've been made to look stupid by a titchy woman armed with a bag of chips. So piss off.'

'I'm not titchy,' Honor protested.

The Tadpoles began to shuffle towards the street, as if hoping Martyn wouldn't spot them. Frog glared, but was obviously inhibited by no longer dealing mob-handed with someone smaller and younger than himself in a quiet corner where nobody could see.

'Freak!' he spat, viciously, in Ru's direction, ramming his hands into the pockets of his jeans and turning to follow his fast-disappearing buddies.

'Wait!' Honor's voice rang out before she'd realised she was going to speak. 'Apologise to Rufus!'

'*What*?' He swung around, wearing an expression of ludicrous astonishment.

'I said, apologise to Rufus,' she repeated, weakly.

Martyn's mouth twitched but he said, 'You heard the lady. Apologise to Rufus.'

'Get stuffed,' said Frog, instead. And, with a final flip of his fingers in Ru's direction, disappeared around the corner of the nearest shop, like an angry bear.

'You may have pushed a little too hard with the apology,' Martyn observed.

'I hope I haven't made things worse,' she said, anxiously, to Ru, who was staring at her, clearly bemused.

'Dunno,' he said. Then added, honestly, 'Probably.'

'Oh, crap.' She felt a sinking sense of shame. 'Are you OK?'

He rubbed his shoulder where his shirt was torn but nodded. His huge dark eyes, so like his mother's above his high cheekbones, were unfathomable. 'Thanks.' He flicked a shy, awkward glance at Martyn. 'Thanks,' he repeated.

Martyn dismissed him with a nod, then frowned down at Honor, as if wondering what the hell to do with her. 'I'm cooking pasta. You'd better come and have some in place of your fish and chips. It'll give the neighbourhood thugs time to clear the area. You didn't exactly diffuse the situation.'

'I didn't know how to.' Anxiety was squirming unpleasantly, now that the heat of anger had cooled. 'If I'd called the cops Ru would have been black and blue by the time they arrived.'

'It's really tough to defeat a pack,' he agreed, turning and beginning back up the metal stairs, his shoes making a *tung, tung, tung* noise on the treads. 'They're hyenas, opportunistic pack hunters, skulking in the bush until they can isolate vulnerable prey.'

Honor began up the stairway behind him. But halted as she realised that Ru was just watching.

At the door, Martyn looked back, frowning to see Honor only a few steps up the stairs. His gaze switched to Ru and he sighed. 'You'd better come, too.'

And when Honor set off again, *tung, tung, tung,* she could hear the echoes of Ru's footfalls behind her.

'Wow,' she breathed, when she stepped in through the black-painted door.

She could see clear through the apartment from the wooden floor and cream walls of the entrance lobby, past a stainless steel kitchen area lit, it seemed, by twenty concealed lights and divided from the living area with a wide expanse of polished silvery black granite, over the cream carpeted lounge area to four French doors in the end wall. A long way off.

It was huge. The apartment extended over the entire block of shops at Starboard Walk.

And a couple of doors and a black-painted spiral stairway leading from the entrance way indicated that there was more to be seen.

'This is quite a place,' she observed inadequately. In a rush, she remembered about Martyn not being just Martyn but being Martyn Mayfair the Model. She kicked off her tennis shoes before stepping on to the carpet.

Martyn was busy throwing handfuls of penne pasta into bubbling hot water and combining tinned tomatoes in a pan with a jar of sauce – no doubt to make it stretch to serve three. She took one of the tall chrome stools on the other side of the counter, checking that there were no studs or zippers on her jeans to damage the butter-soft black leather seat. Beside her, Ru silently followed suit.

Whenever Martyn flicked a glance at Ru, Ru dropped his eyes. Most of Martyn's glances were actually glowers, so Honor wasn't too surprised Ru was abashed.

Martyn moved economically around his – clearly expensive – kitchen and Ru looked like a piece of trash someone had forgotten to take out, shirt ripped, a dirty graze on his arm and his hair hiding his face as he stared down at the silver-black granite counter as if it were showing a brand new movie. Honor's usual effortless flow of conversation dried up. Feeling almost … yes, *shy* of Martyn; Martyn as he really was. All she could think about was that she'd seen him in his skivvies. Like a god up there on the side of the bus, so perfect and at ease with his perfection that he could allow his image to be blown many times life-size and flaunted before the public.

Whoa. She actually felt her palms get hot.

It was ten awkward minutes before Martyn placed glasses, forks and a pepper grinder on the counter, then, from an impressive bank of stainless steel appliances on the far wall, brought out a bottle of chilled water. He dragged a stool up to the other side of the counter and began spooning out pasta on to square white plates.

'Wicked. Thanks,' mumbled Ru.

'That looks great,' agreed Honor, picking up her fork. The sauce was rich with chunks of chicken and studded with broccoli.

Silently, Martyn began to eat.

Ru gazed miserably at his plate. 'I won't say anything to her. I know how she'll be if she knows I've been up here.' He shot a glance at Martyn.

Slowly, Martyn nodded. 'Thanks. That's good to know.'

'I know she's weird,' Ru rushed on. 'I keep thinking that she'll just get over you but she's been weird since Tucker died – weirder. But you know what she's like. She's got this massive thing about you. If I knew how to stop her, I'd do it.'

Martyn forked up some pasta. 'Thanks for understanding that she freaks me out,' he said, ironically.

'Yeah,' Ru agreed, bleakly. 'Freaky, that's us.'

'But it's not Ru's fault,' Honor protested, hearing unwelcome echoes of Frog's *'freak!'* She looked at Martyn, lifting her eyebrows in elaborate expectation, trying to fry him with her stare.

After a few moments of the stare treatment, his eyes gleaming with amusement, he gave in. 'It certainly would make my life easier if you said nothing about visiting me tonight, Rufus. I appreciate that you're in a difficult situation.' One corner of his mouth moved in something that might have been a smile.

Rufus went dark red. ''S'alright,' he muttered.

The grin Martyn sent Honor under his dark brows suggested he was beginning to remember his company manners. And expected her approval. 'Your pasta OK?'

But Ru, gazing into his plate that way, made Honor feel soft with sorrow. He was a good kid in a bad situation and Martyn Mayfair Superstar's graciousness needed work, so she looked at Ru as if the question had been directed his way, obliging him to pick up his fork and taste the food so that he could say, 'Yes. Thanks.'

When they'd eaten and Martyn had filled the coffee machine, he did finally make a proper attempt with Ru. 'You ever taken any self-defence classes? Seems to me that you ought to.'

Ru gave his usual, fatalistic shrug. 'Mum doesn't like me going to classes.' And then, at Martyn's uncomprehending silence, 'She doesn't like me joining things. She says we're free spirits.'

'That's true,' Honor put in. 'I heard her say that.'

'She'd keep me out of school, if she could.' His plate removed, Ru had returned his morose gaze to the granite. 'She doesn't like conforming. I'm probably the only kid you know who sneaks off in the morning to change *into* his uniform. I buy it from the school thrift shop and carry it round in my backpack.'

Honor struggled to understand the school uniform thing. 'So all the kids in your school have to wear a certain thing, and she won't let you?'

'Black trousers and a burgundy sweatshirt,' he agreed. 'But she says a uniform is designed to strip me of my individuality and make me one of a herd. It's important for each person to be valued for how they are and not forced into superficial conformity. She tells me not to be a clone.' He laughed, humourlessly, and Honor thought she caught the glint of tears in his eyes. 'She's certainly made me an "individual". It's no wonder the kids at school call me "freak". They think I live with a coven of witches.'

Martyn snorted. 'It's what comes of being brought up in a non-standard household. People start giving you a hard time for it, as if there's something you could do about it. Your mother seemed OK with Tucker.'

'Yeah.' Ru glanced up. 'It was better when Tucker was alive.' His hair slid slowly over his eyes. 'He was the most normal bloke Mum ever had.'

Honor's heart ached. 'So Tucker wasn't your dad?'

'No. Some bloke she used to be friends with did the business for her when she wanted a baby. He went off to work in South America. They didn't keep in touch.'

Honor sighed. 'At least she wanted you.'

Sliding off his stool to collect the steaming coffee jug and a carton of milk from the fridge, Martyn put out three mugs. His voice was softer, now. 'There've been a lot of blokes, then?'

'Yeah,' Ru said, gruffly. '"Specially at festivals. She's always sending me off "for a walk", or pointing out what tent she'll be in if I need her during the night.'

Honor's anger bubbled over. 'That just stinks! She's a mom and she ought to know better than to embarrass you that way.' But then she caught Martyn's eye and subsided. She wasn't helping, any more than when she'd antagonised Ru's bullies. He was probably wishing her to hell.

Martyn sipped his coffee meditatively, and then, sighing as if making a tough decision, pulled out his phone and dialled with a few touches to the screen. 'Hi, Clarissa,' he said, into the flat, shiny instrument. 'Do any of your mates do self-defence classes?' He reached into a drawer for a pen and wrote a number on a scrap of paper. 'No, not me. Just someone I know.'

Ending the call, he gave the number to Ru. 'Call this number and say Clarissa gave it to you. It's a guy called Hughie. His classes are pretty full but he went to school with Clarissa, so he'll fit you in.' He made a thoughtful face. 'I'm not sure that he knows how to beat up three thugs with fish and chips, though.'

Honor blushed. 'I thought I did a good job.'

His eyes smiled, even if his lips were late to the party. 'You were heroic. By the time I opened the door, there you were, St Georgina taming a deeply unpleasant dragon with a takeaway and impressive American swearwords.'

They both looked around at a sudden squeaky, creaky noise. It came from Rufus, laughing almost soundlessly. 'It was wicked,' he gasped. 'Frog dancing about trying to get hot fish out of his boxers. He looked such a tosser.'

Martyn actually began to laugh, too. 'It's the American hot-fish dance. Frog should be honoured that Honor came all the way from Connecticut to teach him.'

Rufus laughed harder, wiping under his eyes with the heels of his hands. There was something almost hysterical about it, as if he could tip over into sobs any moment. Honor patted his shoulder and Martyn poured more coffee.

When the creaking laugh wound down into hiccups, Honor dialled the phone number Martyn had got from Clarissa. She got through immediately and explained the situation. 'Lucky to catch me! Just off to a class,' Hughie boomed. 'Clarissa gave you my number, did she? I don't do any classes in the Deans but I do a Thursday evening in Kemptown, if that's any good?'

'It's very good,' she said, firmly. 'Do you have enough space for two?' Ru definitely needed support.

Chapter Thirteen

'You're going to the classes, too?' Martyn said, slowly, wondering why he hadn't seen that coming.

Honor nodded firmly, sliding her phone away. 'Ru, the class is Thursday evening in Eastern Road in Brighton. I'll find out where that is and look into the buses.'

Rufus slid off his stool to dump his coffee cup in the sink. He still looked dubious about the whole self-defence thing but offered, 'Kemptown's this side of Brighton. The bus that goes to the hospital will get us to Eastern Road.'

She hesitated. 'What will you tell your mom?'

He quirked his eyebrows. 'That I'm going out. She never bothers. It's the upside of her thing about personal freedom.'

'Great.' Honor beamed and Martyn's heart flipped. It was written across her fine, delicate features that she was set on helping the kid. It wasn't the kid's fault he had a mad mother; Martyn hadn't needed Honor's hard stares to tell him that – but that didn't stop the mad mother making the kid a trouble magnet. Anyone allied to Rufus Gordon was going to attract some of that trouble and what possible reason could Honor have for making herself part of that? He sighed. Any moment now he was going to say something really stupid. He could feel it building in his gut – or somewhere south of that. There was something about Honor that made him come over all helpful.

'So we could get a bus from Marine Drive?' Honor was asking Rufus. 'We could hang around in my front yard until we see it coming, because that way we'd be less likely to run into Frog.'

'Suppose,' said Ru.

Martyn knew what the stupid thing was going to be before he said it. Honor might have the heart of a lion in the body of a ballerina but she was a hell of lot smaller than Frog. 'I'll drive you,' he said. 'It's only a few minutes along the coast road.'

'But—'

He cut across her. 'It's no problem.'

'Oh. Well then, thank you.' Her smile was golden.

It wasn't long before she began doing the polite thing, apologising for invading his home at no notice and insisting that it was time she and Ru left.

'OK,' he said. 'As you have no fish-and-chip cloak of invincibility, we'll walk Ru home then I'll walk you home.'

She laughed as she flexed her feet neatly into her shoes but he noticed that suddenly she wasn't meeting his gaze. He almost reassured her, 'I won't try and kiss you, this time. Even though, that day, I'd never wanted to kiss a woman so much in my life.' To feel her body against his. Had been anticipating the rush of desire that would hit him as he explored the warmth of her mouth and the softness of her lips … The connection had been that strong. Until he'd cut it.

'Thank you. You're sweet,' she said.

'No, I'm not.' A sweet man would have listened when she wanted to tell him about her marriage. Let her talk out her problems, cry on his shoulder if necessary, and take the obligatory step back out of respect for the relationship with its prior claim. Well, he'd already taken the step back. It just hadn't been respectful.

And now she was looking at him with laughter and reproof warring in her green eyes, as if she could read his thoughts. Because the connection *was* that strong.

The evening was clear, the kind of summer twilight that

slides so slowly through the deepest shades of blue that it doesn't meet black until really late. He noted Ru pause on the metal stairs to glance around before continuing nonchalantly on to solid ground. It didn't sit well to see Ru enduring his teen years instead of enjoying them and he remembered how it felt to be different. He'd had the advantage of a wide circle of friends, which was more than Ru seemed to have, but he'd always been aware of the other kids talking about his weird family.

He watched Honor as she skipped alongside Ru on the narrow pavement, talking earnestly. His eyes fell to her round bottom, rolling perfectly. A row of tiny wispy curls had escaped her ponytail at her nape. He made himself look away. Then looked back.

When they'd seen Ru up the passage and into the door that would take him to the flat above the Teapot, they swung around and walked back down The Butts and into Marine Drive. 'I feel real sorry for him,' Honor observed.

'I'd feel "real sorry" for anyone with Robina as a mother. She's a pain in the arse.'

Turning the corner into Marine Drive was like stepping through a door to a new weather front. The wind slapped their hair around and rushed into their ears and they saved conversation until they reached the comparative shelter of the bungalow's patio, tucked in the L of the building.

There, Honor paused, studying her door key. 'So, what does "Wind your neck in" mean?'

'Was that too English for you? "Get out of my face", is the nearest translation, I suppose. Or "Back off". It's used when someone's getting out of order.'

She nodded. The gathering dusk was taking the colour and detail out of her hair and eyes, gradually hiding her from him. 'I saw you today.' She cleared her throat. 'You were on a bus.'

He nodded.

'You're a *model*.'

He frowned. 'That a problem?'

She turned to lean against the door, crossing her arms. 'Of course not. I just feel so stupid.'

'Why?' he asked, blankly.

'Because when your sisters gave you a hard time about only working a few days each month, I assumed you were down on your luck.'

A laugh shook through him. 'No. I do OK.'

'"OK"! I guess you do. I'm *so* glad I didn't offer you yard work. I nearly did, thinking you would maybe welcome a little extra in your pocket.'

'Offer. I might do it.' A picture flickered through his mind of working alongside her in the sunshine on the patch of sandy grass that constituted a lawn, rolling up his manly sleeves to tackle the jobs she couldn't manage.

'Not now I know! That was before you rode past me this afternoon, fifteen-foot tall, looking like the Dolce & Gabbana guy in your skivvies.'

He winced. 'I'm not the face of Dolce & Gabbana, that contract belongs to a big name.' She was looking at him as if he was suddenly speaking in tongues. He tried to explain. 'Don't mix le Dur up with Dolce & Gabbana or Hugo Boss. Le Dur isn't a global brand. It's a UK company with mass appeal – ie the product doesn't cost that much. It's cheerfully aimed at an unsophisticated consumer likely to be impressed by a French name that, literally translated, means "the hard". I'm not "the face of" anything. I'm not those stratospheric guys. Le Dur's campaigns are buses, not performance cars. Weekly magazines, not monthly glossies.'

'I just never met a model before.'

He tried to read her face in the fading light. 'Did you really worry that I was out of work?'

She scrunched up her face in embarrassment. 'Clarissa and Zoë always talked about you only working a few days a month.'

'I do only work a few days a month. On shoots, anyway. Modelling really only takes up so much time, but I do promo stuff, talk to my agent. And do my books, like any self-employed person.'

'And you devote a lot of time to keeping in shape? That's why all the working out and stuff?'

He let his shoulder settle against the door beside her. He could feel her warmth, even though the breeze fluttered around them like an anxious bird. 'I don't really work out. I'm not a gym rat and I haven't had a personal trainer for ages. At school, I ran and played rugby and tennis, and I just accelerated the programme to include stuff like volleyball and swimming when I began making money as a model. It's what I like to do and it stops the pounds from settling. The only thing I have to be careful of is getting tanned in stripes – that's why it's usually either long sleeves or no shirt.'

Slowly, she nodded. 'I have to admit that it makes a whole lot more sense than you being unemployed. I always wondered why your sisters were so mean to you, but now I see it was just teasing.'

Turning, she put her key in the lock. 'You were good to Rufus, tonight.'

'You were the one who pulled his nuts out of the fire.'

She frowned down at her hand, as if waiting for it to turn the key and let her into the bungalow. 'I like Ru.'

'I wouldn't go so far as to say I *like* the kid, with his woeful eyes, obviously always expecting to be left out of everything good. Sympathy, yes. Empathy, even, living with three women, dippy women at that, and no adult male in his life.' But a needy adolescent son of loopy lustful Robina Gordon was strife in waiting; just offering to give the kid a lift had made his instincts howl at him to stay away. 'He's an unhappy kid. Not surprising, with a mum like that.'

'No.' Honor nodded, sadly. She heaved a sigh. 'She's a piece of work.'

'And to think you came all the way over here to find your own mother.'

She laughed shortly. 'Robina's enough to put a girl off having a mother. Maybe meeting her the way I have is meant – telling me to leave well enough alone.'

He allowed himself to be distracted by the way the wind was whipping her hair gradually out of its ponytail. Until–

'Robina's in love with you–'

'No, she's not,' he cut across her. 'Lust, possibly, but it's a lot more stalky than love. Love means that you do the best for the other person, not make life uncomfortable for them to satisfy your own transient and unrealistic desires.'

'She thinks you and she could be "relationshippy".' Honor continued to study the door lock.

'Trust me. Robina's love for me is no more real than the word "relationshippy" is.'

Finally, Honor turned the key. 'Trust *me*. Both are real in her mind. I can't explain how uncomfortable it makes me.'

He walked back along Marine Drive telling himself that she was right not to have invited him in. He'd told her he stayed away from other men's wives; she'd told him that she was married.

End of.

End *of*. Except here she was living under his nose and getting under his skin. And there was no actual husband to be seen …

He rounded the corner in The Butts, feeling for his keys. For a moment he hesitated, looking across the road at where the Fig Leaf's burning bright windows were open to allow the sound of laughter to lift on to the evening breeze.

The idea of strolling in and leaning on the bar for an hour was hugely tempting. There was always someone he knew, someone who would laugh and chat and be undemanding.

But last time he'd gone in for a quiet beer Robina had paid the girl behind the bar to take him over a drink, like in some cheesy movie. So he'd ended up standing there with a drink in each hand, feeling conspicuous and uncomfortable. And Robina had winked at him, which had made people snigger.

He turned across the car park. And then halted. Stared into the black shadow behind the straggly line of bushes that, to someone's mind, constituted the landscaping of the area, positive he'd seen movement. Fuck's sake. Robina? Frog?

He stared into the darkness in silence, the hairs on the back of his neck rising. And, as hesitant as a bird, Rufus Gordon stepped into view.

Martyn frowned, not letting himself relax. 'I thought I'd seen you home.'

Ru nodded. He put his hands in his pockets and scuffed his feet.

'So what are you hanging around for?'

'I'm not waiting for you.'

'So who are you waiting for?'

Ru scuffed his feet again. His trainers looked overlarge for his skinny legs. 'Not anyone. It was you came charging around the corner. Made me jump.'

Martyn stared at him, tapping his keys against his leg, trying to work out what was going on. 'Did Robina send you?'

Ru looked up, startled. Wounded. 'No!' He turned away. 'I'm not here for anything, OK? I just don't want to be there. I'm on my way down to the beach.'

Martyn's conscience pricked. 'Have you had a row with your mum?'

Ru slowed. Shrugged. 'Kind of.'

'Was it anything to do with you coming here, earlier tonight?'

Ru swung back. 'I told you I wouldn't tell her *and so I didn't*. OK? Just take a chill pill, will you? Not everything's about you.'

Unwillingly, Martyn laughed. He let his shoulders unbunch. 'Sorry. So what's the problem?'

'It'll blow over.'

Perversely, now Martyn wanted to prevent Ru from melting into the night. Unhappiness radiated from the kid like a bad smell. 'Why don't you tell me what's wrong?'

Ru looked up at the stars that were just beginning to prick through the sky. He shook back his hair. Finally, he muttered, 'Crusty came out of hospital a day early and Mum and Soppy got drunk on Malibu, to celebrate. Crusty went to bed, probably feeling like shit and wishing she was back in hospital, and Mum and Soppy are being really stupid. They're dying their hair and they wanted to dye mine, too; coming into my room and getting hold of my arms and trying to drag me into the kitchen, giggling like twats. Mum got really stressed because I wouldn't do it. Screeching at me.'

Martyn's lips twitched. 'Crusty and Soppy?'

'Kirsty and Sophie,' Ru clarified impatiently. 'Who live with us.'

'Yes, I know who you mean. So what colour did they want to do your hair?'

Ru began scuffing again. 'Flamingo.'

A pause. 'Like … pink?'

'Yeah.'

Martyn turned for the metal steps. 'Want to come up, then? I've got some stuff to do but you can watch Sky.'

Ru breathed, 'OK.' But it took him a moment to start up the steps behind Martyn, as if he couldn't quite believe he'd been invited.

Chapter Fourteen

On Sunday morning at the Eastingdean Teapot, Honor found Sophie sulking in the kitchen and sporting shocking pink hair. It looked like hell with her ever-pink face. Honor felt laughter ballooning.

'Robina was going to do hers, too!' Sophie wailed. 'She chickened out.'

Robina tossed back her dark curls, then winced. Sullen grey shadows lurked beneath her eyes in an otherwise stark white face. 'There wasn't much dye left. I was worried it wouldn't take properly.'

Sophie pouted. 'You chickened out.'

'You certainly were brave, Sophie,' Honor consoled. 'And how is your friend, Kirsty?'

Sophie's gaze accused Robina once more. 'Exhausted. She could have done with a good night's sleep. But Robina wasn't very well during the night. *Were* you, Robbie? And every time she thundered to the bathroom she banged the door. Poor Kirsty.'

'Poor me.' Robina swelled with outrage. 'I was the one who spent half the night on the bathroom floor.'

Honor washed her hands and tied on her apron. 'Was it something you ate?'

Sophie slammed the oven door shut and set the timer. 'No – something she drank. Because she was greedy, as usual, and drank more than her share – also as usual!' Her pink face quivered as she slammed utensils on the steel surfaces.

Robina screwed up her face in pain and reached for the ties of her apron. 'I'm too ill to work. I'm taking a sickie.'

Instantly, Sophie's anger flipped to dismay. 'Robbie!

That's not fair. OK, I won't bang–'

Calmly, Honor cut across her panicked apologies, reaching around Robina and retying the apron strings. 'No, you're not taking a sickie because if you do, me and Sophie are downing tools so the Teapot will have to be shut and Sunday must be a lucrative day. You're not too sick to work. You and Sophie are going to stop taking swipes at each other and we're all going to be friends and just get the work done, OK?'

Robina and Sophie gaped.

Honor held their gazes. She'd spent too long dealing with Stef's stunts to be intimidated by people throwing tantrums. 'Jeez, what is it with you guys? Grow up. Does Kirsty usually get between you when you fight?'

Robina's glare dissolved. 'Yes,' she admitted, with a grin. 'Kirst is the sensible one, Sophie's the emotional one and I'm the diva. Right, Sophie?'

Sophie giggled. 'Right, Robbie.' But then a stick of a woman shuffled through the door, clutching the doorframe as if her knees might buckle. The laughter died.

'Hiya, Kirsty!' Robina's jollity was horribly forced after the instant of silence.

Sophie shot around the counter and helped Kirsty pull out a chair. 'Kirstee! Are you sure you ought to be up?'

Kirsty propped herself in the chair, looking like an old waxwork, yellowed and shrunken. 'No,' she admitted. 'How about peppermint tea?'

'I'll do it. You guys sit down together.' Honor made peppermint tea for all three of the women after shaking hands with Kirsty, 'Hi, how are you?', pretending not to notice that Kirsty's hand had a permanent tremor.

Kirsty looked so drawn that Honor had to thrust away the words *sick unto death* that rushed into her mind. Customers began to cast Kirsty furtive glances, making Robina joke, loudly, 'I hope nobody thinks she got like this from eating here!' But no amount of wisecracking disguised the shock in Robina's eyes or the anxiety in Sophie's round pink face.

When Kirsty had staggered back up to her room, Robina snapped at everyone for the rest of the morning. Sophie whispered that it was because Robina could see there was no way Kirsty would be well enough to look after the Teapot while Robina and Sophie went to the Global Gathering, but Honor thought Kirsty was so damned sick that even Robina couldn't be quite that self-centred.

She hoped not, anyway.

Thursday and Friday were Honor's free days this week and, by the time they came around, she was glad to have a couple of days off from refereeing spats between Robina and Sophie, facilitating ecstatic encounters between hungry customers and Robina's cakes and breathing in so much sugar that her own sweet tooth took a hike and she began to fantasise about salted nuts or crispy bacon.

She hadn't intended working half the hours Robina rostered her on for but the Teapot was frantic with the tourist season in flood, as most English kids finished school during the third week of July for the long summer break, and the sun shining as consistently as the English sun seemed able to manage. She had to harden her heart about Ru standing in for her because Robina said that the last couple of days at school were a waste of time.

Honor said, 'No, they're not! They're fun!' and felt double bad because his supposed holiday job at the funfair had fallen through and he'd probably end up covering at the Teapot all summer. But a girl had to have the odd free day in which to run by the ocean with the wind flying her ponytail like a kite, mooch contentedly around Pretty Old and haggle a 1960s' Wedgewood cruet from Peggy the hobbit, then hang out over lunch at the Fig Leaf pub before heading home for a hot shower and to fire up her laptop.

Her email inbox had another message from Stef waiting for her, making use of Billie's internet connection again. *OK. You're making me think long and hard about what I've done and I apologise (again) for how it turned out for you. I don't accept that it's all over between us, though.*

She sighed. There didn't seem much point in repeating how over it all was. Stef probably thought he could talk her round now that she'd had time to calm down.

To cheer herself, she caught up with the family news – her dad and Karen, along with Stef's dad, Will, had joined a club, *I wouldn't go so far as to call it a gym*; Jess had new shoes, *it was the turquoise heels that did it*; and Zach was finding his internship in Texas *hotter than hell*.

Facebook caught her up on what was going on with her friends and the former students of Hamilton High, bringing vividly to her mind the sunny streets of Hamilton Drives and the places they'd hung out: the lake; the shopping mall. The picture-book white wooden church; the steeple so white against the blue of the sky and the green of the willows.

Then, on impulse, she searched Facebook for Martyn Mayfair and, as well as his own understated one, found a fanpage with a very proprietary tone. As well as listing a ton of ads that Martyn had been in, complete with images, it led to a slideshow on YouTube. Was this what Robina had done, without even asking Martyn if that's what he'd like? Wow.

A little Googling around and she discovered that Martyn's own web presence was minimal and sophisticated in purple and black and linked directly to a similarly understated page at Ace Smith Model Management, giving few details other than height, weight, colour of eyes and successful campaigns, headed by le Dur. A selection of moody and sizzling images pretty much did the talking. Backtracking to the Google search page she found a whole host of other model agencies to click through. The most successful agencies adopted the same 'less is more' approach as Ace Smith. Not for them tempting bios vaunting *positive approach* and *unique look* or lists of work that would be considered.

Shutting down her machine and wriggling into her combat pants, which felt appropriate for a self-defence class, she felt downright weird that Martyn Mayfair was to be her driver for the evening.

Once the damned class was upon her, she found herself no more enthusiastic about it than Ru. But if she didn't go, Ru wouldn't have anyone to encourage him – or pay for him, in all probability. They found their way into the hall over a pub where *Personal Safety Training* was printed on the sheet of white paper stuck to the door. A dusty stage at one end rose above floorboards and a spongy blue floor mat. The smell of beer tainted the air.

Including Honor and Ru, the class numbered twelve. Seven of the others were women of all ages up to mid-sixties, and each paused to look at Martyn when he walked in. Lifting a lazy hand to Hughie, he hopped up to sit on the edge of the stage and watch.

Honor hadn't bargained on his presence but she could scarcely object, as he'd given them a ride. She and Ru joined the half-circle around Hughie, a tattooed hulk with a buzz-cut who, despite the grey in his hair, balanced on the balls of his feet and looked ready for anything. He had an oddly sweet smile and liked making his class laugh with jokes about his middle-age, 'Blimey, this lad was no more than a twinkle in his father's eye when I left the army and began these classes!' Which put at ease the ladies who had a decade or so on him but made Ru flush. Ru looked how Honor felt – alien and apprehensive. If it hadn't been for half of the class looking even less at ease in elastic-waist trousers and cardigans, Honor might have hissed, 'Let's go!' to Ru and made a break for it.

Instead, she focused on Hughie's growly voice as he bounded into his course introduction. 'I'm not going to ask you all individually why you're here,' he began. 'Because I know.

'Something, at some time, has made you feel in need of a swift and effective answer to violence. You, or someone close to you, has been mugged, beaten up, picked on or sexually assaulted. You're here to learn to defend yourself – not so that you can pick up tips on how to be an aggressor.'

He paused and scanned his class sternly, keen blue eyes daring anyone to admit aggressive tendencies. 'I'm going to show you that even the smallest person can be effective in self-defence by mixing up the pairings.' Rapidly, he divided the class up: young with middle-aged, woman with man, large with small. Ru looked terrified to be partnered by a plump woman with tight grey curls in rows, as if the perming rods were still in there.

'And you – Honor, isn't it? – you're the lightest of us, so you partner me and we'll show these guys how a little woman can overcome a big bloke.'

Honor grew hot with alarm. 'Wow. I'm a complete beginner. Maybe someone else–'

'–would be a complete beginner, too.' Hughie twinkled reassuringly. 'Don't worry, this class is all about empowerment, about vanquishing that feeling of being out of your depth. That's not a nice feeling and we're going to show it the door. Right? We're going to begin with vital point striking, because the brilliant thing about vital points–' he began to tick points off on his fingers, projecting his voice to the class at large, – 'is that we've all got them. Vital points cannot be conditioned. Vital points are as vulnerable on a fifteen-stone hoodlum as they are on a seven-stone weakling. OK?'

Along with the class, Honor nodded. 'Stones' were a bit of a mystery to her, but the principle was easy to comprehend, fifteen being more than twice as many as seven.

'Now make me a fist.' Hughie turned back to Honor and watched as she curled in her fingers and thumb on her right hand. 'Good!' He beckoned the class closer. 'See, the thumb is on the outside of the fingers, parallel to the knuckles and across the front. You *don't* curl your fingers over your thumb. Or stick it out at the side.' He demonstrated each no-no. 'Because you might break your thumb the first time you use a fist like that. Right? Honor, clench it harder. Great. The harder you can make it, the more effective it will be and the less chance there is of you getting hurt.'

He pulled up a banner from a sort of tube on feet that stood on the floor, to show a black silhouette with pink dots. 'Here are the vital points,' he pointed to each dot. 'Eyes. Nose. Ears. Throat. Groin – especially if your attacker's a man. Knees. Instep.

'This isn't a martial arts class and I'm not going to show you classic technique – I'm going to show you how to control a violent situation and get away, right? So you'll use your hand in the easy ways.' He stuck out his own hairy fist to demonstrate each option. 'The back of your fist, the side of your fist, the flat of your palm and the points of your fingers. And you'll put all the weight of your body behind each blow, right? Right?'

'Right,' the class responded, shyly.

'OK, find you and your partner a bit of space and we'll begin with the eyes.'

Honor glanced across at Ru, saw his face finally igniting with something that might be enthusiasm, and felt her heart lift. This was going to work. This had been a great idea. She turned to throw Martyn a grateful look. But then Hughie said, 'Right, Honor. Now I'm going to choke you.'

Chapter Fifteen

Honor stepped back.

Hughie gave a guffaw. 'It's all right. I'm going to pretend to choke you and you're going to pretend to jab me in the throat. See?' Gently, he fit his warm and scratchy hands around Honor's neck. 'Now, your instinct is to put your hands up to mine to try and free yourself. But by far the simplest thing is to strike your attacker.'

Freeing Honor for the moment, he touched the base of his own neck, at the front, turning to show all the class. 'All of you feel, here, you've got a nice little cuppy shape? With a bobbly bit inside, like a button? Just press it lightly.' Several people coughed and Hughie grinned. 'Not comfy, is it? So, Honor.' He returned his hands to her throat. 'You take your two fingers and jab me – a touch will do! – in the trachea, on that button.'

Quickly, Honor lifted her hand and touched Hughie fleetingly where he'd indicated. Though she controlled her touch, he still coughed. And let go of her neck.

Rubbing the area, he turned away, 'OK, let's see you practise that with your partners. Gently, *gently*!'

Hughie strolled away to correct someone's perception of where the vital point was and Honor glanced over to Martyn, who had propped his elbow on his knee and propped his chin in his hand. Even across the hall, his dark eyes were intense. She could see why advertisers loved him smouldering out at women from moody images. One corner of his mouth lifted in the faintest of smiles and her heart gave a great *boingggg–*

'Now, Honor,' boomed Hughie, right beside her. 'I'm

going to grab you by your hair.'

Honor, her eyes still locked to Martyn's, felt her gaze turn into an accusing *Who got me into this?* Martyn's smile widened into a boyish grin. And Honor had the feeling that she was slipping sideways, even though she could tell that her feet were planted on the floor.

Climbing back into Martyn's big black BMW, it seemed that Rufus had discovered enthusiasm for self-defence. 'That was wicked! That button at the base of your throat kills if you press it, doesn't it, Honor?'

'It really does.'

Ru gloated over his new power. 'I hope Frog tries something soon so I can press his button.'

Honor turned to look at him over the seat. 'Have you had trouble with him, this week?'

Instantly, Ru switched his gaze to the view from the side window. 'Not really. He's said some stuff, y'know, that he's got his eye out for me. I said that he nearly had his eye out – when you poked him with a chip. I told everyone at school about you beating him up with fish and chips, so he's been ripped a bit.'

'I didn't exactly beat him up,' protested Honor, uneasily. 'I just kind of ... stopped him. What does it mean to rip someone?'

'To tease,' said Martyn. 'That's the clean version. Ru, I agree it's good to stand up to bullies but do you think it's the best thing to do, to get people ripping Frog?'

'Yeah,' said Ru, dreamily. 'So he knows what it feels like.'

Martyn dropped Ru in Saltdean to meet up with one of his few mates from school, which, handily, meant that there was little risk of Robina seeing Ru with Martyn.

Then he drove the big vehicle up to the bungalow and parked in Honor's drive. It was darkening early, this evening, as inky clouds marched in from the ocean. His face was lit by the various dials on the dashboard, making him look like the cover art for a paranormal novel.

He got out of the car.

Honor slid out on to the drive, and shut the door. 'I guess that as you were so kind as to drive me to that scary class it would be remiss of me not to offer coffee. But I don't have decaff.'

'I'm not religious about decaff. Why was it scary?' He stood back to allow her to go first up the steps.

She began to fish for her key. 'Hughie may be one of the good guys but I don't warm to someone who says he's going to choke me. I wish I hadn't been the smallest person in class, I would much rather have hung out at the back and been less noticeable.'

'Funny how the smallest person there was also the prettiest,' he observed, drily.

'He chose me because I'm lightest.'

He laughed, softly. 'If I had the choice between getting up close and personal with you or with those lumpy pensioners, I'd find some reason to choose you, too.' And then, when she didn't answer, 'Funny that you're freaked by the classes but you dealt with Frog without batting an eye.'

'Anger can do that. It's been said that I have anger management issues.' Stef had said it, as she'd hurled stuff at him. She veered away from the memory of that ugly scene, of Stef trying to laugh off his own unbelievable stupidity and tell her that she was overreacting to a joke. Pretty serious joke!

Martyn followed Honor up on to the patio and waited whilst she unlocked the front door to the bungalow and stepped through the hall and into the kitchen, flicking on lights, whizzing the kitchen blind down, filling the tall, white kettle. She'd gone all silent and abstracted, but there was something satisfying about watching her go through the cosy rituals of coming home, sexy in her combat trousers.

To distract himself from the velvet glide of desire he broke the silence, propping himself against the wall, arms folded and legs crossed. 'Where do you think of as home, these days? Here or America?'

She paused in reaching for two tall, white china mugs. Taking down a jar of coffee, she shrugged and frowned. 'Good question.'

But just as she opened her mouth to say more, the front doorbell went *bing-bong* and she looked relieved. 'I have a visitor.' And before he could unwind his limbs and suggest that he do the big butch man thing and check out who was ringing her bell as the clock rolled around to ten at night, she'd skipped past him.

'Wow! Hello,' he heard. 'Of course it's convenient – come on in.' Then his heart sank. 'I'm just making coffee for your brother, who was kind enough to drive me home. Maybe you'll join us?'

And before Martyn even had time to curse about it, Clarissa, Zoë, Beverley and Nicola came crowding into the kitchen, each distinguished from the others mainly by the style in which she wore her mouse-brown hair. They milled around him like unsteady Munchkins, giving him the opportunity to see that Honor, although daintier, actually stood more than half-a-head taller than any of them. Pink and grinning, his sisters hugged him enthusiastically, yanking down his head to plant alcohol-rich kisses on his cheeks, 'Hi, Martyn!', dragging out kitchen chairs and making themselves at home. Which Clarissa was, kind of, he supposed.

'Didn't expect to find you here.' Clarissa's eyes glittered above a wine-bright smile. 'We've been to the Fig Leaf –

Robina asked after you, by the way. She seems to think you're avoiding her.'

'I am,' he said, frankly.

Clarissa pshawed. 'You're not still paranoid about her, are you? Anyway, I need to talk to Honor, so I thought I'd call.'

'Funny time of night to call on your tenant,' he observed. He cursed himself for leaving his X5 standing in the drive like a big, fat tell tale. That probably had been what dragged them in, merry-eyed and bursting with curiosity. *Didn't expect to find you here*, like hell.

Clarissa's eyebrows rose in the way they did whenever anyone was presumptuous enough to call her actions into question. 'In fact, I rang the bell on the way to the pub, but Honor wasn't here. You were out together, were you?'

Martyn simply lifted his eyebrows to give her back her own astonishment at being questioned.

Honor interrupted. 'Well, now, I know Clarissa and Dr Zoë, but …?'

Clarissa abandoned Martyn and showed him how sweetly reasonable she could be to anybody else. 'The rest of the Mayfairs, my sisters Beverley and Nicola. I'm sorry if we're imposing, Honor. We didn't mean to interrupt.'

'No, we didn't mean to interrupt.' Nicola, Beverley and Zoë threw meaningful grins at Martyn. He tried to frown them down but that just made them snuffle with giggles as they exchanged nudges. It was an incredibly maddening way for grown women to behave.

'You're not interrupting a thing,' said Honor, calmly. 'Suppose I make a pot of coffee, and then you can tell me whatever it is you want to tell me.' She pulled out one of the two remaining kitchen chairs and glanced first at Martyn and then at the chair.

Martyn sighed and took the seat. At the end of the table.

Which meant all four of his sisters could smirk and twinkle at him. 'Looks to me like coffee's exactly what you lot need,' he grumbled.

'So we've turned up at the right time.' Nicola looked pleased, her habitual expression, maybe because she spent so much time delivering bouncing babies.

'Probably, we need two cups,' agreed Beverley. Beverley was one of the most agreeable people he knew, at the opposite end of the spectrum to Clarissa.

'It's actually a fallacy that coffee helps sober you up.' Zoë assumed doctorly mode. 'It makes you feel a bit more awake, which is what fools you into thinking you're becoming sober. You have to give your liver time to eliminate the toxins and there's no way of speeding up the process. A pint of water helps with hydration, ie the hangover.'

'Would you prefer a pint of water?' Honor paused in pouring coffee into cups.

Zoë looked horrified. 'No, I'd like coffee, please. I'm not drunk so I won't be hungover.'

'That's good.' Honor put sugar and milk in the centre of the table, flicking a glance at Martyn that shone with silent laughter: *They look pretty drunk to me ...*

He smiled back conspiratorially, enjoying the way her ponytail wagged behind her as she turned back to her task. The smile flipped to a scowl when he saw all four of his sisters were regarding him with knowing grins. Then, as Clarissa talked to Honor about getting the garden tidied up and Honor confessed that she wasn't used to gardening, Nicola, Beverley and Zoë began to yawn between sips of coffee, and Martyn sighed as realisation dawned that he was going to end his night by delivering sleepy female Mayfairs to various addresses around Saltdean and Eastingdean. Why hadn't he left the X5 in the car park behind Starboard Walk and walked Honor home?

The yawns increased in size and frequency as the coffee cups emptied. Clarissa continued to monopolise Honor with truly trivial tenant/landlord crapola, so he rose, resignedly, to his feet. 'Shall I drop you lot off?'

'Lovely!' Amidst scraping of chairs and thankful noises, Nicola, Beverley and Zoë clambered to their feet. Clarissa followed, but she was never big on thanking him for merely doing what she considered he ought to. Instead, she demanded, 'Why the rush? Working tomorrow?'

'Yes, actually. Doing a shoot in Arundel for DownJo Jeans.' He was pleased to be able to spike her guns before she could fire off a list of jobs he could do to help people in the family who worked 'proper hours'. Like her.

Honor chipped in before Clarissa could arm her next salvo. 'Arundel! I plan to go on the train to Arundel soon to see the castle. I love how the way you guys in England have castles and palaces right in the towns.'

Martyn held the kitchen door for Clarissa. But, instead of walking through it, she said, 'Martyn can take you with him, tomorrow. He can take you on his shoot and then there will be time afterwards to look around the castle.'

'Oh!' Honor's eyes lit up. Then she looked into his face and instantly rearranged her expression. 'No, I couldn't possibly impose that way.'

Clarissa talked her down. 'There's no point you going on the train when Martyn has his big, shiny car and is going to the same place. Eh, Martyn?'

He jumped on his irritation and wrestled it into submission, giving Honor his sweetest smile. 'It's only a small shoot so I'd love it if you'd like to watch, if you don't mind hovering in the background. Then we can look around Arundel when I'm done.'

'Really?' Light flew back into Honor's eyes. 'That would be great.'

Clarissa bounced back in expectantly. 'I'd love to watch a shoot, too.'

Martyn let his eyebrows speak his incredulity. 'Nobody takes their mother on a shoot. Nothing could be uncooler.'

A crackling silence. Clarissa dropped her gaze and strode across the hall. He let the other Mayfair women cover Clarissa's silence by babbling to Honor about joining their Zumba class in the community hall. 'Clarissa's the instructor and it's really fun! And the class needs people or it'll close.'

'Zumba's always fun,' Honor agreed, without committing herself.

Clarissa waited outside, silently. As usual, Martyn would end up regretting striking back at Clarissa, but she jabbed him with every spiky word and never seemed to worry how much that stung, so he wasn't ready to be conciliatory yet.

In the doorway, he looked down at Honor, who was gazing at him, frowning. He knew that he didn't have to explain to her why Clarissa brought out the worst in him. Instead, he winked and somehow found himself dropping a kiss on the top of her head. 'I need to be there by nine-thirty, tomorrow, so I'll pick you up at eight.'

Chapter Sixteen

Honor had no idea what to wear to a photo shoot. The day was fine but the wind was frolicking with white woolly-lamb clouds so she teamed an aquamarine summer dress with a long cream cardigan that fell right the way to the dress's hem, like something out of the sixties. She was no fashion guru but you couldn't go wrong with retro.

Martyn was quiet.

He hadn't shaved. His hair swung spikily around his cheekbones as it usually did and, thinking back to his image rumbling down The Butts on the side of that bus, Honor concluded that Martyn's style of modelling relied a lot on people liking him exactly as he happened, by good luck, to be.

'So, tell me about the shoot,' she tried, when they'd negotiated the village traffic and were on their way, uphill, out of Rottingdean. 'What's it all about?'

'The client is DownJo Jeans and it's for an ad – magazine, website and the lead page of their section in catalogues,' he said economically, eyes on the road.

'Will it be exciting?'

'No.' He accelerated past the mock-Tudor Downs Hotel.

Juice, a Brighton radio station, took the place of conversation. Honor watched the scenery, the roadside bungalows with little windows in the roof and flint cottages with redbrick corners, giving way to grassy hills divided into irregular fields by darker green hedgerows. Sheep and horses grazed. The occasional hill was clad entirely in trees, reminding her of west Connecticut. Small scale.

They fought their way on to the A27 and, periodically,

Martyn glanced at his watch.

'Worried about being late?'

He glanced in his side mirror and pulled into the right-hand lane. Although she'd never driven in England and hated the idea of tackling those endless rotaries – roundabouts – let alone driving on the 'wrong' side, she knew that the faster traffic should be in the right-hand lane and the slower should be in the left-hand. It didn't appear that all of the traffic knew that. 'More mindful than worried,' he said, after driving closer and closer to the dawdling little car in front before, grudgingly, it inched over. 'I could have stayed at the hotel with the rest of the crew but as the shoot's almost on my doorstep I decided not to. Now, of course ...' He waved a disparaging hand at the lines of traffic. 'People trying to get to work are being held up by tourists setting out on their nice day trips. But I've built in a time buffer.'

'And I guess they won't start without you?'

He grunted but didn't smile. Honor translated the grunt into, 'Actually, I'm feeling tense and regretting inviting you so I'd prefer you not to tease me about my job. Let me retire into my own head for a while.' Under time pressure, Stef had not only been as snappy as a dog but, unlike Martyn, who seemed self-reliant, he'd expected her to multitask her way through both their schedules as an unofficial and ultra-reliable PA. She knew how it felt to desire a little silence in which to contemplate the business of the day.

When had she last thought about business? Wearing a suit or studying client files would seem like living on Mars, now. She tried to imagine herself back at her desk with her licences on the wall and her computer screen permanently alight, land line and cell phone ringing all day and her income linked firmly to commission. Driving home with a headache that promised to last until bedtime only to discover that Stef had an evening off from the diner and wanted to go to the Star

Bar where his old high-school buddies' rock band would play and he'd dance all night with a bottle of Bud in his hand. If she mentioned her headache he'd say, 'It's because you have to relax, babe. You've got to learn to chill.'

Time had flown by, in Eastingdean. Was it really only six weeks since she'd taken down her licences and walked out of that life?

Nearly a month since she'd stored her stuff in a storage facility and taken a car to the airport?

In that short time, she seemed to have learned how to chill. Waiting tables didn't pay well but neither did it scramble her brain. Robina and Sophie were just nuts enough and the locals just friendly enough to make her time in England fun. Her old life had fractured and she'd crept out of one of the cracks.

She watched the cars, buses, trucks and vans streaming along the undulating road between tall banks of scrubby shrubs in the morning sun and sank into her seat, content, for now, just to soak up the country that had given her half the blood in her veins.

Even the silence of the man beside her was fine. And, fifty minutes later, when they were approaching a fairytale town on a hill, swinging over a little humped bridge and up towards castle, trees and cathedral, he kind of shook his shoulders and relaxed into his seat and began tapping his fingertips to the music on the radio. 'We're here. This is Arundel.'

Jolted from her reverie, she leaned forward to stare as they cruised past a jumble of grey stone, flint, red brick walls, spires and turrets.

'That's part of the castle, but not where you get in. And, see that kind of mini castle peeping over the wall? That's made of oak and it's in the castle grounds.'

'Wow.' Honor gazed at the jaunty flags waving on each

corner of the 'mini castle', which, she knew from her guidebook reading in bed, last night, was actually called Oberon's Palace, created from drawings by Inigo Jones. Her mind was bombarded with a feeling of entering history, as if all the thousands of souls who had lived in Arundel over the centuries it had stood where the hill met the river were yelling at her all at once. No way had the guidebook done Arundel justice.

The road eased around to the right and into a broad street in which brick, stone and flint were joined by buildings painted white, blue or yellow and a couple of those cute timbered places, lining the slope down towards a monument in the middle of the road.

Martyn found his way around the back of the buildings to park at a red brick hotel. A last glance at his watch seemed to reassure him. But as she gathered her things he said, 'Are you coming to watch the shoot?'

She hesitated. She was, wasn't she? Didn't he invite her last night …? But then she got it. Last night, he'd been put on the spot by Clarissa and, making the best of a bad job, had invited Honor to cut Clarissa out. Aw, shit.

She responded brightly, hoisting her bag on to her shoulder and trying not to look disappointed. 'I don't quite know. I don't want to miss out on seeing around this cute town and all these amazing buildings–'

But maybe her acting needed work because his eyes softened and he actually did the gallant Englishman thing. 'You can come on the shoot. It'll be OK if you don't mind hovering in the background. I should be finished in time for a late lunch anyway, and then we'd have the rest of the day.'

She capitulated in a heartbeat. 'If you're sure no one will mind?' She wouldn't be human if she wasn't agog to see a real live shoot.

He shrugged. 'It's not a big busy shoot.'

Following him through a rear entrance of the hotel she hovered so far in the background that when one of the reception staff showed them to a ground-floor meeting room with a conference table somewhere in amongst the clutter of clothes rails, aluminium boxes, leads, tripods, boxes and people, he had to look around for her. 'This is Honor. Honor, this is Ian, the photographer, and Lily the MUA. Make-up artist.'

With a squeal of joy, Lily flung herself into Martyn's arms, blonde hair flying. 'Martyn! Hello, stud muffin!'

Martyn laughed and hugged her with one arm, shaking hands with Ian with the other. He'd obviously worked with them before.

Ian had dark, slicked-back hair and black-rimmed glasses; Lily was about Honor's age, blonde prettiness spoilt by a peevish expression when she spotted Honor.

A faun-like guy, complete with dark curls and a pointy goatee, merited only a brief introduction from Lily. 'Hair's Leon, today. He's here on work experience.'

Honor gave the faun a sympathetic smile at being so dismissed. But Martyn shook Leon's hand anyway, obviously not catching Lily's subtext that Leon was beneath Martyn's notice.

But the presenting of Leon proved to be almost effusive compared to Ian's single-word introduction of two incredibly young and eager girls wearing skinny jeans and untidy ponytails. 'Assistants.'

Obviously quite used to being the bottom of the heap, the 'assistants' paused in burrowing through the mysterious aluminium boxes and black crates on wheels only to give distracted waves, although one of them muttered, 'Stylist, really.'

Ian and Lily began talking to Martyn and Honor found some background to occupy.

From there, she figured out that the girl whose role was to assist Ian with light boxes and umbrellas was called Ettie and the other, stylist-really-Olivia, was there to look after the clothes and be barked at, with a dual role of keeping everyone supplied with coffee, tea or bottled water from a table set up at the side of the room that, during her weeks at Florence Events Catering, Honor would have known to refer to as the beverage station.

She helped Olivia hand around the drinks, then retired to a seat beside the beverage station from where she could occasionally be useful, see everything happening in the large room, but wouldn't trip anyone up. As a conference room, with red velvet at the windows, red carpet on the floor and brass lights along the walls, the environment was familiar. But, in its current guise as a crew room, she was out of place.

Coffee over, Lily ushered Martyn to a canvas seat that reminded Honor both of a garden lounger and a dentist's chair, tilting him back and covering his chest with a blue paper bib, talking quietly, Lily's giggles ringing over Martyn's soft baritone. After breaking off for a quick conference with Ian, Lily delved in a big pink case and brought out what looked like a razor and buzzed like a razor, but actually merely reduced the length of Martyn's stubble. *GQ stubble*, Honor thought. Then, wow. That's exactly what it was.

Ian was brought to examine the result and they pored over a sheet of paper Ian unfolded from his shirt pocket; Olivia dashed over to listen in, then all parties nodded. Lily beamed. 'OK, the bathroom is through that door. Martyn, can you wash? Finish with cold.'

Martyn disappeared and Honor switched her attention to Ian, who seemed welded inside a leather jacket although the room was stuffy, and who was comparing his sheet of paper to one proffered by Olivia, ticking things off and rubbing his chin, allowing Olivia to coax him over to the clothes rail and study and nod as she took out pairs of jeans and other garments, making the odd note on his paper, pausing Olivia mid-sentence whenever Ettie ran over with a different list or a piece of equipment for a different consultation.

Then Martyn was back in the chair.

Honor tried to see exactly what Lily was applying to his face – it seemed to take a lot of pressing on to his skin for no discernible result – and then almost fell off her chair when Lily took out a long brush with flat, squared-off stubby bristles and began first tapping the bristles into something then touching them to the base of Martyn's eyelashes. So intent was she on her task that she got closer and closer until she finally straddled him in order to get really close in.

'I'm never sure what to do with my hands when you do that,' Martyn rumbled. Lily's whispered response made him laugh, a laugh he covered with a cough.

Lily's voice rose to normal volume. 'Calm down,' she cooed, concentrating fiercely. 'It's only because you're tall.' But then she whispered something else, obviously at home virtually on Martyn's lap. She wore a complicated layering of underwear-as-outerwear covered with a loose green top in swirling Indian print that, falling casually off one shoulder, probably gave Martyn an interesting view.

Honor began to realise that, as a financial advisor, she had missed out on a whole bunch of fun jobs. And that Lily and Martyn were far friendlier with one another than with the rest of the crew. Refusing to become a voyeur to their renewing their acquaintance, she transferred her attention to where, it seemed, decisions had been made and clothes and equipment were being relayed out of the room by Ettie and Olivia like ants carrying food to the nest.

Leon, ready with a smaller black box like Lily's pink box, watched Martyn, who had shed his shirt and was standing, now. Studying his torso, Lily chatted about his chest hair, a shadow between his mighty pecs. 'It goes with the stubble, doesn't it? And flows into the line of belly hair into your jeans. Can you undo your waistband? Because we've got some unbuttoned shots and you'll need powder right down. You're a nice colour. And no tan lines! Good boy. Been sunbathing in the nuddy?'

Honor wondered where or what the nuddy was.

Lily's words flowed steadily as she wielded first a towel over his entire torso and then a big powder puff from the base of his neck in slow circular movements over his belly and down to the waist of his underwear, making his skin glow luminous and supple. Then, with a fresh white towel, she lightly blotted away any surplus.

Martyn, responding with a grunt or the occasional, 'Yeah,' seemed to have drawn into himself, paying attention to what was going on without contributing.

Then Ian was looking at his watch and Lily was apologising and Martyn sitting down again so that Leon could finally get his hands on him – or rather his hair – talking to Martyn earnestly and spending ages rubbing wax between his finger tips to tease Martyn's shining raven spikes and, to Honor's eyes, make absolutely no difference whatsoever, whilst Lily watched critically, muttering, 'He's only half-trained. It's only 'cos his dad knows someone that he's out on shoots. I could have done that.'

Whilst Martyn was fussed over, the room had steadily emptied of equipment and clothes. Honor rose, unsure of what she was expected to do. The movement seemed to make her visible to Martyn again, as he slid carefully into his shirt. 'I'm going in the van with Ian, will you be OK walking with the others?'

Honor studied him carefully but she just couldn't see he looked any different after Lily and Leon's attentions. He was just Martyn. 'Sure,' she said.

Lily led the crew, and Honor, down the hill and across a busy crossroads at a trot. 'Ian wants to begin on the bridge.'

Honor hardly paid attention to their destination because suddenly they were rushing right by the turrets and arch that formed the entrance to Arundel Castle, crenellations and chimneys soaring behind, and her eyes didn't seem to be able to unglue themselves from the solid chunk of history the others were streaming past without a glance. To cross the road she shuffled crab-wise, gazing at the gatehouse and the slot windows where once archers must have defended the person and family of Roger de Montgomery when he built the first castle there, after Hastings. After *Hastings* for Crissakes! Almost an entire *millennium* ago. Holy freakin' Joe, couldn't these people *see*?

Oblivious to being towed along by one elbow, she mentally ticked off the buildings rising behind the gatehouse – Norman keep, medieval barbican, and, towering behind like something out of Disney, the gothic Victorian castle. It was like European History 101 and she could hardly breathe for excitement. 'Holy crap,' she whispered.

Lily swung on her. 'Do you want us to leave you behind?' she demanded, like a mother threatening a dragging child.

Honor jumped, guiltily. 'I was just looking.'

'Only, you can stay and gawp if you want.' Lily began to pant as she picked up the pace. 'But the rest of us have to get to the location because if Ian gets pissed off we'll all have a bad day. So if you're coming, come *on*.'

Oh well, the castle would still be there later … With one final awed stare Honor gave in to the pressure and hustled with the others. Already, she could see a blue van pulled over by a long stone bridge that spanned the river in three graceful arches. Olivia sprang into the open back doors. Lily and Ettie got busy amongst the boxes and Leon stood around, looking lost.

Grimly, Ian inspected the location. 'This is going to be a pain in the arse. A giant pain in the arse. The client wants the bridge but what about the fucking traffic?' Somehow, he arranged his equipment out of the way of the traffic and, finally, placed his model in an alcove, in the eye of the camera.

And Martyn became somebody else.

He reduced his focus until it was all on the photographer, who brought his light meter up close to Martyn's skin and gave Ettie curt instructions to stand for arm-aching periods holding aloft a light box or a big white disc which she could somehow, with a dextrous twist, fold down into a smaller circle in three layers. Lily and Leon ran in between shots with powder and wax and, so far as Honor could make out, still made no difference to Martyn's appearance.

Martyn did a lot of leaning, turning and staring. Honor had had some idea that he would strike poses and hold them but, in fact, he was rarely still. In contrast to his snapping and snarling at the crew, Ian talked to Martyn like a cowboy gentling a horse. Martyn worked hard to give the photographer what he wanted, occasionally with a fleeting smile at a joke. But the camera shutter whirred when he was unsmiling, as if the smiles were only to let his glower relax.

The shoot began interesting but slid slowly and surely into tedium. Martyn kept appearing from the back of the van in various jeans and shirt combinations; sleeves rolled up, sleeves rolled down, but shirt always sexily open around his torso; leaning or sitting on the bridge parapet with the lichen and the moss, then moving down by the glassily gliding water and the reflections of the sky. The reflections, at least, Ian approved, and he spent what felt like years over them.

Crew attention was on Martyn and when Honor volunteered, 'I guess that's the River Arun,' it was met with such eye-rolling apathy that she kept to herself the rest of her knowledge about Arundel for centuries having been a thriving port, and tried to work out where the docks would have been, instead.

Ian's voice began to take on the rhythms of a relaxation tape. 'Look down ... then up. Again. Again. Now left ... and front. Again. Try right. And front. This time, when you look down, don't come up so far ... and up – stop! Let's try that again. Wait. Let's wait for the fucking sun.'

'He's really intense, the camera loves him,' breathed Leon from several yards behind the camera.

Lily unbent enough to giggle. 'What's not to love?' And Leon shivered and smiled for the first time.

At the end of a couple of hours Honor had turned her attention to the town, which looked as if a giant child had opened a toy box marked 'historic buildings' and jumbled them all together on the hillside.

But, just as she was preparing to abandon the shoot and cross back into the town that she was itching to explore, the crew all got busy stowing the equipment back in the van. Ian stretched and yawned. 'Next stop, the castle grounds. And you'd better all find a way to squash into the van because we've only got a crew pass.'

Honor's desire to leave vanished.

Martyn looked her way, apparently not as unaware of her presence as he'd seemed. 'Honor, you can squash in the front with me,' which earned her an affronted look from Lily, who had to crawl into the back with the racks of clothes, photography equipment and the rest of the crew. Martyn took Honor's hand and stepped up into the cab all in one motion, hoisting her on to the seat by his side as if she were a doll. She looked at his face curiously. The make-up was so subtle she probably wouldn't have noticed it if she hadn't watched it being applied. He smelled a little different to usual; powder and hair wax. Other than that he was still Martyn. More remote than she was used to and sitting oddly at the centre of everyone's attention. But still Martyn.

Still warm, as his hand proved when it lingered on her leg as he reached past her to shut the heavy door. She glimpsed his smile. Then he turned back to listen to what Ian was saying about the light and the grey clouds just beginning to move in over the clutter of buildings on the brow of the hill.

Apart from a member of staff who showed them to a roped-off area of greensward in the lee of one of the massive curtain walls, Arundel Castle took no notice of the photography crew in its grounds. The van burst open and spilled its cramped cargo of crew, arms full of equipment, clothes and collective backs to turn on any tourists hovering at the distant ropes, treating the castle as a huge prop that might as well have been made of cardboard as majestic grey stone gathered over centuries.

'This is better!' Ian kept saying, brandishing his light meter. 'We've probably got an hour before it clouds right up and I think we'll get the best stuff, here. I like the light and we don't have to keep stopping for fucking traffic.' In the comparative peace and quiet of the castle grounds, he became almost jovial.

Martyn no longer bothered to squeeze himself into the back of the van to change his clothes. He stripped off his shirt to exhibit a body that deserved to be looked at and Honor felt her breath stick. The sun poured over him, defining every line, and it took her a moment to remember how to fill her lungs.

And then he unsnapped the waist of the dark indigo jeans and eased the two halves open and she forgot again, her eyes helpless but to follow to where the faint arrow of hair pointed.

Oh, whoa …

'Let's work with the wind and get your hair across your face.' Ian was again behind his tripod. 'Don't quite turn all the way back – yes! Exactly like that! Let's have that again … again. OK, now over here.' With an anxious glance at the sky, he kneeled, and then lay, on the ground and shot up past Martyn with a tower soaring into the sky behind him, doing a lot of squirming and rolling and making Martyn laugh.

'Next,' said Olivia. 'Half into the jeans.'

Without comment, Martyn undid the jeans the rest of the way and shucked them down to his thighs, showing mid-grey trunks. Olivia fussed around, arranging denim between his thighs as he said something that made her giggle. Yup. Honor had definitely pursued the wrong career.

'Last set,' Ian said, some time later, relief in his voice, 'the tattoo.'

Honor edged closer to watch as Lily took handfuls of wipes then a towel to Martyn's torso, removing the powder. Then Martyn propped his hands against the side of the van, presenting his naked back to Lily, who opened an alcohol wipe to clean his lower back, then took out a coiled sheet of white shiny paper and began to press it on to his skin, slowly and painstakingly.

Whilst Lily concentrated, Olivia passed around bottled water and muesli bars and Ian studied the window on the back of his camera as he clicked through shot after shot. As his humour seemed to have improved, Honor hovered nearer and he tilted the camera so that she could see the shots in miniature in the viewing pane. 'These are going to be good.'

And, all at once, she understood 'the camera loves him'. It somehow honed the planes of Martyn's face, made his eyes glow like marcasite and emphasised every muscle. He really did look like the personification of a Manga animation. Honor had always had a soft spot for the dark clear lines of Manga men – odd how she'd ended up with tawny-haired Stef because she could almost have written the order for Martyn herself, right down to the deep dark eyes. The massive stone wall was the perfect backdrop, especially the dramatic shots from below with the castle towering over him like a giant chess piece. 'Jeez,' she said, inadequately.

'They'll look fabulous in monochrome. The clients will wet themselves.'

'You've done a great job.' She could see why the crew forgave him his grouchiness if he got results like these.

Above the elastic waist of Martyn's grey trunks, Lily was putting the finishing touches to the transfer tattoo, a pair of intensely staring, slanting eyes beneath curling brows, maybe man or maybe beast.

'Ooh, wicked,' breathed Leon.

Olivia passed Martyn a different pair of jeans and he stepped into them but pulled them up only loosely as Lily squeaked, 'Watch the tatt!' Then she brought out a spray.

Martyn frowned. 'I suppose that's cold?'

She pulled a face. 'It was warm this morning, when I wrapped it in foil but ...'

He sighed and lifted his arms and she began to spray him with water. 'Fucking cold,' Honor heard him say. Lily replied with something reproving and he laughed, choking on the spray. Then he closed his eyes and Lily sprayed vigorously over his head until his hair dripped and hung in his face.

Ian rose to new heights of enthusiasm. 'Leon, get out of shot! I want his hair exactly like that. All right, Martyn, face the wall, drop the jeans a bit then pull them up slowly as you turn your head back towards me, looking over your shoulder.'

Each time he did so, Honor could hear the spitting of the shutter taking continuous shots and Lily breathing, 'Oh my God, oh my God, watch that tatt ...' Down, up. Down, up.

By the time she'd watched it a few times, the tight cheeks of Martyn's ass under those tattooed glowing eyes were etched into her brain and she was pretty sure she'd dream about them that night.

Then, suddenly, it was over.

Lists were compared for a final time. Lily removed the tattoo with more alcohol wipes and then Martyn towelled himself dry and climbed back into his own clothes.

And it was as if he had been released from a serious-spell.

He began to chat and smile and the tension he'd fed on all morning evaporated. The crew relaxed, packing the equipment back into the van with end-of-assignment laughter.

'So, you up for lunch at the hotel with us, Martyn?' chimed Lily. 'Even Ian's staying today.'

Martyn smiled but shook his head. 'Honor and I have plans.'

'OK.' Lily somehow managed to make her carefree smile for Martyn become, by the time it got to Honor, a glare that quite plainly accused her of pushing in and spoiling crew camaraderie.

'I don't really mind—' began Honor.

Martyn took her hand and squeezed it. 'No, you've been patient but I can see the way you've been lusting after the castle all morning. Let's wallow in the history stuff.'

'Oh, you like history.' Lily sounded as if she'd just uncovered a filthy secret.

'I was a history major.' Honor tried not to sound apologetic. 'Actually,' she turned to Martyn, 'I'm a real fool for social history and would rather look around the town. I'll never do the castle justice in just half a day, anyway.' She wondered if Martyn realised that he'd kept hold of her hand.

Once back at the hotel, the turnaround was rapid. Martyn

washed, retrieved his wallet and keys, shook Ian's hand, kissed Lily's cheek and gave her a hug, waved at the rest of the crew, 'Thanks, guys!' grabbed Honor's hand again and strode out across the hotel vestibule and into the street outside.

It felt like an escape.

'You really didn't want to eat with the crew?' she asked.

'Not today,' he said, frankly. 'A coffee-shop lunch OK for you?'

'Sure.'

'Let's find the oldest looking place we can, with sloping floors and a ceiling I bang my head on. Then it can count as part of your history tour.'

She laughed and allowed him to tow her into exactly that sort of coffee shop, down by the monument, where a teenage girl, who blinked when she got a look at Martyn, showed them to a titchy circular table for two under the rake of a staircase, as all the other tables were filled elbow-to-elbow with holidaymakers and day trippers.

Martyn grimaced and tucked himself into the available space, sure enough banging his head.

It was past two but the teenage girl said they served lunch any time, blowing her dark fringe out of her eyes as she passed out cardboard menus, cream with a line drawing of the castle gatehouse in brown. Honor chose something called Smuggler's Pie, which seemed to be a pie of beef and ale and sounded right at home here in Sussex, England. And Martyn chose Chicken Balti and boiled rice, which didn't.

He laughed when they banged knees under the table and even when he banged his elbow, twice, on the panelled wall beside him. 'Ow! Have we wandered into a doll's house by mistake?'

'You've sure unwound,' she observed. 'You're quite different in front of the camera.'

'Oh?' He looked faintly surprised. 'I'm certainly ready to relax. Today there wasn't much hanging around and we've wrapped everything up nice and early, but it's amazingly tiring standing in front of a camera and doing nothing.'

'It looks it.'

His eyes narrowed suspiciously.

'I'm not being sarcastic. You're so concentrated and intense, having to put up with doing the same thing over and over, the make-up artist and the hair guy dancing around you. There were times I was reminded of Gulliver and the folks of Lilliput. They were trying to tie you down with a thousand threads of annoyance.'

Laughing, he shifted his legs and banged her knees again. 'Ow. Sorry. They don't annoy me. We're all working together to get the best results. It's a team thing. Also ...' His eyes crinkled, 'I don't want to come over like a diva. That gets you lots of hate.'

Sitting back to allow the waitress to place cutlery and water glasses on the table, Honor asked, 'So why aren't we eating with the crew?'

'Because I'd rather eat with you.'

'Or because you think I'll save you from Lily?'

'I don't need saving from Lily.'

But something had flickered in his eyes. She tried not to act deflated. 'You have history.'

His gaze steadied. 'True. Because we were both free to hook up, so one night we did. But it was what it was. I didn't invite you to lunch to warn off Lily.'

She gazed back. 'But you didn't want to spend time with her today, that's why you held hands with me.'

A smile formed slowly, lighting his eyes. 'It would have been a good excuse, if I'd thought of it. But I don't need saving from Lily because we hooked up briefly and we parted friends. End of.'

'I expect you have a whole army of make-up artists, stylists and models to pick from.'

'Not an army.'

'But you do go out with models?'

'Of course.' His eyes had half closed, gleaming at her from between the lids. He seemed to be enjoying her questions, as if intrigued to learn where they were heading. 'Why wouldn't I? But not exclusively. I love attractive women but I don't have a "type". A woman just has to interest me, not be a model or a six-foot-tall blonde.'

She didn't ask about five-foot-five and sort of sandy. 'Was Rosie-with-the-hidden-husband a model?'

He shook his head. 'Flight attendant.'

She snorted. 'Just another industry hot on physical perfection and beauty. And I bet you met her when you were flying home from some exotic location?'

'The Maldives,' he agreed. 'Rosie was gorgeous, well-travelled and sophisticated.'

'I guess you miss her.'

'Not once I realised how short on honesty she was.' His eyes became teasing. 'And how unoriginal – she never once sifted through my sex life or got my attention by taking on teenage louts with a handful of hot food and a kickass attitude.'

The waitress arrived, easing the steaming and fragrant plates carefully on to the tiny table. 'Not much room I'm afraid,' she pointed out, unnecessarily. Martyn's fragrant sauce came in a steel balti bowl, naan bread and white rice in another. Honor's pie scarcely left room on her plate for peppery wedges of potato and a mound of peas, making her realise how hungry she was. She was never going to compete with models or flight attendants with that kind of appetite.

'So,' he said, inconsequentially, when her plate was nearly empty, 'what do you really think about my job?'

She lifted her brows. 'I think it's great. You're obviously sought-after and, I presume, earning good money.'

He brushed that away. 'So you don't think it's odd for a grown man to stand around in his underwear all day, being told where to look? You don't think I should be utilising my intelligence in some more worthwhile way? And that it's plain lazy to only work for a few days each month?'

'You sound as if you're the one who has a problem with your job.'

'No. I don't have a problem with it. But I'd like your objective opinion, as someone who hasn't known me long. How does the whole thing strike you?'

Thoughtfully, she stacked her plate and cutlery with Martyn's so that it would be easy for the waitress to swoop up as she hurried by. 'I don't think it's odd. It's interesting. Yes, the stuff at the bridge got repetitive and my attention wandered but it looks a wonderful career. You're using the assets you've been given. If you have so many issues with your career, how come you got into it? Did you go to modelling school, or something?'

His expression relaxed. 'Just fell into it, which must be really annoying for anyone who does go the modelling school route. I was in Brighton and something was going on in the Pavilion Gardens. So I wandered over to look because it seemed to involve a group of pretty girls. They were from a promotions company, scouting for guys to go into a competition to be a model, organised by *In Town Magazine*, sponsored by le Dur. "You are *just* what we're looking for – how would you like to be in a modelling competition?" they said. And, compared to revising for my finals, it seemed attractive.

'I'd never done any kind of performance but I'd swum and played sport and the shoot director began by sticking us all in swimming gear and it didn't seem too difficult. It might have been torture if they'd wanted cheerful, beaming knitting-pattern guys or something but they just wanted someone who would stare into the camera. I found I could do that OK.' His smile was slow, as if waiting for her to butt in with some kind of funny.

When she didn't, he went on, 'Le Dur liked me and offered me work, which conjured up several agents and managers, so I hooked up with Ace. I don't do runway or acting or anything. I do product-led commercial print and I do quite a bit of editorial – you know, a feature in the glossies about some lifestyle thing and they want the right images.

'I think I must have been born three-parts lucky bastard. It's so random that I just happen to look how they want that sometimes it seems almost wrong to make money out of it.'

'Have you ever been in *GQ*?' Her voice sounded shy and awed, even to her own ears.

'British *GQ*, yes, for a company that sold hand-sewn shirts, and in a couple of editorials, but *GQ* uses a lot of top sportsmen and actors in their ads. I've been in *FHM* and *Esquire* and *In Town*, of course. But I'm in more women's or general interest magazines. And on buses.'

She sorted through the subject in her mind. 'Do you have to deal with clients?'

'Not a lot. Ace, my agent, does that. I maintain my website and do Twitter and Facebook. The agency is keen on each of their models having an online presence.'

She wasn't going to admit that she'd already Googled him. 'And what comes after? Can you model for all of your life?'

'People do. They shift their area of operations into ...' He made a face. '... I don't know, ads for vitamins and life insurance. But others become agents or managers or get work on fashion courses. A lot of models are actors or musicians, anyway, so they concentrate on that. But I don't do that kind of performance.' He hesitated. 'I do some web design, which is what I was doing at uni. I look after the websites of several of the models at the agency. And the agency's site, too.'

She studied him. 'And you do that so that you have a career to move into?'

'And I enjoy doing it, I suppose. I don't get it when men say they do nothing but model. I like to exercise my brain. I do a couple of websites for charities, too, because I've got the time.'

He lapsed into silence, chin on his palm. He seemed to want to get something off his chest but he was having a hard time coughing it up.

'Are you telling me some kind of secret?'

'I suppose I am.' His smile stretched slowly, ruefully across his face. 'I don't tell Clarissa.'

She laughed. 'About the web design? But surely she knows?'

He shook his head.

Baffled, 'Why not? It would seem to me that she'd get off your back, if she knew.'

'That's why I don't tell her.' He smiled at the waitress, who looked dazzled. 'I suppose I have some ridiculous idea that she ought to accept me as I am.'

'You know ... last night you were pretty hard on Clarissa.'

He glanced away. Sighed. 'I'm afraid I've always had a highly developed talent for speaking in the heat of the moment and she has an equal talent for pushing my buttons. But, you're right. I was hard on her. And it would have taken away all the sting if I'd just put my arm around her and said sorry, straight away, wouldn't it? If I'm three parts lucky bastard then the other part is irritable and I do recognise it – but not normally until the next day. And then I'm sorry for how accurately I aimed hurtful words. And that's when

I apologise. When it's hardest to do. But, don't worry, I've already sent her a "let's be friends" text.' His eyes were rueful, even as he laughed at himself.

His phone began to ring, getting him out of the confession, and he answered with a brief, 'Hi, Ace.'

He didn't get up and seek privacy so Honor had no real choice but to listen to his side of the conversation, presumably with his agent, as Ace didn't seem a common name. They talked about the shoot. And Martyn said, 'No, I'm not home yet. I'm eating lunch with someone. No, not from the crew. Yes. Yes, she's pretty.' His eyes crinkled at Honor. 'No, I haven't …' He took the phone away from his ear. 'My agent, Ace is coming for dinner tonight. He says he wants to meet you.'

The waitress stopped to clear the table and offer the dessert menu. Honor took it, not so much because she had room for dessert but to give her time to consider. 'Why would he want to do that?'

Martyn shrugged. 'Typical, flamboyant, expansive – slightly nosey – Ace.' A voice buzzed thinly and he put the phone back to his ear, then added, 'And now he's heard your accent, he says he loves Americans.'

'Oh. Well, I guess.' Now that she'd seen a male model in action, it would probably be interesting to meet his 'flamboyant and expansive' agent, too. She imagined someone who wore satin and called everybody 'darling'.

Ending the call, Martyn chose plain vanilla ice cream but Honor said, 'I'll pass. I've kind of lost my sweet tooth, working amongst Robina's cakes all day.'

'One thing that woman does well is make cakes.'

'If she heard you say so, she'd be beating down your door to deliver lemon drizzle or rocky road.'

'Then please don't tell her. I can run off most things I eat but have never dared let myself get addicted to Robina's cakes. And they're positively dangerous if they arrive attached to Robina.'

No trace of Martyn Mayfair the Model remained. He was completely his Eastingdean self, now, leaning into the crook of the wall, his hair drying and tousled as if he'd just come in from walking in the rain. She felt comfortable with this Martyn. The kind of comfortable that had a lasting feel to it. A comfortable she might never tire of … uh-oh.

There was this feeling. As if he was reaching his hand into her chest and stroking her heart. And her heart liked it.

She sat straighter, her breathing quickening like an animal sensing approaching danger.

And the danger was from within herself. A self that already knew that falling for Martyn … wow. Way to improve her emotional stability! She'd have to be a special kind of swivel-eyed loon to make a fool of herself over a pin-up.

Just like Robina.

Chapter Seventeen

She'd come to England to get away from the storms in her life, not to brew up new ones. 'She says she really loves you,' she reminded him.

His gaze sharpened, as if he were trying to read her thoughts. 'I thought we'd covered this – she's just infatuated, which is uncomfortable for us both. Anyway, there's no chance–' he paused, deliberately, –'*no chance* that I'll return her feelings.'

'But I feel bad for her–'

'Why?' He pulled himself up from his slouch and planted his elbows on the wobbly little table, bringing his face close, eyes intense.

She halted, unwilling to formulate an explanation. One would be: *You know what? I'm looking for obstacles to put between me and something that's going to hurt because I was just zapped by this enormous bolt of desire. For you. And it was scary.* Instead, she said, 'She doesn't believe it's infatuation. She thinks it's genuine, hopeless love.'

'It's not, but why should you feel bad for her? You've only known her a few days.'

She paused. 'Do you have to know someone a long time before you get to care?'

He thought about it. 'I suppose not. Not in my experience.'

His smile went crooked and the hand around her heart began to squeeze. What was hanging from the edges of his words? She tried to think about Stef. Stef, who'd once been her best friend and protector and, for many years, had been her husband.

You're fighting mad with Stef, Sensible Honor reminded

her. *Falling for some guy – even if it's a hunky male model with a cute English accent and buns of steel – is stupid. Did your commonsense crumble with every click of the camera? Did you get a CRUSH for goshsakes? Like some pitiful teenager? Don't embarrass yourself. You've just taken a pounding and if you hand your heart on a plate to Martyn, with his uncompromising only-single-will-do lifestyle, it'll end up as hamburger meat.*

The waitress arrived with a tall glass filled with scoops of ice cream as white as snowballs and Martyn released her from his gaze as he picked up a long spoon from the saucer and took a mouthful. 'Mm. Good.'

Honor seized the opportunity to redirect the conversation. 'What's the nuddy?'

He almost choked, covering his mouth with his napkin while his eyes sparkled. 'The nuddy?'

Her stomach crept with embarrassment. She must've said something idiotic. 'What? Lily said it. She asked if you'd been sunbathing in the nuddy.'

He swallowed and cleared his throat with a swig of water. 'The nude. She was asking if I'd sunbathed nude.'

'Oh!' Her face fired up as hot as the day Martyn had first found her, getting sunstroke, and she made herself busy studying the coffee column of the menu.

He turned back to his ice cream. Just when she felt her temperature returning to normal, he drawled, 'I do sunbathe in the nude.'

Involuntarily, her eyes flew to his.

'But not on the beach,' he added.

Her voice strangled, but she had to ask. 'So ... where?'

His eyes were dancing again. 'Come tonight, and I'll show you. Where I do it, I mean. Not me doing it.'

By the time she'd bought a book about Arundel to add to

her collection and they had followed one of the walks that it suggested, up and down the steep little lanes, over cobbles and flags and elevated sidewalks, in and out of quaint shops, it was early evening before they began to make their way back to Eastingdean.

Fresh air and exercise and the passing Sussex scenery had almost rocked her to sleep by the time he drew up in the small lot behind the shops of Starboard Walk. Although she had only tentatively accepted his dinner invitation, somehow she slipped into following him up the metal stairs. Yeah, 'somehow'. Right.

Inside his apartment, Honor again kicked off her shoes in deference to the blond carpet, which felt like velvet on her feet as she prowled around and Martyn took trays from his stainless steel refrigerator and posted them into his stainless steel oven. The sofas, black suede, were angled towards a huge TV on the wall. Cream slatted blinds shielded the French doors that led out on to a curved black metal balcony. She pressed her nose against the glass and saw Marine Drive rumbling by, right below. No nude sunbathing on the balcony, then ...

The open-plan design meant windows all around, overlooking not just Marine Drive and the backs of the houses that ran along the road, and The Butts, but also any cars parked behind the flat. If not for the dips and folds of the land, she might have been able to see the back of the bungalow.

Between the sofas stood a piece of leather-topped furniture that, she guessed, doubled as both table and footstool. A large black laptop computer, the kind that was only portable if you were a weight lifter, lay folded shut, on top. Beside one of the sofas, papers and magazines were piled haphazardly on the floor with untidily kicked-off blue canvas shoes and a khaki jacket that had landed like a parachute.

'Red, white or rosé?' Martyn called.

'Rosé, please.' There was no point asking what they were eating because she could never remember what to drink with what. Rosé meant she didn't have to bother.

Then he was strolling across the acre of carpet, a glass in each hand. The sun, slanting through the rear window, threw shadows across his face. He gave her one of the glasses. 'Cheers.'

'Cheers,' she echoed, suddenly aware that she was alone with him in his apartment.

'Let me show you the rest of the flat.' He led her back to the entrance hall, where the wooden floor was suddenly chill to her toes. He opened a door, 'Downstairs loo.' Mainly white, but for a cobalt-blue-tiled floor.

The next door: 'Office.'

A desk, a printer, a fax machine, some filing cabinets, trays piled high, a roll of tape in a dispenser, a spilling holdall. 'It looks like an explosion happened in here.' She liked the untidiness, liked that he was only perfect when captured by the camera.

'It looks better when I remember to shut some drawers.' He shoved shut one filing-cabinet and four desk drawers, improving the situation only slightly but at least allowing Honor to squeeze into the small square space. Over the desk was a glossy image of a younger Martyn, hair shorter and spiked, staring down at a pouty, tousled female model, gazing up at him. He was easing a strap from Pouty's perfect shoulder with such an expression of hunger that it seemed the shutter must have clicked only an instant before he ate her right up. Honor swallowed. He'd looked at her like that, too, as if she were on the menu. But, in her case, not on his diet sheet – like Robina's cakes.

He shifted self-consciously. 'That was the first ad that got into *FHM*. It's a bit narcissistic to frame it but nobody

156

usually comes in here. It was a career landmark.' He bustled her out as if he wasn't much more at ease with Martyn Mayfair the Model than she was. He steered her towards the staircase that spiralled up from the centre of the floor. 'The other rooms are in the roof, so the upstairs is a touch smaller.'

The stairs were steep, each one a wedge of polished wood on the black metal frame, opening up on to a landing and three doors. The first stood open. 'Spare room. That's where Ace will sleep tonight.'

'He's staying over?' She glanced in at the white-and-cool-green room.

'He's a friend, not just my agent.' Another door. 'Bathroom.' The floor and wall tiles were palest blue and a bathtub in size XXL took up a quarter of the space. The final door he opened and walked through. She followed into a huge bedroom with windows set in the sloping walls, and a super-king-sized-this-is-the-biggest-I've-ever-seen bed. She looked away. Beside the bed, another pair of French doors was set into a dormer. He threw them wide, exhibiting a few square feet of balcony and a great view over the gardens and rooftops of the houses on Marine Drive. 'It's nice to look out but looking down isn't so hot – at the car park and the outbuildings belonging to the shops.'

She glanced down and saw what he meant. But a few flat roofs one level down didn't seem a high price to pay for such a view. The sun, dipping towards the sea beside Brighton, spread an elongated patch of light over the balcony and onward, inside, on a thick blue rug.

'There you are,' he said, indicating the pool of sunlight on the floor. 'That's where I do my nude sunbathing. Nobody can see.' Then, before she could lick her lips and formulate a reply around the burning image of Martyn baking his nakedness in his private slice of sunlight, he clicked shut the doors and led her back to the winding stairs, just as the doorbell pealed out like a fire alarm. Martyn said, 'That will be Ace. We can eat.'

Ace Smith. His silvery suit, black shirt but no tie, looked all-designer; he probably wore nothing but. Hair and beard were buzzed down to the stubble, giving his head a suede look, like Martyn's sofas. He wasn't exactly handsome but had interesting cheekbones and big brown eyes. He smelled of alcohol.

She knew there was an appropriate formal response to his 'How do you do?' but couldn't remember what it was so just said, 'I'm good. How are you?'

Ace looked at her, long and slow. 'Martyn was right, you're pretty.'

Coolly, she responded, 'Thanks.' And sipped her wine.

Martyn poured another glass for Ace and began setting out cutlery and plates. 'She won't fall for your bullshit, Ace. She's too switched on.'

'But she has a real look,' Ace objected, tossing his jacket and taking the stool next to Honor's, edging it closer.

'She does. But she either doesn't know, doesn't care, or takes it for granted. Unresponsive to compliments, anyway.'

Ace fixed his seal-pup eyes on her. 'Interesting. See, in our business, we're more used to women who suck in compliments like the rest of us breathe air.' He let his elbows slide along the polished granite until his arm brushed Honor's. 'You're in good shape. Sure you're not in the biz?'

There was a looseness about his movements that was consistent with the alcohol fumes and Honor guessed he wouldn't pass a sobriety test. 'Biz?'

He waved his wine glass in an encompassing motion. 'Modelling. Fashion. Photography. Are you an MUA?'

'No. But I did think, today, watching the shoot, that there

are worse jobs.'

His eyes widened. 'Martyn took you to a shoot?'

Suddenly, she wondered whether she was not supposed to have been there. Maybe she was getting Martyn in trouble? She had only the haziest idea of the agent/model relationship. 'I was going to go to Arundel on the train and he offered me a ride,' she said hastily. 'I really just hung out on the fringes.'

'Right.' He looked at Martyn and smiled.

Martyn placed warmed plates in front of them and then began to pull dishes from the oven, steaming and sizzling as they met the air. Ripping foil from the top of each he slid them on to the granite. 'Braised lamb, Mediterranean vegetables and roast potatoes. Honor's just here for the summer, looking for her mother.'

'But not too hard,' Honor added. 'I'm beginning to think of that saying, you know? "Don't wish too hard for what you want, or then you might get it."' Politely, she offered the serving spoon for the lamb to Ace.

Martyn took the seat opposite. 'She's met Clarissa and I think it's put her off mothers.' He took the serving spoon from Ace, who was waving it uncertainly, and ladled a lamb steak on to Honor's plate.

'Did you cook this?' she queried, going next for the baby roast potatoes, golden and crunchy and pitted with rosemary leaves.

'I ordered it from a caterer and they gave me instructions for how long to put it in the oven. Does that count as cooking?' He topped up her glass.

Honor remembered Clarissa suggesting his interpretation of 'domesticated' revolved around avoiding real cooking. 'I guess it's domestication Martyn-style.'

Ace laughed. He didn't attempt to put any food on his plate but drained his wine glass and held it out for Martyn to refill. 'We should have had pizza, Martyn – American

Hot, in honour of Honor.'

Martyn began to put food on Ace's plate. 'Tomorrow night we'll have fish and chips.'

'Yeah! Eastingdean fish and chips are the best in the world.' Ace's voice was a touch too loud.

'Honor can take on a gang of thugs armed only with fish and chips.' Martyn tasted the lamb and then reached for the pepper grinder. He told Ace the whole story, making a big deal out of Frog hopping about – appropriately enough – with steaming fish dropping into his boxer shorts.

Poking desultorily at a potato, Ace nudged Honor. 'It's every woman's fantasy, isn't it? For a giant to come striding to the rescue, like Martyn did?' Once more he drained and refilled his wine glass and tried to top up her top up.

She put her fingers over the glass. A smart woman knew when to stay sober. 'In my experience, men's ideas of women's fantasies bear little resemblance to women's actual fantasies. Your caterer can cook up a storm, Martyn.'

Twizzling his wine glass, Ace fastened his eyes on her. 'Go on.'

Her fork paused in mid-air. 'Go on with what?'

'Educate us. Tell us about what women's fantasies really are.' His eyes had slitted and sweat beaded his forehead. The wine was disappearing fast.

'I'll pass, thanks.'

'Ignore him.' Martyn frowned. 'He's taken his winding-down at the end of the week too seriously. Eat, Ace, soak up some of the booze.'

'What, and waste the buzz?' But Ace did pick up his knife and fork.

Taking refuge in silence, Honor addressed herself to her delicious meal – the gravy was to die for – and let Martyn steer Ace into talking shop. She listened to curious phrases such as, 'I've taken a pencil on it,' wondering if it meant the same as, 'I've pencilled it in,' and noticed that Ace heaped praise on Martyn at every opportunity. 'DownJo love you. Everyone loves you, Martyn. I do, every time I look at my bank statement.' Noticing, also, that Martyn never responded, as if he either didn't want or didn't need the ego trip.

She had the feeling that somewhere in Ace's alcoholic pushy bullshit there was a nice guy trying to get out. But he wasn't making it tonight.

As they were in deep conversation, she went into waitress mode, quietly clearing the plates and stacking them in the dishwasher. Then she figured out Martyn's coffee machine, sliding in the little pouch and waiting for the jug to fill as she opened cupboard doors and found bright blue coffee mugs and a jar of sugar. The milk was in the refrigerator. She moved her finds over to the island counter and then went back for the coffee jug.

'You seem at home here.' Ace's eyes were once more fastened to her.

'It's not hard to find your way around a kitchen.'

'So does the kitchen figure in your "womanly fantasies"?' He made stupid quote-unquote signals with his fingers without letting go of his wine.

She made a good-natured *pshaw* noise and slid back on to her stool, taking the opportunity to move it six inches from him.

'Watching you bending over the dishwasher, then, I had a little fantasy of my own.'

She poured coffee.

'Ace–!' began Martyn.

Ace refused to be diverted. 'Come on, Honor, satisfy my curiosity. Rape?'

She looked at him over her coffee cup.

'Bondage? Chocolate sauce? Animals?'

161

'Stop it, Ace.' Martyn's brows had curled blackly over his eyes, reminding Honor of the fake tattoo Lily had applied to the small of his back. His stillness spoke of tension.

Ace smile's slipped. She could almost see his mind ticking away behind his glassy eyes. 'C'mon. Put me out of my misery and tell me what women want.'

'OK.' She let her voice drop like she used to do when she had told Jess and Zach stories at Halloween. 'Right now, my fantasy is about a guy who doesn't speak. Why don't you try it? It's particularly appropriate for assholes.'

Sweat bubbled afresh on Ace's wine-flushed face as he totally missed the point. 'And you've never found a guy who could do that? Well, my little American Hot, why don't you try me? You can do anything you want to me and I won't say a word–'

'She's telling you to shut up, Ace.' Martyn was on his feet. 'I'll walk you home, Honor. No, don't argue. It will give Ace the opportunity to drink a gallon of coffee, just in case Dr Zoë's wrong and it will sober him up.'

Outside, the gulls had gone to bed – or nest or roost or whatever gulls did at night – and even the noise from the traffic had eased. The air smelled fresh off the ocean and Honor shivered as they rounded the Starboard Walk shops and turned into Marine Drive. Martyn strode silently beside her, hands jammed into his pockets but otherwise not showing any signs of feeling the chill up on the clifftop.

Maybe he was pissed with her because she'd been rude to his buddy. It was bad manners not to get along with a fellow guest. She could almost hear Karen: 'Really, Honor. I did my best to raise you as a lady. A lady wouldn't let some creep rile her. Couldn't you have just quietly excused yourself, without the attitude and the cursing?' She sighed as they turned into the drive of the bungalow. She could have. But the word 'asshole' had popped out. She never had been diplomatic with men who suddenly turned into slimy, scumbag sleazeballs.

She trod up the concrete steps to the patio, fishing out her door key. But Martyn's long arm descended over her shoulder and his hand closed over hers before she could fit it to the door. She glanced up at him.

'I'm sorry Ace insulted you.' He gave an almost smile.

She made a face. 'And I'm sorry I called your friend an asshole.'

'I don't think he even noticed, and he was. He's not usually like this or I wouldn't have invited you to meet him. I don't expect my friends to hit on my other friends.'

'Even best friends can be assholes.' Stef – perfect example.

He laughed. 'I hope the night air has helped cool you off. I certainly needed it – or I might have booted Ace off the balcony.' He breathed in deeply.

Silence. He was frowning heavily. She peeped up at him from under her lashes, toying with her key. 'So. Here we are.'

His frown lifted slowly. '"Here we are." I've always wondered whether that actually means anything.'

She considered. 'I guess it can mean a whole range of things. It can draw your attention to my presence, or that we've got to where we're going. It could be an acknowledgement that it's time to say goodnight. When my grandma says it, everyone just seems to get what she means.'

'Right.' He rocked back on his heels. 'I know you're here. I know we've got where we're going and I suppose I'd better say goodnight and check that Ace doesn't need a stomach pump.

'So, goodnight.' Pulling her jacket around her.

'Yeah.' He sighed, not going anywhere. 'I hope that at least you enjoyed the shoot?'

'It was an education. I had no idea what being a model

was about or that guys like you did it. In fact, if I thought of it at all, I guess I thought all male models were gay. You know, the make-up, the posing, the interest in fashion – woop!'

His arm hooked her by her waist and yanked her up against the firmness of his body so that her toes just touched the ground. She gasped and his mouth found hers. Hot mouth, hot body, heat flooding her. He adjusted his stance, cupped her buttocks and picked her right off the ground, letting her feel his hardness against her through the thin cotton of her dress.

His velvet tongue stroked hers and her breasts tightened against his chest, his heartbeat, and he made it something longer, deeper, hotter. The kind of kiss she and her high-school friends had called a 'soul kiss' – like your souls were communicating through your mouths. They used to giggle and hypothesise over how it would feel. And, wow … It felt like heaven – if you were allowed to feel this turned on in heaven.

Slowly, slowly, he put her down.

'I'm not gay.'

Breathless, she shook her head. 'I got that.'

He nodded. 'Good.' And then, 'That didn't cool me off at all.'

She shook her head again. Her heart was pounding as hard as it had on that run when Martyn had amused himself by letting her try and keep up.

Slowly, slowly, he backed away, his hair lifting in the breeze, his eyes very black in the moonlight. Honor felt words flying up towards her mouth, words like, 'We could go indoors …'

He paused, as if waiting for her to say them.

Struggling, she kept the words in.

He let out a long sigh. 'I'd better go.'

Tung. Tung. Tung. Martyn made his way up the metal stairs on legs that felt as if they belonged to someone else. Whoo, she'd tasted like fire, pressing close as if heaven was just a heartbeat away. Those bare legs beneath her dress. He'd always had a thing about bare legs. Could imagine skimming his hands over, up, up ... Watching her eyes turn hotter and more liquid as he went past the point of no return.

He let himself into the flat.

And let the door slam, stalking the length of the open-plan space to where Ace was slumped on a sofa, feet up, an empty wine glass on its side on the carpet. The TV blared. 'Would you like to explain why you turned up drunk and hit on a friend of mine, like a sad old tosser?'

Ace turned slowly from the TV screen. 'Was I a bit over the top?'

Martyn snatched up the empty glass.

Ace flinched. 'I've had a shitty day.'

Carrying the glass to the kitchen, Martyn refilled the coffee machine. In silence, he emptied Honor's cup and stuck it in the dishwasher.

When he returned, Ace was still staring blankly at the television. It got Martyn's attention. Something was wrong. Because Ace wasn't usually ... well, he wasn't an asshole. He let his voice soften. 'What's up?'

With a long sigh, Ace dropped his head on to his hand. 'Seems like Shelli's dumped me. Got home last night and she'd cleared out her stuff and left me a note – the classic one-hundred-reasons-you-don't-make-me-happy note. She didn't answer her phone. Then, this morning, I got an email from the agency's new talent, that young black guy I've been working with for a few months, telling me that *in the circumstances* he's sure I won't want to represent him any more. He's sorry that things have worked out like this but he and Shelli ...'

Martyn dropped down on the sofa, aggravation draining away. 'Shit. I'm sorry.'

Ace picked up the coffee. 'Me, too. Sorry I got out of hand with Honor. I did realise that you like her but I'm in a crazy place. I hope things work out for you.'

He did like her. He liked her a lot. The memory of that kiss was like a demon breathing down his jeans. But Martyn sighed, forcing himself to remember why he shouldn't have begun that kiss. 'No. You know – husband.'

'Ah. Is he over here, too?'

'I don't know where he is, to be honest. She just told me she's sort of married. She wanted to tell me more but I kind of … didn't listen. After Rosie.'

Bitterly, Ace laughed. 'At least you let the husband cross your mind. That's more than Shelli and her lover boy have done.'

Chapter Eighteen

It was a busy week at the Teapot, the last of July and the English school summer holidays in full swing.

Sophie decided to like her pink hair, humming David Bowie songs as she clattered around the steamy atmosphere.

Ru, almost silent, a baseball hat on back-to-front as his nod to hair hygiene, stood at the steamy, soapy sink washing the eclectic white crockery and stacking it in the wall racks to drain. Kirsty made a short appearance each day, scarily skeletal and snapping at everybody, then clutching her forehead and apologising.

Honor got right into her waitress's stride of rapid and economical movement, taking orders, serving, clearing tables, sanitising, watching the tables fill and empty, fill and empty. She was astonished when Sophie, having organised a Finnish student, Aletta, to help serve, opened a door that Honor hadn't really noticed at the rear of the inside seating area to reveal a whole other room. The twenty tables in there began to fill and empty, too.

Very beautiful, with apple-round cheeks and soft full lips, Aletta's English only failed her if a customer showed any hint of irritation, when she would smile gently and drift away, leaving one of the native English-speakers to get yelled at instead of her.

Through the bustle, Robina serenely made cakes, whipping up sugary frostings or boiling glistening jams to sandwich together layers of moist sponge or crispy meringue. Her drunkenly risen scones were treated by many customers as a meal in themselves and so many were baked that Honor was sure that she went home at night smelling like a steaming trayful.

On Tuesday, Clarissa dropped in for lunch. 'Hello, Honor. Baked potato with cheddar cheese and crispy bacon, please. This place can't be good for me. What jam has Robina made? Plum? I'll have a jar, then.'

Honor reached for a stubby jar with its white cotton cap. 'I'm sure you can work it off. You Mayfairs are never still.'

'True.' Clarissa glanced at her watch. 'Martyn says you run, so you're pretty active, yourself?'

Honor wrote the jam on Clarissa's bill and dropped it back on to the table. 'I used to dance and stuff, too. But I haven't got into that here, yet.' The instant the words had left her mouth she wanted them back. Clarissa's face lit up.

'But I take dance classes – tap, ballroom …'

'I'm more hiphop, these days–'

'And Zumba,' Clarissa finished, triumphantly. 'Zumba sounds right up your street. It's tonight, at the community centre.'

'I have taken Zumba classes back home.' Honor made as if to move on to the next table but the hope in Clarissa's eyes made her pause. The economy was bad and Clarissa was probably finding her numbers falling. And then the classes would end and Clarissa wouldn't have a job and that would be awful … 'I'll try to come,' she promised.

By the time she'd finished at the Teapot her feet burned and Zumba class didn't sound like a good cure. She'd just jump in the shower and veg out with a meal from the freezer and a magazine. She liked English magazines. They made room for Z-list celebs who'd never done anything more noteworthy than appearing on a reality show and having their picture taken – bizarre but somehow fascinating.

Even though she could hear Karen saying, 'A promise is a promise,' she wrapped herself in her robe and flopped on the sofa with *Heat* magazine. Russell Brand – nobody's Z-lister – was on the cover, his smile assuring her that he didn't give a rat's ass for what anyone thought of him. An attitude she recognised. From Stef.

She tried not to think about Stef.

But it must be about time for a message to come through cyberspace.

Her laptop was sitting on the table, its baleful blue eye winking at her. She sighed and flipped it open. Tapped a key and the screen sprang to life, already logged into her Yahoo account.

Inbox (3).

One email from her father, asking her to touch base and reassure him that she was OK. *I'm good thanks,* she typed rapidly, *enjoying having only myself to worry over. Hope you are doing fine, too.*

She sighed again. Both the other emails were from Stef, through Billie.

I'm getting real tired of you blanking me. I may have fucked up but I don't think I deserve to be forgotten or ignored. Come on, babe. Lighten up on me and let me know how you're doing.

She opened the second.

Well, guess what! Jessamine, who obviously has a whole lot more heart than you have, came to see me today. And it seems you don't mind replying to her emails or your dad's, or Zach's. So you're really not speaking to me? Thanks a lot. You always find out who cares when you're in a bad place and I'm not only in a bad place, I'm having to worry about my wife. What the fuck are you doing leaving your life behind?

She tried to stem the sour swell of indignation, to delay any response until she'd reflected and cooled down. But … she clicked *reply*. *OK*, she typed. *Here I am. Fine – on my own. You don't have to worry. I'm so mad at you, Stef. Your stunt wrecked my life so that there wasn't a whole lot of it for me to leave behind. The bad place? You got yourself in it. There's no law that says that I have to go there, too.*

You've left it a little late to worry about your wife.

Quickly, she pressed *send*, snapped the laptop shut and rolled restlessly to her feet. Damn him. The sofa and *Heat* had lost all power to relax her. No longer hungry or lazy, what she needed was to get out and get busy and her watch told her that there were only thirty minutes before the start of the Zumba class.

Quickly, she dressed in blackberry-coloured capri dance pants, an exercise bra with a camisole and fleece over, grabbed a bottle of water and set off power walking towards the community hall.

Clarissa beamed over her little cash tin when Honor marched into the wooden hall and paid her fee – and the reason for the warm welcome was pretty clear. Apart from herself, there were three people in the class – plus a whole lot of Mayfairs: Clarissa, Zoë, Beverley and Nicola. And, she saw with a hop of surprise, Martyn, at the back, performing hamstring stretches. She waved at the Sisters of Mayfair but skipped over to where Martyn was folded over to hold his feet, stretching alternate legs.

'You're kidding me! You dance, too?'

He gave an upside-down grunt. 'If guilted into it by Clarissa. It's exercise.'

He was the only man in the class. Most of the women had dressed bright, tight and dancy in sizzling colours of lycra. One looked as if she'd come directly from a hiphop dance-off with slouch pants riding low on her hips, displaying an expanse of bare flesh between the waistband and her tiny brilliant turquoise top. Martyn's Zumba gear was pretty much like his running gear – plain, dark and roomy – but, at least he could wear a T rather than a sweatshirt, indoors.

'I resisted for a while.' Honor unzipped her fleece and tossed it on a chair. 'But then I wanted company. And I like to dance.' She hesitated about whether to hang out with Martyn at the back. But he appeared to be in one of his remote moods again, eyes distant, as if his thoughts were too intense to be shared. And then she was beckoned forward by Clarissa to discuss her fitness, health and dance experience. By the time that was over, the only space left was in the front row between Beverley in green and peacock-blue, and Zoë, who had abandoned her dark doctorly suit for scarlet chevron stripes.

The community centre had an OK wooden floor and high ceiling but was lacking the mirror array of the dance studio back in Hamilton. Still, the Latin rhythms of the music were the same and Honor fixed her eyes on Clarissa as she warmed them up then talked up the class energy level through the opening bars: *Zumba ah ah ay oh!* Then, on *Zumba ah ah ay ah*, shouted, 'Okay-six-seven-eight,' and danced right into the routine. The class went with her, side-step right, right, dot the toes, side-step left, left, dot. In swung the arms, arcing up together, wrists crossing above heads as the feet side-stepped again, *Ay oh, ay oh oh*, wrists down to cross behind, *ay oh, ay oh oh* … head turn right, look up as wrists curve up, left and down at the floor. *Zumba ay oh! Zumba ah, dadda dadda dadda dadda Zumba ah, dadda dadda dadda dadda Zumba oh.*

With a surge of pleasure and a release of tension, Honor felt the music take charge of her feet, easily following Clarissa through a weight and direction change to allow the class to flow back across the room. *Zumba ay oh!*

Suddenly, it didn't matter that she was in a pretty basic amenity in England with no mirror wall, dodgy lighting and windows that needed cleaning, or that the instructor had to pressgang her family into attending the class in order to keep it going. *Zumba ah ah ay oh.* It was just good to be dancing, to be moving in time with everyone else, rhythm quickening, hips rolling, body stretching.

At the end of the first routine her heart rate and adrenaline levels were on the way up, making her whip off her camisole and flip it to the side of the room. If the woman with the slouch pants could show the world a bare midriff, so could Honor.

She was going to dance so hard that there would be no energy left for sour feelings like anger and regret.

On the odd occasions that he allowed Clarissa to drag him to venture into the otherwise, all-women Zumba class, Martyn generally made space for himself by virtue of the length of his stride and the reach of his rotating arms.

Zumba didn't thrill him, although he could keep in time OK – unsurprising as he shared genes with the instructor radiating rhythm and presence from the front of the room. But if he'd known that Honor would show up, he would definitely have stayed at home. He'd almost forgotten – no, disregarded – Honor's husband when he'd kissed her on her doorstep on Friday night. Until Ace had made him see, with painful clarity, what it felt like to be the husband whose wife was getting it on with someone else.

Bad.

He'd decided he'd better keep away from Honor in case he suddenly found himself undressing her.

And now, here she was, a couple of rows ahead of him and wearing so little that he was getting the idea of how undressed would look. Oh mannnn ... why did she have to throw off her top and dance in her sports bra? She was a great mover and those two vertical lines that ran up her abdomen, the sure sign of a taut body, were mesmerising. He'd follow those lines in either direction and like where they took him.

Wiping sweat from his forehead with his forearm, he tried to look away.

But she was right in his line of sight. And her wiggle and swing was a class apart. Her fingers flexed and pointed, her back stretched and arched and her tidy little behind was poetry. Real salsa hips. By the third routine she was beaming and laughing, glowing with the fun of dancing, and he'd worked out that she was able to follow the routines so easily because Clarissa was indicating changes of direction with a pointing finger, or the leading foot by placing her hand on the appropriate thigh. That Honor could interpret placed her on a higher level than the rest of the class.

Clarissa's shouts of 'Zumba!' were usually greeted by self-conscious silence but Honor was quite at ease giving exuberant 'Zumbas!' of her own. The energy level climbed with every 'Whoo!' and 'Yeah!' and Zoë, Nicola and Bev, who generally treated the class as something they played at doing for Clarissa's sake, were joining Honor in a dancing fury. For once, they really needed the drinks they brought in shiny bottles with spouts on top.

Actually, he was glad for Clarissa. He watched her glow with pleasure as she demonstrated – not for the first time, he had to admit – the difference between Cuban motion and waggling your bum. 'Ball-flat,' she called, 'not heel-flat. Tiny steps and then your hips will sway away from the side that's taking the step.' And suddenly, not just Honor's hip action was following Clarissa's. The whole class 'got' it and Clarissa's face was one big grin. 'Yeah! Great! Now, we need to practise our break back. For a break back step, we never put down the heel of the foot that is breaking back–'

Clarissa and Honor seemed set on outdoing each other in the pizzazz department and Clarissa had to keep dropping back into tutor mode to collect the class up and put the less able of them on track. But it seemed as if every one of the women was concentrating hard on keeping up.

Whereas he was concentrating hard to not get hard, with Honor's rolling round behind in constant Cuban motion and the lycra no more than a second skin over her breasts. He'd never sweated so much in a class. Or been so out of breath. He could hardly wait for the cool down and final stretches so he could call a brief goodbye and slide out of the door as he zipped into a fleece and got himself and his aching groin the hell out of there.

Chapter Nineteen

'Hey!' Honor smiled at Ru who was at the sink, where he seemed to have spent most of the last week. Covering off days had morphed into a full-time job, washing steaming dishes, baseball hat reversed and a spike of hair sprouting from the front.

'Hey.' His hands didn't pause in their mechanical repetition and his attention remained on the gleaming white dishes.

She tied her apron with rapid movements. 'What's up?'

'Nothing.' He shoved a plate into the drainer.

Honor paused. She recognised deeply pissed off when she saw it. She checked that Robina was out of the room and Sophie was at the other end of the kitchen, flipping scones off a baking sheet. 'Still not enjoying working at the Teapot?'

His hand clenched around the dish mop. 'Hate it.'

She checked in her pocket for her pencil and pad. 'At least it's self-defence class tonight – that ought to be fun.'

His hands reached for more plates from the stack. 'I'm supposed to be going into Brighton.' He still didn't look at her.

'That's a pity.' She spoke lightly but her mind flicked to 'close attention' mode. Ru had been getting quieter and more morose as the week had worn on. 'The class gave me a lot of confidence, last week. I was intending to go again tonight but I'm not sure I want to – alone.'

Ru scrubbed violently at a burned-on raisin. Rinsed. Sighed. 'Yeah, OK. I'll do the class with you first.'

'Great, thanks.' She slid her pencil and pad from her pocket. When she'd accomplished a circuit to check status at both inside and outside tables, she cleared up after a few early birds, scraping the plates and carrying the stack over to Ru. 'Have you had more trouble with Frog?'

'Not yet.'

Honor moved on to the other likely source of friction. 'So, where's your mother?'

He scowled. 'Upstairs. Arguing with Crusty.'

Aha.

He yanked on the chain to the plug, the grey water running away as if being gulped down by the drain monster. Finally, he looked up, eyes hard. 'She's trying to get Kirsty to look after the Teapot while she goes to the Global Gathering.'

Honor felt her brows shoot up. 'Isn't Kirsty still too sick? When is the Global Gathering? It's just a music festival, right?'

Ru laughed, rinsing the sink with the tap's trunky hose attachment known as 'the elephant'. 'Yes, she's way too ill because the Global Gathering starts tomorrow – and there's no "just" where my mum's concerned, about music festivals. We all realised weeks ago that Crusty wasn't going to be well enough to look after the Teapot but Mum seemed to think that there was a miracle on the horizon. She's all packed up, ready to go. So now she's sulking and whinging because the miracle hasn't happened.'

Watching the fresh water pour into the sink, creating white suds and a million spherical rainbows from the sunlight streaming through the window, Honor frowned. 'Are you disappointed because it means that you can't go, either?'

Eyes saucers of amazement, he laughed. 'No! I don't want to go, I've had enough of tents and queuing for disgusting pooey toilets. But Mum will give everyone stress because she can't go if Crusty won't run the Teapot. Even Mum knows the Teapot has to be open to pay the bills so she can't just shut up shop because she's keeping that in reserve for the end of August, in case Crusty doesn't get better in time for Reading Rock Festival. It'll hurt her to miss the takings from the whole bank holiday weekend but if Mum has to miss Reading she'll probably throw herself off the cliff.' To demonstrate, he dropped a stack of plates into the water, flopping water and suds everywhere.

'So where is this Global Gathering. Here in England?'

He nodded. 'Stratford. They have it in other countries, too.'

'Stratford where William Shakespeare came from?'

He looked vague. 'Dunno. Did he?'

It was another half hour before Robina flew back into the Teapot with a face of thunder and a tongue full of spite. Ru kept his eyes on his washing up and Honor glided off amongst the tables, taking care not to get any closer to the kitchen than the counter.

Poor Sophie looked ready to burst into tears at being trapped between a Robina who spat like the coffee machine and the silent back of Ru as he jabbed and scrubbed with his washing-up brush. It was a tense morning.

At two, Honor took her break, grabbing a scone and spreading it with jam. The Teapot didn't do coffee 'to go', so she took a bottle of chilled water and prepared to put some distance between herself and the Teapot. But Robina caught her as she tried to swing out through the door and head for a bench on the cliff top. 'Honor, I'm really stuck for some extra help this weekend–'

'I know and I'm sorry I can't help,' said Honor, quickly. 'It would mean me working three twelve-hour shifts, at least, when it's meant to be my weekend off, and I've never run the place.' And she gave Robina's arm an apologetic squeeze and skipped out.

'No freakin' way,' she muttered, rounding the corner

of the shops at Starboard Walk and dodging the Marine Drive traffic, rather than pressing the button at the crossing, intending to jog on across the grassy cliff top to an iron bench to watch the sun dancing on the waves and let her back relax.

It was only as she popped out between a bus and a truck that she saw Martyn on the pavement, waiting to cross in the opposite direction. 'Are you trying to kill yourself?' he demanded.

Honor had had about enough of other people's bad temper. 'No. I could find much more efficient ways. What's it to you?'

His snow-white shirt hung out over his jeans and his hair streamed from one side of his head then the other on the whims of the wind. Honor willed herself not to colour up – just because Martyn had kissed her on Friday night as if he was going to drag her off for wild, nightlong sex. But hadn't. And had then apparently forgotten that she existed.

Today was Thursday, which was awkward. Last Thursday, he'd given her and Ru a ride to and from self-defence class and he'd kind of talked as if that's what he'd meant to do this week, too. So, if she took the bus then he turned up it would be really rude. But if she *mentioned* that she was going to take the bus then he might think she was hinting for him to drive her.

His eyes fell on the napkin-wrapped package in her hands. 'Lunch?'

'Got to be some perks to the job.' She smiled politely and began to move on by. She'd take the bus. Chill and Remote Martyn had probably forgotten about the classes.

She trod across the rippling grass, the wind rushing in her ears. At the bench she tried to juggle with the scone and the water to free a hand to brush the seat without dropping anything or letting the wind mix her ponytail up with the jam oozing out of the sides of the napkin. A hand descended over her shoulder and took the water. 'Let me.'

'Oh!' She turned to look at Martyn. The wind must have drowned out the sound of him following. 'Thanks.' With a hand freed up, she was able to tuck her ponytail into the back of her black T-shirt and settle the scone on the napkin, on her lap.

Martyn sat down and perched the bottle on the bench between them. He looked out over the cliff. The tide was in and the ocean was its most beautiful blue.

She broke the scone in half and offered one half to him.

Slowly, he turned to look at her. He'd shaved. Really close shaved so that he looked smooth and touchable. If anything, he was more mouthwatering without the *GQ* stubble. His jawline was a blade. 'I shouldn't.'

'I guess life would be more comfortable for us all if we were never tempted.'

He snorted a laugh and took the proffered half. 'Or if we were better at resisting things. This is your lunch.'

She shrugged, licking her fingers. 'I know the tree that these grow on and I'm going right back to it when I've taken a few minutes in the fresh air.' She stifled a sigh at the thought. Her idea of a job without stress didn't include a boss that acted like a premenstrual pitbull.

After wiping her hands, she offered him the napkin, then the bottle of water. Then they watched the gulls, beady black eyes fixed on tourists to mug for food, as the waves glittered and shushed on to the beach below.

Ten minutes, she promised herself. Ten minutes to chill, to refill her emotional well, before returning to suffer under the black clouds that had rolled into the Teapot. Ten minutes to be aware of Martyn lounging, unspeaking, beside her.

At the end of that time, she climbed reluctantly to her feet. 'Better get back to it.'

He didn't move. Or look at her. 'Shall I pick you up for your class?'

She hesitated. 'I could get the bus.'

'No need. Tell Ru.'

I thought that all I wanted was to get a message from you but, now you finally decide to talk … Babe, I said I'm sorry. Don't you care how I'm hurting? When are you coming back? This is crazy. Maybe you've gone crazy. It can't be the end. I won't let it be. I don't believe you're quitting, Honor, because you just never quit.

Honor stared at Stef's words, wondering why she didn't feel worse for him. Maybe it was the distance. She thought about Connecticut and found it unexpectedly hard to remember living in their apartment with the view of Main Street, because Stef liked to be in the middle of town where they both worked and he could get around the bars and clubs on foot, rather than living out on the lake, as she'd wanted. She tried to walk her mind through the furniture they'd picked out – the chaise with a broken leg from when Stef tried to prove he could still back flip, the rug with the red wine stain after his birthday party, his end of the sofa splashed with beer from when he got excited during ball games.

Yes, she had no trouble picturing Stef on his end of the sofa.

And, yup, she was in the frame, too – bringing home most of the bacon and picking up the groceries on the way, running the household and battling to undo the Stef effect to make the apartment look nice. A reasonable housekeeper. Not a bad wife – Stef had never stopped reaching for her in bed.

Her response was where her imagination got unco-operative. For there to be want there had to be trust.

Instead, she thought about the big clapboard house she grew up in, pale blue with sparkling white trim, the sloping lawns bounded by field stone walls, the heavy colonial furniture, Karen hosting dinner parties or barbeques, Garvin working on one end of the long kitchen table. The house that her dad bought for Karen, which Karen had made a home for Zach and Jessie. And for Honor – not so much, though she'd tried.

This English bungalow would probably fit into her father's spacious lounge. The sitting room was bijou – frankly? She'd had bigger closets – but she felt more at home here, looking out to the ocean, than she had in any other place. She counted up on her fingers. Not even six weeks since she had moved into Eastingdean and she connected as well with Ru, Robina, Sophie and Martyn's thoroughly English lives as with anyone back home. Even compartmentalising her inopportune crush on Martyn, she cared whether Clarissa's Zumba class folded. She cared whether Robina would have got over her snit by tomorrow or if she was making life unbearable for Ru. She even cared that Kirsty looked like a walking horror movie.

She clicked on reply. *Life is peaceful, here. I'm tired of your chaos. I said everything I had to say back in May.* And then, *It's better this way.*

Send.

After that, Honor was glad of the chance to relieve her frustrations in the self-defence class, practising snapping kicks to the front or the side of knees and slamming the palm of a curled hand into vulnerable noses.

As last week, Martyn perched on the stage at the end of the room, but Honor tried to put him out of her mind as she concentrated on joking Ru out of his doldrums. Ru managed the occasional smile but, at the end of the class when she suggested, 'Want to come home for coffee and soup?' he gave her a startled look, grabbed his backpack from the side of the room and shot into the men's room, casting back, 'Can't. Staying in Brighton.'

He sprinted out two minutes later, transformed by shirt, trousers and proper shoes, a strong smell of deodorant and his hair over his eyes like a windblown dog, making for the door. He had to pause as Martyn intercepted him, jingling his car keys, but Ru, muttering something as he pointed to his watch, just wriggled past.

Honor grabbed her jacket and crossed to where Martyn was frowning after Ru. 'Where's he flying off to?'

'I think he said Spangles.'

She felt a spasm of alarm. 'Spangles? Does he mean Ali Spangles? The nightclub?'

Slowly, Martyn nodded. 'I'm rather afraid he might.'

Honor started off in pursuit down the corridor to the stairs. 'But he's way too young to get into a nightclub, isn't he? And I've been to Ali Spangles – it's a dive.'

Out in the street, there was no sign of Ru. Kemptown was a grid, providing any number of corners for Ru to have disappeared around. Honor felt her heart hurry uneasily, in a way that had nothing to do with the exertions of the class. 'Ali Spangles is a dive,' she repeated, frowning up and down the street.

'I'm surprised you know.' Martyn regarded her curiously.

'A guy took me there when I was pretty much fresh off the plane,' she admitted. 'I didn't stay long.' She glanced at her watch. 'I don't know what Ru's up to but I'm going to go after him. That kid can get himself in a fix way too easily.'

'You won't get in dressed like that.'

Impatiently, she glanced down at her sweatpants. 'Right. If you could drop me straight home, I'll change and get a cab over there. I don't know what Ru's doing because he surely

182

can't get into a nightclub, but I don't have a happy feeling about this.'

'I'll go with you.'

They turned for the X5, parked on the side of the road. 'I'll be OK–'

He glared as if she were a giant pain in his rear as he slammed the door and turned the key. 'Like you said, it's a dive.'

In the half hour that Honor had between jumping out of the X5 and climbing back into it, she showered at top speed and wriggled into the only vaguely clubby clothes she had in England, exactly what she'd been wearing when Aaron had taken her to Ali Spangles – the short, stretchy, black dress shot with gold and the rainbow shrug that tied high in front. So as not to feel any tinier beside Martyn than she needed to, she slid quickly into black, spike-heeled mules.

Her hair would take too long to put up, so, with wet hands and a little conditioner she smoothed out the worst of the frizz and then combed it down either side of her face, letting it ripple on to her shoulders. It looked like somebody had been at it with a crimping iron but, hey, people paid good money for that look and she could have it for free. And it left her time to apply blue-green eyeliner and black mascara.

Both the mules and the short skirt made the ascent into the BMW sports vehicle a challenge but she scrambled up and soon the vehicle was bowling smoothly along Marine Drive, past Saltdean and then Rottingdean, the lights from the pier and the Brighton hotels looming closer and closer, twinkling as the sun prepared to dip into the sea.

On this summer's evening every parking space along King's Road was taken, but Martyn found a spot to ease the BMW into in a side street. Honor discovered that, worse than scrambling up, dropping down from the perched-up passenger seat of the big vehicle in a short skirt and high heels was damned near impossible without flaunting her underwear or letting her footwear drop from her toes. Watching her struggle, Martyn swore, seized her by the waist and swung her down, as if dragging a naughty child out of a tree.

'Sorry,' she said, meekly. 'I didn't think about climbing in and out of your SUV.'

Martyn had changed into a midnight blue shirt and he looked exactly what he was – a pin-up. His hair flipped sexily around his collar while hers wiggled around her head like the Gorgon's snakes.

King's Road was thronged, unsurprising in a resort at the height of the summer. Martyn grabbed her hand and tucked her behind him, which had the double benefit of advancing their progress and providing relief from the wind. When they reached the well-worn exterior of Ali Spangles he stopped short, bringing her around beside him. 'Ah. That explains how he can get in.'

Outside Ali Spangles, on a blackboard decorated with silver stars, they read: *Under 18s Nite at Ali Spangles! Wickid DJ! Only £5!*

'Oh ...' Honor deflated. 'I never even thought of that. I guess he's just hanging out with his friends. I just jumped to stupid conclusions. I'm sorry I dragged you out here.'

Martyn studied the three doormen, standing in a row like thuggish penguins. 'Yes, but it is Ali Spangles. As we're here, maybe we should look around.'

They gazed up the stairs and into the entrance passage. Every scuff on the badly painted walls showed. Teenagers straggled in trying to look cool and mainly looking furtive as electronic music pounded and scratched out into the street.

Martyn approached the biggest doorman, a bald guy with two crosses in one ear. 'Is it under 18s only? Or can we get in?'

The doorman raised his eyebrows, looking from Martyn to Honor and shrugging. 'OK with us, mate. You pay your five quid, you go in. Long as you behave yourself.' He smirked. 'They might ID you if you try and buy alcohol.'

Martyn gave him a tiny smile and brushed past, paid ten pounds to a different penguin at a window and drew Honor up the narrow stairs and down the corridor that let out into the bowels of the club. Honor didn't know whether to put her hand over her eyes or her ears at the swooping neon-green lights and shrieking teenage voices over headaching music, trying not to wince at the number of show-off boys barging around squealing girls. It wasn't lost on her that the girls, who Stef would have termed jailbait, were dressed pretty much like her – tottering on heels, hemlines high, necklines plunging.

Her eyes got used to the wheeling lights but there were a lot of bobbing heads to block her view. She had to rely on Martyn, his gaze raking the room methodically. 'I can't see him,' he said, bringing his mouth down close to her ear, 'but there's some kind of big meeting taking place in the far corner. Let's wander in that direction.'

Tucking in behind his formidable height as he wove along the edges of the heaving dance floor, Honor was able to negate the worst of the mob effect of excitable kids crammed into too small a space. A whole bunch of wide girlish eyes drank Martyn in as he made his way through the throng, sliding on then to check her out. She wondered how many of them were thinking: *he could do better–*

'He's right in the corner, talking to two older guys,' he said, suddenly.

Now that they'd made it past the dance floor, Honor was able to step out from behind him and crane up to see that Ru and a group of teens around him were listening and nodding as the two men, one white and wholesome-looking and one black and über-cool, talked. Aaron and Jermaine. Fury flamed inside her. 'Those dumbass morons!'

Martyn's eyebrows shot up. 'How come you're so well acquainted with local dumbass morons?'

She staggered on her tiptoes, trying to become taller even than the spike heels made her. 'The guy who brought me here before? He's Aaron, the white dumbass. The guy who he brought me to see, who seems to control the local grey labour market – he's the black dumbass, Jermaine. Aaron works at an employment agency and if he can't fit someone into a legit job, he brings them to Jermaine to get them work off the payroll. Aaron was so mad when I passed on the opportunity that it's obvious he gets a commission.' She dropped back on to her heels. 'I'm going to talk to those guys.'

Incensed by the trust on the face of Ru and the teens clustered around him, she flung herself through the horde of clubbers-in-training. With a final shove, she burst into the small clearing about Aaron and Jermaine. 'Well, hi there!' She beamed around.

Ru looked astonished.

Aaron and Jermaine looked shocked and wary.

She locked her eyes on Ru. 'What's up?'

'Nothing.' He shrugged. His expression switched abruptly to dismay. 'Wait a min–!' A groan went up from the other kids.

Honor wasn't surprised, when she looked back at the yard of floor that Aaron and Jermaine had been occupying, to see it suddenly empty. Martyn was standing close by, watching their departing backs and smiling.

'They're going!' objected Ru. 'But we hadn't finished.'

Honor sighed. 'Shame. I've had a bad day and I wouldn't have minded trying that pressing the button thing. Were they talking to you about a job, Ru?'

The muttering crowd began to disperse as he hid his eyes behind his hair. 'They said they could get me work in Brighton. I hate working for Mum.'

'Is it really that bad? It gives you a little money in your pocket.'

Ru stopped hiding with a flick of his head and an incredulous laugh. 'It doesn't.'

Honor paused. 'It doesn't?'

'Mum doesn't pay me. That's why I hate it. It's slave labour.'

'I guess it is,' she said, slowly. 'She doesn't pay you a cent?'

'Not a cent, not a penny. Not as a wage. She'll give me money for a particular thing, if she feels like it. But she doesn't often feel like it.'

'Oh.' Honor looked into the eyes that were both wary and trusting. 'Well, I hate to break it to you but those guys, they aren't on the level, either. They specialise in getting work for people who want work but there's some reason that finding it is difficult. Foreigners like me and, I guess, young kids like you. They don't pay the going rate and I'm pretty sure they don't pay taxes or any of those tiresome things. It's not legit. They're bad news.'

Ru's lips set. 'But they would pay me something. Which is better than nothing.'

'Yeah.' Honor nodded. 'But they could get you in a whole lot of trouble. Maybe we can figure something out. Something better. How about you come with me and we talk about it?'

'S'pose.' Digging his hands into his pockets, Rufus allowed himself to be shepherded back through the crowd, shuffling disconsolate feet up the corridor and down the stairs, collecting polite goodnights from the doormen.

'OK,' said Honor, as soon as she'd somehow clambered back up into the X5 – taking the mules off first, which turned out to be helpful. Turning to face Ru in the back seat, she could watch his deeply shadowed expressions in the half light. 'Will you work at the Teapot if I make her pay you?'

Ru stilled. 'Yeah,' he conceded, suspiciously. 'But I bet you can't make her.'

Honor smiled. 'Bet I can. She wants to go to that Global Gathering thing, right? I'm going to make her an offer she can't refuse.'

From the driver's seat, Martyn groaned as he started the BMW up. 'Fantastic. She's going to try and reason with Robina.'

Martyn hadn't been able to talk her out of it. Half-an-hour later, having struggled once more out of his car after he'd parked it behind the Starboard Walk shops, Honor was seated on an iridescent green-and-purple, crushed-velvet beanbag in Robina's lounge.

The whole place – two storeys over the Eastingdean Teapot – was like some old hippy hang out. Web and feather dreamcatchers hung in doorways, crystals stood where they'd catch the light, posters covered entire walls and the ceiling was painted dark purple. Jos sticks burned on the mantel and fat white candles lit a room devoid of TV or any furniture that had legs. Surreal.

Even though sitting elegantly on a beanbag in a micro skirt was no easier than climbing in and out of the X5, Honor didn't feel disadvantaged by her station because Sophie, Robina and Ru were each flopped on beanbags of their own.

Kirsty lay on a futon. On the floor beside her were a couple of crackers on a plate, one nibbled. Honor, dismayed, spoke to her first. 'I didn't mean to disturb you, Kirsty, or tire you out.' How on earth had Robina hardened her heart sufficiently to ask this shrunken wreck of a female to drag herself into the Teapot to work for even an hour, let alone an entire weekend, so that Robina could go off and enjoy herself?

Kirsty's skin stretched tight around her smile. Her eyes were sunk into circular black shadows. 'Nice to see a new face. Newish, anyway.'

'So,' interrupted Robina, 'what's Ru been up to? And why are you done up like a doll?'

Honor was shaken to realise just how chilly she felt towards Robina. When she'd first arrived at the Teapot she'd considered her quirky and fun, and anticipated that Sophie was the one who would irritate the hell out of her. Instead, Sophie had turned out to be a warm-hearted, hard worker, who just happened to hero worship her best friend, warts-and-all, though occasionally was prepared to stand up to Robina if Robina was being extra warty.

Stef was self-absorbed but Robina had him beaten, hands down.

Honor hid her thoughts behind a smile. 'Ru and I, we've just been having a little chat and we've come up with a way that will mean you can go to the Global Gathering.'

'Fantastic! How?' In an instant, Robina was as shiny-eyed as a kid who had just discovered Santa Claus.

Honor put up a restraining hand. 'Whoa! There's a deal involved. So don't go agreeing to anything until you've heard it. OK,' she began. 'Like any other teenager, Ru doesn't just need a job – he needs to be paid for doing it.'

Robina shrugged. 'But he's family.'

'So what? It's not written in stone that you have to be mean to your family.'

They stared at each other. Robina's eyes glittered. 'What has little Ru got to do with a deal? And why are you making me one?'

Honor ignored the last question. 'The deal is this: I'm

prepared to work whatever hours it takes to run the Teapot this weekend while you and Sophie swan off to your music festival if you'll leave Ru behind to work with me – and you pay him the same hourly rate as you pay Aletta, not only for this weekend but for every hour he works for you from now on. This weekend is just about doable if we don't open the back dining room and I think I can make Aletta work a little harder than she has been doing.

'*And* you and Sophie have to get downstairs now and make enough scones and cakes to see us through whilst you're away.'

'That'll take all night,' Robina objected.

'But we could do it!' stuck in Sophie. 'Let's, Robbie! I want to go.'

Robina considered. All attention was on her. Her eyes moved from Honor to Ru, to Kirsty. 'Maybe if you, Ru and Kirsty pitched in tonight–'

'No.'

'Ru isn't as old as Aletta so I can't pay him the same–'

'You can. He works twice as hard as her. It's the only deal on the table, Robina. And if I find out that you've dragged Ru or Kirsty down there tonight, the deal is off. You ought to be downright ashamed of yourself even thinking of making poor Kirsty work, anyway.'

Angry roses bloomed in Robina's cheeks.

But Sophie clapped her on the shoulder. 'Come on, Robbie, we can do it! Then we'll get straight in the van and head off to Stratford and grab a few hours once we've got the tent up.'

'OK then,' said Robina, with bad grace. 'It's better than missing it.'

Honor waited, but she obviously wasn't going to get a thank you. Neither was anybody going to ask whether she really felt that she could run a tearoom after working there as a waitress for less than two weeks. Maybe they simply shared her confidence that she'd had enough experience of making things work out to know that she could avoid complete disaster.

And at least gratitude was shining from Ru's eyes.

She struggled up from the depths of the beanbag. 'Leave the keys with Ru and I'll be here at eight in the morning. You, too, Ru, OK? If you're on the payroll, you have to be punctual.'

'All right.' Ru walked her down to the front door, tucked away up the walkway from the street. 'You were wicked,' he said, simply, before he shut the door behind her.

Chapter Twenty

Martyn had been waiting in the dark for thirty minutes but he wasn't tired or sleepy. When he saw the slight figure emerge from beside the Eastingdean Teapot he let her totter on her huge heels down The Butts, then started the engine, flicked on the lights and wheeled slowly out of the car park.

At the side of the road, Honor paused, and he eased the big vehicle up beside her, rolling down the window. 'Everything arranged to your satisfaction?'

She grinned. 'Just about.' Her hair lifted from around her face in the breeze.

'Hop in,' he suggested, opening the door and putting out a hand to help her up the tall step. He didn't trust himself to get out to do it, getting behind her in that short skirt ...

With a laugh and a whoop she made the jump, her eyes gleaming in the light from the street lamps. 'Did you hang around just to save me a five-minute walk home? You're a regular knight in shining armour.'

He shook his head, letting the X5 roll down the street past the silent shops. 'I hate the idea that you may judge Brighton by Ali Spangles. Brighton's a fabulous place. I thought you might like to see somewhere a bit nicer.' He turned right, on to Marine Drive.

'OK,' she said, cautiously. 'But I've sold my soul to the devil and agreed to look after the Teapot until Monday so I can't be real late.'

'OK. Just an hour or so to enjoy yourself before the hard graft begins.'

He drove back towards Brighton. The coast road at night always did something for him; the sea black and oily below, glittering with yellow lights, the pier's skeleton exposed by a million bulbs. Turning right into the Old Steine, following the traffic system up through Marlborough Place, he eventually turned off into a quiet nook above the North Laines and parked behind wrought iron railings.

One of the fabulous Regency houses with a curved front and several storeys, it could have been almost anything behind the big black door with *4 Fox Square* painted in white. He keyed in his pass number, swiped his card and the door buzzed him in.

'What's this place?' Honor gazed around at the high moulded plaster ceiling and glossy tiled floor.

'Somewhere quiet.'

A steward in black materialised. 'Dining, sir?'

'Just a drink in the lounge.'

The dark figure nodded and faded away, leaving Martyn to lead Honor up carpeted stairs, past the bar on the first floor, loud with talking and laughter, glasses clinking. Past the second floor where diners clustered around tables with snowy cloths, the whisper of cutlery a grace note to the murmur of voices. On to the top floor and a small lounge, empty but for sofas and chairs upholstered in shades of gold and low wooden tables where newspapers had been dropped as if half-read. Martyn chose a curved sofa in an alcove beside a tall white fireplace with plants instead of a fire basket.

A waitress materialised and he ordered beer and once Honor discovered that they served both Budweiser and Schlitz she said, 'Beer for me, too.'

And whilst they waited for the drinks she gazed around at the room with its worn wooden floor, chair arms burnished to a gentle shine. 'So, here we are,' she said, when the waitress had left the drinks. 'Should I be worried?'

The low lighting painted starbursts in her eyes. He was

intrigued. 'Why?'

She lifted the Bud, served in a condensation-coated stemmed beer glass. 'This place. It's kind of secluded, isn't it?'

He let his lips curve. 'It's just a club. There are private members clubs all over England. Fox Place is mainly for people in the media and the arts – kind of an East Sussex Groucho Club. A lot about Brighton is centred on tourists. I like to know a couple of places that aren't. And it's somewhere I can count on never finding Robina.'

A group of four women and a man surged into the lounge, splintering the hush, choosing facing sofas in another corner and ordering champagne. One of the women was pink under her smart silver hairstyle and kept protesting, 'Oh, this is silly! A proper engagement, at our age.' But she didn't seem to be able to stop admiring her ring finger.

'I think I've heard of the Groucho,' Honor admitted, relaxing against the back of the sofa after watching the new arrivals. 'So why are we here?'

'To chat over a beer. I think you thought I'd brought you to some den of vice? To introduce you to all my deviant practices?'

'Of course not.' But a quirk in her smile told him that maaay-bee such a suspicion had crossed her mind.

It wasn't what he'd planned to talk to her about but his heart stepped up its beat at the thought. 'Any particular deviances you have me down for?'

She tilted her head. 'I haven't really thought about it.' But she smiled.

He was tempted to pursue this interesting avenue but, as the champagne arrived for the group in the corner, he dragged his focus back to the conversation he meant to have.

When he'd pulled the X5 into her drive this evening and her bare legs had danced down the steps, right in his line of vision, that dress clinging to all her neat little curves, he'd been reduced to foolish silence. And when she'd taken four goes at hopping up into the passenger seat, her bobbing breasts apparently tied in place by that multicoloured little cardigan thing, he'd nearly had a heart attack.

It would be way too easy to submit her to the clumsiest lunge in the history of man …

Instead, he took another drink. 'So,' he began. 'Done any more about finding your mother?'

She wrinkled her nose. 'The internet tells me I have a bunch of alternatives. Lots of people willing to help – some charities, some businesses. But it seems there's no need for either. I can go to Brighton Town Hall and read the Electoral Register, and if she's around, she'll be on there.'

'But you haven't done that?'

She rolled her eyes. 'I've been kind of busy, with the Teapot and with just hanging out in England.'

'But you're going to give it a try?'

She shifted to face him across the curve of the sofa. 'What if I don't like her?'

'Isn't there only one way to find out? Go see her and say, "Hi, I'm Freedom, remember me?"'

She laughed, but looked pained. 'Come on, I asked you to forget that Freedom stuff. Freedom Lefevre didn't exist for more than a few weeks and I've only ever known myself as Honor Lefevre or Honor Sontag. And introducing myself is not the kind of action that I can easily undo if it goes bad on me. I might just leave things as they are.'

'Does that mean that you're going home?'

She looked surprised. 'I rented your sister's place for four months so I guess that's how long I'm here.'

'I just thought that if your mission was to find your mother …'

She looked away. Watched the group in the corner,

drinking their champagne, on to the second bottle now, getting louder, clinking glasses and drinking to the future of the happy couple. 'I don't think I ever said it was my primary purpose, did I? Mainly, I needed space.'

He waited. Watching her, sitting there, looking as if her dress had been vacuum packed on. 'So you're not rushing back to Mr Sontag?' he prompted.

Her eyes swivelled to his. She finished her beer and sank back against the sofa, twisting her hair, thoughtfully. Her smile had been replaced by a wary notch between her brows. 'I guess not.'

It was the opening he'd been probing for. 'I was rude when you tried to tell me about your marriage, before. How about you tell me now?'

Chapter Twenty-One

She didn't look away.

He gazed steadily back. Waiting her out. Watching a debate taking place behind her eyes.

She made a face. 'I'll need another beer. I hadn't scheduled a Q and A.'

He got her two, so as not to invite a further interruption, and, conscious of the car keys in his pocket, chose water for himself.

She took a deep draught and licked her lips. 'My husband's name's Stef. Stefan Sontag. His dad, Will Sontag, and my dad are partners in the same law firm in Hamilton Drives, which is where I'm from, a small town up on Route 7 in west Connecticut. When we were children, our dads joked that one day we'd get married because we were inseparable. But something happened to Stef at puberty – he turned into a hellraiser.

'And a hellraiser can be an embarrassing member of the family for someone in the legal profession. His relationship with Will deteriorated, and my dad began to warn me off him. But, thing was, Stef was still my best friend.' She smiled, her eyes warm with memories.

'Define hellraiser.'

She lifted her brows. 'For a long time, he didn't do anything that was so bad. Well, OK, it *was* bad, like putting fireworks in mailboxes and dying someone's white cat pink – I felt bad about the cat because it was in the paper and a lot of people wrote to say what a cruel trick it was – but his pranks were kid's stuff. And all the other kids in town loved Stef because he was so funny and he always stuck up for underdogs. I never had any trouble in high school because he always watched over me, you know, and nobody messed with Stef. And on weekends he'd teach me how to ride a dirt bike or get everyone to the lakeside for a cook out. We played up, on those cook outs, but nothing other teenagers didn't do; just strip poker or outrageous dares. Getting drunk, making out. Stef was always trying out new haircuts or getting a tattoo. Stef was fun.

'And then he decided not to go to college. Just flat out refused. He didn't really give any reason, just no. He had good brains but Dad used to say that they'd been wired wrong. I went off to college and he did a variety of jobs – car shops, delivery, making pizzas. My dad wrote that Stef was in more trouble, because he'd added joyriding to his repertoire. But when I came home, he seemed just the same old Stef. We dated. He was still my best friend as well as a date but we dated other people. After a while, I began not to like that and when I came home the summer I finished school, I told him. We'd been out to the lake and … Anyway, he said that if I wanted "exclusive" then we'd better get engaged. I wasn't quite ready – but I did want to be exclusive. So we got engaged. Dad didn't know what to think because he knew Stef could be off the wall but he did like him, and at least it made me plan to stay in Hamilton Drives. And, who knew, maybe Stef would settle down and put his wild years behind him. So Dad put in a word for me at VPV Finance and, over time, I took my exams to be a financial advisor – which meant years of night school. It took a while for us to get the money together to get married but that was OK. We were young.'

Other people had begun to drift into the room, late diners choosing the lounge for coffee. But Honor wasn't paying attention to anyone else, now that she was into her story.

'While I'd been away, two things happened. One was

that Stef had found a job he liked, managing a diner. We used to hang out at the Drives Diner when we were kids and it always attracted a lot of oddballs. Well, you know,' she laughed suddenly, eyes alight, 'Stef is "oddballs R us" so he was happy. He stuck to the job. And if his dad was disappointed that Stef wasn't a lawyer or a doctor, he didn't go on about it too much. So their relationship improved.'

'What was the other thing?'

Her smile slid off her face. 'Some of his pranks got a little out of hand. I think it was the internet.'

He loved how she said that. *Inner-net*.

'You know, if you search for "pranks" on the internet you find a whole bunch of stuff. Like how to make bombs or make people ill. Stef kind of gave our dads false hope by beginning a computer science course at night school. But he wasn't looking to make a career, he was improving his skill set so that he could play better pranks. And, between the course and the pranks sites, he learned how to do stuff like sending emails that look like they're from someone else. So, he'd send a guy an email, apparently from another guy, saying he's always had the hots for him and what about it? Or send an email, apparently from the school, telling a lot of parents that school's closed on Tuesday, when it's not. Then he'd sit back and watch the fall out.'

Martyn nodded. Her frown kept flicking in, signalling that her memories were getting uncomfortable. 'So was he still fun?'

A sigh. She sipped at her beer. 'Mostly. Because he didn't do that kind of thing all the time. He did get in trouble for riding his dirt bike around inside a rival diner, though, putting tyre tracks on the wall and breaking things up. That was one night when he was off and I was at night school and he got bored. He said it was a dare and a joke but the police said it was a crime and he got community service.'

'Ouch.'

'Yeah. That was just after we got married. We had an apartment in town and some of the time it was great because wherever Stef goes, there's something happening. I remember coming home just before Christmas and he'd trimmed a Christmas tree with ornaments he'd made himself by cutting up Budweiser cans. It was a work of art – kind of. I don't think he got the hang of letting go of his childhood so the rest of us got more responsible and he got less, which seemed to make him mad at everyone and more determined than ever to act like a juvenile. His pranks got more and the fun got less. By then, I was unhappy with his personal code.'

The frown had become permanent now and the second beer was on its way down. Her hand lay on the sofa and he reached out and took it, feeling the length of her fingers and the smoothness of her fingernails, still neat and pretty, even though she was working in a kitchen and waiting on tables. 'Am I asking too many questions?' he said softly. 'You can stop, if you'd rather.'

After a moment, she shook her head. 'I'm so mad at him. I've never been this mad at him before. I don't think I've ever been this mad at anybody, ever. He took our whole life and threw it in the trash. He got out of control. That's not the way I want things to be.'

He squeezed her hand.

'He got more community service for taking a car,' she continued, looking at their linked hands as if she wasn't seeing them. 'He said he was hiding it, to pay a woman back who dumped his friend, and it's true he only moved it a block away. But that's when our relationship began circling the drain.

'Then he did something so stupid.' She shook her head and drained the last of her beer. The hand that held the glass was shaking. 'One of his staff, Billie, she's a lovely person. I liked her a lot. And she was getting a whole load of grief from her boyfriend. Stef got into an argument with him because the boyfriend got the idea that Stef was having a thing with Billie and it all got ugly. The boyfriend is a dumbass, spending all his money and most of Billie's on junk from the internet and from shopping channels. Anyway, the boyfriend began sitting in the diner on Billie's late evenings, so that there was no chance of her going anywhere with Stef.'

'Is that what was happening?'

Slowly, she shook her head, eyes troubled, the frown now a furrow. 'I don't think so. Stef just seemed to feel really protective of Billie. She's one of those pretty, dainty little things, you know, that bring out a man's protective streak.'

He smiled. 'You're a pretty, dainty little thing yourself.'

She looked surprised. 'Oh.' Then continued, 'Anyway, the boyfriend used to sit there, just in case, and Stef couldn't do a damned thing because the boyfriend was a paying customer. The boyfriend even used to ask for the diner TV to be turned to the shopping channels, if not many people were in.

'Then, one night, when all the other customers were gone and Stef and Billie were just finishing up, the boyfriend called the shopping channel to buy something. And he gave all his credit card and security details right over the phone. Stef was writing up work sheets or something so he had a pen in his hand and he took those numbers down. Next time he heard the boyfriend being mean to Billie, he rang the shopping channel and used the information to order ten portable commodes. Then because he always gets carried away with his stupid ideas, he went on to the internet and ordered a ship load of viagra, incontinence pants, penis extenders, blow up dolls – you name it. They all arrived at the boyfriend's house.'

Martyn tried to hide his smile.

'It's OK. You can laugh.' Her own smile was only a twist of the lips. 'We were all meant to laugh. But there were thousands of dollars involved and you know what? The police said it was a felony.' She blinked, hard. 'That was how I stopped wearing my wedding ring. I took it off and I threw it at him.'

'I'm sorry.' He held her hand tighter.

She looked surprised, as if noticing for the first time that their hands were joined. 'So,' she ended, resignedly. 'Hamilton Drives is a small town. People don't like it if their financial advisor's husband is charged with identity theft. They start taking their business elsewhere. I knew that my boss was going to have to make somebody redundant so I volunteered. I wasn't making commission worth a damn, anyway, with my client list shrinking like cheap socks.'

'So you left your husband to think things over while you were away?'

She lifted her eyes to his. 'He's away, too. He was away before I even came out here. He got 180 days in county jail. He's in Bridgeport Correctional.'

Chapter Twenty-Two

'Wow,' he breathed.

She examined his eyes. He looked astonished. But not disgusted. He didn't take his hand away. 'He gets to send out letters and postcards or make phone calls. He sends them to my sister Jessamine or to Billie – who finally dumped the boyfriend – and they send them to me as emails.'

She could see his mind working. Computing. Coming to the obvious conclusion. 'So, what's Billie to him, now?'

'I think she's still just his friend, because if she's more, why is he sending me message after message and saying he wants to see me? But the town certainly thought that there was something going on between her and Stef, judging by the looks – sympathetic or knowing – that came my way.' She stopped. Dropped her eyes to her watch. 'Look ... I'm tired and I have to be at the Eastingdean Teapot at eight–'

Instantly, he let her off the conversational hook. 'Of course. I'll take you home.'

The night was much cooler, now, and she crossed her arms and scrunched her shoulders as they hurried back to his SUV. He reached across and pulled her up into the seat again. 'Thanks.'

It wasn't until he stopped in her drive that she spoke next, words that just seemed to have made their own decision to be spoken. 'I told him that I couldn't put up with things any more. I'm tired of it and we're over.'

His face turned to her, in the darkness. She could smell his clean, warm smell. 'No one could blame you,' he said, gently. 'Effectively, he lost you your job. And you've lost face in front of the town where you live.'

'To the point of humiliation,' she agreed. 'But the main issue is that I don't trust him any more. I don't expect a man to look after me in the old-fashioned way but I don't expect him to drag me into his crappy mess, either. He shouldn't expect me to wallow around in his dirt. He keeps sending messages about me being his wife and visiting him in jail and I'm just not going to do it. That wasn't in the vows.'

Tears prickled, suddenly, and she fumbled with the door catch, hearing Martyn's door opening and shutting as she struggled with the weight against the ever-present clifftop wind. Screwing round in the seat, she tried reversing out to see if it was any easier than going forward, muttering, 'Holy crap,' as she battled with her bag and the stupid mules that, she vowed, she would never wear again in any vehicle more than one foot from ground to seat.

And, as if the gremlins were listening in, the heel of her right mule caught on the sill and was wrenched off and she was suddenly hurtling backwards into space.

'Oof!' said the solid body she collided with. Hot hands grabbed her in mid-air, an arm around her chest and a hand on her thigh for a long, still moment. 'Sorry,' he muttered. Then lowered her to the ground.

But, 'Ow!' she yelped, as spiteful stones bit into her tender soles. 'I lost my shoes.'

His hands grabbed her waist, lifting and turning her carefully until she was back on the edge of the passenger seat, her hands falling on his shoulders as she fought for balance. 'Thanks–'

But the words stuck in her throat when, instead of moving away, he moved closer, and his hands slid down from her waist to her hips. Nearer, nearer, as if drawn by a string, so that her hands slid past his shoulders and her arms went around his neck as his body nestled against hers in all kinds of places.

The chills she'd experienced since exiting the warmth of that swanky club gathered into a giant shiver. Yet heat emanated from him in waves, as his hands tightened. He groaned. 'Wow, Honor–' Then, despairingly, 'I've tried so hard to do the right thing. But I want you so much, all the time.'

She knew she ought to pull away, pat his cheek and say, 'A pretty thing it would be if I told you that I want you, too, with my husband in jail. They have names for women like that, you know.' And she ought to think of Robina's feelings, too. Not that Robina cared a whole lot about anybody else's.

But her heart was flying and her insides fizzing, and her thoughts turned to words. 'I'm so tired of doing the right thing. I've done the right thing all my life. I've made a point of it. It really hasn't made me happy. How about we do the wrong thing and see how it works out?'

'Yes!' He yanked her right out of the seat and held her in his arms as she gripped her arms around his neck and he pressed against her as if trying to burrow through her clothes, kissing her harder than she'd ever been kissed, his tongue in her mouth, smooth and sweet. She heard the car door slam behind her and beep as it locked. The kiss just went on and on as he swung around and began carrying her to the house.

She broke away to squeak, 'My shoes!'

'Tomorrow. I'll get them tomorrow.' He pulled her legs up and around him and she gasped and pressed against him as her skirt pinged up around her waist revealing, the heat of his hands and the deep noise in his throat told her, more naked buttock than panties. She entrusted him with navigating the steps in the dark whilst she fumbled behind his head to get her door key out of her purse and gave it to him. 'Quick,' she whispered.

'Quick seems to have deserted me.' He cursed as he fumbled behind her back.

'If you put me down–'

'Not an option.' The lock gave up the fight, the door sprang open and they fell into the hallway. Having had it drummed into her by Karen that a woman coming home alone should take sensible precautions, she'd left a lamp burning in the bedroom, and Martyn followed its light like a moth, his arms fending off the walls to protect her from bumps.

The walls faded from blue to grey outside the oval pool of light and the bed quilt glowed white. He came to a halt, hands hot, breathing fast. She kissed his throat and he groaned. 'This is where I'm supposed to give you time to think–'

'Don't do that!' she gasped, scared that thinking might wake her conscience.

He kissed her again, urgent, almost savage. Then pulled back. Slowed down. 'I've wanted you since that first day.' He let her slide down his body until her feet touched the floor and then he was stooping over her, fingers busy as he unknotted her shrug and slid it down her arms. Touching her with his eyes as well as his hands. 'I'd love to undress you slowly but I don't think I can bear to. This dress has been begging all night to be whipped off over your head.'

She reached for the hem.

'Don't! That pleasure's mine. Lift up your arms.' And as she did, the dress whooshed up past her face and her hair flew around in a blast of static. For several moments he held the dress around her wrists, just looking. Then he let her hands down and turned her so he could slide open the catch on her bra. He slid the bunched fabric off her arms and she found herself in nothing but her panties.

'Whoa,' he breathed. 'You are beautiful.' He wrapped his

arms around her, gave a quick breath out and suddenly she was standing on the end of the bed, her breasts level with his mouth. A mouth that was hot. She forgot to breathe as he used it to explore her, plucking gently at her nipples with his teeth then sucking them hard, making her jump and thread her fingers through his hair, just in case he had any ideas about getting away.

His hands ran up and down her back. 'OK?'

She gulped. 'Sure am.'

He stroked her waist, her hips, her buttocks; his fingers against her skin awaking her to almost unbearable sensitivity. His fingertips ran around the high leg line of her underwear. 'What do you call these? They leave so much of you uncovered. I love them. If I'd known they were all you had on under that short dress, I think I would have exploded.' His breath shivered across the wetness left on her breasts by his tongue.

'Cheekies,' she gasped. 'Cheeky panties. Don't you guys have Victoria's Secret, here?'

'I don't know but it ought to be made law that we do. We don't have panties, we have knickers.'

'Knickers?' She didn't mean to make it a question, she knew perfectly well that the British called them knickers, but his prowling hands made her voice somehow squeak up at the end of the word.

'Mmm. As in, "I'm going to take your knickers off."' His fingertips hooked themselves in the elastic, drawing them down.

'But you're getting all behind,' she protested, shakily, making her fingers, which had been gripping his shoulders, move to the top buttons of his shirt.

'Let's catch me up.' He began working up the buttons as she worked down, his mouth keeping up a deliciously damp contact with whatever came close enough, her wrist, her nipple, the inside of her elbow, until he could shrug the shirt on to the floor. Then, in the impatient way of men, flicked open belt, button and zipper and somehow the beautifully cut trousers hit the deck, and he was running his tongue up and down her abdomen as he swung her up and fell with her sideways on to the bed. 'Height difference more easily overcome when horizontal.'

In college, Honor's roommate had invariably referred to sex as 'rolling around in the sack'. Until now, Honor had never been able to equate the phrase with the act, but Martyn was so relentlessly physical, hauling her around until she hummed with excitement, that she totally got it. The pillows scattered and slid, the quilt joined their clothes on the floor and Martyn complained, 'This bed's way too small,' as his long limbs kept ending up in thin air.

Then, suddenly, he changed gear.

The night went into slow motion.

He stared into her eyes. He positioned himself. And began a slow slide, hot, hard, until he was inside her. Transfixed by his gaze and by the sensation of him taking her over, she stilled. And just allowed herself to feel.

'I've wanted to do that for so long.'

'Yes,' she croaked. 'Oh, fuck. Oh, wow. That's good.' Her muscles flexed around him, accommodating, feeling, wanting.

His eyes flickered as his breathing increased. 'Yeah. Do that again.' He dragged in air. 'No, you'd better stop! There's only so much–'

But then he was moving, helplessly, 'You're still doing it! But don't stop.' And his eyes closed as slow became fast, then faster, and she held on tight as she was picked up and carried on his wave, and they crashed, together, into a whole new world.

During the night, when they'd made love again, slow and intense, he curled around her on his side, hooking her legs over his so that he was snuggled nicely against her behind, his chest rising and falling warm against her and joked, 'I was right, you're hot, Freedom Lefevre.'

She stilled. It made her feel toe-curly to hear him speak that name out loud, so casually, as it might have been used if her life had run along a different track. 'I've always been Honor. Not Freedom.'

He kissed her ear, then licked it. 'I like Freedom. It's part of you, the whole you. The you that you were born to be as well as the you that life made you.'

She stared into the darkness. 'I guess I'm acting a lot more like Freedom than like Honor, right now.'

Chapter Twenty-Three

Alerted by the muted ringing of her phone, Honor groped for the bag she'd abandoned beside the bed last night, screwing her eyes up against the morning sunlight. Behind her, Martyn moved to close the space that had opened up between them. She held on to the edge of the mattress so as not to fall.

And, in her ear, Ru complained, 'So I'm here and Aletta's here. Where are you?'

And she was awake. 'Oh crap, I overslept! Give me fifteen minutes and I'll be there.' She let go of the mattress cording to touch 'end call' and fell from the bed, rolling on to her feet as she ran for the shower. No matter how short of time she was, a shower, after the night, was a must. With a towel turban over her hair she washed briskly, wincing as parts of her protested because she hadn't used them for too long.

A fierce scrub of her teeth and she was flying back through the hall to the bedroom, ignoring Karen's best stepmom voice in her head: 'No way can you deal with your daily hygiene routine in that amount of time, young lady!'

Martyn still sprawled across the sheet, eyelashes resting down on his cheeks, each individual muscle in his body defined by the morning sun. She drank him in as she tried to ease open her underwear drawer. Surreal to think that the reason that he looked like something from a magazine was … because he was something from a magazine. 'Ow! Fuck!' she hissed, as the drawer shot out and banged her knee.

'I love to hear you say fuck. Right now, it's my favourite word,' observed Martyn, without opening his eyes.

'And if I'm not out of this door in five minutes, you're going to hear me say it a whole lot more. I was such a hero when I sent Robina and Sophie off to their music festival and said I'd be there to open the tearoom. And now I've spoiled it all by being late–' Robina. Her heart hopped to think how Robina would feel if she knew what Honor had spent the night doing with Martyn.

'*Fucking* late,' he augmented.

She laughed as she pulled on her white T-shirt and buttoned her black skirt. No time to do anything much with her hair and last night's fairly glam crimped look had, with sweaty sex and sleeping for only about three hours, turned into a haystack. She brushed it into a ponytail high on her head and jammed a black baseball hat over it, hoping it wouldn't make the Teapot look as if it got its staff from McDonalds. Snatching up her bag, she shoved her feet into her favourite-for-waiting-on-tables flat soft sandals and dropped a kiss on his hair. ''Bye now.'

He opened one eye and reached out a hot hand to her bare leg. 'Hang on and I'll drive you.'

She stepped out of reach. If she let him touch her she'd never get to work. 'In the "nuddy"?'

He grunted a laugh. 'That sounds *so* wrong in your accent.'

'I don't have an accent, honey. You do.' She blew him a kiss.

Although she'd made a lousy start by catapulting into the tearoom, red-faced and breathless and nearly forty-five minutes late, Honor quite enjoyed her first day 'in charge' at the Teapot. With no cakes cooking and no Robina taking up all the room with abandoned utensils, obliging everyone else to act like her kitchen porters, much of the stress and irritation was gone. The already cooked slabs of cake stood waiting and there wasn't even a mammoth clean down to do, although Honor had realised with regret that she hadn't specified Robina clear up after her middle-of-the-night bake-in. Probably Sophie had taken care of it.

Whilst Aletta rolled cutlery into yellow paper napkins, Honor and Ru cut the cakes horizontally and sandwiched them back together with the frosting Robina had left in a huge jug in the refrigerator. A shake of chocolate flakes and even without Robina's artistic chocolate leaves and roses on top they looked delicious.

Honor washed her hands, looking around to see what had been left undone. 'So, Aletta you concentrate on waiting tables, clearing tables and sanitising, me and Ru will fill orders and clean dishes, OK? We should be able to dash out and clear or take orders sometimes, too.' Aletta, looking incredibly wholesome and apple-cheeked, was too dreamy to be let loose in the kitchen, where teamwork and organisation was the way to a right mind.

Aletta agreed with a smile and a wave of her pen and order pad.

Honor's eye fell on the potato oven, cold and empty. 'The baked potatoes! Can you wash some, Ru, please?'

His ball hat on back-to-front, Ru stuck his head around the corner to inspect the potato rack. 'Only got two.'

'Damn,' Honor groaned. 'One of us better take some money from the cash register—' She dived into the pantry and fetched the wooden cash drawer from the shelf where it usually spent the night. Every compartment was empty apart from those containing small change. 'Oh.'

Looking as if he was trying not to laugh, Ru patted her shoulder. 'I suppose Mum needed some spending money.'

Reaching resignedly for her purse, Honor sighed. 'Your mom can be a real pain in the ass, do you know that? We better hope the first customers have change.'

By the middle of the day, in between thinking about the night before and wondering where the thing with Martyn was going, Honor had cried, 'Holy crap!' more times than she could count – especially when Kirsty made it downstairs, looking like a nightmare, to order a white china pot of peppermint tea and point out that the potatoes might only be meant to take an hour-and-a-half, but took at least two so a blast in the microwave would be helpful, the frosting should have gone back into the fridge and that Aletta was letting half the neighbourhood youth hang out around one of the tables outside without buying anything to eat or drink, behinds on table and feet on the chairs. 'And it's frightening off the paying tourists.'

'I thought we were goddamned quiet, all of a sudden.' Abandoning a stack of clean plates noisily on the counter, Honor marched outside, flapping her arms and shouting, 'Get off that table! Go!'

The teenagers laughed and scattered as if they were used to being shooed away like a flock of seagulls. Even Frog just grinned, 'Chill, Yankee Doodle,' and mooched away down the street without getting in her face about it.

By six o'clock, Honor was dead on her feet. Aletta had left on the dot of four-thirty, evidently feeling no need to pitch in and work extra. 'Let's put up the closed sign,' Honor yawned, when she saw the time. Staying open till six easily fulfilled her end of the deal, as Robina's usual policy was to stay open until she felt like doing something else.

Honor definitely felt like doing something else. Almost anything. Her feet burned, her back ached, her eyes watered from massive, uncontrollable yawns. She had had way too little sleep, which was fabulous in some ways but pretty damned hard in others.

Ru vanished the moment they'd cleaned down, leaving Honor to count the takings and retrieve what she'd paid for the potatoes, throwing a tea towel over the drawer and locking it in the pantry – Robina's idea of overnight cash security.

The sun was still shining as she locked up and the salt air tasted so delicious that she filled up her lungs over and over. Setting off down The Butts, she saw Martyn instantly, perched halfway up his metal staircase in the shade. As she drew near, he came down to intercept her. His hair was shower-damp and he looked great, as if he'd slept all morning and run all afternoon.

His smile was a caress as he tipped up her face and kissed her. Taking his time. Deepening the kiss, settling her against him so that they touched in the maximum number of places. 'You look seriously cute in that hat.'

'I feel seriously exhausted and icky. I'm going home to shower, then sleep until it's time to get up in the morning and open the Teapot again.'

Horrified eyes opened wide. 'That's a terrible plan. I have a better one – come upstairs to my place. I have to be at a shoot in Paris at dawn on Sunday, which means setting off Saturday afternoon. *Tomorrow.*' He kissed her again, a gently coaxing kiss that sent such a tingle through her that she half-expected a shower of stars around her head, like a fairy waving her wand in a Disney cartoon. *Turrrrrring!*

'What's so good about your place?' she mumbled, leaning her cheek against his chest to feel the steady *bmm-bmm-bmm* of his heart.

'Big bed,' he whispered.

'Mm?' She pretended to be considering.

'Sleeping all night in my arms after hours of sizzling sex. I'm feeling very ... attentive.'

'Mmmmmm.'

'Creative.'

'*Mmmmmm.*'

'There's wine chilling.'

'Mm.'

'Fish and chips for supper–'

She pushed herself away and planted a kiss beside his mouth. 'OK, you got me. I'll be back in an hour, when I feel clean.'

His eyes gleamed. 'So that I can make you feel dirty?'

With that thought whizzing around her head, she needed less time to recharge her batteries than she'd anticipated and it wasn't even the hour she'd promised, when she returned with a smile and an overnight bag.

The instant that she stepped inside his front door, he trapped her between his body and the wall. She turned to spaghetti. And his kisses were the boiling water.

Slowly – because he didn't seem inclined to unwrap himself from around her or to stop with the kisses – he guided her to one of the big, squashy sofas, pausing briefly in the kitchen area for chilled white wine and glasses. His big, swanky laptop stood open on the table, ticking away to itself, demonstrating how busy it was with a download or an upload or something as a blue line grew slowly across the screen.

He poured the wine then swooped her up and on to his lap, nodding at the screen. 'I've been doing a revamp of Ace's agency site. I'm uploading files. Now I've started I need to stick with it for a while.'

'Sure.' She smothered a yawn and tucked her cheek against the hollow beneath his collar bone.

'Tired?' He traced her jawline with a fingertip. 'It's damned Robina's fault. You could have stayed in your bed all morning. Like I did.'

She widened her eyes, fighting their demands that she should let them close. The first sips of wine, however crisp and chill on her tongue, had let fatigue press down on her eyelids. 'You slept all morning while I slaved? I knew it, you rat bastard.'

'I'd had a hard night.' His lips touched butterfly kisses to her forehead.

'You bet.' Despite her best efforts, she heard her voice fading into the distance as sleep began to melt her. Then jumped awake when his doorbell rang.

He sighed. 'I really hope that this is someone I can either get rid of quickly or push down the stairs. Not a sister. Sisters are like limpets when you don't want them around.'

She let him pour her into a corner of the sofa, where she curled like a puppy. But her eyes reopened when she heard Ru's voice. 'Ru? What's up?'

He slouched across the carpet towards her, hair falling over his face and hands so far in his pockets that it looked as if his jeans were going to slide off over his bony hips. 'Nothing,' he shrugged, aimlessly. 'I just saw you coming up here so I thought it would be OK if I said hi to Martyn, too.'

Martyn, she could see from the frustration burning in his eyes, wasn't totally appreciating Ru's neighbourliness. She smiled at him, hoping she was telegraphing, *don't throw him out; he's just an insecure kid.*

Ru dropped on to the sofa, next to Honor. 'Cool laptop. Your download's finished.'

Martyn took the remaining place, on the other side of Ru, with only a tiny sigh, lifting the computer on to his lap. 'It was an upload. I've been working on someone's website and the image files are so big I'm uploading them one at a time.' His fingers moved over the keys and soon a new blue line began growing slowly across the screen.

Apparently hypnotised by its progress, Ru nodded. 'Is it Front Page?'

'No, that's old hat now, it's Dreamweaver–' But then Martyn's voice began to dissolve and, like syrup sinking into the dents in a waffle, Honor sank into sleep.

Swimming back to the surface, a couple of hours later, she found the computer had changed laps and Ru was tapping away happily, while Martyn kept one eye on him at the same time as watching a documentary about snakes on the enormous TV.

She yawned and stretched. 'I fell asleep.'

Martyn turned a slow smile on her. 'You certainly did. Ru's raring to get the fish and chips.'

Ru shoved the laptop aside with an accusing, 'Yeah, we're starving, Honor.' Clutching twenty quid from Martyn, he disappeared through the front door like a man on a mission.

Martyn regarded her sternly as he slid up the sofa towards her. 'I'd better get some good hands-on reward for being nice to him while you slept our evening away.'

She glanced guiltily at her watch – it was after nine. 'I was just so tired.'

He laughed, pulling her against him. 'Evidently.'

She let her fingers wander inside his shirt, grateful that he hadn't got rid of Ru with heavy hints as Stef would have done. Even if those hints were dressed up as jokes, they could still sting. 'I owe you.'

His eyes half closed as her fingertips brushed his ribcage. 'I will collect. I take it you don't want him to know about us?'

Her conscience twanged, even as her heart hugged itself at the idea that she had got herself into an 'us'. Then anxiety rolled in like a stomach ache as she followed his reasoning. 'Robina. Holy crap, she's going to be upset.'

He squeezed her, reassuringly. 'Why worry about a stalker when we could worry about a husband?'

She hesitated. 'She's more than a stalker.'

'OK, she's your employer. But let's not stress about it

tonight, OK? Let's just live in the moment.'

'Never works,' she said, gloomily. 'Stef always wanted to live in the moment if I worried about tiresome things like getting enough sleep before work or paying the rent ahead of the entertainment budget. The bad stuff just waits till the moment's over.'

He nudged her hand, which had suspended its stroking beneath his shirt. 'At least until I get back from Paris.'

'OK.'

She tried hard, eating scalding fish and chips straight from the paper, laughing at Ru's disgusting combination of vinegar, tomato ketchup and mayo on the side, refusing to believe that he would have topped the lot with cheese, had there been some. After, Martyn logged on to his Twitter and Facebook accounts, lazily dictating posts while Ru's fingers flew over the keyboard. She even cheered when Martyn observed, 'Ru, you're an IT wizard. Would you be interested in taking over some of my routine on-line stuff? I'd pay you.'

Ru breathed, '*Wicked!*' before Martyn had finished the sentence. Then Ru wanted to see every one of the sites Martyn designed and kept up, avid for information, for opportunity, to have something better to do than work in a tearoom.

Still, Honor couldn't rid herself of the spectre of looming trouble.

It was hovering like one of the biggest, beadiest gulls down on the undercliff, just waiting for a tourist to come along to be crapped on.

Chapter Twenty-Four

Saturday began agreeably as Martyn, reasoning that he could catch up after Honor had begun her day at the Teapot and she had surely banked enough sleep by now, woke her with his mouth on her prettiest curves.

'Whassa time?' she muttered sleepily, shifting accommodatingly.

'Six.'

She shuddered as he let his lips trace the lines down her abdomen, exactly as he'd pictured when he'd been lusting after her in her sports bra, exhibiting a body that was his definition of perfect. Taut. Pretty. Curvaceous to just the right degree. 'Six? What are we doing awake at six?' But her fingers threaded through his hair in a way that encouraged him to continue doing exactly as he was doing.

'We're making time for a fabulous sexual encounter before you go to work and I go to France.'

She groaned. 'I was too tired to ask, last night. Tell me what's in France.'

'Paris.' He blew gently over her damp skin, rewarded with a shiver and a pathway of goosepimples. 'Eiffel Tower, Arc du Triomphe, the Seine, Avenue Montaigne, Rue St Denis, Boulevard St Germain, Moulin Rouge ... all the backdrops essential to sell mock-French cologne.'

'Oh right.' She shifted, as if planning to return his attentions. He moved his weight to keep her where he wanted her. Because he wanted her a lot.

Afterwards, when she was curled tightly in his arms, hair like ripples of caramel across the pillow and his shoulder,

he said, 'When I get back on Thursday, we'd better talk.'
Because there was a guy called Stefan Sontag whose first job
when he regained his liberty was going to be to try and put
his marriage back together.

He felt her heave a sigh.

Fitting his fingertips neatly into the dimples either side of
the base of her spine he kissed her. 'I know. It's not easy. But,
you know. If we want things to go on from here ...'

She kissed his shoulder and he felt her cheeks move as if
she smiled.

He tried to see her face. 'Have you had any more emails?'

She snuggled closer with a groan. 'I didn't look. I told him
before I came out here that it was over. But he doesn't want
to hear. And right now isn't the best time to yell it at him.'
She began to uncurl and sit up. 'And then there's the Robina
issue. Martyn, that's probably trickier than you thi–'

Hastily, he yanked her back down against him, skin on
skin. 'Oh no. I refuse to let *her* into bed with us!'

The Teapot was calling and she had to leave, in a flurry of
kisses and one long, hard hug, her hair bright in the morning
light. He wanted to hold on to her and kiss the tiny freckles
spangled across her nose but she laughed and wriggled away.
'I don't want Ru to have to call me again to tell me to get my
butt over to the Teapot.'

He leaned on the doorframe and watched her check out
the street before she left, running lightly down the metal steps
then up the street towards the Eastingdean Teapot, ponytail
streaming above her backpack. It seemed faintly ridiculous
that she should be sneaking around to avoid Ru – and
therefore Robina – learning that they were sleeping together.
Honor was being way too careful of Robina's feelings, in his
opinion. Robina was becoming more and more of a pain.
He was organising too much of his life around her.

Although pleasantly heavy of limb, he was too restless to go back to sleep. He showered and packed instead, checking out his diary notes to see how the client wanted him ... stubble, which was pretty much standard. He hadn't shaved for the last couple of days in anticipation.

Then Ace rang. 'Everything OK, Martyn? All set?'

'Airport at five, I'm booked into a Hyatt. How's everything with you? And Shelli?' He felt a twist of guilt that he hadn't spoken to Ace since last weekend, when Ace had been so broken up. And he was intelligent enough to know why. It hung before his eyes. *Husband*. Ace was a betrayed husband.

'Absolutely all over.' Ace was obviously trying to keep his voice light. But. Still. Definite wobble.

'I'm really sorry to hear that, man.' The word hanging in the air changed to *hypocrite*. It followed him around as he finished the familiar task of packing, nipping and gnawing at him like a nasty dog.

And then, as he was throwing his small black case and suit carrier into his luggage compartment, Clarissa pulled up into the car park. 'Going somewhere?' She looked relaxed and cheerful, for once.

He snapped the hatchback shut. 'Airport. Working in France this week.'

'Oh, good. I can pinch your car-parking space for an hour, then.'

Obligingly, he backed the X5 out and let her pull into the space, waiting as she hopped out, beeped her car locked and ran over to his vehicle. As always, she was on her way to or from a class, pink training shoes bright against her black leggings and long black T-shirt knotted at one side. 'Have you seen Honor? She's not home.'

He kept his voice neutral. 'She's working at Robina's tearoom, isn't she?' And then, curiosity aroused. 'Something up?'

'Only that she's still not cutting the lawns. If she doesn't want to do it then she'll need to find someone to do it for her. It's in the lease. Have a good trip.' Through the open window, Clarissa squeezed his forearm, then turned and whisked around the corner, into The Butts.

As he drove away, he reflected that, by some miracle, Clarissa had neither sneered at his work nor tasked him with some of hers. And it was a while since she'd made an affectionate gesture towards him, too.

Months. Pretty much since she lost her husband to somebody new and, after screaming at him for being Rosie's 'other man' – hadn't that been fun? – had collapsed, sobbing, into his arms.

Switching his mind to the job in hand, he drove to Gatwick airport, leaving his car with the north terminal valet parking and checking in, enduring the boring lines of travellers at security, the familiar routine under the bright terminal lights, until he was seated in a traveller's lounge with a newspaper and a cup of coffee, passenger announcements crackling and departure screens flickering. His flight to Charles de Gaulle was on time. All he had to do was relax and wait.

But relaxation wouldn't come. He gazed at the print, but his thoughts chased each other around. Clarissa. Ace. And the way that he was hiding his relationship with Honor from them, as he dealt death blows to Honor's marriage. All this sneaking around didn't sit well with him at all.

But, Honor!

The coffee in his cup sloshed suddenly. Body like a dancer, smile like a fallen angel, heart like a lion. In his head, in his bed. The past couple of days had been a dream come true and what was done was done. But there was part of him – not that part – that wished he hadn't lost control when he had found her in his arms in that tiny, stretchy excuse for a dress; that he could have put her down and hung in until she'd been able to wind things up properly with her husband. Been strong. He'd sworn after Rosie had made an idiot of him that he would run a mile rather than get involved with a married woman again.

Conveniently forgetting that running a mile was something he did with incredible ease.

Chapter Twenty-Five

By Sunday, Robina's cakes had run out. Honor let Ru and Aletta do all the prep in the morning while she made chocolate cupcakes from the recipe she remembered from school, times five, and cherry scones from a recipe she called up from the internet on Ru's phone. She used the last of Robina's chocolate frosting from the fridge to swirl over the cupcakes, hoping she wasn't contravening any health regulations and crossing her fingers that no one would get sick.

There was plenty of jam for the scones, which, because she included a little extra baking soda, rose every bit as majestically and drunkenly as Robina's ever did.

The cake table still looked empty, by Robina's standards, so, cursing, remembering a recipe from Jess's time at girl scouts, Honor mixed up apple and cream cheese with chopped Snickers bars and dolloped the mixture into more cupcake cases and cooked them.

When she emerged from her mad bake-in, hot and bothered and muttering, she realised that Ru had filled the potato oven and opened the tearoom and he and Aletta were serving, everything under control. 'You guys are so great.' She opened the back door and fanned herself, gulping iced water, then called Ru into the kitchen to tackle the washing up whilst she whizzed through the mini clean-down necessary after her efforts. Just in time for the "elevenses" trade to morph seamlessly into the lunchtime trade.

By three in the afternoon, she was flagging. With Martyn in France, she'd gone to bed early on Saturday evening. But then he'd called from his hotel room and what began as a quick goodnight became, 'So, what are you wearing?' and ended up as phone sex. Fabulous, but it didn't fulfil the same function as sleep.

But the teagarden was busy and she was making a couple of pints of fruit slush by throwing fat red strawberries into the blender with ice cubes.

'Honor!' Aletta scuttled in from the garden, eyes wide in alarm.

'What's up?' Startled to see Aletta moving at more than a serene amble, Honor twisted the blender jug from its base and halted.

'Those ... those ...' Aletta's English deserted her. 'Big boys! And they push Ru–'

Throwing open the counter flap, Honor raced outside to find Frog and his Tadpoles gathered in a threatening knot around Ru, whilst customers exchanged looks of alarm and drew away.

Ru stood, unmoving, his hands by his sides, eyes on Frog. His hair was pulled off his face by his reversed ball cap and it made him look vulnerable. But he was clearly composed as he said, 'No. Not without the money up front.'

'*No*, freak?' Frog sneered, his back to Honor, his jeans hanging low to reveal the swirling black pattern on his boxer shorts and his shoulders menacingly broad in a tight black T-shirt. '"No" isn't the right answer. Get your arse indoors and get me a drink. I know your freaky mummy isn't here to cast her scary spells on me.'

Honor knew that she should give Ru a chance to sort this out on his own. This is what the classes had prepared him for, given him the confidence to face. If she charged in then she was undoing all the good that Hughie the instructor had done.

Ru smiled into Frog's face. 'No.'

Delicately, as if preparing to enjoy himself, Frog put his

fingertips on Ru's chest. And shoved.

As he was forced to step back, Ru's gaze dropped to the 'button' at the base of Frog's throat, his smile stretching into a big grin of anticipation as his right hand drew back.

And suddenly, Honor didn't want him to make that jab that would stop Frog in his tracks and even throw him, coughing, to his knees.

She didn't want him to drop to Frog's level, to get the badass reputation she'd once wanted for him, or maybe even get pleasure from the violence, get a taste for it. She'd watched Stef stand up for an underdog and enjoy it; she'd had a hard time calming him down afterwards and preventing him from turning all vigilante. Being a badass could be bad.

Even for the badass.

With a squeak, she leapt forward, yanked out the elastic waist of Frog's boxer shorts and tipped in the contents of the blender jug. 'Watch your ass, buddy.'

Frog screamed, spinning around to face her, gyrating and glaring, plunging his hands into his pants. 'You fuckin' Yankee!'

'Good one!' Ru began to howl with laughter.

The Tadpoles started to snort, shoulders shaking.

Customers joined in as Frog jiggled and danced and ice rained out of the leg of his jeans, until the teagarden was swept with gales of laughter.

When he had finally pawed what he could from his underwear, ice and crushed strawberries lay glistening on the ground. He glared ferociously at Honor. Honor glared right back, swinging the jug gently.

Slowly, laughter was replaced by silence.

'That,' said Frog, with perilous dignity, 'was fuckin' 'orrible.' But his lips twitched as he looked down at a damp patch spreading over the crotch of his jeans. Gingerly, he wiggled his hips, reigniting some giggles. His mouth actually curled up at one corner. Without his habitual teeth-gritted snarl, he was nearly good looking.

Then Honor stepped forward and enfolded him in a great big hug, somehow recognising that, beneath the façade of adulthood, the heart beating was still that of a child. 'Please stop bothering Ru because we don't want to have to hurt you. If you want to earn a drink and a cake by doing half-an-hour's washing up, there's plenty.' She stepped back to gauge his reaction.

Frog's jaw was suitably dropped and the tips of his ears had gone red. 'Earn?' he repeated.

'Sure.' Encouraged, she linked her arm in his and turned him towards the tearoom. 'We're real shorthanded so you'd be doing me a favour. You wash up this load that's waiting and it'll be worth a drink and a big cake. What do you say?'

Frog paused. Then said, gruffly, to the Tadpoles, 'Catch you later.'

In the kitchen, he surveyed the stainless steel sink full of steaming water, a stack of plates ready beside it. 'Two cakes,' he stipulated.

She sighed. 'Well, OK. Just this one time. Because I have to make more strawberry slush.'

He looked at her and laughed. 'OK, Yankee Doodle, how much do I have to do to get a cheesy potato?'

'A lot.' She gave him an apron and began to rinse more strawberries in the other bowl of the sink. Then, seeing that Ru had come into the kitchen to stare, 'And you have to get along with Ru while you're here. Rufus, Toby is going to be helping us this afternoon, as we're shorthanded.'

'Frog,' said Ru.

'Freak,' said Frog.

'Whatever. Just play nice.' Honor switched on the blender.

After showering out a head full of hair wax that, in his view, had been totally unnecessary on a windless day, but the hair stylist had 'wanted definition', Martyn emerged from the all-white hotel bathroom with an all-white towel hooked around his hips, and checked his phone. He'd become a compulsive checker on this trip, greeting every text with a skip of anticipation in case it was from Honor.

But this one was from Ru. He read and reread it, half-convinced that Ru must be suffering from hallucinations. Electing to go straight to source, he dialled Honor. 'Ru tells me that you beat Frog up, again.'

Her laugh was little more than a breath down the line, raising the hairs on the back of his neck. 'I didn't! It was a satisfactorily non-violent intervention. I suddenly didn't want Ru to prove that violence breeds violence.' She yawned.

His eyes ran over the text again. 'So you tipped ice down Frog's boxers? And then hugged him? Are you bonkers?'

She yawned. 'I guess you had to be there.'

Laughter bubbled up from his chest. 'I can't tell you how much I wish I had been. You're something else, Freedom Lefevre.'

Chapter Twenty-Six

Honor, not due at the Teapot until ten, was drifting in an agreeable somnolence of half-dreamed dreams when her cell phone rang. She scrabbled it somehow to her ear and groaned, 'Yeah?' discouragingly.

Ru sounded diffident. 'Mum and Soppy only got home about six this morning and they're in bed, wrecked. Shall we open up? Or stay closed?'

Honor kind of wanted to snap, 'Stay closed!' But, sometimes, her conscience just insisted that she live up to the name her father gave her. And she hadn't slaved and contrived for the last three days to keep the Teapot running just to have Robina come home and mock all her efforts by leaving it shut. The tearoom was meant to be open. So she would make somebody open it. She swore. 'I'll be there in thirty minutes.' She was beginning to totally appreciate why waitresses wore their hair in tight knots or braids. It wasn't hygiene. It was so no one could tell they had unwashed, unbrushed, unstyled hair because they had *no* time for all that.

She banged into the Teapot like a child in a snit, where Ru was already scrubbing potatoes. 'Come on,' she snapped. 'Let's get your fu– your mother up.'

Ru, who hadn't put his hat on yet as the Teapot wasn't open for business, grinned through his curtain of hair. 'You won't wake her.'

'You just watch me.'

'Love to.' Ru let her in the door in the side of the building. Honor stormed up the two flights of stairs to the bedrooms. 'Which is your mother's? This one?' And burst into the room.

She paused to let her eyes adjust to the gloom.

A giant yellow caterpillar lay on a double mattress and the curtains swayed lazily in the breeze from the open window. 'Robina.' Honor addressed the sheeted caterpillar, politely. 'You need to get up and open the tearoom. You need to bake the cakes.'

The caterpillar lay still.

Honor cranked it up a notch. 'Robina, *you need to get up and open the tearoom. You need to bake the cakes!*'

Still, the caterpillar didn't move.

Honor grabbed one edge of the sheet, braced her foot against the mattress and yanked. 'ROBINAYOUNEEDTOGETUP ANDOPENTHETEAROOM!YOUNEEDTOBAKETHE FUCKINGCAKES!'

The sheet ripped. Robina lay, exposed and blinking through a storm of hair. 'No,' she moaned.

'YES!' roared Honor. She seized Robina's hands and dragged her from the mattress and, with superhuman strength, to her feet. 'Yes,' she repeated, quietly. 'You do. Oh, good, you're already dressed; we needn't waste time with fresh clothes. Yesterday's will be fine. Put on your shoes.'

Kirsty had appeared in the doorway beside a grinning Ru. She looked like a scarecrow in pyjama bottoms and a wrap-over robe, and laughed like a growly dog. 'I never thought I'd live to see that.'

'And how are you?' Honor asked her, not releasing Robina's hands as she led the older woman to the bathroom like a geriatric. 'Do you have everything you need?'

'Thank you for asking.' Kirsty smiled, thinly. 'It's refreshing. But I'm OK.'

Sophie was easier to rouse and Honor presided grimly over face washing, teeth cleaning and the pulling back of hair before dragging the pair downstairs to at least get the cakes baked before she allowed them back to bed to pass out. 'And, Sophie, don't forget to put Ru on the payroll. He has worked his butt off all weekend while you guys have been mainlining alcohol.'

'Payroll?' Sophie blinked.

'Yeah, remember? Robina promised that Ru would get paid the same rate as Aletta. I'll write down for you how many hours we've each done, to make sure you get it right. OK?'

'OK.' Sophie smiled, gently, humouringly.

Although Sophie and Robina were in the kitchen in body, their minds were quite obviously still afloat in the ether. 'I should have left the place shut and you two in bed,' Honor told them, disgusted, when she hadn't been able even to take a break to shove down a scone to fill her empty stomach because she had to act like a sheepdog to keep the orders moving.

Robina's eyes cracked a touch wider open. 'But the Teapot has to open. Or we don't make any money.'

Honor planted her fists on her hips. 'So you just assumed that I'd open up for you? And Aletta would give up her day off?'

'I thought that's what we arranged,' she fibbed, weakly. 'I'll pay you a bonus.'

'Yeah, damn right!'

But not even Honor's energy could keep Robina and Sophie on their feet indefinitely and she returned from clearing tables at two o'clock to discover only Ru in the kitchen, busy at a steaming sink. 'Don't tell me they've slunk off!' Honor exploded.

'OK.'

Honor waited. Then, 'They've slunk off, right?'

'Yeah, out the back door.' Ru shrugged philosophically

and smiled. 'But they were crap really, weren't they?'

Even if she had to laugh and give Ru's skinny shoulder a mock punch, Honor was aggravated to find it was once more nearly six by the time she was free to go home, past the shops of Starboard Walk – with a longing glance up at Martyn's front door, uncompromisingly shut – turning her face to the sea breeze, half surprised to realise that, once again, it had been a pretty day.

Here they were in the last few of days in July and she was working through the days, making her too tired to enjoy the long, light evenings. Was this really what she'd come to England for? She didn't think so.

She awarded herself a long soak in the bathtub, scraped around the kitchen and ended up with an unsatisfactory meal of pasta with cheese sauce – she hadn't had time to shop over the last few days – and, finally, flopped on the couch with a book on the history of Sussex, one she'd bought in Arundel with glee but had hardly snatched a glance at.

Across the room, her laptop waited like an accusation.

She tried to concentrate on the book and the chapter on the Sussex smuggling trade illustrated with atmospheric monochrome line drawings of shifty looking men with ragged shirts, cuddling casks of brandy like stolen babies.

She texted Martyn: *Hey, how's it going?* But then remembered him telling her of tonight's late evening shoot at the Louvre with its spectacular backdrop of fountains and reflections; the glass pyramid twinkling with golden light.

He suddenly seemed a long way from her. More than miles. It was a big shoot, this time, with other models – female – and a bigger crew than Honor had witnessed in action at Arundel, underlining how little a part of his world she was. While she sprawled on a rented couch with a history book, he might be standing in the fountains in his underwear with a gorgeous model in his arms, smouldering down at her whilst she returned his gaze with an adoration created by le Dur cologne. She thought of the framed advertisement in his study and the hunger he'd injected into the pulling down of one teeny shoulder strap.

She tossed the book away.

In a consumer society, those moody, sexy shots of beautiful people with fabulous bodies and convincingly lustful expressions were everywhere. Magazines, bill boards ... buses.

She'd never wondered how the lovers and partners of those beautiful people coped with the way those shots were captured. The models had to get up close and very personal.

For distraction, she grabbed the laptop and booted it up.

There was a message waiting from Stef.

Honor, listen. You're too good a woman to leave me. You just wouldn't. The guys who get left while they're in here, they're pitiful. You couldn't go back on your wedding vows that way. Not even I deserve that. You'll wait until I get out so we can talk, because that's all that's fair.

She read messages from Jess and Zach and her father without really taking in their words about what was going on in their jobs and their relationships.

You just wouldn't whizzed her pasta around uncomfortably in her stomach. *You'll wait until I get out so we can talk, because that's all that's fair.*

Fair. That's what she'd always been. Honourable Honor. Always fair.

Slowly, she tapped out a reply. *Were you fair to me?*

Chapter Twenty-Seven

The morning was bright and beautiful and Honor floated from the bungalow to the Teapot in a happy dream. OK, the official end to her marriage was going to be painful and she had to figure out how and when to make it happen – which was going to be a can of worms, even if she argued that, by making bad decisions, Stef had, effectively, chosen jail over his wife.

Honor knew she would just have to steel herself to handle those worms, no matter how slimy. If Stef hadn't been in a correctional facility, she would simply have filed for divorce.

But *if* Stef hadn't been in county jail then the end of the relationship might never have happened, and if, and if, and if …

But there he was; and here she was, living in England 'at the seaside' (mentally, she put on an English accent to say that) and working for a couple of crazy hippies in a cute English tearoom. Today was Wednesday; tomorrow Martyn would be back and she'd worked yesterday to make it so that tomorrow and Friday were her days off, this week. And she was glad to be alive. Glad she didn't have to go through life not knowing what it felt like to be touched as if she was the last woman he'd ever touch. To be kissed with ferocious hunger, to make love with a man who used his mouth as his main means of exploration. A gourmand. Pretty damned incredible.

As if on cue, one of the cream-and-red double-decker buses passed her going the other way, and a huge Martyn glowered down at her, a god in boxer shorts. Whoo. Funny, funny feeling …

Stepping up her speed, she turned up into The Butts, past Starboard Walk, where Martyn's BMW should magically reappear tomorrow, past the butcher's shop, past the greengrocers, past the pub on the other side, across the road into the Eastingdean Teapot.

The counter flap was up and she breezed into the kitchen, reaching automatically around to the hooks where her apron hung. 'Hi, Sophie!'

Sophie looked up from pricking potatoes that looked like big brown pebbles. 'Um, Honor–'

Robina shot out from the pantry. Her huge dark eyes overwhelming her face, so absolutely white. Her hands shook. Honor stared, wondering whether Robina was ill or eating the wrong kind of mushrooms. 'Are you OK?'

Robina swallowed. A tear broke free of her eye. 'You fucking bitch.'

Chapter Twenty-Eight

Honor recoiled.

'You fucking bitch,' Robina repeated, advancing slowly, pointing her trembling finger like a weapon. 'You know how I feel about Martyn. You know I love him. You *know*. And as soon as my back was turned you stood right out in the street, touching tonsils with him. Did you think nobody would see? Because half the customers of the Fig Leaf must have been looking out and they couldn't wait to rub my nose in it when I went in there, last night.'

Honor's heart plummeted. 'But,' she began feebly.

Robina's face twisted into a snarl, tears streaming. 'I don't want to hear any of your fucking excuses.' Which sort of solved a problem as Honor had no idea what she would have said after 'But'. Martyn was a free agent, considered Robina a total nut job and had made it clear that he would set fire to himself sooner than get in her bed. But it was difficult to know how to convey those sentiments without making the situation worse.

'Get out.'

Honor took an involuntary step towards Robina. 'Can't we just–'

Robina clenched her fists. She hadn't tied up her hair and it streamed out from her head and over her shoulders like springs. 'Get. Out. Sophie will make up your wages and post them through your door. I don't want to see you in here again.' The tears had become a flood but, eerily, Robina's voice didn't even shake, though the misery in her expressive eyes made Honor feel bad clear through to the pit of her stomach.

'Robina, I'm so sorry. I didn't mean to hurt you–' Honor had to push her voice past her heart, which had jumped to her throat.

'Of course you did. Get out of my tearoom.'

Honor stood her ground, unhappily, searching for something, anything, to say, to make things better. She glanced at Sophie, whose flamingo hair had faded to a gentler party pink. Sophie shrugged and shook her head, her arms folded as if to fence Honor out. 'You knew how she felt.'

Slowly, Honor hung her apron back on its hook.

She trailed out of the tearoom, threading between the chairs and tables of the teagarden, dazed. Aimlessly, she wandered down on to the undercliff and walked into the wind, watching the ocean, and the gulls wheeling over everyone who had chosen to walk, run, ride or skate along the undercliff this morning.

She walked. Past Saltdean and the entrance to the park; past Rottingdean and the White Horse Hotel; on and on as the path narrowed and became separated from the stony beach by a wall and a rail. The sea was in, rolling and roaring over enormous concrete breakwaters, rattling the pebbles. When the walk finally rose and curved up to the main road, she found herself nearly at Brighton Marina. With sore feet.

On the opposite side of the main road was a café and she took her tired self to a table by the window and drank coffee as she stared through the rushing traffic at the sun glittering on the ocean, like the anger and misery that had glittered in Robina's eyes as she'd declared her love for the man Honor had just fallen into bed with.

She heaved a great wretched sigh.

Then she set off back. By the time she reached Eastingdean, her legs were almost too heavy to carry her up the steps on the side of the cliff and across the road to the bungalow. She let herself in, feeling lonely and unloved. Her hand hovered over her phone. Martyn was only a call away but he had a heavy day's shooting planned – and some conversations should only take place face-to-face.

She sighed. As well as talking to Martyn about Stef, she had to explain all about Robina.

Thursday wasn't exactly the ecstatically happy day that she'd planned. It began with an unwelcome phone call from Martyn. 'No planes taking off from Charles de Gaulle. The air traffic controllers are protesting about something.'

She tried to be philosophical and grown up and not flounce down on her bed wailing, *Ooooh noooo!* 'How long do you think it will last?'

'No idea.' He sighed. 'If it goes on, I'll try to get a place on the Eurostar, although it'll be a pain because my car's at Gatwick. And the Eurostar and the ferries will be crazy because of the strike.'

'Guess so,' bleakly.

His voice dropped. 'I'd better end the call because I haven't got that much life left in my battery. And, in an airport lounge that's filling up but not emptying, privacy's negligible.'

She forced a laugh, but the day dragged from that point. She tried to put into effect the once-attractive plans she'd made for her day off and wandered up to Pretty Old to poke around amongst all the deliciously interesting stuff that smelled of dust and age. But she couldn't raise enough interest to buy a thing, despite Peggy's expectant expression on her gnomy face, which dissolved into disappointment as Honor left empty handed.

Unless she deliberately took a roundabout route, she had no choice but to pass the Eastingdean Teapot, glancing wistfully at the teagarden full of chattering tourists and waving to Aletta, who was wafting between the tables. Aletta's eyebrows lifted clear into her hairline and her eyes opened wide, telegraphing, 'What's going on?'

Grimacing in return, Honor elected not to pause and explain. If she set a foot on Teapot property Robina would probably race out like a snappy poodle to sink her fangs into Honor's leg. Or she'd fire Aletta just like she'd fired Honor, and Honor would hate for that to happen.

She tried to peer through the teagarden and into the Teapot, hoping to catch a glimpse of Ru. She swallowed, dismally. Would she ever get to see Ru, now? Robina would probably hate them hanging out together and Robina had proved to Honor that it wasn't necessarily in a real mother's job description to put your kid first, even though Honor had always assumed it would be and that her own mother, her real mother, would be better than her stepmother. But Robina and Ru had shown her that a real mother wasn't necessarily a good mother.

She paused, studying herself in a shop window, hair frizzed in the wind, forehead furrowed. Did Karen used to look at Honor's features and wonder about Garvin's first love? She smoothed the lines away, hearing in her head the English saying: *if the wind changes, your face will stay that way*. The wind, swirling up over the cliffs, never seemed to know which way it was going.

She knew how it felt.

Drawing level with the Starboard Walk shops she glanced automatically at Martyn's car space, even though she knew there was no way he'd be home. But the space wasn't empty; Clarissa was just locking up her car.

Clarissa raised her eyebrows. 'Not slaving over a hot teapot?'

Honor summoned up a shaky smile. 'I guess I got canned.'

Clarissa halted, frowning. 'Fired? What on earth for?'

Belatedly, Honor realised that she couldn't exactly say, 'Oh, it was because I'm having sex with Martyn and Robina has the hots for him. But I dismissed her feelings because Martyn calls her his stalker.' Because ... well, because too many reasons to count. Maybe not a mother to Martyn in the conventional way, Clarissa had nevertheless given birth to him and might well not appreciate Honor's candour. And Martyn might not want Clarissa – or anyone at all – to know he was involved with Honor, or might want to tell her himself. It was just plain awkward. So she muttered, 'Robina and I, we had a fight.'

Clarissa looked startled for a moment. 'Not a fist fight?'

'Just words,' Honor confirmed, managing a smile at this latest evidence of the differences between UK English and US English. But if she'd stayed around Robina much longer, she reflected, she wouldn't have put money on it staying just words.

As always, Martyn had to queue to get through the traffic signals in Rottingdean. He yawned. It had been a long, crappy day and he'd never been so glad to get on a plane in his life, the French Air Traffic Controllers having been persuaded back to the negotiating table – and the control tower – late in the day.

He glanced at his watch. His phone battery had died on him and he hadn't won the scrabble for power sources on the plane, at a premium on such a short flight, nor thought ahead to bring the gizmo to let him charge in-car, so he hadn't been able to call Honor since he landed. Travel worn, he'd stopped at a service station to freshen up and now was probably just too late to swing by Hughie's self-defence class and see if she and Ru needed a ride home.

But then, as if he'd wished her into being, there was Honor, jogging across the lights in front of the waiting traffic, ponytail bouncing behind her, her movements easy and economical, a pace a runner could keep up for miles. Then, like a shutter cutting her out of a photo, the shop on the corner put her out of sight. He waited, impatiently, for the signals to turn to green and a driving school car to dither left around the corner like a geriatric beetle as he cornered the X5 at a crawl into Marine Drive.

His headlights picked her up straight away and he pulled up beside her, rolling his window down. 'Are you running uphill for the sake of your beautiful bottom? Or would you like to climb in here with me?'

Surprise blazed across her face as she laughed. 'I think I'll just climb in there with you.' She tugged the large door open. 'I let one of the ladies at the self-defence class show me where to catch the bus. Unfortunately, it was a bus that only came as far as Rottingdean before looping back.' She hopped up into the passenger seat. Then paused, blinking at him, as if suddenly unsure.

He gazed back into those gooseberry eyes. Then let his eyes drop to her pretty mouth. 'This is where you kiss me,' he suggested.

With a strangled laugh, she threw herself into his arms, as well as she could above the steering wheel, and hugged him as if she were a child. Hugging him and hugging him, hugging him hard, desperately.

'That's almost as good,' he murmured, wrapping her up in his arms and pressing his lips to her hair. But he frowned. What was with such desperation? Had her lips trembled? He stroked her neck, her shoulder, followed her spine with the palm of his hand. 'You OK?'

She withdrew slightly and he was able to see that she was gathering herself. 'Sure.' She smiled. 'It's just good to see you.'

Her smile was a fake if ever he saw one. He lowered his

lips to hers, taking his time, letting his fingertips follow the shape of her arm, her fingers, then back up to trace her jawline. 'Ru not with you?'

A shadow dropped across her face.

So it was something to do with Ru. Surprise, surprise.

But as traffic was having to squeeze past the BMW, pulled up inconveniently at the side of the road, he just kissed the tip of her nose and said, 'Let's get out of here.' In a few minutes he was turning left into her drive, the bungalow perched above them.

He flicked off his seat belt and went to give her a comforting hug. But she turned her face up for his kiss and suddenly he was all over her, her smooth lips and hot tongue passing a thousand volts through his heart and his groin. He savoured the heat of her body, the incredible softness of her skin, ignoring the centre consol digging into his knee as one of her breasts pressed tantalisingly against his chest.

Her fingers fastened in his hair and he groaned aloud. 'It's so hot when you do that. How about we take this indoors? Even a big car can get tricky for a tall guy, however horny.'

'Mmm,' she agreed, but kissed him again. Slowly, sloooowly.

His hands slid up and inside her T-shirt, skimming the smoothness of her back, discovering the clasp of her bra, fighting the urge to find a way, right now, right here.

Five steps from the road? With supreme effort, he controlled his hands, breathing faster than if he'd been for a five-mile run. 'Let's get inside. Before something explodes.'

'Always better to get inside before exploding,' she agreed, groping behind her for the door handle.

He couldn't get out of the car fast enough. Tricky with his arousal to work around but he caught her halfway up on the steps, threading his hands back under her T-shirt, heading for that bra strap. She laughed and put in a wiggle to make his job harder.

He had to put in a giant stride to get his hands around her waist and spin her around and catch her up against him, so that he could possess her mouth again as he steered them up the last couple of steps and slowly across the patio, lifting and trapping her between himself and her door while she wrapped those shapely legs around him. He couldn't drag his mouth away, couldn't stop holding her against him while he settled snugly exactly where he wanted to be. 'Where's your key? Get us through this door.'

But self-preservation did make him turn his head when he caught movement from the corner of his eye. Because, like a harbinger of doom, a dark figure was rising up from the wooden lounger at the side of the patio.

And the harbinger of doom had a voice. It said: 'Say, buddy, you want to take your hands off my wife's ass?'

Chapter Twenty-Nine

Honor found herself deposited suddenly on to her own two feet.

She closed her eyes. She was falling down a lift shaft. She opened them again. Nope. She was still here, the figure was still there and she had to force suddenly frozen lips to work. 'What the hell are you doing here?'

Thumbs hooked in the belt loops of his blue jeans, Stef strolled closer. 'Getting here in the nick of time, seems to me.' His voice was deceptively lazy.

Martyn didn't move or speak. Honor felt as if her insides had turned to worms and every single one of them cringed away from how he must feel about being caught in exactly the situation he'd been trying to avoid from the first. She touched his chest. 'I have to speak to him.'

Slowly, he turned his eyes to her. His expression was unreadable as the last of the light began to leach from the clear summer sky. 'I suppose so,' he said, stiffly, as if he actually didn't think so at all. 'I'll wait in the car so I know you're OK.' He nodded, shifting his weight, ready to step back.

Stef laughed, stepping out of the shadows so that his face caught the light from a street lamp. He was harder, thinner and looked weary. 'Why wouldn't she be? She's my *wife*! Listen, you're really not needed here. I don't know what Honor let you think but, believe me, I know her. She's mad as hell at me, right now, but she'll cool down and come home. I know her.' He rocked on and off his heels. 'Didn't I know exactly where to find her, right here in liddle ole England? As soon as she left town on her high horse I knew she'd be heading here to meet her long lost mommy. So, what's she like, Honor? This Robina Gordon?'

And Martyn let go of her hand.

His shock was like a cold breath between them, curling and chilling as fog. 'Your mother's *Robina*?' Even through the twilight, Honor could feel his disbelief.

She nodded, miserably. 'I was going to tell you, tonight.'

Stef laughed again. 'Oh, pardon me. Was that a secret?'

'Why hadn't you told me already?' The disbelief became anger, sharp as a blade.

'Because – because she's–' Honor was horrified to feel hot tears spilling from her eyes. 'I was so disappointed. All my life, I'd thought that she'd love me like a proper mom and would have some fantastic, justifiable reason for leaving me when I was a baby.' The tears tracked down her cheeks and her heart began to beat in huge great thuds. 'But when I met Ru I began to realise that biology and maternal instinct are not the same. She lets Ru down in so many different ways.

'And she's your *stalker* for goodness' sakes!' she finished, shakily. 'That made it a little awkward.'

'But you've known all the time that you've been living in Eastingdean?'

Honor opened her mouth but Stef beat her to it. 'She's known a hell of a lot longer than that.'

Martyn turned to him. 'How?'

Stef shrugged, scuffing closer. 'Years. It's the kind of thing you can find out on the internet for fifty dollars. Every so often she'd talk about coming out here to meet her mom and I'd tell her what a bad idea it was, how they probably wouldn't even like each other.'

Martyn was looking down at Honor as if he wasn't liking what he saw. 'Why didn't you want me to know?'

She made herself confront the pain in his eyes. It was hard but she wanted him to see she wasn't trying to hide anything, now. But she couldn't prevent her voice from emerging tight with tears. 'To begin with, I didn't want anyone to know, in case it got back to her before I figured out what I wanted her to know. My dad warned me off ever searching her out. He said that I would be hurt, that Robina was nobody's happy ending. He called her a flake. When I traced her and her son, Rufus, everyone was against me coming here and making her real. So I didn't.

'Then ... I lost my job,' she glanced at Stef, 'and I had my severance money and I thought I'd come and do it anyway.'

'It was a "fuck you",' stuck in Stef.

'No, it wasn't! It was *for me*,' she fired back. 'I just pleased myself for once, OK?' Shakily, she turned back to Martyn, forcing the tears back, wanting and not wanting to crumble, to fling herself into his arms. Good guys tended to console crying women. But if Martyn hadn't read that memo and pushed her away ...

With superhuman effort, she swallowed the sobs down. 'It seemed possible and reasonable to come here and just get a look at Robina. At my mother.' She had to swallow again. 'To maybe get to know her and judge for myself. After all, the Robina my dad knew was no more than a kid. It was thirty years ago that she left me and I knew that she could have found me, but what if she hadn't just because of all the same doubts I had? What if, when we met, we had gotten along?' Her voice was wavering but she held her gaze steady. 'So I came. I took a look at her. I found a way to get to know her a little. I planned that, afterwards, I would probably just go on home with my curiosity satisfied and pull my life back together and move on.' She found herself clutching Martyn's hand, willing him to understand. 'All these years, all my attention had been focused on her and I didn't think properly about Ru. He was the one with the real mom, right? He was the lucky one.

'Turns out I was wrong about that. Turns out he could really use a hand from his big sister. And I felt something for him that I really didn't feel for his mother. Our mother. It complicated things! Should I tell him? Should I tell her? Could I tell one without the other? It seemed safer to tell no one, at least for a while. *And*,' she went on because she couldn't let him speak before she confessed the whole mess, 'she knows about me and you. And she fired me. Which was unexpectedly painful.'

Slowly, he nodded. Computing but not commenting. Probably he saw his stalker getting a dose of reality as unimportant right now. Or he just thought that Honor had been served right. His eyes were unreadable. 'Now I see why you didn't want me to call you Freedom.'

Stef looked at him sharply. 'My, you have gotten intimate, haven't you? That's something she doesn't tell everyone.'

'It seems as if there's a lot she doesn't tell everyone.'

'I'm sorry,' she whispered. 'I was going to tell you about Robina.'

He sighed. 'Maybe you were.'

'I tried to talk to you about her just before you left and you said–'

'I remember what I said. A nice easy out for you, wasn't it?'

Chapter Thirty

Martyn's SUV backed out of the drive like an angry badger. Honor felt an agonising pull as it gunned up the road and away, as if it were attached to her heart by a thread. She gazed at her husband, standing calmly, here on her patio in England, gazing back, tense but not letting his emotions take charge of his mouth. For once. His hair was short for the first time since high school. The smile lines bracketing his mouth had deepened into grooves, making him look uncompromising.

Anxiety slithered down her spine but she moved coolly past him, lowering herself on to one half of the lounger and gesturing to him to take the other.

He sat, without arguing. Also for once.

'How did you know which yard to hang around in?'

That laugh again. It was beginning to make Honor wince. Stef used to laugh all day long – but it never used to be a bitter punctuation to his conversation. 'Babe, this place is minute. All I had to do was buy myself a beer. I told some guys at the bar how I was in trouble because I'd come here to meet my wife and must have left the address on the train. And could anyone save my ass by telling me where an American woman called Honor was living? They sent me right along here.'

'Right. And your release is scheduled for November 2nd but you're here on August 1st because ...?'

'I made full restitution and one of the charges was reversed on appeal. Straight release with no conditions. I'm a free man.' His smile was chill.

Honor, the daughter of a lawyer, translated, 'Your dad paid them off.'

Again, the laugh. 'You know better than to use words like pay off, babe. I made the victim whole again. Or, rather, my dad did. At first he said I'd just have to serve my jail time but when he saw me all caged up like that, the old man finally came through.' Then he added, deliberately, 'Of course, you never saw how miserable I was in jail, crawling the walls and hating the entire world.'

She ignored the barb. 'Your poor dad. That must have nearly wiped him out.'

A sharp breath. 'I've paid him back a little already. But, you know, I needed to keep enough money back to come chasing after my wife and I haven't had a pay cheque in a while. You made things pretty tight, disappearing like that.'

She settled her back on the wooden slats, cool now the last of the sun was dipping into the sea. 'You've cleared out our savings account and you're here after my severance cheque?'

'I didn't say that.' But he didn't deny it, either. More softly, 'I came to find you, babe. I miss you. And I'm not giving up on you.'

She made her voice soft. 'I'm sorry, Stef. But you have to. I told you, when you got yourself put in jail.'

'You sure did. Right around the same time that your ring came whizzing through the air.' His elbows were planted on his knees, hands hanging loose, as relaxed as if this was a summer Sunday out by the lake. 'What you omitted to mention was you were going to sublet our apartment, store our furniture and dump all my gear in the loft over my dad's garage.'

She hugged her knees against the ocean chill rolling up over the cliff. 'If you'd been released on time, the tenants would have been out of the apartment. Whether you moved your gear back in would have been your decision.'

Slowly, he nodded. 'And would your stuff be in there, too?'

She stared. 'No. I *told you*.'

Silence. Then, 'You're really that mad at me? Shit.' He let out a long sigh that seemed to come right up from his boots. He glanced at the bungalow's front door. 'Would you mind telling me what we're doing sitting out here in the dark and the cold when your rental's right there?'

The bungalow was her refuge. Damned if she was going to take what she was running away from right in there with her. 'I think you need to find yourself a room somewhere.'

'Are you shacked up with that guy?'

'He doesn't live here, if that's what you're asking.' Her voice shook, though she told it sternly not to.

'I don't know, Honor. *Is* that what I'm asking? Or am I asking you whether you and him are having sex?' He paused. His voice hardened. 'I guess I don't have to ask. The way he had your ass in his hands and his tongue down your throat pretty much tells me all I need to know.'

'Well, then.' Honor hated hurting Stef, no matter what he'd done; marriages begun with joy shouldn't end in pain. But it was beginning to seem as if there was no other way.

He shook his head. For the first time his voice softened and he sounded more like the Stef that Honor used to love. 'I would never have believed that you'd cheat on me.'

She didn't try to explain that she saw it more as leaving him than cheating on him. 'And I would never have believed you'd become a criminal. So neither of us got what we signed up for.'

He snorted. 'Babe! I'm not a criminal. It was a prank. You know about me and pranks. You *know*.'

Weariness settled heavy hands on her shoulders. 'Stef, identity theft is a felony in the state of Connecticut. You used someone else's credit card details to buy a shit load of embarrassing stuff for the guy.'

He couldn't quite hide the laughter in his voice. 'Exactly.

For the guy. Billie's boyfriend. It all went straight to his address, so how is that theft? It was a prank, not a crime – I'm not a criminal – I'm a prankinal.'

'You know damned well–!' Automatically, Honor prepared to explain how it was immaterial where the goods went; it was buying with Billie's boyfriend's credit card that was the issue. But she clamped her lips shut on the hot words. An argument was just what Stef wanted. He'd make her laugh and cajole her by saying it was just a joke. Funny. Ha ha. Everybody ought to be able to take a joke. Jokes were Stef's way of dealing with everything. Even when she could see from his eyes that he was really hurting.

She took a breath. Let it out. Slow. Slow down, Honor. Keep calm. 'OK, so you're a prankinal. Here's the thing, Stef – you're the only person in the world that recognises the word. Your *prank* got you 180 days in county.

'And that wasn't nice for me. The good people of Hamilton Drives didn't want their investments handled by the hands that had been given in marriage to an inmate. And half the town thought you'd just made a fool of yourself over Billie and the other half thought you were actually sleeping with her.'

Stef shrugged it off. 'That didn't happen between me and Billie.'

'Before all this happened, whether you did or whether you didn't would have been important.'

He frowned. 'So it's not important, now?'

'Why you chose to punish Billie's boyfriend so thoroughly has always been a mystery. The fact is that you did. I don't know if you did what you did for Billie but, sure as hell, it wasn't for me. I'm just the poor fool who suffered.'

He inched closer, until he could lay his hand on hers, warm and remembered. Yet no longer familiar. 'So, you cheated on me. You had to get back at me. I think I understand that.

It's a hard thing for me to get over, but I will get over it.' His voice was a plea, trying hard to make her see things his way. 'Same way you'll get over me doing jail time. I guess we'll have to find a way to forgive each other.'

Gently, she slid her hand out.

Courtesy of the street lamps that marched up the hill, she could read his expression. The wanting. The determination. The certainty that Honor belonged with him and he might have some grovelling to do, but everything was going to be OK.

It hurt to snuff that certainty out. She was as gentle as could be – but she still said it. 'You turning up here today was a shock, but it has made things easier for me because I can tell you to your face what I decided this week.

'I want to get a divorce.'

Chapter Thirty-One

The sound of the doorbell, early in the morning, at first made her heart leap. But reality took over.

It wouldn't be Martyn.

She'd called and texted him the night before but he'd evidently been observing voicemail silence.

Talking – yelling, crying – things out with Stef had taken into the early hours, leaving both her head and heart thumping. It was only when it sank in to him that she really wasn't going to let him into the bungalow and they'd spend the night shivering on the lounger outside, if necessary, that he'd admitted to having already taken a room at the Fig Leaf, 'In case things didn't work out right away.' Tossing and turning for what was left of the night, she'd strained for the ringing of her cell phone or even the *turr-ree* of an incoming text message, wrestling with the temptation to run up the road and bang on Martyn's door. But when a girl had left both voice and text messages and a guy didn't respond ... he probably wasn't ready to see her in the middle of the night.

When the doorbell sounded again before she could even get to the mirror to check out how bad the bags under eyes were, she paused. Impatience. Stef?

So she opened the front door cautiously. Then flung it wide, with a glad smile. 'Ru!'

His hair curtained one side of his face but the half she could see showed the hint of a smile. 'I've got the money Mum owes you.' He exhibited a folded brown envelope, obviously much recycled, *Honor* scribbled above other crossings out.

Pulling at his arm, she dragged him into the kitchen, almost forcing him to take a seat at the table. 'How about breakfast? You like eggs?'

His eyebrow lifted. 'Yeah, great. Thanks.'

She poured him orange juice and broke eggs into a jug, whizzing through the meal preparation in case he suddenly tried to get away. In ten minutes, rafts of toast and creamy hillocks of egg were on the table. 'When you didn't turn up for the self-defence class I made up my mind that your mom – mum – had forbidden you to see me.'

He cut a corner from his toast and snow-ploughed a froth of eggs up on to it. 'She has.' He popped the forkful into his mouth.

Honor's heart sank. 'Oh.'

He shrugged as he chewed and swallowed. 'But Soppy put your wages out, ready to post through your door, so I decided to do it for her.' His half a face smiled again. 'They're always on at me to be helpful.'

Relaxing, beginning on her own breakfast and realising how long it was since she'd eaten properly, Honor grinned. 'I don't want you to get in trouble with Robina, though.'

His cheeks bulged around too much food for one teenager's mouth and he shrugged again, wrinkling his nose, too, which she assumed to convey that he didn't mind being in trouble with his mother. Or that it was a situation too familiar to cause anxiety.

He didn't slow down until there was nothing but crumbs and a sheen of grease left on his plate. Then he swigged back his orange juice and wiped his mouth on the back of his hand. 'Mum's mega pissed at you for getting it together with Martyn. I warned you how she'd get.'

'I know.' She lost her appetite for the rest of her scrambled eggs, dropping her fork untidily on the plate. She wasn't that certain whether 'together' and 'Martyn' were destined to end up in many of her sentences. She propped her chin on her fist. 'I hate it that I can't hang out with you any more.'

He shook back his hair and for a moment she saw his whole face and its set expression. 'We can hang out,' he said, gruffly, sliding his chair back. 'Unless Mum puts a bad spell on you or sticks pins in an Honor doll or something. Better get back.' With a quick grin, he loped across the hall and out of the front door before Honor could even begin to compute the effect if she told him that Robina was her mother. Too.

Martyn opened his front door to find Ru hovering, hands in pockets, brown eyes fixed on him uncertainly.

Inside, Martyn heaved a sigh gusty enough to blow Ru right back where he came from. But he didn't allow his frustrations to make it to his face, just stepped back and let Ru in. 'I thought you'd be working in the Teapot.'

'Yeah, soon.' Ru made no attempt to go further than the foyer. 'Um …'

Martyn waited.

Ru shuffled. Then spurted, 'Will it still be OK for me to do stuff on the computer for you? Only, I really want to. You know.' Ru gave a great, exaggerated shrug, making the time-honoured *it's a woman thing* face. 'Now Mum knows about you and Honor.'

Martyn was stirred by curiosity. 'What happened, exactly? Honor was obviously upset and I didn't ask for details.' In fact, it hadn't even been near the top of his *things that have gone badly wrong* list.

'Someone told her they'd seen you kissing so she sacked Honor. She really doesn't want you guys to be together. I mean *really*. I've just seen Honor and she looks as if she's been run over by a train.'

'She's upset,' he repeated. And could have added: *You don't know the half of it. Honor's husband has shown up and – listen to this, it's good – turns out that Robina is Honor's mother. So you're Honor's brother, which explains why she took you under her wing. She didn't tell you? I know exactly how that feels because she didn't tell me.* And, maybe, *Did you happen to see the husband over breakfast at all ...?*

But he couldn't let his sparks of anger and hurt ignite the whole box of fireworks because it was Honor's decision whether to tell Ru.

And, whoever's fault this sticky mess was, it wasn't Ru's.

He managed a smile. 'I'm working on a relaunch of a site this weekend. Come round on Sunday evening and upload all the files – if you can do that without pissing your mother off.'

'Wicked. I just won't tell her.' Relief ran across Ru's face like a flicker of sunshine. He opened the door and backed out on to the space at the top of the stairs. 'I'll be–'

'*Ru!* What the *flying fuck* are you doing with him?'

Ru's and Martyn's gazes locked, neither looking down at the street from where the bellow of rage had come. 'Oh, shit,' they said, in unison.

Then Ru shoved his hands into his pockets and turned reluctantly to clump down the stairs. '*What?*' he demanded, in his best belligerent-teen, mothers-are-so-crap voice.

On the ground, Robina's eyes burned with rage as they flicked from her son to Martyn. 'What are you doing with that bastard?'

Ru's steps halted. 'Don't be lame, Mum–'

'I said, *what are you doing with that bastard?*'

'I'm going to help him with some stuff,' he muttered, defensively.

'Like hell you will!' Robina's voice achieved the pitch and volume of a whistling kettle.

Male solidarity wouldn't allow Martyn to abandon Ru. Somehow, he found himself shoulder-to-shoulder with the kid, who was looking as if he could literally be blown against the wall by Robina's screams. 'What's the problem, Robina?'

Robina swung on Martyn and he was shaken to see venom where he was used to seeing the fawning hot looks she'd been sending him for what seemed forever. 'You take your American bitch and fuck off. Ru, go home.'

Martyn tried to make his voice conciliatory, because poor Ru had to live with Robina, at least for the next few years. And surely Robina's erstwhile crush couldn't have been buried so deeply, so quickly? 'Robina, there's no need for this—'

'Touch my son again and I'll call the police,' she snarled.

He recoiled. 'Don't be ridic—'

'I mean it.'

They glared at one another. Slowly, Robina turned and yanked Ru along by his elbow, away up The Butts in the direction of the Teapot.

Bursting with impotent wrath, Martyn hurled after Robina, 'I've heard stalkers can turn on their victims!' Then he noticed a denim-clad figure across the road, leaning on the wall outside the Fig Leaf and drinking in the whole scene. Stefan Sontag.

Martyn locked on to his gaze. 'Want something?'

Stef grinned. 'Not a thing.'

And then, as if his day wasn't the pits already, Clarissa's voice rang out from the car park. 'Mar-tyn May-fair!'

He swung to face her. '*What?*' He sounded just like Ru. He even felt like adding, *Don't be lame!*

Clarissa hesitated. A dozen expressions flitted across her face, as if she were trying each emotion out for size before wearing it. Finally, she settled for rueful disapproval. 'From Robina's remarks, I suppose I know now what Honor and Robina quarrelled about.'

Martyn suddenly realised that he was standing in the entrance to the car park in bare feet being given a talking to by his mum. He wanted to roar with fury. Instead, he turned and sprang up the stairs.

Clarissa's voice followed. 'Honor's lovely but there's no point getting involved with her, Martyn. She's only here for the summer. And how much do you really know about her?'

Stef watched as the door at the top of the metal stairway slammed and the woman in the blue athletic gear glared at it, before tucking her car keys in her bag and marching up the street and into a shop.

His gazed moved on to the place that the crazy woman and her kid had disappeared into, with tables and chairs set outside.

So now he'd seen them: Robina and Rufus Gordon. Till now just names on Honor's lips.

Not surprising that Honor hadn't opened up to a mommy like that. Robina Gordon was a spitting wildcat with poison-tipped claws.

His head swivelled back as Martyn's front door banged open and he stormed back down the stairs, cast Stef a freshly honed glare, then set off down the street in the opposite direction and crossed the busy road at the bottom. He'd changed into running gear and paused on the stretch of grass beyond the road to stretch out his hamstrings. Then he ran towards some railings and disappeared from view.

Stef thought toxic thoughts, shaken by a daylight viewing of Martyn. He saw that Martyn was what women would call *a hunk*. That was bad.

But toxic thoughts, however satisfying, were unlikely to have any actual effect. Thoughtfully, he straightened, and began to saunter towards the collection of chairs, tables and flowerpots through which Robina and Ru had made their way. Above the little white door was a sign that said *Eastingdean Teapot*.

Inside, apparently one of the day's first customers, he chose a round wooden table and a chair with its back against the wall, facing the kitchen where a red-eyed Robina was drinking from a thick white mug, both hands wrapped around it, as if for stability. She was listening to the whisperings of a woman with pink hair. The kid, Rufus, was making cutlery scratchy noises at the back. After a minute, the kid emerged to take Stef's order.

Stef glanced at the menu and was glad to see that an English tearoom actually served coffee. 'I need black coffee, please.' Ru flicked him a curious look when he heard the American accent but filled the order without comment.

The coffee was good and rich, maybe Costa Rican, and Stef breathed in the steam as he watched kitchen activity step up as customers arrived, calling greetings, and some of them even nodding to him, a stranger. Here, next to the ocean in this small place, folks were friendly. On his one previous visit to England Stef hadn't really cared for it, maybe because Honor acted as if 'England' were another word for 'paradise'. Or maybe it was because they'd never left London and he wasn't a city boy, let alone thrilled by history, like Honor and Garvin. For him, old soon got old.

By the time he'd drunk two cups of coffee he'd thought things through. Robina had begun to work, albeit with nothing of the frantic pace set by the pink-hair lady. Nearly every table was occupied and Rufus threaded backwards and forwards with the orders. Stef stopped him as he breezed by. 'Would you please ask the owner if she'd spare me a moment?'

Rufus looked suspicious.

Stef smiled. 'Tell her that I won't keep her long.' *Brother-in-law.*

Shrugging, Rufus swung back into the kitchen, tearing an order from his pad as he paused to speak to Robina.

After a lengthy and evidently dubious sizing up, Robina emerged from behind the counter. 'Can I help you?' It was difficult to believe that this was the same woman who had been screaming the F word up and down the street not much more than an hour ago.

Stef rose, extending his hand and making his voice low and rueful. 'You certainly can. My name's Stefan Sontag and I'm having awful trouble with my wife, Honor. I know that you've had trouble with her, too, and I'm hoping that between us, we can persuade her to come home to America with me.'

Robina's eyes widened. 'Honor's *husband*?'

Stef took his seat again, making his movements relaxed and non-threatening, smiling boyishly. 'That's me.'

Slowly, Robina slid into the chair on the opposite side of the table. 'I didn't know Honor was married.'

Stef made his smile wobble. 'She seems to have forgot, doesn't she? Maybe–' He lifted his hands in a gesture that said, *I'm looking for ideas.* 'Maybe if you could tell me something about this Martyn Mayfair guy she's … with? It would be a huge help to me to know what I'm up against.'

The spark of curiosity in Robina's eyes ignited into a flame of eagerness. 'I can probably tell you more about him than you'll ever need to know.'

When Stef finally left the Eastingdean Teapot he'd drunk enough coffee to float a boat and eaten a chunk of incredible cake.

In his room above the bar of the Fig Leaf pub, he fired up his laptop, opened a new document and began to tap, retrieving from his agile mind just about every detail that Robina Gordon had told him about Martyn Mayfair, adding in his own observations about Martyn's property and lifestyle.

Plenty to work with.

Chapter Thirty-Two

Since yesterday and Ru's visit, Honor hadn't seen a soul she knew; not anybody from the Eastingdean Teapot nor any of the Mayfairs. Not even Stef. And especially not Martyn.

The day had been long and tense, not helped when she – belatedly – logged on to her email account and found a message from her dad: *Stef's jail time is over early. He's looking for his wife and I think he knows where to look. I assume you're in England, searching for your mother? That's what we all thought when you took off. Did you find her? Is she still a flake? I'm afraid that if you're looking to Robina to solve all your life problems, you're in for a disappointment, unless she's changed a lot.*

But I'm still here, honey. Nothing will change my love for you. Nothing at all.

She'd had to blink back tears. Typed, *Good guess, Dad. And coming to England's not a decision I can regret. Except that, yeah, Stef's here ...*

Honor put on her running shoes and black lycra shorts. Running along the undercliff would release those endorphins to brighten her mood, expand her lungs and send oxygen-rich blood to her brain – hopefully allowing her to work out whether she ought to call on Martyn. 'Hi!' And, maybe, 'As I realise that you're avoiding my calls and not answering my texts I thought I'd coming banging on your door ...' Yes, why not make a guy feel cornered and defensive? Way to go.

It wasn't that she was hoping to encounter him out running, on neutral territory or anything ... But running the route he ran every morning, at exactly the time he usually ran it, wouldn't hurt. She could run it two or three times before she fell over from exhaustion, probably.

The weather was very British. Patchy August sun but a chill breeze, tourists sticking obstinately to their summer clothes as if that would warm up the day. Honor paused at a bench down on the Undercliff Walk to do her stretches, taking her time and stretching right out. Then she set off slowly, to warm up, but soon she was running comfortably, weaving gently between strolling tourists and young families with bikes and buggies, teenagers with skateboards.

And other runners.

Her wish came true when a runner who threw a long shadow drew level and slowed his pace to match hers. She risked a glance up at him, his hair streaming back from his face and managed, 'Hi,' without disturbing her breathing.

He responded, 'Yeah, hi,' neutrally. He wasn't even breathing fast, yet.

They completed the distance to Rottingdean together and ran up the steps and down the slope, up the steps and down the slope. When Honor felt as if the bones would slide out of her legs if she had to do one more circuit, Martyn jumped down on to the stones and set off back in the direction they'd come. *No way!* Lungs beginning to burn, she forced herself to keep up on the concrete. When he jumped back up and ran into the underpass, she followed, their footsteps magnified and echoey, then out of the underpass, around the corner, across the parking area and into the park.

Martyn took only one run up the grass slope, then walked along the brow, beside some houses, cooling down. Shakily, Honor flopped down on to the grass, chest heaving.

Presently, after he'd performed a load of sensible stretches, he crossed his legs and folded down beside her.

From their vantage point, they could look down on the children's play park, the skateboard park and some courts where men were gathering, stringing up a volleyball net.

One shaded his eyes and looked up to Martyn, shouting a question.

Martyn waved and shouted back, 'Five minutes, Jamie.'

Only five minutes. Words began to burst from Honor's mouth. 'So, aren't we even friends, now?'

For the first time, he looked right at her. 'I don't know what we are. I've been thinking about nothing else but that you didn't even trust me enough to tell me Robina's your mother.'

She'd had over a day to mentally run this conversation and had her bullet points all ready. 'You said I was tainted even when I went to work with her. You call her your stalker.'

He ripped up a handful of grass. 'Fuck it, Honor! Having an imperfect mother isn't a foreign concept to me. I would have understood.'

She kept her eyes on his face, on the well-defined profile, set and grim. 'You're pissed with me. And I don't think it's because I hid my unsatisfactory parentage. It's because Stef turned up – even though I had been open with you about my status.'

Silently, he turned and watched the men below tossing around a volleyball, boosting it up into the air with forearms, punching it down again with fists. He chewed a stalk of grass. Finally, 'Maybe you're right. Maybe it's unfair but, actually, you're right and it's all about your *"stattus"*, and yes, I am pretty pissed. Maybe more at me than you. Because I knew you were married and what the potential for trouble was. Now the trouble has arrived, it's eating me.' Climbing to his feet, he set off down the slope.

'I told him I want a divorce,' she called after him, without moving.

He halted. She watched him trade off his curiosity against his dudgeon. Then he reversed his route and let himself back down beside her on the cool grass, closer, this time. 'What did he say?' His brown eyes were cautious.

Scrunching up her knees, she laid her cheek on them, holding his gaze. 'He said no way. It was awful,' she admitted. 'He stayed and stayed, arguing, and he's hanging around, still hoping to change my mind. He says he loves me. I told him I can't live his life any more but it's hard to hurt him. I guess it goes against my character.' A tear tipped, unwanted, on to her cheek.

He let his fingertips touch her arm. Pause. Hover. Stroke. Warm. Delicious. His voice was soft. But regretful. 'That sounds like too much Honor, not enough Freedom.'

'And you sound so good-mannered about not taking something that's not yours. So fucking *English*.'

His thumb was drawing tiny circles on her arm, creating goosebumps. 'I am English. Which brings me to the small matter of us living three thousand miles apart.'

'People make it work.' She slid her hand on to his.

'Like your parents?'

'Your parents lived in the same country and that didn't work a whole lot better, did it?'

'Fair point,' he admitted. 'But you need to sort yourself out. I don't want some half-arsed triangular relationship with me as the villain, the adulterer. I hate that kind of guy, the weasel who sneaks around. I should have kept a lid on things because, where you're concerned, I don't share. I want all of you.' He leaned in and kissed her nose.

She sniffed as he jerked suddenly to his feet and the tears began to trickle down her cheeks. 'Martyn?'

He turned.

She tried to swallow away the misery that made her throat stiff. 'I'd already told him that I wanted out, before … you and me. You believe that, don't you?'

She heard his sigh, even though the breeze was hissing in her ears and whipping his hair across his eyes. 'Yes. Does that make a difference?'

The volleyball men were shouting again. Martyn acknowledged with a wave and began to trot down the slope.

Honor watched him go, muscles rippling under his running clothes, long-sleeved and full length so that his tan wouldn't get diced up. 'Yes,' she whispered. She sighed and climbed to her feet. If she wasn't too much mistaken, Martyn had just told her that what he wanted was commitment. According to the rules, that was meant to make her happy. Funny.

Back home, Sunday was one of Stef's favourite days to work at the diner because it would be jumping with kids out of school and Monday to Friday workers who'd broken free from their treadmills.

But the Teapot, he discovered this particular Sunday, boasted the same number of grey heads, tan cardigans and sensible sandals as it did any other day.

Comparing the quaint Eastingdean Teapot to the chrome and plastic Drives Diner was like comparing a tinkling music box to a jukebox blasting out Springsteen.

Robina smiled vaguely in his direction but didn't stop work, if you could call it work, decorating a cake. Customers read fat Sunday newspapers or murmured their way through tedious conversations, putting *ly* in words that didn't need it, like *real* and *quick*.

Stef couldn't stand to watch that much nothing happening. He left after one cup of coffee.

He wandered down the street, crossed the busy coast road and gazed at the ocean for a while, hugging his jeans jacket around him. It would be over eighty degrees in Connecticut, right now. He ought to be there, enjoying the sun, celebrating his freedom, not chasing around liddle ole England. The sooner he made Honor see sense, the better he'd like it.

So he turned and made for Honor's rented house. But when he reached it, it was empty. Or, at least, if Honor was there, she wasn't answering the door of the dull-but-cutesy, white-painted, single-storey house. Mooching back down the stairs, he took a seat on the second step. He'd wait.

He waited for quite a while, giving himself a numb butt, bored to tears with the view of untended garden. Finally, he was rewarded not by Honor running up the drive but by a small white car pulling in. A bug. And, well hey, the woman who hopped out was the other one he'd watched giving Martyn Mayfair a hard time right after Robina-mom-in-law had finished screaming at him. Stef's nose for trouble twitched. He rose to his feet as she made for the steps. 'Hi.'

She pulled up short, eyeing him speculatively.

'I'm Honor's husband, Stefan Sontag.'

Her eyebrows snapped down. 'Honor's *husband*?'

He sighed. 'Yes, ma'am. But I guess you didn't know about me, right?' He pinned on his best rueful-and-harmless expression.

'That's right.' She didn't look any too pleased to be in possession of the knowledge and it took her several seconds to digest it. 'I'm Clarissa; Honor's renting the bungalow from me,' she said, eventually. 'I called to ask her to get her grass cut. Again.' She glanced down at where the grass had grown so long that it had fallen over the edge of the drive. 'She keeps promising ...'

Stef smiled, scenting opportunity. 'I don't think Honor cares for yard work. But, now I'm here, I'd be happy to do it, if I can find a machine to use.'

She brightened. 'No problem. There's one in the garage.'

'Do you have another key? Honor only has one but she said she'd ask her landlady for another – and that's you, right?'

'That's right. But she should have a spare.' Her lips pursed in fresh suspicion.

He grinned. 'That's what she said! She was sure she had a spare. But you know Honor, she's forgotten where it was. Just like she's forgotten the time, now, most likely.'

'The key should be hanging up inside one of the kitchen cabinets.'

'Great.' Stef stood back and gestured Clarissa ahead of him. 'If you can just let me in, I'll search for it.'

Clarissa hesitated. 'I ought to wait and ask Honor if it's OK.'

Damn! But Stef was too shrewd to complain. He just made a performance of settling himself back on the step. 'I appreciate you looking out for her safety. I've been real worried while she's been here in Europe and I won't be happy until she's home in Connecticut with me.'

For several moments, Clarissa just looked at him. 'You've come to fetch Honor home?'

'That's my plan.' He laughed, as if stating the obvious.

She tapped her keys on her palm. 'I see.' She tapped some more. Faster. 'It's just that Honor rented the bungalow for four months.'

He went for sincerity. 'And if Honor signed up for four months' rent, that's what you'll get.' He launched into a eulogy about Honor being so honourable that she'd travel across continents just to return a few cents she owed.

'How about if I just give you the garage key, so that you can cut the grass?' she interrupted.

'That would be great.' He leaped to his feet like a waggy dog. 'It's boring just waiting.' He followed Clarissa as she opened the garage door and showed him the mower, the electrical outlet, the door out of the end of the garage to give him access to the back yard and a green bin on wheels for the grass cuttings.

He wheeled the mower to the lawn, pressed the button and tweaked the handle, and it roared into life. While

Clarissa watched, he cut two swathes of grass then raked up and dropped the long stalks into the green bin. 'This is not grass cutting, it's haymaking.'

Such a feeble joke seemed to reassure Clarissa that there was no harm in him and she said her goodbyes. As soon as she'd backed the little car out and whirred away up the road, Stef let the mower fall silent and whisked through the garage and up more steps to the back yard, where the long grass was falling over with neglect. He glanced around, checking out the degree to which the garden was overlooked, which turned out to be not much. Just another bungalow, really, its back to Honor's place and just about every blind still rolled down in Sunday morning laziness.

Grateful for late sleepers, Stef began to feel around the opening edge of each window. The top one, in the way of many wooden frames, had some play in it. He began a rapid tattoo with the flat of his hand, just where the long window catch hooked on, pausing periodically to ease the opening section to and fro. The catch began to jiggle. All he needed was patience and a little time.

Honor, to avoid Stef, had risen early and taken the bus into Brighton. It wasn't one with Martyn projecting sex appeal from the side, but a sparkling woman and a cute child peeking through fashionable spectacle frames.

From the bus stop on the Old Steine, Honor walked down on to the shingle of Brighton beach, past the fairground rides to where a series of arches under the promenade parallel with the sea were filled with gift shops, beach cafés, and watercolour artists' studios. She browsed through postcards and prints, pulling up her jacket collar against the breeze.

Families had staked their claims on the beach and, as it was low tide, there was even a ribbon of damp sand for the children to play on. Only the final few of the pier's stilts were in the water.

Behind the breakwater a noisy group, probably students, sat around a young guy who cradled a guitar. He grinned up at Honor as she crunched past, goatee beard and blond curls making him look like the result of an imp catching an angel at a weak moment, and kicked a jacket over an impressive beer stash. From the *Argus*, Honor knew that Brighton police had the power to confiscate alcohol being consumed in public places. Returning the smile, she hoped that kids only eight or ten years her junior didn't think she looked as if she could be the Beer Police. She hesitated. What if she stood and listened to the imp angel's music? Maybe they'd widen their circle to admit her and offer her a beer.

A new song began and she hovered but the circle remained closed. OK. On past the little shops, the sculpture that looked like a curved segment of a monster Easter egg, the row of little boats that constituted the Brighton yacht club, a skate park and playground, the great rusty frame that once was the West Pier and a bandstand straight out of Dickens. Finally, she walked up from the beach to find that the esplanade had widened to encompass gardens and statues and she'd crossed the boundary into Hove. Angling away from the ocean, she strolled through gardens surrounded by buttery yellow Regency houses and found herself in a crowded and busy shopping area for a late lunch and to browse the afternoon away around the shops.

At the end of the long solitary day, she caught a bus towards home, content to watch the city go by as the bus crawled through the busy traffic in Hove and Brighton, seeming never to progress more than a few yards without stopping for traffic signals, junctions or bus stops, until it began uphill to Woodingdean. There, the view was more suburban and she was almost asleep when it finally swooped down to Rottingdean.

She clambered down opposite the White Horse Hotel, where the bus would loop around and turn back, crossed the intersection and started down the slope to the Undercliff Walk – it being a lot flatter than Marine Drive – glad that today she didn't have to go through Martyn's up-the-stairs-down-the-slope routine. The sea was well on its way in, now, sucking and gobbling at the pebbles and then falling back for a breather.

Rounding a fold in the cliff, she came across Frog and the Tadpoles, toeing a soccer ball around one of the widened areas of the Undercliff Walk. She grinned. Her last encounter with Frog had gone well – once the ice down the shorts incident was behind them – ending in eating cake together.

Although he didn't grin back, he half-lifted a hand in greeting. 'Hey, Yankee Doodle.' His hair was so short that it didn't move in the breeze but the loose material of his top flapped against his body.

'Hey, Toby.'

She paused to allow the ball to cross in front of her. As she went forward, she tensed, *juuuuust* in case the ball flew back via some part of her body.

But Frog just tapped the ball behind her then fell into step alongside. 'Know what? There's a Mr Yankee Doodle hanging round. Says he's your old man.'

Honor sighed. 'Yeah.'

The ball dribbled past them and Frog trapped it with his foot. 'He asks a lot of questions.'

'About me?'

Frog tried, and failed, to flick the ball up and on to his knee, then tried again, scowling. 'About Martyn Mayfair.'

'Oh.' Disquiet trickled through her stomach. Martyn would hate it if Stef's questions got him talked about. Particularly in connection with Stef's wife. 'Did you tell him anything?'

Frog managed to flick the ball up, on to his knee and back to his foot. 'Yeah.' He grinned. 'I told him to piss off.'

'That really works for me.' Honor was filled with relief. 'Thanks for the heads up. I owe you one.'

Frog began to fall behind, lining the ball up for a mighty kick. 'Make sure it's not an icy one.'

With the last of her energy, she pulled herself up the cliffside stairway by the handrail and crossed the road on aching legs.

In her driveway, she halted. Wow – somebody had cut the grass. A wriggle of guilt. Bet Clarissa had got sick of asking her to organise it and had sent someone herself. Honor had better call her up and arrange to pay her back. She yawned and let herself into the bungalow, which was quiet and still and felt like home. And smelled like coffee.

Coffee? She hadn't been here to make coffee.

'Hiiiii honeeeee. Had a good day?' The voice was full of laughter and jubilation. And was all too familiar. And all too damned close.

Honor's head spun right so fast that she hurt her neck. And there was Stef, lounging on her sofa, his laptop open on his knee, grinning like a chimp and waggling a door key in the air. 'With me living here,' he promised, 'we'll be able to work things out.'

Chapter Thirty-Three

Martyn half-regretted agreeing that Ru could upload files for him. It wasn't that he minded Ru lounging on the sofa and gazing beadily at the laptop screen as blue lines grew and shrank to reflect progress. It was just that, however tedious he generally found it, tonight he actually could have used something to focus on.

He would have bought the iPad he'd fancied if he'd thought about Ru hogging his laptop and his password book, preventing him from working on anything else or even checking his bank account or posting on Twitter or Facebook.

He tried to read, but all he could see in front of his eyes was Honor's face, in Saltdean Park, when he'd explained to her what kind of a (sanctimonious? up himself?) guy he was. And how, having enjoyed (some of the hottest ever) sex with her, he was leaving her to scrub away her troubles until she was shiny clean enough for him.

He'd been crap at volleyball, staring blankly as the ball boinged past him. Jamie had asked him if he was hungover or getting the flu. But he was feeling worse than that. All the hurt and anger that had sustained him during the past few days had flickered and died as, from his customary post at the back of the court, he'd watched Honor climb to her feet and trail away across the grass.

He'd hadn't quite anticipated the huge sense of loss.

That slow sinking feeling that told him he'd just fucked up had stayed with him for the rest of the day. An hour ago, he'd sent her a text. *Can we talk? x*

And she hadn't replied, which probably was what he

deserved. Turning to the television, he flicked through the satellite channels, from the nature channels to Fashion TV to movies, with zero interest. Noticing that Ru's gaze had flown to the screen like a starving child outside a sweet shop, he tossed over the remote. 'You choose.' Leaving Ru flicking blissfully to South Park, he prowled into the kitchen, switching on the coffee machine, gazing into the fridge without interest.

A knock on his front door. He let the fridge swing shut. He supposed it would be Clarissa; she didn't take any classes on Sundays and was prone to turning up. He truly hadn't expected it to be Honor waiting at the top of the metal stairs, a bright red suitcase in one hand, her hair falling half-free of the band that was meant to secure it behind her head. He stared blankly, baked to the spot by a hot rush of pleasure and want.

'Hi,' she quavered. 'Can I just–?' Her lower lip – her beautiful lower lip – trembled and she bit down, ducking her head. 'I–' she tried again, but the rest of the words were strangled into a kind of unintelligible song.

'Sorry, I'll–!' With a hiccup, she spun on her heel, she and the suitcase teetering dangerously.

His hand snaked out and fastened on her elbow. 'Come *here*!' And in a moment the door was shut and Honor was this side of it, shaking with sobs, clinging, trembling, her suitcase on its side on the floor. Holding her tightly, he murmured, 'It's OK. It'll be OK,' kissing the top of her head and quashing his instinct to batter her with, 'What's wrong? Who did it?' questions.

'I'm sorry,' she gulped. 'I shouldn't have come. You've got a strong view on my situation and I respect that. I just– When I got your text–' Her fingers gripped his shirt, her words squirting out between gulps and sniffs and gasps. 'Stef broke into the bung-bungalow and he's moved his stuff in … *and won't leeeee-eave*. He was hate-hateful.'

Breathing in the fresh air that she'd brought in with her, he let her cry. Holding her was delicious, even with her heart pattering against him like a trapped bird and her tears soaking slowly into his shirt.

Finally, her head rolled and her shoulders bunched and fell on a huge sigh. 'I should-shouldn't have come to you, putting you in a situation where you'll go all English and sacrifice your principles by not sending me to find a room somewhere. I'd better go.' Her arms slackened, as if she truly did think that she was going to disengage herself and leave.

Yeah, right. His own arms tightened like wire. 'Listen,' he murmured. 'Can you hear that?'

She tried to swallow her tears to listen, tilting her head. 'What?'

He laid his cheek against her hair. 'It's the sound of my "principles" getting counselling. They've just reached the bit where they're having to face the fact that they're not principles, but jealousy.'

She shook her head. 'No. I truly respect the kind of guy you are–'

'I'm the kind that needs to review his loyalties. I've been sitting here feeling like the King of all the Dumbasses for my possessive reaction when Stef turned up. I hung my anger on the truth about Robina because it was easier than admitting that I want to rewrite your history and erase Stef from it. I'm sorry. I've got over myself, now, and I know we have to cope with reality, not wishes.'

She gave a watery gasp. Her cheek was turned against his chest, her head tucked comfortably beneath his chin. 'But I do have way too much reality. It's pretty challenging.' She sniffed. 'I don't know what to do about Stef squatting in the bungalow for free when I'm paying good rent. I don't even know how he got in. I came home and found him sitting

274

there with a big grin, and when I told him to leave he said, "No way, babe! I'm here so we can work things out." And all the time I was packing he kept saying it didn't matter how many times I left him, I should face the fact that he wasn't just going to go away.

'I had no clue about British law, whether I should call the cops or get a lawyer. I just knew I didn't want to spend the night with him.'

He sighed inside, seeing the inevitability of it leading to Clarissa's involvement and her very probably blaming him. 'I suppose Clarissa needs to know, first.'

'I didn't even think of that.' She sounded mortified. 'I panicked, I guess. Yes, I'll call Clarissa.' She fished in her pocket, as well as she could whilst still hugged close against his body, as if to make the call right there and then.

Finally, he told his arms that they could safely slacken; that Honor was OK and he had her safe. Kissing her head, he tugged the band gently from the half of her ponytail it was still clinging to, combing out her hair with his fingers and smoothing it behind her ears, down on to her shoulders, letting it run like threads of silk against his skin. 'Take it easy on yourself, you don't have to do it right now. I'll speak to her for you, tomorrow. Have you eaten?'

'Not since lunch.'

'You need something, then. Ru's here.'

'Ru?' She scrubbed at her face with her cuff. 'Oh hi, Ru,' she called, sheepishly, peeping around Martyn to where Ru was still slouched on the sofa at the far end of the apartment.

'Do you want me to go?' Ru sounded stiff and excluded.

'No, stay and eat,' Martyn said, easily. 'Cheer Honor up while I organise food.' Occupying himself with plates, bread and a big tub of his favourite Marks & Spencer pasta salad, he watched Honor trudge across the carpet and drop like a stone on to the sofa beside Ru, giving him a spontaneous hug. 'I left my husband. Turns out he didn't want to be left. He showed up.'

Ru's eyes grew round. 'You've got a husband? An American guy came in the Teapot and I wondered if he was anything to do with you. He was talking with Mum for ages.'

'Ohhhhhh shit. That sounds bad.' Honor dropped her head against the sofa back and gave a sigh from right inside her soul. 'Ru. There's something I've got to tell you because I want you to hear it from me. It will probably be a shock.'

Chapter Thirty-Four

While Martyn moved around in the kitchen, giving them space, Honor told him her story and Ru stared at her as if she'd just told him she was the Queen of England. She ended, 'So. I'm your half-sister.'

His enormous brown eyes didn't even blink.

'I guess it's a lot to take in.' She wanted to hug him again but while that had seemed fine two minutes ago, her confession had created a gulf. She needed his reaction to act as a bridge. Labouring under his stare, she tried to fill the silence, answering all the questions he wasn't asking. 'I haven't told your mom because I'm not sure she wants to know. She didn't show any signs of liking me even before I hooked up with Martyn. Just because she gave birth to me didn't guarantee she would like me, I knew that, but I was still disappointed by there not seeming to be any connection at all. She's never tried to contact me, even though it would have been easy, through Dad, who's still living in Hamilton Drives, so that should have given me a clue but ...' No reaction.

'So that made me pretty cautious about identifying myself. And as I didn't tell her, well, it made it tough to tell you. Even though I wanted to because you and me seemed to get along real well. I guess I never counted on meeting you and ... caring. I thought Stef might have told her – or you – by now but maybe he doesn't want to give me reasons not to go back to him. Not that there's any chance, but he's still hoping. Or maybe he's keeping it up his sleeve in case he needs it.'

Ru was like one of those creatures from a wildlife programme that think immobility is the same as invisibility.

Honor took a fresh breath, then went on talking, about

how it was to be brought up by her dad and grandmother and then her stepmother, Karen, about Jessamine and Zachary, trying to explain that she'd always felt a piece of her was missing or undefined and how that would be resolved by meeting the mother that had abandoned her when she was three weeks old.

Finally, he reacted. 'A real mum isn't necessarily a good mum.' It came out as a croak.

She laid her hand on his arm and he didn't snatch it away. Her chest ached with sadness. 'I've come to realise that.'

He gazed at her, blinking. 'So what's going to happen?'

'I wish I knew.'

Still talking, they drifted over to the high stools, eating just because Martyn put the food in front of them. Ru came up with questions, getting it straight in his mind who knew what about whom, and why. Tasting the relationships with his tongue, just to shake his head each time and pronounce, 'Weird.'

Honor kept blotting her eyes and felt ready to explode over the tangle of her life. With Stef squatting in her house, Martyn sitting across from her with so much remaining to be resolved, and Ru – her brother – staring at her as if wondering if she was for real.

After eating, he became quieter and even when Martyn tossed him the book of passwords and dictated wildly silly status updates to his Twitter and Facebook pages for Ru to type in, he managed only faint smiles.

Then he slapped shut the laptop, muttering, 'I better go,' and made for the front door, pausing only to shove his feet into dirty, untied running shoes before grabbing for the doorhandle.

Jumping up to watch his flight, Honor called, 'Ru! Are you going to tell her?'

Ru didn't pause. 'Nope. Course not.'

Chapter Thirty-Five

From halfway down the iron stairs, Honor could see that Stef was sitting in the teagarden of the Teapot, staring down the street, just waiting.

Obviously, he knew she hadn't spent the night at the bungalow and was smart enough to know where she'd go. Tucking Martyn's spare key in her purse and squaring her shoulders, she padded the rest of the way down to the street. As she approached, Stef pushed out the empty chair at his table with his foot. She sat, planting her elbows on the wooden top.

He grinned. 'Showdown time.'

'Fine. Then I'll shoot from the hip. You know what, Stef? It's over.'

He chose not to hear. 'You ready to come home to Hamilton Drives?'

A picture swam into her mind of her dad's blue clapboard house. And in it her father. 'I'll be going back in a while – you know, to start divorce proceedings.'

His tousled fair hair lifted in the wind. His eyes were hard. 'That's not going to happen.'

'It is.'

Ru came out with his baseball hat on back-to-front and a tea towel tucked around his waist. He hesitated when he saw Honor. She smiled at him. 'OK?'

He nodded.

'Could I get a coffee?' She realised she'd phrased it as if she was in the States and wished she'd said, 'Coffee, please,' like the English, to show Stef how well she fit in.

Ru looked from Honor to Stef.

'For me, too,' snapped Stef.

They waited, in silence, for Ru to reappear with a round tray and two tall white mugs, a milk jug and sachets of sugar. 'Thanks, Ru.' Honor watched him through the door into the tearoom and caught sight of Robina looking at her. Robina smiled. She wasn't smiling at Honor; it was just the kind of smile people give when their thoughts amuse them. But Honor still smiled back.

Stef followed the direction of her gaze. 'You know how weird she is, don't you? She knows everything there is to know about your Englishman.' He said the word *Englishman* as if it tasted bad. 'She knows when he runs and where to intercept him on his route, all his social networking platforms and that he does web design. I'll bet she has a scrapbook of his ads. Doesn't it creep you out that *she* feels like that about *him*?'

What was creeping her out was that he was talking about this right outside Robina's tearoom. Keeping her eye out for Robina to appear, Honor added milk and sugar to her coffee and took a sip. 'It's certainly an awkward situation.' She met his gaze steadily. 'My life seems to be filled with them, right now. I have stuff to sort out and changes to make.'

His brows snapped down. 'Don't you count me as one of those changes! I'm your husband. You made vows.'

'I did,' she admitted. 'But I made those vows to a different Stefan Sontag and I don't think even vows are designed to allow a woman's husband to run wild while she just has to put up with the consequences. You've chosen a life I don't want a part of.' She shivered. 'I curled up and died of humiliation, seeing you in the dock, and when they took you away to jail I felt disgust.'

He dropped his eyes, fiddling with a tube of sugar. 'It can be put in the past, Honor; Martyn Mayfair and all of my pranks. I'll mend my ways, I swear. I'll never make you feel humiliated or disgusted again.' Suddenly, his eyes were tawny bright. 'Our life is still waiting for us. We can go home and get our apartment back, put our lives back how they were. Only better.'

'With neither of us having a job?'

He scrabbled for arguments. 'OK, we'll start over, somewhere new.' He looked less sure of this idea. 'You still have all your licences, you can get a job, and maybe I'll start my own business so my record won't count against me with an employer.'

'Doing what? You never got yourself a career or a skill, Stef. And we don't have enough money to open up a diner.' She fumbled her way to her feet before the tears of pity came and Stef thought she was weakening. 'I hate that I'm pouring cold water over everything you offer. But, I'm sorry, it's not going to happen.'

He jumped up, screeching his chair back. 'Then I'll just have to make it happen, won't I?'

Martyn returned from his run, cooled down, stretched, and showered. Honor was out, so he picked up his phone and called Clarissa.

'I thought your phone didn't make outgoing calls to mine and that's why I always call you,' she greeted him.

He wasn't in the mood to be guilted. 'Honor's got a problem with the bungalow. She has a squatter.'

A pause. Clarissa sounded guarded. 'Squatter?'

He hesitated, alerted by her uncharacteristically mild reaction. 'You don't sound shocked or horrified or outraged. I thought you'd go ballistic.'

'I just–' She seemed to be choosing her words. 'Would the squatter be Honor's husband, by any chance?'

His heart gave a thud. 'How did you know?'

She sounded uncomfortable. 'He was there when I called. About the lawns.'

'In the bungalow?'

'Um … outside.'

He let a silence grow, hoping she'd fill it. She didn't. 'He's inside now,' he prompted, helpfully.

'I didn't let him in. Or not into the house.' Clarissa sounded defensive.

'So where did you let him into?'

'He said that he'd cut the grass so I let him in the garage.'

'And I suppose he found a window open at the back,' Martyn finished, grimly. 'And now he's in, he's refusing to get out.'

Clarissa sighed. 'Then, evidently, I've unintentionally caused a situation. But if he's her husband–? Martyn, it's obvious that you've got a thing about Honor, it's been written on you all summer. But she's married. I presume there's been some issue, for her to have come here without her husband, but he's here now, so he wants to patch things up. Don't get involved! You know how I feel about people who interfere in other people's marriages.' Her voice tightened. 'If I gave him access to the bungalow it was inadvertent but it's probably for the best. I'm not going to apologise if it's stopped you getting mixed up in their problems. And I can't quite blame him for fighting to get his wife back. In fact,' she ended, defiantly, 'I applaud it.'

Martyn took a deep breath. He counted to ten. He reminded himself that Clarissa was his mother and she loved him. And that it wasn't long since her own marriage had ended and it had caused her enormous pain. 'But Stef could be as mad as a box of frogs. You don't know why she left him or what he did once he got Honor alone in that bungalow. So she's moved in with me.' He ended the call feeling he'd been as polite as he could be, under the circumstances.

After Honor had gone – back to her fucking fancy, male-model boyfriend, presumably, Stef sat for a while, letting the white heat fade. It had seemed like a good idea, planting himself in her rented house, but it had backfired big time. He hadn't thought it through. Underestimated Honor's desire to keep distance between herself and him.

Finally, he picked up the order check that Ru had left on the table and wandered into the tearoom, pausing inside the door and letting his eyes adjust to the dimmer light. Ru, enveloped in a cloud of steam, was busy at the steel sinks with his back to the kitchen. Pink-hair lady was cutting crosses in baked potatoes and piling in cheese. Conveniently, Robina was closest to the counter.

He walked soundlessly to the open flap, leaned in and touched her sleeve. When she glanced up from balancing little silver balls on whorls of frosting, he jerked his head and stepped back, so the others couldn't see him.

Robina followed him out. 'All you need to do,' he said, 'is ring her when I give you the word. That OK?'

Robina smiled like a mischievous child. 'Aren't you going to tell me why?'

He made a conspiratorial face. 'Honey, that would be no fun at all.'

Paying her for the two cups of coffee, he left, wandering along The Butts, stopping and gazing into shop windows – many of which, he thought, needed the salt cleaning off of them – and then crossed to the other side of the road and dawdled like a tourist, turning his face up to the sun, which had decided to grace Eastingdean with its presence, watching white fluffy clouds drift by.

When he reached the Starboard Walk shops he meandered, idly, into the car park, glancing around. And then up. Around the outbuildings and the dumpsters. Then he wandered out, looked at a few more shop windows, and rambled back off to the bungalow.

Chapter Thirty-Six

Honor had been staying with Martyn for several days. Having flown from the bungalow in a snit, she found herself with an ill-considered mish mash of possessions and a feeling of camping in someone else's space.

When her phone rang, displaying the number of the Eastingdean Teapot, she answered cautiously. And was shocked to hear Robina's voice. 'Honor? I need you to come along and sign some crap the taxman wants, to cover the time you were working here.'

'OK.' Honor made her voice neutral. 'I'll be along this afternoon.'

'I need you to do it now.' Grudgingly, Robina explained. 'Certain stuff has to be in on certain days, in this country, so I need to post it quickly. And the last thing I want is the taxman taking an interest in my business because of you.'

'I guess I could come now.' Martyn was out running.

Honor entered the cool interior of the tearoom ten minutes later with mixed feelings. Some of the time she'd loved working in the sweet atmosphere of the Teapot; some of the time she'd been frustrated, put upon and frazzled. She looked around for Ru but saw only Aletta, patiently filling bowls with tube sachets of white and brown sugar.

Robina and Sophie were staffing the kitchen. 'Oh, you're here.' Robina snapped. 'Sit down and I'll get the paperwork.'

Honor sat, listening to the slamming of drawers and cupboards.

Then Sophie half-smiled in Honor's direction, and followed. 'But, Robbie,' Honor heard. 'I don't know which forms you mean.'

And Robina growling, 'Those *forms*! I've seen them; they're here somewhere.'

It got noisier. Robina's voice got louder, Sophie's more plaintive.

After twenty minutes, Honor lost patience and called through, 'Call me again when you've found them.'

Robina snapped, 'I need you to wait. They can't have gone far.'

Fifteen more minutes crept by. Sophie came out and filled orders, looking upset and puzzled. Honor got tired of waiting. Then she left. When Robina had the forms to hand, she'd return.

Apart from that tense little scene, Honor thought she was approaching pretty close to heaven. Martyn not having a shoot until the following week and Honor being currently unemployed gave them a lot of time. He took her walking on the Downs, the rolling moors just inland of the coast – he called this being 'up on the Downs', which made her giggle. They spent a day on the pier – riding four times on the roller coaster, rattling around higher than every other ride, swooping over the sea, screaming as they looped the loop. Well, she screamed, he laughed and called her wussy. They swam, wandered around The Lanes and watched a gay wedding in Kemptown. Martyn even went into Pretty Old with her and shamed Peggy into gifting her a glass inkwell that had come as part of a house clearance, because, he said, he was sure that Peggy must have ripped Honor off plenty in the past, her being an American.

'Not that much,' was Peggy's defence, 'because she's not completely American.' But she chuckled and wrapped up the pretty inkwell for Honor. It stood on a windowsill in Martyn's bedroom, collecting rainbows from the sunlight.

They ran together a couple of times, although he still took most morning runs on his own, harder, faster and further than Honor could manage.

They made love. A lot. In his bed, on the floor, on the sofa, in the pool of sunlight that came through the French doors in his room – also harder, faster and further than Honor had before. But she kept up with that OK. He made her feel so hot she thought she might melt.

Sometimes they then scrunched up together in the big corner bath, soaping each others' bodies and exchanging stories from their lives.

What they didn't do was face up to reality.

Honor knew she had to – and soon. Using Martyn's computer because she'd left hers when she'd packed so haphazardly at the bungalow, she'd just received an email from Jessamine. *Is Stef still there? Are you OK? I miss you. Dad's worried – he's about ready to get on a plane to England.*

She responded, *Tell Dad not to worry. I'll be back for a while, soon, and I'm guessing if I go home then Stef will surely follow.*

She gave a huge sigh. Martyn sat down on the sofa beside her, swooped her up and arranged her on his lap, kissing her cheekbones. 'Trouble?'

'Oh, you know. My sister emailed. My dad's worried. And I know I have to go home soon and deal with stuff.' She let her head settle back into the crook of his neck. 'I'm getting my head around it.'

His warm arms tightened as if he didn't want her to go, even as he said, 'I suppose so.'

She fiddled with the laptop, shinily black, running her fingers around the keys. 'I want to see Ru before I go. I know he was freaked by what I told him and I need to know he's going to be OK in the end.'

'Text him.'

'Hm.' She drew more patterns. 'It's Thursday but I don't

feel like going to self-defence class. And I'm kind of hoping that Ru doesn't need it any more.'

'So invite him for fish and chips. I'm sure he'll take that bait.'

'OK.' Still snuggled on his lap, she took out her phone. *Join us for fish n chips tonight? Martyn's, at 7.*

In only a few minutes she received, *OK.*

She was ultra-relieved when Ru arrived at seven, easing himself into the room with just one familiar smile, half-seen behind his hair. Honor gave him a quick hug. It was like hugging a plank that wouldn't get its hands out of its pockets but he didn't actually resist.

'I'm starving,' was all he said. 'Shall I go and get the chips?' And Honor realised that he didn't want or didn't need to talk about what she'd told him. He just wanted everything to be OK.

'Great,' she said. 'I'll give you the money.'

Afterwards, they arranged themselves around the sofas, too full to do more than sit for a while. Ru reached for Martyn's laptop. 'Can I do my Facebook and stuff?'

'Of course.' Martyn had begun flicking through the movie channels on TV. He pulled Honor's legs over his.

Honor watched Ru, his mouth half-open as he focused on the screen. 'So, how are things with Robina?'

Ru shrugged. ''Bout the same.' He tapped briskly. 'I didn't tell her.' It was the first indication he'd given that Honor's confession had ever happened.

'Probably best. Has she said whether she's found that form she wants me to sign?'

His eyes were still glued to the computer. 'What form?'

'She called me and told me I had to sign some form for the British tax authorities.'

Ru frowned.

'Then she couldn't find it and slammed around, quite

287

obviously not wanting me there and blaming me for the fact that I had to be.'

Ru's eyebrows shot up.

'So I left her to her snit. She didn't mention it to you, at all?' Honor persisted, nudging him with her foot to break the spell that had glued his eyes to the laptop.

Ru put his head on one side. 'Martyn? Are you gay?'

'Don't think so.' Martyn winked at Honor. 'I don't even think I'm confused or curious. Why?'

Ru read from the screen. 'Your Facebook status update says that you are. And that you're grooming *me* for ...' he squinted, '"delicious discoveries". And you're going to change your name to Mary.'

Slowly, the grin faded from Martyn's face. 'I hope you're joking.'

Turning the laptop around, Ru passed it over.

'Fucking *hell!*' Martyn exploded. 'What the hell is going on?' He tapped rapidly at the keys. 'A whole series of status updates has been posted about my supposed interest in adolescents "of either persuasion". And – holy *fuck* – slagging off clients I've worked for and saying they haven't paid me or they test their products on puppies!'

'You've been fraped,' Ru observed.

'What's frape?'

'Facebook rape – frape,' Ru clarified. 'You must have left your accounts open on your machine and someone decided to post a lot of stuff pretending it's you. It happens.'

Martyn frowned at him. 'But I've never done that.' Grimly, he returned to the computer. Then he sat back. Stared at Ru. 'The Facebook and Twitter passwords have been changed.'

Honor swallowed. She opened her mouth but Martyn's phone began to ring and he pulled it out of his pocket, glancing at the screen. 'Hi, Ace?'

Ace responded at such a volume that no speaker phone

was needed for Honor to hear, 'Martyn, what the fuck is going on? When I try and open the Agency website it clicks me through to a website called www.allmodelsrperverts.com, full of porno images of you and some of my other clients!' He paused, and his voice dropped a decibel or two. 'They're Photoshopped images, of course, sticking your head on to an image of some porn star's body – hard porn at that. The agency's Facebook and Twitter pages are full of supposed confessions from you about your perversions.'

Martyn's knuckles were white. 'My Facebook and Twitter pages have been messed with, too.'

'How have you let it happen?'

'It hasn't come from me,' Martyn rapped. 'Did you think I'd found a "destroy your career" button on my laptop? Some bastard has hacked everything.' His fingers were busy on the keys as he talked. 'Shit, it looks like he's hacked into every single site I maintain. Leave it with me, Ace and I'll sort it.'

He threw down the phone and stared, white-faced, at the screen.

Honor forced herself to speak. 'It's Stef,' she croaked.

Martyn didn't look at her. 'Fits with what you've told me. Bastard.' He breathed hard. 'The only missing part of the puzzle is how he got my passwords.'

And he looked at Ru.

'No!' Honor, exhaled her outrage, jerking upright.

Ru looked startled and then affronted. 'I didn't give them to him! Fuck off.'

Shaking with rage, Martyn turned the laptop towards Ru, showing him the naked figures cavorting across the screen under crude headings. 'You're the only other person who's had access to the passwords. Did you give my notebook to him? Did he pay you? Or is this some sick way of getting back at Honor, and you timed it to happen whilst you were here, so you could watch the fun?'

'The book's right there.' Ru pointed to the slim black book, lying in its normal place on the footstool.

'Martyn, I'm sure it wasn't Ru,' Honor began, hotly. 'How could you think it was? Stef must have got in here and–'

'Don't talk such bollocks, my front door is next thing to Fort Knox. It's too convenient that your new-found baby brother knew where to find my passwords and your ex-husband has used them to try and destroy both my careers in one swipe.'

Ru jumped up, looking much more child than adolescent. In a few quick strides he was at the front door and gone.

Honor stared at Martyn. 'I'm so sorry. This is all because of me.'

All his attention was fixed on his computer. 'No, it's my fault. I know that married women always fuck everything up.'

'I'll go see him and make him change it all back.'

'He won't just be waiting there to be discovered–' he began. But Honor snatched up her bag and followed Ru out of the door, clanging down the metal stairs, swinging around at the bottom and setting off at a dead run for the bungalow.

Chapter Thirty-Seven

She was too late. Of course. She hadn't held out much hope; Stef was too neat in the execution of his pranks not to have left himself time to jump ship.

In the silent bungalow, Honor strode past the sitting room, strewn with magazines and empty beer cans, and the kitchen with its sink full of dirty dishes and a bulging bin of cartons. In the bedroom, the bed was unmade. On the pillow was a note. *See you in Hamilton Drives, babe.*

It blurred before her eyes. Her instinct was to phone a cab and set off in pursuit.

But she knew she would be too late.

The damage was done. Damage to Martyn and his careers. Because of her. He had been right about her all along.

Stolidly, she rang American Airlines and was able to switch the round trip part of her ticket to a flight at eight thirty in the morning. The internet got her a room overnight close to London Heathrow and a further phone call got her a taxi to get her there, leaving in one hour.

Eyes boiling, she switched off the UK cell phone.

Then she straightened up the little bungalow, washing the dishes, throwing out the cans and cartons, packing the things she'd left when she had run to Martyn's, and was standing in the drive when the taxi arrived.

In the cab, she closed her eyes, unable to bear to see the last of Marine Drive, the ocean or her route down to the Undercliff Walk. She'd hate to glimpse somebody she knew – Frog scowling, one of the Mayfair sisters looking curious, Peggy wistful at the departure of a lucrative customer.

Taking out her US phone, she checked with the driver

that it was OK to plug it into the car cigarette lighter, then switched on. She checked her watch. At home, the working day would be ending. All at once, she longed to be back in the thickly wooded hills around Hamilton Drives, Connecticut, where families would be taking picnics out to the lake to cool down after the hot August day; clapboard houses, the white wooden church where she and Stef had had a pretty June wedding, field stone walls, familiar traffic systems where everybody drove on the right side of the road. She clicked on **Jessamine** in her phone book, waiting out the silences and clicks until the ring tone sounded in her ear.

'Honor?' Jessamine answered with that peculiar mix of delight, irritation and worry that family members reserve for other family members who don't call often enough.

Honor coaxed her voice to emerge on the light side of neutral. 'Hi, Jessie! Guess what? My flight gets into JFK at eleven-twenty tomorrow morning, local. I'll get the airport shuttle to New Milton. It would be great if you could meet me.'

Jessamine didn't hesitate. 'What's wrong?'

Honor forced a laugh, swaying with the car as it breasted a rise and swung hard left at the same time. 'Why should anything be wrong?' She felt slightly sick. Maybe it was the fish and chips that she'd eaten too enthusiastically. Or motion sickness.

Or she was just sick with sorrow. She forced her eyes wide open so she wouldn't see visions on the insides of her lids, of Martyn, beyond angry as his careers disintegrated, Ru haunted and sad. And suddenly her in-breath turned to rags and the out-breath was a sob and once she started she couldn't stop and she could hear her sister's voice, across the miles, crooning in her ear, 'Don't cry, Honor! I'm so sorry, I'm so sorry for whatever has made you so unhappy. Come home. You come home right away.'

And she cried harder than ever, because that's exactly what she was going to do.

Martyn worked grimly through the tedious processes of hacking out the hacker.

If it had been just his own web presences compromised he would have gone straight after Honor. But with the agency and other agency clients involved …

It took him about ten seconds to realise that both Twitter and Facebook were all-too-wearily-familiar with compromised accounts and that one only had to reset passwords and delete the crap to right the whole thing.

The endless posts were sexually imaginative, defamatory and eye-watering in turn – or sometimes all at once – but in an amazingly short time he had returned normality and sanity to the social networking pages, the agency's and his own, and plastered apologies and explanations all over the place.

Ace rang again. 'Martyn, DownJo are going out of the stratosphere! Twitter and Facebook are alive with stories about child labour being used in the manufacture of their products.'

'Yes, I get it, Ace!' Martyn almost shouted. 'I've put up explanations – for God's sake, get Tweeting those links. Tell DownJo to do the same. And leave me alone to fix the mess.' As he worked, he was savagely aware that he had – again – hurt Honor, her white, shocked face swimming in front of his eyes. Drumming his fingers as he waited for emails full of security questions and long involved password replacements, he promised himself that the moment he'd gone through the excruciating 'compromised security process' with his web host and returned all of the sites to normal, he would abase himself with grovelling apologies.

His host company advertised on their site that they would

respond to security problems within an hour and that certainly was when they began their co-operation.

But he couldn't believe how long it all took. Ace rang every twenty minutes demanding progress reports, driving Martyn nearly demented. Then the host's helpdesk rang him and that kept him tied to the machine, glancing at his watch, but at least reduced Ace to a 'call waiting' beep that he could ignore.

He tried to ring Honor but got only her voicemail.

He stabbed at keys and clicked on links, fielded phone calls, personally reassuring an irate executive officer from le Dur, dragged away from an evening out, agreeing to record an explanation to go on the le Dur website and on YouTube, swearing continuously under his breath, feeling as if his head was going to explode with information frustration overload, fingers fumbling. Waited for new emails with fresh instructions. Rang Honor again, heart thundering. Where the hell was she?

Finally, finally, his hosts used their back-up files to restore all sites to the previously unsullied glory and he sagged in relief. He already had the laptop half-thrown down, ready to race off to the bungalow to begin his search for her when realisation hit him that if Stef had all his passwords for websites and social networking, it followed that he would have the password for Martyn's email account, too, and would be able to gain possession of *all the new passwords mailed over the past few hours* and repeat the whole appalling process. He snatched the machine out of mid-air and raced through the re-resetting of all his passwords – beginning with his email – and then clicked furiously through each site.

He groaned with relief. No further meltdown.

Then, to his fury, he saw an email drop into his inbox from **Stefan Sontag.** The subject line was: *Nothing's foolproof.*

The bottom dropped out of his stomach. His brain

screamed *virus!* at him. But he couldn't make himself delete the email unread. Slowly, he clicked on it.

In case you're wondering, pretty boy, I climbed up to your French doors in the roof. You ought to keep them locked. Your security's hardly foolproof – not for this talented fool. Then followed images of the relevant pages of his password book, including one of Stef holding the book and beaming to demonstrate how the pages had simply been held up in front of the laptop's own webcam. Easy enough, then, for Stef to email them to himself.

Tomorrow – he looked at his watch: *today* – he would take his machine into his computer whizz in Brighton and get it checked out for viruses. But he was at the limits of his patience, endurance and talent and until then the machine could stay off.

He texted Ace to tell him all the dials should now be set to zero, texted Ru: *Really sorry, I know it wasn't you, I just lost my temper.* Then rang Honor and, again, got her voicemail.

Ru replied: *Yeh OK cd c u were freaked.* Martyn squinted at his watch. Past four in the morning? He checked with the clocks in the kitchen, incredulous when they said the same. And felt worse than ever that his text had probably woken Ru up.

But the time didn't stop him pulling on his shoes and setting off for the bungalow, knowing that he'd hardly be welcome when he got there. But he *must get to Honor*. He knew Stef wouldn't still be at the bungalow. If Honor had found him, she would have phoned Martyn. So she was hiding out from him. And he couldn't blame her. And he hated himself for making her feel like that.

Breathing much faster than the exertion demanded, he made the distance in two minutes, scarcely noticing the palest blue-and-apricot dawn and the steely sea. His feet slowed as he reached the drive. There were no lights on in the bungalow and, unlike the houses either side, no closed curtains. Taking the stairs in three giant strides, he pressed on the bell and pounded on the door.

Nothing stirred.

He tried Honor's phone again. *It has not been possible to connect your call …*

Cursing, he cut the connection, pressing so hard that the screen bowed. He rang Clarissa. She sounded alarmed. 'Martyn? What's the matter?'

'I need the key to the bungalow.'

'Now? It's the middle of the night, Martyn, has Honor locked herself out? What about …?' She trailed away.

'Exactly,' he agreed. 'What about her husband, who got into the bungalow without her permission? What about if Honor's locked in there with him and he won't let her answer the door?'

'I'll come right down.'

'Good. Because in ten minutes, I start smashing windows.' Martyn paced the patio and glared at the hawthorn bushes that filled the space between the bungalow and its neighbours, almost impossible to penetrate, squeeze past or climb over. As a key was about to arrive, he decided against trying to scale fences in and out of neighbouring gardens or doing anything else to wake the neighbours. The last thing he needed right now was a patrol car wailing up with its lights flashing.

Bad enough that the key arrived clutched in the hand of Clarissa, who had woken up enough to want to cling on to it whilst she hissed an interrogation into the early morning hush. Martyn listened for five seconds, decided that that was about four too long, and snitched the key out of her fingers. 'You stay here,' he instructed, jamming the key into the lock. But, of course, she followed him in.

It didn't take him long to race through the few rooms, seeing them neat, clean … and empty. In the bedroom, he threw open the wardrobe and the drawers. Empty. Empty. Empty.

Fighting the urge to roar with rage, he picked up a note from the floor. *See you in Hamilton Drives, babe.*

Bastard.

Underneath Stef's words, Honor had written, *It's time for me to go home. xxx*

She'd known that he'd come looking – the message was undoubtedly for him.

It seemed as if the world had hit the pause button.

Clarissa came up quietly and, without a word, he showed her the note, hot with shame.

She made a small, inarticulate noise of pain. 'Martyn, what I did was wrong–'

He shook his head. He'd done enough blame shifting. He did something he should do more often and put his arm around Clarissa. 'It's my fault that she's gone.'

Chapter Thirty-Eight

Honor felt as if she hadn't slept for days. In fact, she calculated fuzzily, battling a luggage cart that wanted to travel in circles, it was only about a day-and-a-half. It just felt like more. After lying awake all night at the hotel, she hadn't been able to sleep on the flight, staring at movies without taking them in and picking at the airline food, tension banging inside her head.

Still, it was good to be home. Even if it was odd to be home.

Most of the voices around her were American, but she'd grown used to the pecking English accent and the ironic humour. And everyone was dressed for summer here because there would definitely be one, unlike the crazy English weather that would fry you one day and drown you the next.

Exiting the Arrivals hall she sagged, wishing she'd booked her transportation between the airport and Hamilton Drives ahead. But then she heard her name and suddenly there was long-haired Jessamine in shorts, waving, and even grinning Zach home from Texas, looking too big and manly in black denim cut offs to be her little brother.

And her dad, buttoned up in a tan golf shirt, who crossed the polished floor, yanked her from behind her luggage cart and into a bear hug. 'When Will rang last night and said that Stefan had just gotten home, alone, I nearly lost my mind. If Jessamine hadn't found out about the same time that you were on your way, too, I would have jumped on the first plane to England.'

He sounded so fiercely protective that Honor felt fresh

tears prickling. 'Well, here I am,' was all she could whisper.

The arms tightened. 'It's so good to see you, honey.'

In no time, she found herself packed into the front passenger seat of her dad's blue Ford Escape, though Zach-long-legs should have been awarded that prime spot. Zach tugged her ponytail and said, 'Did you get to see many castles, Honor?' And everyone talked about England and history and Honor's trip, lightly, neutrally. Nobody mentioned Stef or jail or the way that Honor had taken off without a word.

Next thing, they were drawing up outside the double garage doors at her father's house and Honor realised that somewhere, as the Escape rolled soporifically along route 7, her eyes had closed. She'd zoned out of the family conversation, missed the sunlit lake flickering through the trees and missed driving through her home town and seeing the mall and the church and all the places that she'd known since she was a child. Already, Zach was dragging out her cases while Garvin put his arm around her and steered her indoors.

In the large, well-remembered kitchen, Honor stood still, just letting home flood into her. A tall woman was waiting, smile at the ready. 'Karen! How are you?' Guiltily, Honor realised that she hadn't asked after Karen on the whole trip north from the airport.

Karen gave her a hug. 'Hi, Honor. Welcome home.' And, miraculously, she didn't give out any lectures. Karen might have a certain 'my way or the highway' aspect to her personality, but at least she wasn't asking why Honor had run home. Like, had she done anything stupid. Like falling in love with someone when you weren't completely free to. Like messing up that person's life. She just glanced at Garvin with something like relief.

In an instant, Honor saw not a partisan mom – or not only a partisan mom – but a woman who had taken on someone else's kid, a kid who had never hesitated to remind her that she wasn't her real mom, even though she was the woman who had made Honor's dad happy.

She felt a twinge of shame. 'It's good to see you, Karen. I guess I'm imposing on you–'

'Not on family,' said Karen, simply. 'I got your room ready for however long you want to stay.'

That's when Honor began to cry.

Jessamine dragged her into her arms. 'Do you want to talk about it?'

Wildly, Honor shook her head.

Garvin: 'You maybe ought to, honey.'

Zach: 'Can any of us do anything to help?'

Honor gulped. 'No-o-oo.' But their sympathy and love made her cry harder, blubbing great sobs around sentence fragments. 'Ru won't know I've gone ... I feel so bad about him.'

'Is Ru a guy you hooked up with?' asked Jessamine, so obviously trying her hardest to understand.

'Nooooo,' howled Honor, laying her head on Jessie's shoulder. 'My bro-oth-ther. Rufus Gordon.'

'Oh, yeah, Rufus the brother,' breathed Zach.

Jessamine patted Honor's back. 'Oh no, another brother! No wonder you're upset.'

'This must seem really weird to you two,' Honor hiccupped. 'But he's fourteen and Robina isn't the ideal mom. I got to really love him.'

'It's only a little bit weird,' soothed Jessamine. 'We know what a good big sister you are.'

Honor unwound from around poor Jessie, who must be feeling hot and damp, and took a deep breath. 'I have to find Stef.' She ignored the exchange of dubious glances around the table. 'Dad, do you know if he's staying with Will?'

'I guess he is. Should I call Will and check?'

Honor rubbed her eyes. 'No, I'll just go on over. There's no telling what he'll do if he gets advance notice I'm going to show up.'

She borrowed her dad's car, even though she knew by that spaced-out, distant, grit-eyed feeling that she was way too exhausted to drive. Her dad knew it, too, because he'd said, 'I'll drive you when you're ready.' But she waited until he was on the phone and slipped his keys off the row of hooks in the kitchen and sneaked out.

Now she thought that maybe she ought to have sneaked Jessamine or Zach out to drive for her, too, because driving when she was too tired to think straight couldn't be good.

Luckily, Will's house wasn't far – what was far, in Hamilton Drives? – and so she wasn't a public menace for more than a few minutes. And, whaddya know, there was Stef, sitting on the porch on the swing seat, eating ice cream with one hand and tapping away on his laptop with the other, looking up with a crooked grin as she barrelled into the drive and as close as she could get to the porch without running over the flower beds.

She put the car in park and jumped down.

'Hey, babe,' Stef called, cautiously, as if weighing up her mood.

Set-faced, she marched up and glared down at him. 'Put them back.'

He paused. 'Put what back?' Thoughtfully, he gave a couple of taps to the keyboard.

She sent him a death glare. 'Don't mess with me over this, Stef. Put them back. Put all those websites and Twitter and Facebook accounts back exactly as you found them. Get rid of the porn and the fake sites. Put. Them. All. Back.'

Stef lifted his brows, his eyes calculating as he absorbed her words. Then he smiled. 'If you're going to get a divorce, why should I do anything for you?'

'Because what you've done is wrong, you've threatened someone's career and you want to put it right?'

He pulled a considering face and then shook his head. 'Nope. That isn't it.' His fingers tapped some more. Then a slow smile spread over his face. 'OK, I'll make sure all those sites are exactly as they used to be. All you have to do is stay away from that pretty English boy and give our marriage another go. Come back to me, babe. You're "Honor-bound" to.' A joke, but his eyes told her that he was deadly serious.

Chapter Thirty-Nine

'My mother called me Freedom.' But, slowly, resignedly, she took the seat beside him, sinking into the dark green cushion of the swing.

He sat absolutely still, as if she were one of the wild squirrels that skittered up and down the nearby sour gum trees and he knew that any sudden movement would send her whirling from the porch.

'Your mother doesn't even know who you are. Babe, we're childhood sweethearts and I love you. I'm sorry that my pranks got me sent to jail and I get how hard that was on you. But I'm straightening myself out. I swear. We can begin with a clean sheet and I'll be the man you want me to be. Stay home, Honor. Let's try again. We can work things out.'

The softness of the swing cushion surrounded her, as if it thought she was back where she ought to be. She looked into his face. His tousled hair and eyes the colour of ginger. Thought of never seeing Martyn again and her heart gave a great spasm. She swallowed, noisily. 'OK,' she whispered. 'I guess now Martyn's careers are screwed because of me … You put those sites back as they were, right now.'

His smile turned to satisfaction. 'OK, babe. It'll just take me a few minutes.'

He put the bowl of ice cream on the floor to free both hands, his fingers flying over the keys. Honor watched, remembering Martyn's face when he'd discovered what Stef had done to him. The thunder. The distress. And she knew that what she was about to do was worth it, to save his career. Careers.

It didn't seem to take Stef long. He spun the laptop around and passed it over. 'There.'

She checked out Martyn's site and the site of Ace Smith Model Management. Martyn's Facebook page. No porn. No defamatory messages. Her shoulders melted with relief and fatigue fizzed at the periphery of her vision like a waiting black swarm. 'That's good.' She stooped to lay the computer down on the wooden porch floor, the planks shrunken and separated from decades of Connecticut summers, and picked up Stef's ice cream bowl.

With a swift movement, she inverted it, dumping the contents on the computer keyboard.

'*Honor–*!'

She squished the melting blobs right between the keys, rubbing circles that forced it, creamy, shiny, into every crevice.

Stef rose slowly to his feet, his voice shaking. 'That's not even funny. My laptop – I spent a fortune on that, I doubled the RAM, the graphics card is–'

She clambered to her feet, swaying with weariness. 'It's a prank, Stef. Pranks *aren't* funny. They cause pain and they screw with people's lives.'

'It's criminal damage–'

'Yeah.' She folded her arms, leaning a hip on the porch rail to keep herself on her feet. 'Call the cops. I have to speak to them anyway. To tell them about you committing identity theft again.'

He scowled. But there was uncertainty in his eyes. 'They won't be interested in something that happened outside of the state.'

'Let's just put it to the test.'

Standoff. She stepped forward, so that he could read in her face how deadly serious she was. 'But I won't talk to the cops – for you, *babe*. If you sign those divorce papers when they're served and forget all about us giving our marriage another go.'

His face set like stone, eyes flat. 'OK,' he conceded, eventually. 'I guess I don't have a choice. What in the hell's happened to you? This isn't "Honor-able".'

She pushed the laptop closer to him with her toes, the ice cream melting and dripping from the edges. 'Sometimes, I'm really not in that "Honor-able" little compartment you try to squeeze me into.' But her heart ached for him. For the Stef he used to be and all the Stefs he wouldn't be, as long as he could only turn his intellect to mischief instead of making a life. She made her voice gentle. 'There can't be a marriage where there's no trust or respect.'

She left him standing on the shady porch as she climbed into the car, turned around in the drive and headed for her father's house.

By the time she pulled up, she was so tired she could hardly see. Her last shreds of energy had gone into the final Honor-Stef confrontation.

Karen was at the stove, sizzling something in a wok, and had already set one end of the table while Garvin worked at the other. He sprang up, lines of anxiety all over his face. 'Where the hell did you skip off to this time?'

Honor hung her tired arms around him. 'Sorry, Dad. I guess I stole your car. Do you mind if I don't talk about it, just yet? I'm going upstairs and I'm going to sleep for a week. Karen, that dinner smells delicious but I can't eat a thing.'

Garvin hugged her, hard, with all the unconditional, unquestioning love she'd had from him all of her life. 'OK, honey. You go sleep.'

Chapter Forty

Her cell phone informed her that it was 07.13 Eastern Daylight Saving Time, Saturday August 10th in Hamilton Drives, CT, USA. The weather was sunny and already 72 degrees.

She had slept for more than twelve hours. She lay under the single sheet that was all she needed in the summer and blinked at the sun edging the blinds, trying to orientate herself. She was in her childhood room at home, pearly pink and ivory, and the blind rattled in the morning breeze in the old familiar way. She swallowed. Her phone might as well have said, *You're back where you started. Now what?*

She closed her eyes again.

The next time she woke it was nearly ten and the household was alive. She could hear her father and Karen laughing downstairs and Zach's voice from his room, probably on the phone.

She'd hardly noticed last night that her old bathroom had been made into a wet room, with a big chrome showerhead and a crystal clear screen. Now she stood beneath the deluge and let the water rouse her, before dressing in shorts and a T from the bags Zach had brought up for her, and drying her hair. She hadn't answered the question *Now what?* yet but figured it could be left until after the weekend. Then she'd have to decide, and maybe do something sensible like get all her belongings in one place–

She thought of the red suitcase she'd left in Martyn's apartment and turned her mind swiftly away. There was nothing there that couldn't be replaced if ... If he didn't contact her when he saw all his sites restored to perfection.

Sometime today she was going to have to get all superhero

and turn her UK phone on and see if he'd been trying to call. And hope it wasn't to say, 'Let's just call it quits.' That would plunge her into an abyss of grief she wasn't yet strong enough to plumb. Her heart already felt leaden enough to drag her to the edge.

Whatever happened with Martyn, she would call Ru, soon, maybe tomorrow. She would call Ru and keep calling him, because she was a continuing thread in his life, whereas, in Martyn's, she could be no more than a loose end. Maybe one he wished he could unpick.

She shook away those thoughts and concentrated on her hair, braiding it to one side of her neck and capturing it in a white band.

Pasting on a serene expression, she ran downstairs to join her family. Judging from the sympathetic looks, the serene expression wasn't fooling anyone, but at least, even if they were bursting to, nobody said, 'So how *are* you?' or 'What went wrong?', which would be guaranteed to melt her to tears.

In a kitchen that went with someone who liked to cook – a range, copper pans and lethal looking knives – Karen, her blonde hair loose around her head, poured Honor coffee.

Jessamine had ready one of her customary massive hugs. 'How about a movie, later? We might even let Zachary come with us, seeing as he's home till he goes back to college.'

'Gee, thanks, a chick flick,' mocked Zach, tugging Honor's hair.

She ruffled his, which he'd let grow long in front, in return. 'So how was Texas?'

Zach grinned from behind the hair she'd dragged over his eye, reminding her of Ru. 'Hot. I fit right in.'

Garvin held a file as if he'd meant to work, looking over his reading glasses. 'It's good to see you kids all together.' Which produced a ball-sized lump in Honor's throat and she had to blow her nose.

Karen shook chicken breasts in a bag full of something to season them and then put them in the refrigerator, taking out salad to wash.

'Looks to me like a barbecue,' Honor commented, joining her at the sink, as she always would have.

Karen smiled. 'I thought it would be nice, while everybody's together. It's too hot to cook in here. But I can do this if you want to talk to your dad – Oh, there's the door.' She slipped away up the hall.

Honor took over the washing of the salad, half-listening to Zach's account of his internship with a global engineering concern, showing him that he had a whole lot to learn.

From the hallway, she heard Karen say, 'Hi there!' as she might to a stranger.

A deep rumble answered her and Honor's hands stilled.

Then Jessamine looked up through the kitchen doorway and said, 'Whoa!' under her breath, as Karen stepped back in, her voice the same mix of curiosity and admonishment with which she used to greet one of Honor's new dates. 'Honor, you have a visitor.'

And Martyn stepped in behind her, tall and impressive in black jeans and white shirt, a holdall in his hand.

Zach rose and so did Garvin. Martyn, usually so much the courteous Englishman, ready with his handshakes and his slow smile, didn't take his eyes off Honor to acknowledge that there was any other person in the room.

So everyone turned to look at Honor, standing at the sink with her cupped hands full of cold, wet lettuce.

She heard Jessie say, 'Aren't you going to introduce us, Honor?'

But her tongue had stuck to the roof of her mouth. All she could do was stand there with water dripping from her wrists and on to her bare feet and the floor, her gaze pinned helplessly to Martyn's dark eyes. Vaguely, she heard her dad's voice. 'Honor? Is this someone you want to see?'

Helplessly, she nodded. *So much! She wanted to see him so much.*

After a moment, Garvin said, 'I think maybe now's a good time to get that barbecue fired up, Karen. But we'll be just outside, Honor. *Just* outside.'

Honor nodded again.

And things happened; the refrigerator opened and closed, as did drawers and cupboards. Plates clattered, voices murmured and the lettuce was coaxed from her hands. Then she and Martyn were the only ones left, eyes locked across the room.

'I already made him change it all back,' she blurted. 'Every site. You don't have to find a way to make him do anything. You just have to change all your passwords and–'

Surprise shot across his face. 'But I sorted everything out the same evening. All the porn is gone and the passwords have been changed. I didn't come for him. I came for you. It's only taken me this long to get here because clients were furious at some of the claims about their products on my social networking sites. I had to stop off and see their press officers and Ace set up a video thing. I–' He paused. 'I decided to tell them I had no idea of the identity of the hacker. It seemed safest. For you.'

A wave of heat began at her ankles and surged up her body. '*You* sorted everything out? Why, that bastard, he made me–'

'What?' Softly, as if fearing the answer.

She gulped. 'He made me promise that if he undid all the harm he'd done to you, I'd give our marriage another try.'

Martyn's face drained of all colour. She'd read the phrase in books, but she didn't think she'd ever witnessed it close up, a face turning perfectly white. He pulled out a kitchen chair and, slowly, as if he were ill, folded into it, his holdall dropping to the floor. 'Tell me you didn't agree.'

'Truthfully? I *did* agree,' she acknowledged. 'But then I, um … wriggled my way out of it. We're going to get a divorce.'

And, like flicking a switch, his normal colour flooded back to his cheeks. His eyes even began to smile. 'What did you beat him up with?'

She laughed, her heart lightening, as if it might actually have cause to float up from the pit of her stomach where it had languished for the past couple of days. 'I didn't–! OK, there was ice cream involved. And an ugly, manipulative, unfair threat. Because I'm not worried about what's safe. I'll give him up to the cops, if I have to.'

He rose; came closer. Until she was looking up into his face. 'I love the way you fight for things,' he said. 'But I don't ever again want you to fight with me. I'm sorry. Sorry I left you to run down Stef on your own. I just saw what had happened and I freaked – but I shouldn't have blamed it on Ru or you. It was anger talking and I have to learn to shut it up.

'We can live here if you don't want to live in England. Ace can get me work in New York and I'll force my way through the red tape and get the right permits. Just don't run away from me again, no matter how much of a fuck I turn into when I lose my temper.' His eyes were sombre and black.

'I didn't run away,' she protested. 'I went after Stef, to make him undo what he'd done.'

'But you weren't coming back.' It wasn't a question. 'I went into the bungalow. You didn't leave anything to come back to.'

She blinked as a hot tear formed at the corner of her eye. 'I was the cause of so much trouble–'

Suddenly, he was close enough to gather her gently up against his warm, hard body. 'Stef caused the trouble. I knew that. I'm sorry.' He tasted like mints as his mouth touched hers and it made her glad to imagine him coming straight off the plane, buying Life Savers at the airport as he set out to find her.

'It really is over, with Stef,' she whispered, as a flame of joy licked through her and she felt her feet leave the floor.

'I'm almost disappointed not to have to fight him,' he whispered into her hair. 'When you'd gone, I couldn't believe that I'd let you. I came here all fired up to kick and claw for you. I love you.'

'I – I love you,' she gulped. 'But–'

'But that's all that matters. We can work on the details.'

And he held her harder, as if he was ready to turn and run with her if she disagreed. She didn't disagree.

'I guess I'd better introduce you to my family,' she breathed, eventually. 'They must be wondering what the hell is going on.'

'OK.' He kissed her eyelids, her lips, her cheekbones and her throat.

'So you'd better take your hands off my ass.'

He touched his tongue tip to the corner of her mouth. His hands stayed put as he began to carry her. 'Where are we going?' she gasped, as they moved smoothly over the floorboards, past the coatstand, past the bureau. Not outdoors, where her family were no doubt waiting.

'Upstairs. Which is your room?'

Her breath left her in a giant wave of wanting as they began up the staircase. 'What? In my *room*? With my family right outside?

'OK.' He lowered her on to a step, dropping his mouth to her neck, her breasts, his hands arranging her so that he could nestle right in. 'The staircase is fine. I can get inventive on a staircase.' His mouth skimmed lower.

She let her head fall back. 'I guess my family is pretty understanding.'

Chapter Forty-One

He stopped. Closed his eyes in frustration. 'No family is that understanding.'

'Not really,' she agreed, regretfully.

He sank back to the stairs, managing to land her on his lap. 'We ought to do things the right way.' A huge, long-suffering sigh, pausing for one more lingering kiss. She met his mouth, hungry for the heat of his velvet tongue on hers, her heart beating.

'Family,' she reminded him, on a breath.

He groaned into her neck. 'You're going to have to get off my lap for several minutes before I'm fit to meet them.'

When Honor finally stepped out into the backyard with Martyn, she felt incredibly self-conscious at the silence that broke as the screen door clicked shut.

Garvin paused mid-sentence, barbecue fork in hand. Karen set down a stack of plates. Jess and Zach looked up from the page of the newspaper they were arguing over. Four pairs of eyes fixed on Honor, then switched to Martyn. Then dropped to where Honor and Martyn's hands were clasped together.

Garvin gripped the barbecue fork and narrowed his eyes.

Honor cleared her throat. 'This, um, this is Martyn Mayfair, everybody. We've ...' She ground to a halt.

Before so many silent stares and faces written with questions, Honor's cheeks grew hotter and hotter. 'Dad,' she blurted, 'Did I tell you that I'm going to need to get a divorce? '

Slowly, deliberately, Garvin stowed his fork on the barbecue rack. Then he turned back and his eyes were twinkling, though his voice was grave. 'Would you like some help with that?'

'Yes, please.' She cast around for words. 'I already, um, arranged for Stef to sign the papers.'

'Good.' Garvin's eyebrows lifted. 'I kind of guessed it was Stef you weren't ready to talk about, and I've been waiting for you to come to me for help in dealing with him. But I should have known you'd find your own way.'

Honor glanced sideways at Martyn. 'I had incentive.'

Slowly, Garvin's face creased into a smile. 'You'd better bring him over here so that I can meet him.'

And then everyone was laughing as Martyn shook their hands and Garvin threw extra chicken on the grill and Karen fetched another plate. For the first time in an age Honor felt absolutely, absurdly happy. Each time she looked at Martyn he turned and looked at her. And he smiled. A dark, handsome, full-on smile that made her wonder why the advertisers all demanded Martyn Mayfair wore a glower when his smile could make hearts dance. He sat right down with her family and let them get to know him, telling them about his career, making them laugh about how Honor had thought that he was unemployed. Garvin scrutinised him keenly, but smiled and seemed to like what he saw.

Jessamine leaned over and touched Martyn's arm. 'You know, when I was little, Honor used to tell me bedtime stories about how she was going to marry an English prince and live in a castle.'

'*Jess-sseeee!*' hissed Honor, boiling with horror. 'How could you drag that stupid kid stuff up *now*?'

'But aren't the British princes all spoken for?' put in Zach, grinning at his big sister's discomfort.

Jessie agreed. 'Of course – if not spoken for then too old or too young for Honor. So I guess a model's not too bad. And I always thought that the English accent is to die for.'

She beamed at Martyn. 'I think you'll do nicely for Honor.'

'Hey, not so fast – you haven't interrogated him about the castle,' protested Zach. 'Remember, Honor really likes castles. It could be a dealbreaker.'

Martyn didn't seem to mind how much teasing he got or how long the Lefevre family gathering went on, as long as he could pull his chair close to Honor's and hold her hand. Only his eyes spoke to her and her alone. Making promises that made her shiver as a casual finger swept up the soft skin of her arm, as intimate as a kiss.

Finally, the others began to make their plans for the evening. To make sure that they didn't somehow end up dragged off on a family trip to the movies, Honor walked Martyn to the stream that ran right out to the lake, through the wildflowers in the long grass, carefully far away from the picnic areas, where Honor might see someone she knew and have to make polite conversation. All she wanted was Martyn, to herself.

'So,' she said, when they'd found a place to sit and watch the water, sparkling in the afternoon sun but small and trickling compared to the restless English ocean that she'd grown so used to. 'At least you seem able to get along with the non-flaky side of my family.'

He touched her ear with his lips, making her shiver. 'They love you very much. So we have plenty in common.'

She turned and drowned in his eyes. 'I'm incredibly happy.'

His smile was slow. And hot. 'Jessie said that I was the one who could make you happy. But I'm sorry about not having a castle.' He picked up her hand and began to kiss each fingertip.

She closed her eyes and groaned. 'I could have died when she came out with all that stupid teenage dream stuff.'

He stopped kissing her hand and just held it very tightly.

'I'm really not sure you'd like living in a castle. They seem cold and inconvenient. And what if you decide you want to live in America? Just ...' He swallowed. 'I would like you to marry me.'

Her eyes flew to his, so dark and intense, and her breath hurried from her lungs. 'If I was married to you, I think I'd be very happy living in an apartment in Starboard Walk,' she said, softly. 'And maybe I could get to work in a castle?'

He pulled her close, closer, limb against limb. 'We could always get married in one.'

She tried to pull away, to see his face. 'Seriously? People do that?'

'Of course. Get married, have the reception, stay for the whole weekend. The only thing is ...' He looked suddenly rueful.

She waited, dreading some disappointment that was going to come along and spoil things for her. 'What?' she whispered, eventually.

His kissed her lips. 'I'm no prince.'

Epilogue

The Teapot looked and smelled the same. Honor stepped in through the door, holding tightly to Martyn's warm hand, trying to quiet her butterflies. Aletta was clearing heaped tables, but not rushing herself as she sprayed and wiped. She smiled rosily.

Ru and Robina were behind the counter, cleaning down the kitchen, Ru with his back-to-front baseball cap and Robina in her bandana. Without looking up, Robina called, 'I'm sorry, we're just closing.'

'That's OK,' said Honor. 'We came to talk.'

Ru's head whipped up. His grin was a blaze of pleasure. 'You're back!'

'I guess I am,' Honor agreed, beaming back. She'd called him whilst she'd been away but been deliberately vague about her plans, needing to settle her mind and get used to things working out with Martyn. And file for divorce. Martyn had rescheduled a shoot for the first time in his career, so that he could stay while she tied up loose ends like that.

Robina frowned, her eyes flickering coldly over their clasped hands. 'What about?'

Honor pulled out a chair and sat down. 'I think you'll be surprised.'

Aletta untied her apron and hung it on the hook just inside the kitchen. 'Time,' she told Robina, tapping her watch to show her hours were up. Robina just nodded. Honor wished that she'd been able to get Robina trained like that.

Expectantly, Ru took a chair at the wooden table and then, with a put-upon sigh, so did Robina. 'I suppose you expect me to apologise,' she began, ungraciously. 'Little Ru told me about the tricks Stef played. He guessed it was from me Stef got all the information he needed, so I suppose you've worked it out, too.'

'I figured you must be involved.'

'He got me to ring you and pretend there was something for you to sign, so that you'd be out at the right time. While he,' she indicated Martyn with her head, 'was out running. But I didn't know what your husband planned. You can't pin anything on me.'

'Ex-husband. Almost.' Honor nodded, slowly. Martyn was cradling her hand in both of his as if he were an earth, there to absorb any shocks Honor received. 'So, what was it you thought he was up to?'

Robina shrugged, looking down at her fingers, short nailed and red from cleaning. 'I don't know. It's not my problem. I have enough of my own crap to deal with.'

'Soppy and Crusty have gone,' Ru put in, chin resting on one palm.

Honor switched her attention to him. 'Gone? You're kidding me.'

He pushed off his ball cap so that his hair fell forward. 'Just for a couple of weeks. Crusty said she needed to be somewhere where someone would take care of her, so she was going to stay with her parents in Bristol. Then Mum and Soppy got in a massive row and Soppy said she would take Crusty in her van.'

Robina's bottom lip trembled. 'They'll be back, soon. When Kirsty is better and Sophie cools down. They're my family.'

Honor shifted, awkwardly. Took a huge breath. Screwed up her courage, gripping Martyn's hand. 'Really ...? That would be me.'

Ru made a small noise. Honor saw that he was grinning.

And with Martyn's solid, warm presence beside her, it gave her the nerve to say what she should have said at the beginning of the summer. 'My name's Freedom. Freedom Lefevre.'

Robina stared. She looked from Ru to Honor. Expressions flew across her face. Denial. Curiosity. Then, finally, dawning realisation. 'I didn't know.' Her voice was high with surprise. 'I didn't know it was you.'

'I know. And it doesn't matter. I don't want anything from you – I just wanted you to know.' Her eyes grew hot. Martyn slipped his arm around her, kissing her temple, looking steadily at Robina, as if daring her to say anything that would hurt.

Robina leaned forward and stared into Honor's face. 'Wow,' she said. And, 'Wow,' again. 'You do look a lot like Garvin. I don't know why I didn't see it before.' Her brown eyes were huge and luminous. She frowned at Ru. 'You *knew*?'

Honor jumped in. 'Don't take it out on him!' She took another deep breath. 'I'm going to be around to check on more than just how much you pay him.'

'Around?' Slowly, resignation settled across Robina's face. Her eyes moved to Martyn. 'Oh, shit. Am I going to be your *mother–in–law* or something?'

Honor felt his familiar shake of laughter. 'I suppose you are. That puts a hell of a spin on things, doesn't it?'

'It certainly does.' She pulled a horrified face. 'It's too freaky, even for me.' She turned back to her daughter. 'Why do you call yourself Honor? I named you Freedom.'

I named you Freedom. Despite everything, it was a sentence that Honor wanted to keep in her heart, enshrined in crystal and edged with gold. Her laugh was strangled. 'Well, you know Dad. He has his own ideas about what's important and he added Honor. Freedom Honor Lefevre.

And Honor's what he had me called.'

Robina scowled. 'He would.' She kept looking at Honor, big eyes bigger than ever as she processed what had just happened. What it meant and what it could mean. 'I suppose you want to know why I didn't keep in touch.'

Honor let her head lean on Martyn's shoulder, enjoying the feel of him, the way that he felt, how his flesh and muscles gave just the right amount to make her comfortable. 'Actually, no, it's OK – well, OK, it *isn't* OK, and I would like to talk to you about it sometime – but I have you, as well as Dad, in my make up. And I do accept that you are what you are.

'Because, now, I know what it's like to choose freedom.'

About the Author

Sue Moorcroft is an accomplished writer of novels, serials, short stories and articles, as well as a creative writing tutor and a competition judge.

Her previous novels include *Want to Know a Secret?*, *All That Mullarkey*, *Starting Over* and *Uphill All the Way*.

She is also the commissioning editor and a contributor to *Loves Me, Loves Me Not*, an anthology of short stories celebrating the Romantic Novelists' Association's 50th anniversary and the author of *Love Writing – How to Make Money Writing Romantic or Erotic Fiction*.

www.suemoorcroft.com
www.suemoorcroft.wordpress.com
www.twitter.com/suemoorcroft

More Choc Lit

From Sue Moorcroft

New home, new friends, new love.
Can starting over be that simple?

Tess Riddell reckons her beloved Freelander is more
reliable than any man – especially her ex-fiancé, Olly Gray.
She's moving on from her old life and into the perfect
cottage in the country.

Miles Rattenbury's passions? Old cars and new women!
Romance? He's into fun rather than commitment. When
Tess crashes the Freelander into his breakdown truck, they
find that they're nearly neighbours – yet worlds apart.
Despite her overprotective parents and a suddenly attentive
Olly, she discovers the joys of village life and even forms
an unlikely friendship with Miles. Then, just as their
relationship develops into something deeper, an old flame
comes looking for him ...

Is their love strong enough to overcome the past? Or will
it take more than either of them is prepared to give?

ISBN: 978-1-906931-22-3

Revenge and love: it's a thin line …

The writing's on the wall for **Cleo** and **Gav**. The bedroom
wall, to be precise. And it says 'This marriage is over.'

Wounded and furious, Cleo embarks on a night out with the
girls, which turns into a glorious one night stand with …

Justin, centrefold material and irrepressibly irresponsible.
He loves a little wildness in a woman – and he's in the right
place at the right time to enjoy Cleo's.

But it's Cleo who has to pick up the pieces – of a marriage
based on a lie and the lasting repercussions of that night.
Torn between laid-back Justin and control freak Gav, she's a
free spirit that life is trying to tie down. But the rewards are
worth it!

ISBN: 978-1-906931-24-7

Money, love and family. Which matters most?

When Diane Jenner's husband is hurt in a helicopter crash, she discovers a secret that changes her life. And it's all about money, the kind of money the Jenners have never had.

James North has money, and he knows it doesn't buy happiness. He's been a rock for his wayward wife and troubled daughter – but that doesn't stop him wanting Diane.

James and Diane have something in common: they always put family first. Which means that what happens in the back of James's Mercedes is a really, really bad idea.

Or is it?

ISBN: 978-1-906931-26-1

Why not try something else from the Choc Lit selection?

'Refreshing, funny and romantic, it's like a breath of fresh sea air with a cast of terrific characters.' KATE HARRISON

Turning the Tide

CHRISTINE STOVELL

All's fair in love and war?
Depends on who's making the rules.

Harry Watling has spent the past five years keeping
her father's boat yard afloat, despite its dying clientele.
Now all she wants to do is enjoy the peace and quiet of
her sleepy backwater.

So when property developer Matthew Corrigan wants
to turn the boat yard into an upmarket housing complex for
his exotic new restaurant, it's like declaring war.

And the odds seem to be stacked in Matthew's favour.
He's got the colourful locals on board, his hard-to-please
girlfriend is warming to the idea and he has the means to
force Harry's hand. Meanwhile, Harry has to fight not just
his plans but also her feelings for the man himself.

Then a family secret from the past creates heartbreak
for Harry, and neither of them is prepared for
what happens next …

ISBN: 978-1-906931-25-4

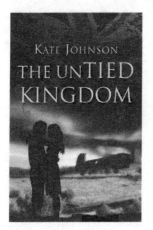

**The portal to an alternate world was the start of all
her troubles – or was it?**

When Eve Carpenter lands with a splash in the Thames,
it's not the London or England she's used to. No one has a
telephone or knows what a computer is. England's a third
world country and Princess Di is still alive. But worst of all,
everyone thinks Eve's a spy.

Including Major Harker who has his own problems. His
sworn enemy is looking for a promotion. The general wants
him to undertake some ridiculous mission to capture a
computer, which Harker vaguely envisions running wild
somewhere in Yorkshire. Turns out the best person to help
him is Eve.

She claims to be a popstar. Harker doesn't know what a
popstar is, although he suspects it's a fancy foreign word for
'spy'. Eve knows all about computers, and electricity. Eve is
dangerous. There's every possibility she's mad.

And Harker is falling in love with her.

ISBN: 978-1-906931-68-1

JANE LOVERING
Please don't stop the music

How much can you hide?

Jemima Hutton is determined to build a successful new life
and keep her past a dark secret. Trouble is, her jewellery
business looks set to fail – until enigmatic Ben Davies offers
to stock her handmade belt buckles in his guitar shop and
things start looking up, on all fronts.

But Ben has secrets too. When Jemima finds out he used
to be the front man of hugely successful Indie rock band
Willow Down, she wants to know more. Why did he desert
the band on their US tour? Why is he now a semi-recluse?

And the curiosity is mutual – which means that her own
secret is no longer safe …

ISBN: 978-1-906931-27-8

CHRISTINA
COURTENAY

Trade Winds

PASSION

Marriage of convenience – or a love for life?

It's 1732 in Gothenburg, Sweden, and strong-willed
Jess van Sandt knows only too well that it's a man's world.
She believes she's being swindled out of her inheritance by
her stepfather – and she's determined to stop it.

When help appears in the unlikely form of handsome
Scotsman Killian Kinross, himself disinherited by his
grandfather, Jess finds herself both intrigued and infuriated
by him. In an attempt to recover her fortune, she proposes
a marriage of convenience. Then Killian is offered the
chance of a lifetime with the Swedish East India Company's
Expedition and he's determined that nothing will stand in
his way, not even his new bride.

He sets sail on a daring voyage to the Far East, believing
he's put his feelings and past behind him. But the journey
doesn't quite work out as he expects....

ISBN: 978-1-906931-23-0

Introducing the Choc Lit Club

Join us at the Choc Lit Club where we're creating a
delicious selection of women's fiction.
Where heroes are like chocolate – irresistible!

Join our authors in Author's Corner, read author interviews
and see our featured books.

We'd also love to hear how you enjoyed *Love & Freedom*.
Just visit www.choc-lit.com and give your feedback.
Describe Martyn in terms of chocolate and you could win a
Choc Lit novel in our Flavour of the Month competition!

Follow us on twitter: www.twitter.com/ChocLituk